Only the Good Times

Bruce-Novoa

D0809192

Arte Público Press
Houston, Texas
1995

LEIS
FIC
BRUC
ONL

This volume is made possible through grants from the National Endowment for the Arts (a federal agency) and the Andrew W. Mellon Foundation.

Recovering the past, creating the future

Arte Público Press
University of Houston
Houston, Texas 77204-2090

Cover design by Gladys Ramirez

Bruce-Novoa, 1944–
    Only the good times / by Juan Bruce-Novoa.
      p.   cm.
    ISBN 1-55885-078-3 (paper)
    I. Title.
    PS3552.R793055   1995
    813'.54—dc20   95-9770
                                       CIP

Para Juan García Ponce

Only the Good Times

I

Ann Marisse

The first time I saw Ann Marisse, she was coming towards me, laughing and running, hand in hand with another girl, across the school playground. Though only twelve then, her breasts already bounced like my big sister's. Her blond hair, gathered back into a ponytail, was tossing from side to side. The blue jumper and white blouse, far from hiding her body as our chaste-minded nuns intended, revealed it perversely. Perhaps she had run by me many times exactly that way, but now the budding warmth of spring stripped away bulky school sweaters, exposing a new season's flowering promise. Alonzo, Dick, Billy and I were waiting near the girls' side of the playground for the afternoon bell. I don't recall Alonzo's comment as the two girls passed, but without cause—I couldn't even place her name then—I reacted like a protective boyfriend, swinging my right fist from where it hung at my side in a smooth, ascending arc, guided more than driven by a swivel of my upper body. It hit the target cleanly: the mouth which for years had grated on me like fingernails scratched across a blackboard. Not vicious—I didn't mean to kill him, not yet—but sharp and efficient. Unfair, maybe, but it paid off later. Much later, because the immediate result made me wish I could take it all back.

The spring of 1957 and Elvis was staking out his kingdom of Rock among us. Everybody wanted sideburns, a ducktail, turned-up collars and a squirmy knee, but most prized was his smile. While most of it proved relatively easy, cosmetic, to coax your lip to lift just slightly on one side was anything but. By the time Elvis hit the Ed Sullivan show, I had it pat. Added to the body moves and the right clothes, my imitation so convinced my older brother's car club buddies that they paid me to mime "Money Honey" at a party. Alonzo, to my content, wasted hours snarling into a mirror and twisting his knee, only to look like a spastic Bugs Bunny. "Is this better?" he'd ask through gritted teeth. I'd destroy him with a hissed denial spit from below a perfectly half-arched upper lip. The ultimate in satisfaction.

Well, the day after noticing Ann Marisse for the first time, Alonzo's face floated in behind me in the mirror of the boys' head. He broke a new smirk with his lip, swollen with my mark of sharp revenge, slightly puffed a la Elvis. How I wanted that swing back, or maybe to add a few more, well placed, like a plastic surgeon's scalpel. Alonzo disappeared out onto the playground to take refuge next to Sister Faith, kissing ass for her smiling protection. I began to learn that rewards sometimes have to wait.

The following year, when they divided us into one class of all eighth-graders and another of seventh-eighth mixed, I stayed with the first group taught by Sister Dolores, the principal—nicknamed Sweets—while Alonzo got sentenced to the terror of St. Catherine's hallways, Sister George, who delighted in slaying young dragons, piercing the heart of their insecure adolescence with harsh words and after-school essays, usually on her favorite topic, the temptations of the opposite sex. Tradition had it that Sister Dolores polished the rough edges from the most promising young minds, while St. George doled out sledgehammer blows of remedial ed to the slower kids in a last desperate effort to prepare them for high school. I felt liberated and somewhat avenged.

"I reeeeally feel for you," I needled him the first day.

"Thanks, man," he replied. "It's big of you, but guess whose tits hang in the row next to me?"

Ann Marisse! I pretended not to remember or care.

At football practice I tackled him so hard in head-ons that Coach Purdy congratulated me, supposedly for improving over the summer, but I bet he couldn't stand Alonzo either. Alonzo limped to the end of the line, one hand massaging his lower back, took off his helmet and whined that I should save something for our first game. I pretended not to understand and rejoined the opposite line, but Coach kept us from facing off again the rest of the week.

Actually, other than a quick "hi" every so often at school or Sunday mass, Ann Marisse and I still hadn't talked. My models ran to the aloof quiet types: Johnny Saxon in *Rock Pretty Baby*, or, of course, the prince of inarticulate rebels, James Dean. By the way, I met her during *Giant*—that is, I always remember having really met her during *Giant*.

The team had reported to league weigh-ins Saturday morning, and making the 120-pound limit had me ecstatic. Two weeks of extra laps after practice and morning jogging around the lake, starving on nine eggs a day, three a meal, had skimmed off twelve pounds, sliding the scales down to the tottering limit. Meanwhile, Alonzo followed Coach's orders to load up on the pasta if he wanted to play heavyweights.

My mother had the promised reward waiting at home: doughnuts, a baker's dozen. The movie, however, was a week-ly ritual, and the team met at the drugstore four blocks from my house to walk down together. The Union Theater marked the corner of thirty-eighth and Union, the intersection of sev-eral Catholic and public school territories, not particularly dangerous, but we always went in groups just in case. The last doughnuts disappeared on the way to the show, shared with Billy and Dick, but none for Alonzo.

With the film barely starting, Liz Taylor riding her sleek black stud across rolling green fields, the kind California kids like us saw only in the movies, Alonzo reached up for the ponytail, the one on the girl in front of him. Yes, who else? She flashed a dirty look over her shoulder, but he kept right on, enjoying the irritation he produced. There, in the semi-dark, Ann Marisse sort of looked like Taylor: flashing green eyes and barely contained anger appraising the horse-trading Rock Hudson, larger than life in front of us. Hudson was admitting to owning half of Texas when Ann Marisse, fed up with the continual tugging, turned and, in a voice the whole theater could hear, threatened: "Leave me alone or I'll have Paul beat you up again."

The usher's flashlight exploded in our faces: "Out, you little hoods, now!"

Fifteen minutes of *Giant* lost convincing the manager to let us stay. He relented, but only if we separated, which for me represented some consolation. Alone, I returned to the same seat. Minutes later Ann Marisse went out to the lobby, returned, worked her way to the seat next to me and silently offered to share a box of popcorn.

After the movie as I walked her home, she told me how for years she had watched me on the school grounds. Ann Marisse underscored words with her hands and took quick glances back over her shoulder as she kept a step ahead of me and barely out of reach. In the past she might have watched me, but now she seemed entranced by something moving just in front of her like an image projected by her own words. Once, she pivoted around on her left foot to bring us suddenly face to face, catching me off guard and making me take two quick steps back, which she instinctively followed with two of her own before intuiting a full stop. She resumed walking towards her house, but backwards facing me—the maneuver carried out to inform me I had broken my promise to call her. Impossible, I thought. You can't break promises to someone you've haven't met. But we had, and she described my Halloween costume for Alonzo's party the year before: a Mexican Bandit.

I had improvised a costume from old toys, strapping a gun belt around my hips, then sliding it up waist-high, Mexican fashion; another belt with the holster cut off crossed over my chest. Under a torn shirt sleeve, a white scarf borrowed from my sister's room showed a generous smear of lipstick blood; her new eyebrow pencil drew a drooping moustache, a bit too Chinese, but I was running late, so it stayed. The mirror told me it still lacked something, so from a closet came my old Charro hat, an ignored present from my never seen godparents in Mexico City. It didn't fit, but dangling behind my neck it provided just enough local color. When I kissed my mother goodbye, she asked who I had made myself up to be.

"Pancho Villa," I informed her.

"But he was a general," she said, "and you look like a bandit."

Ann Marisse described me in detail. Alonzo had forgotten to warn me that girls were invited—our first mixed party, with music and dancing, mostly girls with girls, but dancing. As we walked home from *Giant*, I watched her tell me all this in quick spurts and searched for an image to offer as proof I hadn't forgotten. But I had, and she knew it. She pivoted back around with the same easy motion and stopped, letting me come up next to her. We were standing on a sidewalk, facing the same direction, and she began to dance as if we were alone and not out in the open where anybody could see us.

"Remember this?" She began to clap her hands and move her feet in small rhythmic steps, then a turn, steps, another turn, repeated until she had formed a square, ending up where she started, and it flooded through to me on that most basic of R&B guitar riffs and the wailing saxophone of "Honky Tonk": everyone dancing together, yes, and this Geisha Girl telling me *watch my feet*, then surprising me with the first turn, yes, the porcelain-doll face, as white as a mime's, framing darkly slanted eyes, a tiny red mouth, and thickly rouged cheeks...of course!

"Yeah, now I remember."

"But you forgot to call, after you promised."

"I didn't know your name."

Already walking ahead of me again, she shot an incredulous glance over her shoulder before renewing her litany of memories through which, apparently, all was forgiven, though never forgotten.

She played out information like her Japanese party fan, panel upon panel of my life, individual anecdotes forming a story line held in her hands, displayed in part or in total at her whim, and always she preserved for her eyes only the reverse angle through which small holes were cut for her to hide behind and peek through. She reconstructed incidents I thought no one knew, like the time in sixth grade I got so mad I cried after three guys from eighth jumped me at the creamery for beating one of them out of his position in football. I could feel my cheeks warming to embarrassed red, but they cooled quickly as she also recounted, in more detail than I could muster, how I got even with them one by one, until I broke the last one's leg at practice with an open-field block. Now, writing this after all these years, her version returns the stronger of the two memories, like a voiced-over narration of the actual event.

"Crack! It sounded just like that, like...like a dry branch snapped in two," she said quickly, her voice sparked with wonder. She stopped walking, turned and looked at me, melding whatever image she had been following into my own, staring, relentless and waiting. I suppose it was the way she claimed to have stared at me in school, but for the first time I felt the full force of her intense eyes. Ever so deliberately she added, "It bounced around the park, like an echo. Crack, then nothing, no crying or...just all of you standing around. Till the ambulance came and Coach Purdy sent the team home."

"Crack," she repeated, then we were walking again. Ann Marisse talked on as before, her light, playful tone returning after the solemn interlude. The difference focused in the touch of her hand holding mine as we continued now, side by side.

By the time we reached her house, on a corner surprisingly near mine, we were going steady and she kissed me for the first time. By then I had realized my mistake: she resembled Lana Turner more than Liz Taylor, and her eyes, more than green, played with light along a spectrum from grayish blue to emerald.

❋   ❋   ❋

Two things were necessary to go steady: a girl and a ring.
Now I needed the latter. Dick knew a place where I could get
one—real silver he said—for five bucks. Alonzo suggested a
pawn shop, but I couldn't see placing just anybody's old ring
on Ann Marisse's finger.

"Shit, it's not like you're going to marry her," Alonzo spit
from across the lunch table.

"Flake off, man. A lot you know," Dick shot back. "My sis
started going with Larry right here, six years ago, and they
got married this summer."

"Yeah, and how old's their kid?" Alonzo taunted him.

St. George broke up the fight with a few stinging slaps of
her own, then hauled them both off to the principal, ordering
me along for good measure, refusing to believe I had nothing
to do with it. A five-hundred-word essay on table manners
made the three of us late for practice. Later, after running us
extra laps, Coach Purdy sent the other two ahead, then lectured me on taking leadership seriously, making me ashamed
of letting him down—all because of Alonzo's foul-mouthed
sense of humor.

Early Saturday morning, with a meager five dollars from
cutting lawns and Dick along as guide, I acquired a silver
horseshoe ring set with imitation diamonds. A bit western-
looking, but it shined and gleamed. Not a scratch or nick on
it—brand new. It took the whole morning for the number five
bus to run us back to her house. Dick waited at the creamery,
sipping a cherry Coke I bought him in thanks, while I went to
Ann Marisse's with my first material symbol of steady love.

"Where is it?" she asked, as if she hadn't noticed it on my
hand as soon as she came out onto the porch.

"Right here."

The effort to work it over my knuckle vanished in the
ease with which she slipped it onto her upheld thumb. She
rubbed her fingerprint smudges off against her blouse before
admiring it at arm's length, her thumb up like a painter scru-
tinizing her canvas for flaws in perspective...then frowned.

"What's wrong?"

"Nothing, really," she replied, simultaneously pressing the ringed thumb tightly between her breasts. "It's beautiful. I love it, just..."

Sensing my disappointment, she moved quickly to prevent a misunderstanding, stepping forward to bring her body almost against mine while resting one hand gently on my shoulder and the other open on my chest. In a voice somewhere between a whisper and a sigh she explained, "I love it, Paul, really, but Sister George doesn't allow any jewelry, not even our own. Remember what she did to Marilyn at midnight mass? And her mother gave her that bracelet for Christmas."

We sat on the porch to think up a way around the rules.

"A chain," I said.

"Even if it's long enough to hide under my blouse, she'll notice it sooner or later. Besides, then nobody else will see it."

"It's not for the ring... You'll see, don't worry."

We met Dick and Janice, his girl, at the creamery and walked to the movies, meeting more kids at the drugstore on the way. Ann Marisse held the ring well in view. The girls admired it, ooing and ahhing congratulations, while the guys pretended indifference, preferring to throw rocks at signs or watch the street for the first sighting of a Chevy Impala, the newest car for 58, fins swept on the bias and dual headlights, signs of things to come. We saw *Loving You* and claimed the theme as our song.

The following Saturday, with the end of my Elvis money plus two dollars donated by my ever-supportive mother, I went to the Catholic bookstore to purchase a short, delicate chain with a fine sterling cross. Not even St. George could question a blond angel's piety symbolized in such a modest, simple icon. Ann Marisse said she had seen the exact one, but hadn't dared ask for it. My double display of affection in so short a time left her speechless. I promised to have it engraved before she moved up into Sister Dolores' eighth grade.

In her classroom, St. George imposed a button-up-to-the-collar code in retaliation, but on the playground our cross gleamed silvery against Ann Marisse's throat. The kids knew. Sister Dolores, too, though she never let on. Within a few weeks, other couples followed suit. Never have so many pious girls displayed such a rash of devotion to the holy cross.

The ring appeared on weekends, at games, movies or parties, with the hesitant approval of Ann Marisse's parents. The first time her father saw us about to leave the house together, he objected to her wearing it. She plied him with the same tactic of approach and soft pleading, except she didn't stop short as she had with me. Leaning her body fully against his, she encircled his waist with one arm while pressing the other hand to his chest, then lingered just long enough to elicit consent. Before she rejoined me at the front door, Ann Marisse kissed her mother on the cheek, a thank you of sorts, whether for the approval implicit in her smile or for having taught her a lesson well applied, I couldn't tell. But my admiration for Ann Marisse doubled, as did my anticipation of a time when she'd erase the subtle distance between us she then so accurately drew with the line of her body.

The pride with which she wore the ring, the tip of her thumb tucked into her fist against slippage showing it off all the better, never failed to stir equal pride in me. One image stands out over the rest: seconds after winning our last game, with cheerleaders, pep squad, parents and friends surrounding me, some feet away she simply raised her closed hand so the ring touched her lips, and she stared at me through slightly narrowed eyes.*

With more foresight, Ann Marisse got me a serpent ring, eyes and tail studded with emerald. With its adjustable triple

---

*My editors say I can't end chapters this way—too clichéd, they complain—but it happened like that, kiss, squint and all. Anyway, there are no chapters because I'm not sure where anything ended once our relationship began; lines of distinction bleed across borders. Ours was an amorphous life, reconstructed now from memory-shards broken and buried by time and resignation, pieced together here as best I can.

coil and sexual ambivalence, it lent itself to exchange. I removed it solely for practice and games, at Coach's insistence.

All that year, Ann Marisse found herself under attack by the girls in my class who resented "the bitch" who had dared to steal one of their boys. How could the team captain prefer a seventh-grader? Ann Marisse's presence insulted them personally, so they plotted her destruction as a group project, even selecting volunteers to seduce me out of our relationship. I enjoyed each effort, but none of them came close. Ann Marisse inventively stayed one step ahead, offering delights like free bowling at her uncle's alley, a movie with her parents, teaching me to dance, or the most irresistible bait: her mother's homemade pasta. If all failed, she waited for me to come by her house after whatever for a hushed good night at her window. After I joked about having to whisper and touch fingertips through the screen, like prison visitors in the movies, it was off the next time. I stood on tiptoes to kiss her from outside.

"Isn't it freezing out there?" she asked, holding out the promise of something much warmer inside the open window, if I would only take the chance.

"Maybe, but your folks..." Their window yawned darkly just steps away, as did her little brother's on the other side.

"You're right," she agreed with childlike resignation.

The six blocks between our houses, walked in midnight darkness, are still one of my happiest memories: my body was wound so tight that I could feel the blood pulse in my throat.

"Next time," I'd promise myself out loud, "next time..."

"You'll what?" interrupted Alonzo's voice one night from behind a tree. After that he often tagged along, waiting in the shadows to accompany me home before continuing on across the park to his house on the far side. He'd listen to me talk out my peaked desire in terms of romantic ideals, speaking more openly and sincerely than I probably have with anyone since. We got the closest to being friends during those walks, or at

least to me thinking of him as a real friend. His single-word
responses or grunts of agreement probably contributed more
to my impression of nearness than any shared ideas. It was
like talking to the night itself, wrapped up in the body of Alonzo sauntering mute at my side. A dog would have done as
well, a faithful German shepherd—better, in fact, because a
dog couldn't have said anything, ever. But then, you could say
Alonzo was a dog cursed with speech, and one night it
betrayed him.

"Shit, quit jackin' around and just get into her pants."

He strode on a few steps more before realizing I had
stopped. He hesitated a fraction of a moment without looking
back, then broke into a full run, streaking through the yellow-
ish cone of light cast by the arc lamp as he crossed the street
in front of my house and tunneled into the park's peaceful
darkness. I didn't chase him. His speed out of the blocks and
the couple of inches he would grow in high school were his two
advantages over me in sports. I could have run him down
eventually—already he smoked on the sly and never could
reach peak condition—but I let him go. A small stick-like figure reemerged under another street lamp on the park's outer
edge. Lanky gait, arms held out from his body, he looked back
over his shoulder once, probably breathing hard and surely
chuckling between gasps. Lucky for him basketball season had
arrived, or he might have died at practice. A sharp forearm to
the ribs was all I delivered, and that by accident, really.

Sure, I'd thought about it, that is, making out with Ann
Marisse. Who wouldn't? But never in those words. Alonzo's
problem was always bad phrasing, the wrong word at the
worst time. He might have made a decent actor, given the
proper lines, but never a scriptwriter. He did make me more
determined though, to take advantage of the window.

Unfortunately, Ann Marisse's father had designs of his
own. He'd been working construction since high school and, as
he pleasured in explaining to me many nights over ice cream

at the creamery, he had learned more than enough about the business to go it on his own.

"The money's in having your own business. I could've stayed in the army to work for a boss. The trick's to do the same work, but for yourself, see?"

It made perfect sense, and I nodded in agreement.

"Nothing to it. Just takes cash to get started."

Ann Marisse's mother would watch him talk to us, her head tilted to one side as if seeking a little more distance to take him entirely in, agreeing and urging him to do it and quit boring us kids with a dream he had been talking about since 1946. She looked so young that, despite her jet-black hair, people confused her for Ann Marisse's older sister. Her parents were our generation's ideal: high school sweethearts, marrying when he received his draft notice right after graduation, the last year of World War II. Years later, Ann Marisse confided to me that her mother hadn't even turned sixteen yet, barely a junior and a few months short of legal age, so they married secretly before he left for boot camp. Nine months later, Ann Marisse was born, so her parents were well acquainted with young love. To us, a decade later, they still looked the part.

"Do it," she'd tell him. "Nothing ever stopped you before, not even Captain Thomas's threat to have you shot if you didn't tell my father where I was."

"Your mother knew."

"You'll never get her to admit it."

And they would kiss, right in front of us, and drink Cokes or sip malts, not much different from teenagers.

Ann Marisse reveled in their stories, not the least embarrassed by her parents' public displays of affection, taking them as a model, never a warning. But then, they weren't that exceptional. All their friends had married right out of school as well, or soon after the war. The same pattern fit almost everyone we knew. My parents, twenty years older than Ann Marisse's, didn't share their history with me, but until learn-

ing differently I supposed it had been similar. Not knowing for
sure made me envy Ann Marisse. Her parents were so perfect
in our eyes: young, together and happy, living proof it could all
work out in the end. Only, her father wanted his own business.

"It's easy," he'd insist, turning to talk to me, man to man.
"You start with one house, a duplex to help pay it off. Then
another, bigger, and move into it. Build and move, build and
move, until you have the house you've always wanted, paid for
by selling the ones you live in along the way, that turns out
not costing you a thing. Right?"

"Yes, Daddy, do it," Ann Marisse urged, her head on his
shoulder, her hand in mine on the table, happy in her parents'
happiness, nurturing it as her own and imitating it in ours.

So in search of his happiness, he did it, which in turn
delayed ours. About when I started marshaling courage to
climb through Ann Marisse's window, a new sign appeared on
her father's Ford pickup: his own construction company. Then
with dizzying speed, the family settled into the first of his
dream houses: a modest, though thoroughly modern duplex
near the park—distance never caused our problems. But the
bedroom windows of the ranch-style home were small, high,
and located at the rear, not suitable for secret entries, or even
conversation. Faced with modern architecture, *Romeo and
Juliet* might have become a farce instead of a tragedy. "Young
love, our love," as Tab Hunter sang it, demanded sharing at
closer quarters and in private.

The show and parties were too social, even with everyone
around making out as well. It just wasn't the same, though,
since neither of us had experienced anything else, we didn't
know for sure what it was not the same as. The short ride
home after parties, crammed together in the back seat of cars
or in our favorite, Billy's mother's station wagon, could have
allowed brief explorations of petting beyond the limits, but
none of the girls wanted anyone to know just how far she
would let her boyfriend go, so we needed a private setting.

The chance came simply. An old trick, but still reliable. Comparing family routines, we matched our mothers' days out and then played sick. Mine spent Wednesdays with her painting group, while Ann Marisse's had her bowling club every other week. Timed right, we could have two hours alone. If only no one would see me, or, worst scenario of all, her father might drive over from his new construction site nearby. Anything could go wrong, so we worried, postponing it twice. Of supreme importance: *No One should know, not even best friends.* She made me repeat the promise each time we talked, sometimes in the middle of entirely different subjects, and always after saying goodbye.

"Remember," she would say with ominous urgency as I'd begin to walk away, reaching out to take the fingers of my right hand in her left long enough to stop me, then relaxing her grip without letting go, cradling my fingers lightly in hers, like a bird held softly. I didn't need to turn around to know she was staring at me with an imperative look not devoid of pleading. I didn't have to, but I'd turn every time in a smooth choreography which spun us face to face, her right hand rising to meet my left. Turned to find her eyes again, waiting, insisting, "I promise," I would chorus, squeezing her hands twice for emphasis.

When the day came, I'd worked a cough into laryngitis. Ann Marisse feigned cramps, a foolproof excuse my big sister wielded almost monthly. My mother, however, lingered caringly, making me fear my role had been too well played. Sitting at the edge of my bed, she probed. Had anything happened that I might want to discuss with her. She offered to stay home if I needed to talk. I pointed to my throat, implying talk was exactly what I did not need. Write it out, she urged. But with a final goodbye, delivered with a hot cup of sage tea and honey, she departed. I took my bike for speed.

Ann Marisse opened the door, whispered to me to hurry in, and then embraced and kissed me with the full emotion built up over weeks. One last peek out the window to check for nosy neighbors, and then, "What's that?"

"My bike."

"Why not just hang a sign for the neighbors?"

For the first time I saw the exasperated expression I'd get to know over the years. A deep breath, a relaxing of her body into a gentle undulating vertical curve with a slowly released sigh, head tilted to one side and down, the eyes rising to me before tracing a line towards a spot on the floor next to her feet...entirely disarming. Overacting, too, but as devastating then as the many times I would see it later.

With my bike disposed of down the alley next to Billy's garage—his mother was unique in that she worked away from home—I rushed back to start over. My blunder had upset her, but she didn't let it rob us of scant time. "We'll argue about it later," she said, though we never did.

An hour and half of firsts. For starters, we fully explored French kissing, only timidly experimented before out of fear friends would notice. It surprised us how much we liked tasting each other, a little like children offered a suspicious, new candy only to find it delicious. Its delights occupied us for quite some time, our bodies held in suspension just inches apart, my hands moving strictly within the allowed regions familiar to us for some months. She broke away and offered me a Coke, returning to share it mouth to mouth as her parents did with wine. When I gagged on the bubbles, she apologized, patting my back to help me catch my breath, then reclining back on the sofa and pulling me down toward her. My hand slipped over her breast, a motion dared once or twice in the past, always as if by accident and prepared with ready excuses. This time I let it linger, not fully knowing what to do and a bit startled by the sudden tensing of her entire body, followed by a turning towards mine along its whole length. I moved my hand in circles, more palm than fingers. For the first time my hand felt a girl's breast, and she wasn't trying to stop me. Quite the contrary.

"No," she whispered when I slipped my hand under her sweater, but she kissed me again without pushing my hand away. Perhaps by rolling onto her back she meant to keep it from rising further, but this pulled my body over, my leg slipping between hers. She squeezed her legs together with an instinctual movement that left us facing each other, her arms around my neck, bodies pressed tight.

I slipped my hand around to her back.

"Don't," she pleaded, but didn't withdraw.

The hooks slipped loose so easily. Beginner's luck.

But as I tried to bring my hand back around, I could feel her moving without really moving—a motion contained within herself, like a gentle earthquake pulverizing the earth so far below the surface that you're not sure it's really happening, but you feel vibrations pulsing through your body strongly enough to scare the hell out of you.

In the following days, when instead of arguing about my bike we would sit and recall over and over every detail of that day, she admitted wanting to do more, but she didn't know what. She expected me to know, but no one had told me either.

"When you touched me, something went off somewhere in me... It scared me and then I...I don't know."

"What?" I asked, wanting to hear her talk about it again, never tiring of watching her recall it, fascinated by repetition, listening for variations, the slightest new twist, or just engrossed by the growing familiarity of her words.

"The first time you touched me," she said, and I reached out to stroke her breast, imitating the memory, making her tense up again and look towards the living room where her parents sat watching television.

"We can't now," she insisted, whispering, just as we had whispered the entire hour-and-a-half that afternoon. "Be good," she pleaded, gently guiding my hand away. "When you unsnapped my bra, I was so surprised I didn't know what to say."

"You said, 'don't.' I remember."

"Really? Are you sure?"

"How could I forget. It's not like I've done it before."

"No? I thought you had tons of experience, the way it popped just like that."

But it had been my first time and could have proved too difficult. Back then a stubborn clasp could have been disastrous, producing one of those embarrassing pauses I experienced more than once later.

"What's really scary, though," she added, "is that feeling, all nervous inside, and wanting to stop but go, at once, you know?"

"Yeah, me too."

"Then you touched me. I didn't want to stop you. I think I wanted you to stop on your own, without me telling you. But I'm glad you didn't."

"I've never touched a girl there before," I told her many times over the next few weeks. She probably didn't believe me, but it was true, just like it had been the first time I had come while making out.

"When you wouldn't answer me, I thought you were sick," she told me.

When I came, it was like losing my breath. Then like falling, as if my body was collapsing straight through itself. I hugged her even harder and felt myself drain away.

"You haven't told anyone, have you?"

"No," I reassured her.

"Please don't. It would ruin everything."

I took her plea seriously, but it really wasn't hard for me not to tell anyone. Much later I discovered, however, that even during those years Ann Marisse shared most everything with her cousin...but I'm skipping around too much as is, without bringing Marianne in now. She'll have to wait a bit. Anyway, I told no one, not even Billy when he asked how my bike ended up in his backyard. I forgot it in the rush to get home. His father tripped over it and raised holy hell with Billy. He recognized my bike, but covered for me and didn't insist on an explanation. Unlike Alonzo, Billy never pushed when he sensed you didn't want to talk. He unquestioningly served his friends when they needed help, going out of his way to back you up. Eventually, in Vietnam it won him a Bronze Star and, they tell me, permanent and bitter disability.

On the other hand, Ann Marisse and I talked about that day a lot, yet we never tried it again. Perhaps we had scared ourselves, touching the edge of what neither one felt ready to deliver on. How could we be ready if we didn't know exactly for what? So neither of us did anything to make it happen.

In the den, while her brother played with toy soldiers on the floor, we listened to records and talked about what we had felt, and I'd touch her when her brother wasn't looking. Perhaps then I discovered it didn't really matter what part of her I touched, the back of her neck, her arm, her fingers. Every part of her body excited me. You'd think intensity would diminish over time—not just the excitement, but the memory's intensity—but believe me, it hasn't. Every time we got back together, it resurfaced. She came to recognize it, use it, to reach over and skim the hair on my arm or let her knee touch mine or run a finger barely over my lips, not across, but down in a hushing motion, knowing exactly what she wanted and how to achieve it with me, and enjoying it thoroughly. Her favorite touch of seduction she improvised a little later, in the den of their second house while dancing to "Loving You."

"Let's dance," she said, not expecting refusal.

"No, come here," and I tried to kiss her. Her little brother was watching T.V., leaving us alone for a change.

"Please, for me," and she leaned close, looking at me through barely narrowed eyes, a gesture of pleading and promise, less than inches away, looking into my eyes. Her index finger came to rest gently on my nose.

We danced, close, '50s style, to Elvis on a 45, hardly pausing as the needle rose, swung out and back to resettle and repeat. Somewhere in that dance, she leaned back, looked up and let her hand travel lightly up my spine. Then, in one simultaneous motion, as she rose up on her toes and brought her head alongside mine, her fingers played over the nape of my neck. And the shiver that razored through my body was a whispered word: "Pauly."

No one calls me Pauly, not even my family. My mother, maybe, when I was very young, but she said it in Spanish, so it didn't sound the same. No one else, because I wouldn't have liked it. Ann Marisse knew it, too, and back then, when someone might have saddled me with it, she guarded it, cultivating its uniqueness by reserving it for when we were alone or on a dance floor where no one else could hear: a totally private word.

I never knew what to say when she did it. Luckily, she usually didn't expect a reply, just embraced me tighter. But that first night, that first time, she pulled her head back, surprised or amused by my reaction, watching my eyes close in a sort of fadeaway, feeling my breath draw sharply, then release like a sigh. I shook my head slowly and pulled her back into my body, hugging her completely and feeling her respond in kind, our feet still moving to our song:

> "*my whole life through,*
> *loving you,*
> *only you...*"

And although I couldn't see her face, I knew she was smiling.

*   *   *

I wasn't aware she discussed everything with her cousin Marianne. I didn't even know her cousin, although I had seen her once when we played her school in our second-to-last game. That Ann Marisse's cousin went there meant less to me than knowing they had a good and very big team. I spent the afternoon banging heads with their star player, who obviously had cheated at the weigh-in. Fifteen minutes after the game had ended, out in the parking lot, I thought I could still hear cheers ringing through my head in waves. Then Dick asked me if I knew the girl with Ann Marisse, and when I turned to look, something inside my head kept spinning when the rest of me tried to stop; my stomach followed suit, but end over end. A voice shouted for Coach Purdy, while I watched my gargoyle reflection in a chrome hubcap, vomiting. Some dozen head X-rays later, I was securely tucked into a bed in a semi-private room of Saint Anthony's. A voice was assuring my mother that my injury looked mild, not to worry, but a couple days for observation wouldn't hurt. When she came in with Coach Purdy, she looked as if she had been praying for a miracle cure, but she smiled to hide her fear.

"I've taught you a million times, the head's for thinking; shoulder's for hitting," Coach Purdy repeated, "if you wanna have a brain when you're through. There's life after football."

My mother supported him with a nod, except she would have liked me to quit right then. She suffered through every game. The same with my brother, but she had never had to visit him in a hospital. She knew God had destined me to be her undoing, as she told it sometimes, when I weighed in at ten pounds plus at birth. Now I lay in the hospital bed, even though I felt fine and just wanted to go home. School I could do without, but how could I miss practice? Worse, there was no phone to call Ann Marisse.

"*Paciencia, hijo,*" my mother said, speaking to me in Spanish as usual.

"I've gotta get out. The championship game is coming up." And a party on Saturday, but this I didn't say.

"Just the weekend," she tried to console me.

It stretched into almost a week of torment: food, terrible; Holy Communion, before dawn; an old guy next to me who claimed he would die soon despite his doctor's diagnosis; and visitors restricted to family members. Plus, no television. The weekend inched by while I discovered boredom at thirteen, reading *The Catholic Register* and *Boy's Life.*

Monday, when my mother broke the bad news about extending the observation a few more days, she apologized, taking my disappointment as her personal failure. As she talked, she kept arranging my hair with her fingers as she used to do on the way to mass in earlier years. Then, finally, after looking at me with what seemed a much too melodramatic expression, she made the sign of the cross over my forehead, lips and heart, kissed my cheek, and said in a loud voice, "I'll return tomorrow. By the way, your sister came to visit you, *hijo*," and she left the room.

Out in the hallway she was instructing, "Don't be too long now. He needs to rest." I glanced over at my roommate across the room and he rolled his eyes. His wife had launched fully into her ritual of knitting and making plans for a vacation on which, according to him, she would squander his life insurance. We smiled in mutual sufferance.

"Hi," came a hushed voice. Waiting some feet away, as though requesting permission to approach, stood Ann Marisse.

"Hi," I answered, glad I had brushed my teeth. "Come here."

She took my hand and kissed my cheek—not exactly what I had in mind. Noticing my frown, she nodded towards the door, where right on cue a nursing nun bobbed her head into the room, glanced around and disappeared. Then she kissed me with a tenderness I had known only in her fingertips until then.

My amazement must have shown, because she returned a puzzled look and asked, "Does your head still hurt?"

I slipped my arm over to suppress my erection, explaining she had surprised me totally and asking how she had managed to get in.

"You won't believe it. Your mother called me! Really. Don't laugh, it scared me. I thought something had happened to you, but when she said that you were okay, I thought, God, she's mad...or something. She talks like, real formal."

She continued to whisper, sitting on the edge of the bed, leaning her body halfway over mine, her hair, falling over one shoulder and down to dance just above my chest, giving off tiny sparkles of golden light as it vibrated to her words. She was turning me on, but didn't seem to notice.

"About what?" I asked.

"Gee, anything. Who can tell with mothers? They find out everything sooner or later." She looked over at the older couple and said almost inaudibly, "...That we're going steady."

"She doesn't care," I assured, although I had no idea what my mother thought about her, except that she had asked, "The blond one?" when my brother teased me about having a new girl friend. She called her nothing else for years, in Spanish or English, varying her intonation to convey her appraisal of our relationship at a given moment. That first time, it was flat and noncommittal.

"She said if I wanted to see you I had to pretend to be your sister. So, brother, here I am." The last words rose noticeably in volume. My roommate nodded, while his wife didn't even pause. "And this you really won't believe. Today, Sister Dolores sends for me about two o'clock." Her eyes danced with excitement at the memory. I could imagine her walking to the principal's, wondering what rule she had violated. "Sister George gave me her meanest look when she got the note. Anyway, Sister Dolores tells me she's heard you'll be out a couple more days and, just in case you're worried about keeping up, I could tell you that you can miss this week's tests, but don't forget the essay on Thanksgiving due next Monday. Isn't that too much?"

"What?"

"Oh, Pauly, she wanted to say hello, or...I don't know, but wasn't it sweet? Strange, but sweet. She really likes you."

"And you, too."

"Of course." She shook her head, pleased with herself and us together. The white sheets and stark light gave her clear skin an almost translucent glow, her hair a metallic shimmer.

Then, for the first time, she mentioned her cousin's name: "Marianne told me the big guy from her school got hurt, too. He missed school today."

"Who's Marianne?" I asked, but the bobbing nun reappeared to remind everyone visiting hours were officially over.

"I've got to run," she said. "I miss you."

"Is that all?"

She kissed me on the mouth again with the same startling tenderness, barely grazing my lips, touching my cheek with her fingertips, and then opening her eyes to look at me, very close, a worried expression in her gaze.

"And I love you, Pauly," she whispered. "So get well. It's awful not to have anyone to talk to." Then she turned to leave, but paused at the door.

"And you?" she asked.

"Me too."

"I know. Bye."

Later, my cell mate omitted his usual ranting about his wife in favor of a short comment and a recommendation: "If I had a sister like yours, I'd gladly go to hell for incest. Don't let that one get away."

Next morning the nun came by to tell me my sister had left me two books, handing me one of Ellery Queen mysteries and a second, *The Diary of Anne Frank*. From the former I lifted the iconoclastic facts I rewrote into my Thanksgiving essay, while the latter, postponed for nine months, became my reading for Ann Marisse's vacation.

I did intend to read Anne Frank, being a gift from my own Ann, who for a short while signed her notes to me with a significant "e" appended to her name. Until I read the book, her implicit message would remain a mystery to me, but eighth grade in Catholic school is graduation year, with so many activities to fill the time. When the calendar cleared in June, I still hadn't read Anne Frank and, what's more, had forgotten all about it, the prodding "e" having slipped away sometime before spring, traditionally my reading season.

I hated baseball. Still do. Only movies about baseball are
more boring. Adolescent independence meant, among other
things, the right to refuse to be dragged by my father to games
where he would spend three hours talking to friends or
strangers alike—his generation attended baseball as one
might a revival meeting. Some kids took a glove and hoped for
foul balls; I took a book and prayed for rain, unlikely in Southern Cal, so I read a lot. Given my right to choose, spring
became my non-sports season, time to do nothing, mostly with
Billy, who shared my taste in sports, and Ann Marisse.

Also high on the agenda, higher than everything except
Ann Marisse, figured scheming to get a motor scooter for my
fourteenth birthday. I wanted a Vespa, quick-silvered like all
Vespas, but the customizing designs I endlessly worked out on
paper would make it unique. My earnings would never cover
it, not even hoarding every cent from working inventory at
Dick's dad's store and dollars paid me for imitating Elvis.
Besides, I blew it on a box of Valentine candy and the largest
stuffed animal I could afford, a spotted puppy with a heart-
shaped dog tag for writing a message to your girl. The candy
vanished by March, bribes doled out to Ann Marisse's brother
for minutes of absence. The puppy disappeared as well, into
her bedroom to rule over the menagerie I caught glimpses of
only when one or another ventured out into the house's more
communal spaces. So, my summer loomed bleak: no scooter,
no real job, lawn-cutting for a couple of bucks a yard, and just
hanging around. Ann Marisse was my only consolation.

It started off both good and bad, before tipping to worse.

"She what?" The phone had to be on the blink. Who would
want to meet Alonzo? "Your cousin wants to meet a guy she's
never seen."

"She has, at our baseball game."

"Tell her he's a creep."

"He's not so bad, Paul. Marianne thinks he looks like Sal
Mineo, but smiles like Elvis."

"Alonzo?"

"Please," she turned on persuasion I could feel even over the phone. "For me?"

The first Monday of vacation, Billy, Alonzo, Dick and I took a bus downtown to see *King Creole* at a first-run theater, just happening to run into Janice, Judy, Ann Marisse and cousin Marianne, the four of them in Sack dresses, 1958's joke on fashion. Nevertheless, Marianne looked impressive; no Ann Marisse, but close. Next to the cousins, Janice and Judy fared badly, but as Dick's and Billy's steadies they had nothing to prove. Marianne, on the other hand, had come to trap Alonzo, who rushed to surrender. Thirty seconds, maybe less, and his hand was on her shoulder. At the theater he bought her ticket, making the rest of us look cheap. We arrived for the earliest showing, claiming a section of the balcony as our exclusive territory. Making out with Marianne kept Alonzo from his annoying games, which struck me as the best aspect of their affair. She distracted him so well he didn't even object to sitting through the film twice.

About a quarter of the way through the second showing, Ann Marisse whispered, "Are you mad?"

"No, why?"

"You act a little strange, like you'd rather not be here."

Not want to be there? Nowhere else I'd rather be than watching Elvis in his best movie ever with Ann Marisse next to me. I'd go back there now if someone would show me the way.

"No, the movie is just so good." I couldn't explain it then, but I related to Elvis. His father was a drag, too, wanting Elvis to be like him; wouldn't give Elvis a thing unless he did as he was told. But Elvis works at what he does best, singing. And he meets this sweet girl who he wants to make love to, but he respects her, while this dark vamp with the fast body falls for him and lets him do whatever he wants, because she's that kind, you can tell by her short, straight black hair. At the brink of fourteen I saw life as the mirror reflection of *King Creole*. But Elvis did something with his anger, warning the world, "If you're lookin' for trouble, you came to the right place." No one had done it as well since James Dean in *Rebel Without a Cause*, but Dean didn't have a back-up band or cool lyrics, whereas Elvis sang it straight out. *King Creole* played up Elvis' dark side much better than *Jailhouse Rock*, because who wants to see himself as an ex-con creep, even if he turns good in the end? *King Creole* was different. He had to hang around with creeps, but he wasn't like them, never a creep himself, and someday he'd take his girl and move far away. The guys with him might steal out of a Five and Dime, but he only played his guitar to distract the people because he had no choice. I could relate. Like after practice, at Murray's Corner Store, some of us would buy Twinkies while Alonzo and Jerry lifted whatever they could hide in their jackets. Though they never shared it, I guess we were all to blame, but that's just the way you have to live sometimes. Elvis knew. You could tell in his smile, in his look, kind of like, they're with me, but I'm not with them and I'll blow this place some day. That was me, all over. But no matter what, his girl, the ponytailed angel, waited for him, right there, accepting him no matter what, taking him back and seeing him through it, just like in *Loving You*. I couldn't explain it to Ann Marisse back then. Besides, I was getting ready for the start of the second time through the "Lover Doll" routine in the Five and Dime.

With her hand, Ann Marisse turned my face, gave me a quick kiss on the lips, then rested her head on my shoulder.

"Watch," I said, looking back to the screen where Elvis was entering the store. "This song tells it all: 'From the first time that I saw you, I fell for your girly charms.'" I sang along. "Just another song, right?, until, see, she's the only one who notices the gang shoplifting," I whispered. "So he works his way over to her, ends the song, sits down and they meet, and he falls for her."

Ann Marisse lifted her head a little and said, "Yeah. And she doesn't call the cops because she loves him, too, before he even notices her."

"You know how he can tell she's a good girl?"

"Aha, her ponytail and because she's smart."

Ann Marisse was always a quick study; give her a clue and she'd jump to the ending. I went on narrating scene by scene, but she didn't mind. "Now he takes her to the hotel, but he knows he shouldn't, 'cause she's a good girl, so he changes his mind."

"What if he doesn't? What do you think she'd do when she finds out there's no party?"

"Go along, because, like you said, she loves him from the start. But he'd still back out."

"How do you know? Maybe she wants to..."

"No, she can't. I read it in my sister's movie magazine. Elvis' manager made them change it."

"Too bad," Ann Marisse said.

I glanced over, but she kept her eyes to the screen. When I looked back too, she added, "It might be more interesting, at least the second time around."

"God, what a great idea, movies that change the second time you see them. You could rewrite scenes over and over..."

"Watch the movie," she ordered.

After seeing *The Fly* a week later, Alonzo and Marianne were going steady, too. When they were together, I didn't mind him so much. She diverted his attention from the jokes and cleaned up his speech. Actually, he did it on his own, because I never heard him say anything obscene around her. He acted almost human. For my birthday, he and Marianne gave me a Ricky Nelson album; Ann Marisse, the 45 extended plays of the *King Creole* sound track. We kept the records at her house, and she wrote her name on them before taking them to a slumber party. One of them is still in my record collection.

Then, right after my birthday, Ann Marisse's father decided his family deserved a vacation. None of them had requested one, but to a man who never took no for an answer, who knew you have to take things in their proper time or lose them, the opportunity to combine business with a vacation in Colorado was nothing to turn down just because three out of four people in the family didn't feel like going. She broke it to me at the creamery.

"For how long?" I asked.

"Until school starts, maybe."

Silence. I looked down into my chocolate Coke, feeling betrayed.

"We have tons of family there, and my uncle Joe wants to build a house. He'll even pay Daddy to get it done."

"Parents always screw things up."

"It's not true," she protested, and I could tell my words had hurt her. "My parents like you. They've been really good to us, so don't say anything mean about them."

"All right, I take it back." I tried to kiss her, but she turned away, tears in her eyes.

"I'm sorry," I whispered, catching out of the corner of my eye the soda-fountain attendant giving me dirty looks for making my girl cry. "Really," I tried to convince her. She turned back, but only halfway, offering just a moist cheek for an apology kiss.

The walk back from the creamery took twice as long as usual while I persuaded her to forgive me. As long as I blamed no one for the separation, we could face it like ill-fated lovers of the screen making the most of the short time left to them. Kisses took on more passion. Whatever movie we went to that Friday, we saw little of it. Sitting on the porch swing Sunday night after dinner with her family, she let me slip my hand up under her short top and undo her bra. But then she got scared.

"Don't. When you do that it's too hard to stop."

"Stop what?"

"I don't know. Please, Pauly, fix me back up. But don't let them see you."

We sat almost in semi-darkness, promising to write and miss each other, until her mother's voice came from the front room. "Ann Marisse, it's getting late, honey."

"Yes, Mom."

Cue departure scene: dark porch, picture-window curtains drawn, the television's tenuous glimmer filters through the front-door screen, like reflections playing across a moonlit pool. Two young lovers face their first separation, he, barely fourteen, she, almost thirteen, with none of the perspective more years could provide to tell them they can't be ready for real emotions, much less love; that they are a cliché to be avoided. But they know what they feel, although they don't know what to do about it but kiss and touch. So they do, but not long, because subtle inflections in a mother's voice convey escalating imperatives.

As he moves off the porch, she says, "Don't get bored. You get sad when you're bored, and I don't like to think of you sad."

"What should I do, see other girls?" regretting the words before completing the sentence. "I didn't mean it."

"You better not," she menaces, threatening with a fist into which she tucks her ringed thumb. "If you want something to do, read Anne Frank. And write."

Stepping quickly across the porch, she kisses him ever so lightly as her hand slips from his cheek over his chest to his stomach, to linger there barely a second. Then she disappears inside the door, shouting, "He's gone, Mom."

With the bag of homemade noodles her mother was sending home to mine cradled into my arm like an imaginary football, I began the sprint home, switching it from side to side depending on the position of the trees as they lunged from the darkness to head me off, planting a foot as close to the trunk as possible, feinting one way to cut to the other, a stiff arm thrown for good measure, hand open wide, knee arched high, like the cover of our Pee Chees; or clearing hedges like Johnny Latner hurdling Army tacklers on his way to the Heismann, tossing the ball high to catch it over one shoulder on the run, fingers reaching skyward in model form, whipping down into a fullback tuck, shoulder lowered against the last tackler between me and the goal line, no hot-dogging, just All-American effort, through the door and into the light.

My mother looked up from her *Vogue* when I burst in, puffing from another hard game played across the neighborhood lawns, my pant legs wet from the sprinkler old man Lombardi used to lay out just to trap me. I held up the bag of noodles and explained, "From the blonde's mother." She smiled and nodded.

"Your father has a surprise for you," she said, and went back to reading. When I didn't react, she closed the magazine halfway in her hands to point the top of the spine towards the kitchen, insisting with her eyes. "And don't forget to thank him."

My father didn't respond to my greeting. He just stood up and signaled for me to follow him to the garage.

"I am sorry it didn't get here for your birthday," he said. "The shipment got delayed."

One generous purchase transformed my Scrooge of a father into a momentary Mr. Cleaver. When he gave me a car two years later, the feeling reprised, but these were isolated gasps in our normal silence, tokens from across a widening chasm, sincere but futile efforts to avoid the schism.

A motor scooter—a gray Lambretta, not a silvery Vespa— but a scooter. I straddled the running boards, bounced on the seat, pumped the foot brake and squeezed the clutch. The speedometer read 100 MPH. I couldn't believe it.

"Gee, Dad, how did you know?"

"Alonzo said you really wanted a Lambretta."

Lambretta? I was too happy to argue. I wanted to test it out, show it to Ann Marisse, but my mother came out to remind my father that I needed a license to drive it. So I rushed inside to call her with the news. Her mother said she had already gone to bed.

Dear Paul:

You're lucky it's not "Dear John." No letter! Another broken promise. Remember me? Ann Marisse, the girl with your silver horseshoe on her thumb and a cross with your name on it. The one who taught you to Continental and Stroll. With relatives in Colorado. Enough? I miss you, so don't be mean, write!

When Mom said you had phoned, I wanted to call, but we left so early. It put us in Arizona around noon. It was too hot to even breathe. But Colorado is lots cooler and so green. My cousins are really great. We went to the mountains to swim, but I like the beach better. That's where I wish Daddy would build us a house. Not yet, of course, because then we couldn't go to the same high school.

Mom and I are working on Daddy to leave soon, but it depends on how fast the house goes. Mom tells him he only has to get them started, but you know how he is. Meanwhile, I miss you, though I don't think you miss me, because then you would write. HINT HINT.

Love,
e
Ann^Marisse

p.s.: The pictures are to remind you.
p.p.s: Marianne told me about your scooter. Can't wait to ride it.

I still have three of the original four pictures, in a strip, the photo-booth kind. Black and white. She wore a light colored, boat-neck top, our cross worn on the outside to show it off. Her ponytail flipped from one side to the other in the two center pictures, playful reinforcement for the smiling face. Perhaps in those shots I first noticed how her upper lip formed a thin double arch over the fleshier lower one, giving all her expressions the hint of a girlish pout, even in the woman she became. In the first and last of the sequence, however, she stared at the camera directly, head erect, motionless—passport-style pictures, stern, businesslike. Poses to match her letter. In sequence they formed an animated play of the mercurial shifts she has used to fascinate me all my life, claiming they merely reflected my actions and moods, as if I were in control of her happiness. She sent them intact, the four together, with *Anne Marisse* written diagonally across the bottom, like one work signed by the artist. On the back, in contrast, in her graceful script, she had written:

> *From your future wife*
> *Ann Marisse*

Later I cut this last one off the series and placed it in a wallet she gave me for Christmas. From there it passed to a couple of others until my senior year in college, when she managed to steal it. The others turned violet and then progressively faded, some sinister chemical process absorbing her features until scarcely the outline and some darker details remained, like her eyes. They lingered stubbornly untouched for the longest time while around them her face, body, clothes and the background melted away into a parody of abstraction. The letters, in contrast, have survived remarkably well, stored in an old English Biscuit tin the origins of which my mother alone would have remembered, but I never got around to asking her.

It wasn't true I'd forgotten her. But the motor scooter expanded my field of action so widely that it took almost all my time to explore the possibilities. Then Dick's father got him one—the right kind, a Vespa—and we were gone all day, riding and discovering new neighborhoods. He took Janice and I usually carried Alonzo on the back to round it out. Alonzo had one favorite place to go: Marianne's. I'd play football with her little brother, while they talked or made out. After he nagged me for days, I relented and let him take her for a ride, which Ann Marisse then mentioned in a letter with an ambiguous phrase. I couldn't tell if she was upset about not being the first girl on the scooter, or because I hadn't told her about it in my letter. I defended myself by reminding her that my letter, other than a few lines to bring her up to date on my own travels, had been dedicated to Anne Frank's diary, which I had knocked off in record time. Granted there were extenuating circumstances.

My mother painted with a group of women who met at
the home of an aging Austrian refugee steeped in impressionism. Their conversations flowed from French to German to
Spanish or Italian in cosmopolitan fashion, returning to English especially for me. This was, of course, years before, when
my mother would drag me along for the group to use as a
model. Somewhere lie dozens of drawings and paintings of a
boy whose face must display the wonder of the linguistically
isolated child. My mother's, however, don't reflect that at all;
perhaps she never noticed how lost I felt, at least until I grew
accustomed to the sound of other languages.

Influenced by her Austrian mentor, my mother wanted to
try her hand at rural landscapes. My father and brother
couldn't take off from work, but my sister and I, she decided,
would accompany her, for our own good. She firmly believed
that children required rural vacations to insure healthy development. I had always resisted being sent to camp, but this
trip presented itself as a no-choice matter. She booked us into
a bed and breakfast in a gold-rush mining town. Its claim to
authenticity made allowances for electric lights and indoor
plumbing, but fell short of television. "Picturesque," described
it. My mother could have copied the rooms in faithful detail
and still achieved quaint distortion. Floors bulged and dipped
over and between supporting beams; not one straight line or
angle remained in the building.

The town offered two distractions: a public swimming
pool and a nine-hole miniature golf course. My sister vetoed
the first—that time of the month again—and the second was
continually occupied by kids from the surrounding area in
which, unbelievably, there existed towns with two less distractions than this one.

So, this is how I finally came to read Anne Frank,
stretched across a sagging brass bed, while my mother and
sister searched for virgin vistas. I might have learned something about location scouting if I had tagged along, but I
would not be tempted away from disposing of the haunting

Anne. I wanted no more complaints about broken promises. As I said, it read quickly, the thin volume giving out with the evening light of the second of our five-day country sojourn. Actually, I saved the last page until the next morning, for reasons I understood only in writing them to Ann Marisse. That third day I spent composing the letter she had been expecting for weeks.

Ann Marisse:

I'm trapped in *Gunsmoke*. I hope the Pony Express can avoid the Indians to get this letter to you. Seriously, THIS PLACE IS DEAD! Lucky I brought ANNE FRANK'S DIARY!!!! Now, reading a girl's diary didn't sound too cool. The bit about what to call the diary is just like my sister's. But it got pretty good. Interesting, as Sister Dolores says. Seriously, I like it. I can't imagine being cooped up with my family for years. Three days with my sister is driving me nuts. And then to live with other people. With my luck Alonzo's family would hide with us. Makes Nazis look good! But at least she had her boyfriend with her. Might not be so bad being trapped with you, but away from everybody. I really like how she watches him, like she's trying to make something happen, but she's not sure what. I know the feeling. But strange, while I was reading I kept seeing you writing the diary. Do you have one? Sister Charity made us do a journal in fourth. I made it up the night before it was due. Sometimes Frank is hard to believe. She sounds too old, you know what I mean? She had the right to still be a kid if she wanted. Who wants to be an adult? You know, I didn't want it to end, so I left the last page till today. When I like a book I wish it could go on, never end. Maybe she did too.

> Love you lots,
> Paul

p.s.: Frank should drop the "e" in her name, because it's you I saw.

Alonzo had been whiling away the time waiting for me, unable to get out to Marianne's. He was sitting on our porch when I got back, ready to go. I wanted to see her, too, because she must have heard from Ann Marisse.

"Sounds to me like Ann Marisse is having loads of fun," Alonzo yelled in my ear as we cruised Main. "Picnics, water skiing, riding horses, hell, could be Spin and Marty on *The Mouse Club*."

Marianne interpreted the basic facts differently: they had so many cousins that there was always something going on. Besides, she asked, do you want her to be bored? Standing behind her, his arms around her waist, Alonzo mouthed "oh sure" as she explained the innocence of what I had heard. She caught him and slammed an elbow into his stomach, doubling him over.

"In fact," she said, as she helped him sit down, "my dad's gonna let me fly out there next week." This verbal blow finished Alonzo off, leaving him speechless.

How they performed their departure scenes I have no idea, because I spent my time grooming the lawns I had put off for a week and cruising with Dick on our scooters. I thought about Ann Marisse, too, getting madder all the time, but Dick kept me calm.

"Don't get all shook up, man. Like she's your chick, right? So what else matters? Remember how Liz Taylor did things Hudson didn't dig, like talking to Mexicans, but never anything really bad?"

I liked Dick's way of fitting us into movies we had seen, rehashing them endlessly. He lived in films and rock music.

"Hick Texans want their wives to do nothing but sit. Real square. No wonder they get such fat asses." Unlike Alonzo, Dick used obscenity sparingly to good effect. "You should dig my relatives in San Antonio, like hogsville." He waddled around, arms out and hands cupped to simulate gigantic butts. "They need pick-up trucks to get around." How he could always make me laugh. "My mother says it's the water, so I stick to Dr. Pepper when we go." Then he broke the news: "And dig, man, we go, like tomorrow."

"No!"

"My words exactly, but who listens to me? You don't know hell until you've driven to Texas in August."

That night, after storing his scooter in the garage, he walked back out to say goodbye.

"When I get back in a week, man, we'll start running the lake every day. Football's coming!" he said, firing a quick fore-arm shiver at my shoulder. Then, burying his hands in the back pockets of his jeans, "Remember how James Dean tried to get to Hudson, making it look like Taylor had been messin' around? That's Alonzo. He's out for only himself. Take it easy, man. Dig ya later, if I live."

Years later, his cool speech suppressed, and along with it his insight, Dick would call Alonzo my best friend. Strange that as a kid, with movies as his reference, he was a keener judge of character than as an adult, when he stopped seeing the world as an epic film and tried to live it as reality.

The next day, at noon, there was Alonzo sitting in the kitchen, eating a sandwich and talking to my mother in the same polite voice he used to con nuns and priests. Once in my room, he got to the point.

"Lets go to Malibu."

"You're crazy."

"Shit, it's not so damn far on the scooter, if we leave early."

"I'm too busy," I lied.

"There's this chick, man, Sharleen! The knockers on her! She's from, get this, Hawaii, visiting Valorie, the one from St. C's who changed to Horace Mann Junior last year. Shit, if she's anything like Valorie, gees, we've got to go! They're stay-ing at Sharleen's brother's near the beach and we're invited any day this week. Come on, come on, what do you say?"

"No."

"*Madon'*, don't be a drag. Pass this up for what? A steady a million miles away who's having so much fun my girl goes to join her? Who's to know? Valorie's going to Jefferson High. And nobody from St. C's hangs around at Malibu?"

Later, when the Surf Sound and Hollywood popularized the beach scene, they never showed August crowds, just wide vistas of open sand, room for everyone to dance or make out. Ever hear The Beach Boys sing about sharing every grain of sand with twenty people? You know, crowded? Back-to-back, belly-to-belly crowded? Everyone but the girls we were looking for. Fifteen minutes exceeded my patience. I hate public beaches.

"Don't crap out, Paul. We shot lots on gas to get here."

"We?" I asked, but he kept eyeing the crowd from the back seat, pretending not to hear me.

I pulled a U-turn to give up, actually relieved.

"Okay, let's try one last thing." He jumped off the scooter and crossed the street to a hot dog stand. From the nodding head and pointing fork I could tell he was getting directions to Sharleen's brother's.

From the beach it was just a few minutes. What looked like a small house from the curb, opened up into more luxury than we had experienced outside of a movie. The crowds had driven the girls back to their private pool. Valorie led us out back to introduce me to Sharleen, the image of a real Hawaiian: straight black hair down to her hips, her skin a deep mahogany—all over, as her bikini revealed. In comparison, Valorie's suit seemed modest, almost chaste. Where Sharleen's rode low on the hips, a small triangle of cloth exposing her lower stomach, Valorie's covered from her navel to her thighs, like shorts. While two tiny triangles of sheer blue and crimson cloth accented Sharleen's breasts, Valorie's were entirely hidden under something like a halter top. The key difference lie in one detail: Sharleen's bikini tied—and untied—at the neck, back and hips; three hooks locked Valorie's top at the back, and the bottom gripped like a girdle,

which it closely resembled. But, both of them, each in her own
way, were more than we had imagined. And there we were,
the four of us alone.

The first hour we played badminton—if you can imagine
the spectacle—swam and had lunch; then we got down to the
purpose of the trip, making out. That's just how Valorie put it,
as if offering us dessert.

"Want to make out?" she asked me, right in front of Alonzo and Sharleen.

"Why not?"

"Where?" Sharleen asked Alonzo.

"Your choice," he responded politely.

We got the living room sofa. I really can't swear where
they went, but to hear Alonzo tell it, they ended up in the bedroom. No matter, it wasn't for long, because I had to get home.
I wanted to.

On the way back, Alonzo shouted himself hoarse. Fortunately, the wind muffled his words, because I didn't want to
hear them. I caught snatches of "snatch" and bits of "tits," and
more exclamations strung together than grammar allows,
laced with persistent, "What did you get?" or "How'd you do?"

"Shit, what a day," he rasped when I left him off.

Smiling and bobbing his shoulders to some inner beat,
wound tight and spinning his wheels, he felt happy and
shared it with me, probably assuming we now shared something important. When I felt he was about to ask one more
time how I had done, I beat him to it with: "What are you
going to tell Marianne?"

His face went blank, eyes wide open, body freezing, as if I
had lifted the needle off the turntable in his head. "Nothing.
What they don't know can't hurt 'em. Why?"

One could admire his absence of conscience. He saw no rela-
tion between one girl and the other. They existed in different
worlds. Most likely he was right, but I wasn't ready for it yet.

In spite of my nagging guilt, we repeated the trip twice
that week. Our homebound conversation did become a little

less one-sided as I fed him a few choice details. In the end, neither claimed to have gotten his first lay, but what we did get seemed more than we could have dreamed.

Valorie kissed like a fish. Sounds unromantic, admittedly, but we're not talking romance yet. Lust—little league, but nonetheless, lust. This I shared with Alonzo: She had a way of opening her lips that made me feel she could swallow me down. She explored my mouth with her tongue, not softly like Ann Marisse the few times she followed my tongue back with hers when we Frenched. I excluded, of course, mention of French kissing with Ann Marisse. That Valorie's breasts required another set of hands to do them justice, I also admitted, again with no reference to the anatomy of mutual acquaintances. Alonzo, on the other hand, included Marianne freely in his comparisons. It irritated me to hear him pronounce her name next to Sharleen's and I told him.

"They're all the same," he corrected me. "Just keep them apart if you want to keep them at all."

Those were his last words our final Malibu afternoon. Sharleen flew back to Hawaii and Dick returned from Texas. The next weeks, we focused on football and facing competition three years older and bigger. Alonzo bragged about Sharleen for a while, but, like everything, it got old. A few times he referred to another girl, but he didn't mention names. Not yet, anyway.

❋　❋　❋

The first night back from Malibu, my mother handed me an envelope from Colorado. The letter had gotten mixed in with her uncle's mail, so Ann Marisse had remailed it with a second letter. The first and longer of the two was a this-is-how-we-spend-the-days kind of letter where she surveyed, almost in Marianne's exact words, all the things Alonzo had tried to turn sinister. This confirmation of the cousins' identical stories doubly canceled Alonzo's version. There was nothing she couldn't or wouldn't tell me.

Like on a split screen, images from Malibu—Valorie, the kissing fish—flashed in my mind next to those of Ann Marisse, her fidelity reconfirmed, and I felt tremendously guilty. Worse, Dick had been right. How could I have ignored a real friend? Finally, towering ever larger: Ann Marisse could find out! I felt like going to confession, though it was only Tuesday. I could get up for six-o'clock mass, but then I'd draw my mother's questions. No, it would have to wait, but it worried me a long time, especially when I reread her letter.

Dearest Paul,

I'm supposed to be at a picnic, but I begged Mom to let me stay so I could write to you. She called me a silly and foolish child, so I said, do I have to start acting like an adult so soon? She gave me the strangest look, but it worked. Good thing, too, because Marianne comes tomorrow, so it's my last chance to be alone. You're to blame. I had to answer your letter. I love it, Pauly, especially the part about *Ann Frank's Diary*. You're right, she's very mature, but we already do more. Do you think Peter touched her? I hope so. I'd hate to think of her dying without feeling what I do when you touch me, even though the first time I thought I was going to die. Did I tell you? My insides knotted up until I couldn't stand it, and when you got all excited, I got even more. But then you stopped. I was shooting into the sky, but you were holding me down, saving me from getting lost. You know all this, but do you think Ann did? Because you have to feel it to know. Like I don't know what IT feels like. Marianne says it must be awful, but poor Ann and Peter never found out. They didn't have time, and that's so sad. Maybe I am silly and foolish. Do you care?

Yes, Ann was lucky to be trapped with the boy meant for her. Sister Faith says God chooses one person we're meant to marry. That's why divorce is a sin. Once you know who, nothing else matters. I can't bear to think of them apart. What if they lived, got lost and didn't find each other, maybe even married someone else and ruined everything? Lucky it can't happen to us.

Yes, sweet Pauly, I saw you in it, too. Cuz I've watched you forever. I saw you play and fight, and everything. I watched till you noticed me. It took so long, but now you can see me, even in Ann Frank. That's scary, too. Marianne says we shouldn't let boys see what we really feel, none of you can be trusted.

Sister Charity's journal! I wrote about a fifth-grader, leader of his own gang, but a cute choir boy. She wrote on it, WRITE ABOUT YOUR LIFE, NOT BOYS!, but she was wrong. It was already only one: You. Since always.

I wished for you when I was so little you couldn't notice me. I wanted to grow up fast before you went to high school and found someone else. When my chest started to get big I was happy, because boys notice girls like that. Now I have my wish. I love you, Pauly, so very much.

Your Ann Marisse

p.s. If we were trapped, I'm not sure I'd want you to wait. We might die and never know.

Guilty. Miserable. I accepted that I had acted like a real rat. Nevertheless, it didn't keep me from making two more trips to Malibu. While my better judgment told me not to return, something else much stronger pulled me back.

That first day, I had wanted to go home. Valorie kissed great, but so did other girls who didn't live close enough to become a problem. When I sat up and shouted to Alonzo that it was time to go, Valorie asked me to hook her top back. She leaned forward and placed her hand where none but my own had wandered before. She left it there while I hooked her suit, moving her palm and squeezing her fingers slightly, causing me to miss the first couple times. That's what took me back: the chance Valorie might do it again. And while her hand never slipped inside my suit, that possibility, too, drew me back. Valorie was my dark vamp, sucking me in, just like Elvis in *King Creole* singing to the world, "I'm evil." But my ponytailed angel would always be there when I realized bad girls aren't worth losing good love over. Especially if she didn't find out, which, other than making high school varsity, became my biggest worry for the next few weeks.*

❋   ❋   ❋

Holy Trinity H.S. We approached it in attack-wing fashion, my Lambretta flying point, Dick's Vespa covering my right and Billy's, my left, each manned with a co-pilot to scan for surprise attacks as we entered what for years had been enemy territory. The first confrontation came when we tried to park in a lot upperclassmen considered exclusively theirs. It wasn't the last...but that's not the point here. Ann Marisse had stayed at St. C's and the separation presented problems of when and where, compounded by volumes of homework and longer practices after school. Nothing I saw among the freshman girls tempted me, except maybe a dark-haired Mexican riding the back of a Vespa, sidesaddle, her tight skirt inching up over her knees, her black hair cut short and straight. In the fashion code of the day, she had to know what she looked like. Her dimpled, come-on smile confirmed the impression, and the change into a loose school uniform the second week couldn't dispel it. But I hardly saw her, and frankly didn't care.

---

*Thinking back now, as I review proofs of this book, I realize the fascination arose precisely from seeing Valorie. Other than my sister's, I hadn't seen a naked breast. I had caught glimpses of Ann Marisse's, but that was something different, special. Valorie's breasts were simply breasts, and she exposed them naturally, sitting up to drink a Coke or just to cool off, making no effort to cover herself. If she caught me looking at her breasts, she didn't try to prevent it. She could have been alone and not act more unrestrained. Her breasts showed a rosy tint from having tried to get an all-over tan like Sharleen's, an effort abandoned, she told me, because it hurt. I wondered if her lower stomach was the same shade of pink, but never found out. Against the fading sunburn, her nipples were like crushed berries I hadn't learned to savor yet. I hadn't gone beyond palming, rubbing, and pressing. If she knew better, she didn't teach me. Her recommendations were limited to "not so hard" and "don't stay in one place"—good advice for beginners. But with Valorie, looking at her was better. I remember nothing of how she felt, but the way she let me see her remains clear. If offered the choice, I take the visual over the tactile in most cases.

Ann Marisse had returned the weekend before school. She looked different, shorter, but then I had grown an inch and half. Since Marianne came home with them, Alonzo had accompanied me as well. While the reunion fell short of what we had planned, it accurately predicted the up-coming year: we would try to be alone but find few opportunities.

Everything seemed a plot to keep us apart. The first day, my Latin teacher picked up Ann Marisse's picture I was using as a bookmark and, without interrupting our sing-song recitation, tucked it into the fathomless folds of her habit and refused to give it back. At P.T.A. she showed it to my father and asked what he thought should be done about it. Through the grapevine I heard he answered, "It's normal, leave him alone." A consistent man, that's exactly how he had always delt with me. But she neither returned the picture nor followed his advice. If anything she rode me harder. She victimized others, too, her dictatorial mien winning her the nickname Little Caesar, which she probably secretly relished.

Sister Augustine understood algebra backwards and forwards, as it should be, but expected us to do likewise out of sheer instinct. She didn't teach, just assigned problems and glared, offended, if you asked for help. Teaching existed somewhere below or above her, and she stubbornly remained on the horizontal of the algebraic equation. The source of my refusal to balance symbols in equal proportions she attributed to the evil presence of a rectangle of Kodak paper she whisked off my desk one day, tore to shreds over my head and made me pick up to throw away in the principal's office, from which I was to bring a note documenting my visit. By the time I returned, class was over and my books scattered in the hall. I never managed to catch up and didn't much care. Ours became a daily struggle of wills. I passed because, as sweet Sister Dolores used to say, God is good and provides for the faithful in strange ways. Copying Phyllis Brenner's homework and off her tests must have figured into the divine plan, because I never got caught.

In Religion, Phylo and I sat side by side in front of Father
Porta's desk. She was cute, smart and playful, a good friend.
Junior year, when her boyfriend dumped her and she borrowed my shoulder to cry out her hurt, I discovered she could
make out better than anyone in my class. But as freshmen we
only played footsy, taking off our shoes to rub each other's feet
in the aisle. If Porta suspected, he didn't care. He was fond of
repeating that, after eight years of catechism, we already
knew enough about sin to make the rest of our lives miserable.

English and speech after lunch salvaged my day. Sister
Rose, so intense, so seriously romantic, could flash light and
frivolous, an emotions-on-the-shirt-sleeve-style teacher. She
insisted we take *Romeo and Juliet* to heart and she ripped her
habit reciting the pound-of-flesh scene from *Merchant of
Venice*. She wept for Desdemona and mouthed a silent curse
on Hamlet for sending Ophelia to a nunnery, but refused to
discuss how her death and entering the convent seemed related. What she called Dick's and my imminent cynicism so
upset her that she called in Father Madlen to discuss freedom
and free will. We watched her dismayed expressions as she
realized that not only was he a fool, he was grammarless fool.
She assigned us *Wind, Sand, and Stars* and forevermore
trusted only in great literature to sway young minds. When
Father Mad ran away with his housekeeper, Sister Rose probably offered a prayer in relief.

English, fun and unpredictable, warmed us up for the
main act: Sister Kate, so named after *The Taming of the
Shrew*. We were steeped in Shakespeare. Sister Kate could
come on like a shrew, but she seldom needed to. The biggest
woman I've ever seen, a hulking six-eight, maybe more. She
thought nothing of picking football players clean off the
ground, as she did me at the slave auction for Mission Relief
during her all-girls class. For a good cause, girls bought a boy
for a day to carry books or lunch trays. Bidding lagged, so Sister Kate gave it a boost, lifting me two feet into the air. I

brought a record price, sold to Karen, the cutie with black hair.

If Sister Rose's forte was allowing herself to be moved by readings in class, Sister Kate's lay in moving us from one emotion or thought to another through words and voice. She directed the drama club, too, but in class she insisted on the word's power sustained only by the range of the voice and minimal gestures. She also moved many of us into speech club through pure inspiration. Dick and I teemed up for debate, spending hours devising arguments on the virtues of Soviet education. Saturdays, I found myself at the library or attending speech meets when I should have been at a movie. But no one forced me.

Sister Kate was my only great woman teacher I didn't fall in love with. There was just too much of her. But learn I did. Hunched over an adult-size desk reduced to preschool proportions by her voluminous mass, she worked with small groups of us, taking a speech apart line by line, laying bare themes, propositions, strategies, logic, suspense, sequence, images— the architecture of a convincing text.

In mid-November, between football and basketball seasons, she called me to her desk to announce I no longer would debate, revealing to me my true genre: poetry recitation. The idea sounded crazy to me, but no one argued with Sister Kate. "Something forceful yet moving," she said, "to take advantage of your voice," and handed me a leather-bound volume opened to "Dunkirk." My father commented that at least the theme was proper for a man. Years later, while filming a reenactment of the battle, I imagined her rising immense over the beach, above blazing tanks and strafing Stukas, a hand barely held out towards the "haze in the east that looked like smoke," her words clear and resonant over the din of precisely planned explosions. I won six ribbons and placed in state finals, surprising both of us, although she wouldn't admit it.

At final exam time, in mid-June, the room stuffy-hot, when we were tediously reciting our best piece to classmates who had heard it so many times before, I chanced my grade on a reading from Anne Frank's diary. Sister Kate looked up from her scoring pad, shook her head, but didn't smile until the end, when my heatstroked mates lavished me with a brief, apathetic applause. Not bad, considering no one else received any at all.

Her last words to me that day were, "Some risk nothing and survive, others risk little only to fail, but, ah, those blessed few who risk it all on a prayer, such a blaze of glory in their tragic descent." Nuns are trained to spring sayings like this on you. She gave me an A, then died of cancer over the summer before we knew she was sick.

❋ ❋ ❋

With all this going on, things between Ann Marisse and me couldn't but change. And I've left out a lot: Dick and I lettered in varsity football, none of us got beyond B-team in basketball, and I missed every dance but Homecoming—the latter exception a result of Alonzo's manipulations. I would have skipped it, too, gladly, but Alonzo insisted that his senior—we each served a senior player on the team—threatened to kill him if he didn't show for the dance. I, for one, welcomed the thought of his death.

"That's your problem," I said. "I'm not going."

Dances were closed to outsiders, especially grade-school girls better stacked than most of the seniors. We had tried to smuggle Ann Marisse and Marianne into a sock hop, but two nuns blocked the door. It did no good to introduce them as future students; they made no exceptions. So I wasn't going to Homecoming, that is until Ann Marisse convinced me. Whenever Alonzo dipped his spoon in the crock, you could count on bitter brew—and an aftertaste to last for years. Alonzo pleaded his case to Marianne, who interceded with Ann Marisse, who agreed to persuade me. It took an extra charming "Please, for me" assault, but she won. Lucky for Alonzo he practiced with the B-team, or he wouldn't have been able to move, much less dance, after what I would have done to him, especially when I found out who he had set me up with.

"Karen says you can work off your slave contract by taking her to the dance. Some deal, huh? I'd like to work her out."

Dick's father drove us to the dance, then mine picked us up and took all three couples for a hamburger and Coke before dropping them off. Alonzo played it cool until Dick got out to walk Janice to her door. She knew Marianne, so he took no chances. But as soon as Dick closed the door, Alonzo pounced, necking and groping. Sitting up front with my father, Karen between us, we rode silently to her house. At her door I started to thank her.

"For what? I didn't do nothing, and neither did you."

"I'm sorry," I apologized for a transgression I had apparently committed.

She let me have it straight: I had paid no attention to her, not really talked to her, nor even tried to kiss her. Her investment, she complained, had been poorly repaid. I offered the excuse that I hardly knew her, so what could we have in common? I sounded like a snob and hated Alonzo for putting me in this position. Maybe we had a lot in common, she protested, and asked me what I liked most. All I could think of was Ann Marisse waiting for me to go by after the dance. I mumbled, lots of things, then made the mistake of asking her what she liked to do. She responded by kissing me, rubbing herself cat-like against my chest. We instantly found a common interest no doubt, but I had to get home, so I promised her another chance to explore our mutual interests and escaped.

Just before one o'clock I switched off the scooter's engine to coast into Ann Marisse's driveway. According to plan, she'd sneak out after her parents were asleep and wait in the dark living room for me to tap on the window. It took three before the curtain parted a sliver. I probably would have given up after the first one, but Karen's goodbye had me turned on. Finally, the front door opened.

"Hi," she said through a full screen door, a night light in the kitchen hollowing out a tenuous glow in the darkness behind her.

"Can I come in?"

"No. I promised my mother we'd only say good night through the screen. She guessed—what else could I do?"

"Great. What about me?"

"Yes, what about you? I've been thinking about you all night, Pauly. How was the dance?"

"A real drag. I thought about you all night, too."

"Good. Oh, can you come over tomorrow? It's corny, but my mother's making a birthday cake and some kids from school will be here. It won't last long, since it's a school night."

We touched fingertips through the screen, recalling old times at the other house, our first year together and how different things seemed now. She looked so tired in the dim light, her eyelids floating dreamily in spite of her best efforts, like a child resisting sleep. Her hair, combed out and free of the ribbons usually holding it, fell over her shoulders. The lace trim of her nightgown rested just above her knees. The street light illuminating the porch where I stood filtered through the full-length screen to where her figure emerged from the shadows, drifting half in and half out, at times barely visible.*

I had forgotten her thirteenth birthday! That's what I mean. The high school routine, with its constant demands, seemed like a plot. The year before, I had had the books under control, sports slotted into manageable hours, and lots of time for Ann Marisse. I liked it that way. But I couldn't get it worked out during freshman year. My salvation lay in knowing that the next year she'd be there, too, going through the

*Years later I would remember her image that night, floating ethereal, like a Pre-Raphaelite virgin, the night light haloing her head in an aura that seemed to emanate from her hair. I wanted to recreate the effect for a film we were shooting in Paris. It proved difficult, even for lighting specialists. I wanted her then, and the image improves with memory. At that point she was more a girl than a woman, but desire diminishes not one degree.

same things, but we would be together for at least three years there, and then forever.

Most weekends the four of us—Alonzo and Marianne, Ann Marisse and I—ended up at a movie, or dancing and making out at one of their houses. The two cousins, reflections in a family mirror. Ann Marisse the original image and Marianne the darker, more brittle duplication, almost exact around the mouth and eyes, but her nose less finely drawn. So similar, until they smiled and the illusion would shatter, leaving Ann Marisse suddenly alone, centered as in a tight close-up. Looking at me across space... We were caught up in something I still can't explain... She watched me, but I learned to watch her watching, to expect her there when I looked up. It became the proper ending to any action, to look up and try to find her gaze across any distance, a basketball court, an assembly or a church congregation. It became a habit I've never lost. I learned to see her the way she wanted to be seen by me; in return I came to depend on her gaze.

※　※　※

Christmas Eve, Ann Marisse's clan gathered at her grandmother's home before going on to midnight mass. It was also the traditional time to present prospective new members of whatever age. She lived in what was then still a semirural area, in a Tudor-style house along a two-lane road, one of those tree-lined routes hiding from developers out in the valley. The closest neighbors were a quarter of a mile off. A driveway led past the house to an old barn turned garage. Cars already lined the drive and the road's unpaved shoulder for a good distance in both directions when my brother dropped Alonzo and me off. We walked stiffly, consoling each other for the tight collars and choking ties, feeling anxious about confronting the whole family at once. A couple of kids stopped shooting their toy guns at each other when we climbed the steps to the porch and rang the bell. I glanced over at Alonzo, who stared at the door, frozen, looking more scared than I had

ever seen him: body rigid, the fingers of one hand cupped over
the edge of his coat sleeve, holding his breath. Just as the door
opened, his tongue flicked over his upper lip and he spoke a
startled hello.

Once inside, however, I found myself next to a stranger in
Alonzo's body, one very much at home with the rest of the
strangers surrounding me, smoking with one hand and sipping from tall drinks with the other. Alonzo sprang from
immobility to perpetual motion, as if he had stepped in front
of a camera. He retained just enough Italian to cross some
boundary I hadn't suspected before entering this house.
Maybe it had been there all along, invisible to me, but its discovery made me feel betrayed. Meanwhile, Alonzo sucked up
to male relatives with *cumba* this and *cumba* that, and a million *madon'*. His hands jabbed and sliced air like a boxer's,
accenting a foreign cadence in his voice. I'd heard it before,
sure, had seen him bob and weave, but this performance was
pure ethnic shtick, laughable had Ann Marisse's relatives not
responded in kind. I felt caught in a dance to which I didn't
know the steps.

"He's great," a stocky man said to me, putting a hand on
my shoulder. "Real funny. Yous guys cousins?"

"I'm not Italian," and I wondered why it sounded so like
an apology.

"You're forgiven," Alonzo condescended. "Nobody's perfect."

Then Ann Marisse took my right hand in her left and
began to lead me across a large living room, rescuing me from
further inquisition. Just as I understood the direction and reason of our movements, she pivoted on her left foot to face me
in a motion so familiar that my left hand instinctively rose to
find her right coming to meet it. Instantly, I felt at home within the small circle she formed out of our bodies cupped around
a space reserved for only us.

"Except you," she said, glancing up at me, her eyes narrowed a trifle, on her lips the faintest trace of a smile. Before I

could answer, she was already dissolving what had scarcely
had time to become a pose, spinning back out on her right heel
to renew our trajectory across the room.

We were approaching a low, wide sofa where the venera-
ble Donna Costanza held court, with Ann Marisse's mother to
her left and Marianne's to her right, a matriarchal triumvi-
rate. In the bronze-veined mirror tiles covering the wall
behind the sofa, I could see our dual image drawing toward us
until coming to stop in front of the women, like kids reporting
to the principal. The Ann Marisse in the mirror winked and
puckered her lips, but caught herself, biting the side of her
lower lip in a gesture of recomposure. Ann Marisse: her hair
freed again like the night before her thirteenth birthday, but
now radiant under an overhead, crystal fixture which sprin-
kled it with tiny highlights. Ann Marisse: in the mirror next
to me, taller in high heels, the top of her head even with my
eyes, a blue velvet dress cut tight in the bodice to flair at the
waist. She looked older and we... we looked so fine together.

"At her age, I was married off to a man I didn't even
know," the old woman lectured her daughters. "And neither of
you were much older," and with a sharp look back to her left,
added a biting, "especially you," which snapped Ann Marisse's
mother's head down in deferential recognition of a distant, but
not forgotten infraction.

Then, accepting my hand, she listened to Ann Marisse's
introduction, studying me all the while. When Ann Marisse
finished, Donna Costanza tightened her grip and pulled me
down to bring my face close to hers.

"But the world is different now, *mio figlio*, so you will
have to wait, *capisce?*" A burst of laughter came from across
the room where Alonzo continued entertaining. She looked
over at the source of the disturbance, frowned and tugged
slightly on my hand again. She seemed about to kiss me on
the cheek, but instead brought her lips next to my ear to whisper, "We are all Americans here." She released her grip and

sat back against the sofa. The ritual was over, and, apparently, I had been approved.

Christmas night at Marianne's, Alonzo and I opened identical boxes from the cousins revealing identical Perry Como sweaters. We, too, had bought them sweaters. I had taken Alonzo to Bullock's where we looked over the selection, wishing we could afford the beautiful turtlenecks on display. After agreeing on a fifteen-dollar maximum, we browsed the appropriate racks and picked different colors of the same style. When they opened the boxes, however, Marianne's held the turtleneck we had both found too expensive. No matter what Ann Marisse ever said to me over time about Alonzo, this one act revealed the essence of our relationship. More than the homework borrowed to copy but returned after my session of class had ended, more than forgotten messages that made me miss appointments, more than the missed blocks that got me thrown for losses, even more than the way he slid in behind me to take advantage of my momentary absences, this summed it up best. We had agreed and he had acted out the agreement to the last moment, then let me look cheap. When they left us alone to try them on, I swung, this time full force, hitting him in the arm and sending him sideways into an armchair.

"You chicken shit. You've had it this time," I said to him, trying to control my voice if not my temper.

Rubbing his arm as I stood over him, one hand clenched and the other signaling for him to get up, he made up some lie about his sister needing the first one and offering him the extra money if he would get another. I didn't want to let myself be convinced. I wanted to kill him, smash his foul mouth, make him take back both sweaters and start over again. But the cousins returned, wearing their presents, and we pretended nothing had happened.

Marianne's mother reappeared from the kitchen with eggnog and sat down to drink with us, hers smelling distinctly of rum. After a few more glasses, she asked me if I really got paid for imitating Elvis. She wanted to see me, even offered to pay, but I did it free, to reclaim the spotlight I felt had shifted to Alonzo over the last few days.

At the time, we didn't know Elvis would never come home from Germany, not the real *King Creole* Elvis, just some imitation less authentic than mine on Christmas, 1958. No one knew yet, so it was possible to imitate him without nostalgia. It was still the real thing, the record player blasting, Ann Marisse and Marianne sitting on the floor screaming, Marianne's mother holding a hand up to her mouth, perhaps wishing she hadn't made the request, and Alonzo slumped into a chair, rubbing his arm and pretending not to watch. Ann Marisse kissed me on the cheek when I finished and whispered, "I could tear your clothes off and blame it on Elvis."

"Do you do anything, Alonzo?" Marianne's mother asked him.

"He's a born salesman," I answered for him. "He'll sell you anything."

❉   ❉   ❉

Easter promised the next ordeal, another gathering of the clan. On New Year's Eve, Ann Marisse mentioned it to me, but I begged off. To her inquiring look, I responded, "No thanks, I don't belong there."

"Because you're not Italian," she said in a low voice, as though talking to herself and weighing a problem. We were dancing in her den. Sliding her hands up to rest on my shoulders, she leaned her upper body back, then she whisked her hair away from her face with a toss of her head and stared up at me, but said nothing until the song ended. Then, she leaned her body back against mine to hug me with both arms, tightly, her smooth cheek pressed to my neck.

"Okay," she said. "Don't go. I'll miss you. So will my Nonna, but she won't forgive you, so you'll have her curse on your soul forever."

"I'll go, already," I gave in, pulling back to look down at her.

"Good. Maybe we can make it more fun for you."

The day after New Year's, we rode out to Donna Costanza's on my scooter. Ann Marisse directed me around back and led me into the kitchen where her grandmother sat drinking coffee and talking to a neighbor, in Italian, of course. Ann Marisse joined in, but her vocabulary far exceeded the few ethnic flags Alonzo had waved to fake his way through. She greeted her grandmother and the neighbor, presented me, and then, standing with one arm around her grandmother's shoulders, continued in the conversation, mixing English where the Italian words escaped her. Neither of the old women reprimanded her hybrid speech; on the contrary, the effort pleased them. When I heard my name and saw the two women glance over to where I sat eating a cenci, I knew Ann Marisse had said something about me. Other than that, I felt as lost as the first time, yet now at least not excluded. I was both subject and object of their conversation.

"So you want to learn Italian, Paul," her grandmother stated more than asked, giving me no chance to respond. The affair had been discussed and decided. Why consult me? Ann Marisse smiled in impish delight, her ponytail flipping from side to side as it had in the pictures from Denver. Donna Costanza said something to her friend, provoking all three women to laugh. Infected by their mood, I joined in, wondering all the while how I could manage Italian lessons on top of everything else.

❋ ❋ ❋

Classes started again for spring semester with much the same routine. Basketball instead of football, but all else familiar. With my poem memorized, enough Latin to pull me through weekly calls to the blackboard, and the basic algebraic skills necessary to understand Phylo's homework when I copied it, matters were well in hand. I never missed an assignment—not even math, thanks to Phylo's reliable assistance.

There was one incident just after Christmas, when the principal caught Karen and me behind the stage curtain during play practice. She guessed at what her eyes had barely missed, despite my believable, because true, excuse about measuring the stage for the set. Karen held a pad and pencil, and I, a tape measure with which I had been taking her measurements when we started making out. Sister Kate confirmed our assignment, but the Principal drew the curtain herself and issued instructions over the intercom later the same day that it should always remain open.

Even so, making time for Italian lessons turned out to be no easy trick. Friday nights and Sundays afternoons we had basketball games, while many Saturdays were taken up by speech meets. That left Saturday nights, and then Alonzo and Marianne insisted on doing something together. We managed to put them off several times, but not enough to make me fluent. Nightly on the phone, Ann Marisse repeated crucial vocabulary—*Ti amo*—and when we were together, she tried to keep my mind on language, but her mouth, its thinly drawn upper lip and lush lower lip, shaping sensual syllables inches from my own, spoke messages impossible to resist. So we practiced kissing—*Mi piace molto, cara mia*. The few times we did drive out to her grandmother's were like meetings of a secret club.

As the weather warmed towards March, the old woman began to work daily in her garden, tending herbs and preparing the soil for spring planting. She would receive us out back with a table set under the tall oak near the old well. There were plums, cherries and even apple trees because her husband had wanted to remember the old country, the mountains of northern Italy where he had grown up without citrus. He planted oranges, lemons and kumquats along the sides of the house where he didn't have to see them out the front or rear windows. There were grapes, of course, for homemade wine.

Now her sons-in-law worked them for her—as I might be expected to do someday—but she supervised every step.

The first Saturday, Ann Marisse made me shout *Bon giorno* to Donna Costanza. She signaled us over to the table where she had bread, cheese and fruit waiting, with a pitcher of ice tea and an uncorked bottle of wine, a strip of masking tape in lieu of a label, *Zinfandel* scrawled across it in faded bluish-violet script. She joined us, peeling off her soiled work gloves. As regal and dominating as she had appeared at Christmas, now she played the role of a rural, old-world widow, a serene matron in a black dress, black apron, black stockings and shoes. She sat down between us at the head of the table, took a sip of wine and spoke to Ann Marisse, who then leaned forward and kissed her on the cheek. Turning to me, she repeated the command: *"Dammi un bacio, Paolino."* When I didn't move, Ann Marisse began to laugh. In what exploded like one long fiery word, her Grandmother must have scolded her, because she stopped abruptly and apologized to me in English. Her grandmother's harsh look faded, and she placed a dark hand over Ann Marisse's much paler one.

"No one laughed at you, *Anna Marizina*, no matter what foolish things you said. With you, yes, but never at you."

She repeated the command, and this time I imitated Ann Marisse, leaning forward to kiss the old woman on the cheek. As I relaxed back into my chair, Ann Marisse's eyes held me in a steady gaze. She seemed fixed on a thought and my face simultaneously, but the lesson allowed for no questions unrelated to the subject. Donna Costanza ruled here. Already she was formulating another phrase for me to fathom.

We managed to visit her several more Saturdays, repeating our approach and greeting exactly, a ritual of schemers in a maturing plot. After the first session, they decided to cover only the bare minimum for effect. Donna Costanza preferred to talk with us about other things. Her life, her trip to the United States after World War I, her marriage to a man she could barely understand because he came from another region of Italy with its own strange dialect, not Italian according to her. She blamed that mixture of regional groups in the United States for the failure of her children to continue speaking the language. How could they be expected to speak Italian when their parents spoke two different languages they both called Italian? But then with a flick of her fingers, she dismissed her own thought, admitting that she had wanted her children to speak English, so they could grow up and be understood.

"So my daughters could talk to their husbands without an interpreter," she said, and laughed. "And good thing, because just like me, they all married men who speak Italian like pigs."

"Nonna, that's terrible."

"Try talking to your father. That *is* terrible."

She turned, looked at me, then nodded her head a few times, as if she had estimated my value and found it neither too great nor hopelessly lacking.

"And now *mia nipote* can talk to her young man in perfect English and a little Italian, too, and it's all right if you do or if you don't."

Ann Marisse hugged her and then reached across the table to kiss my cheek. It surprised me, unaccustomed to displays of affection in front of adults; in the dark back seat of a car on the way home from a party, yes, but not in their full view in daylight. She, however, moved secure in her spontaneity. We were in her space; she felt no need to weigh her movements.

"It doesn't matter what language you say I love you in," Ann Marisse said.

"For some in our family it still does." Sounding ominously like a warning, her words produced a momentary pause. "At least you two must agree what it means," Donna Costanza added and then, as an afterthought, continued, "More than language, it's a matter of the heart; but the head and body, too, especially later, when you make a family. Like the land, your grandfather used to say. He meant me. For him I was like the land, something to care for...well, he loved to make things grow. But he resembled the land more than me. He needed constant cultivation, or the fruit turned wild. I didn't know him. God made the choice, so I learned to lived with him, and together we made this. But your life, children, is no longer like a farm, more like tiny plots of land and new houses every year. No room for all the plants you want or time to watch them grow. So choose the ones you need most and keep them in small pots to take with you, like gypsies. Maybe someday you'll find a place where you can be alone together, and then plant them in your own ground."

Ann Marisse started to ask her something, but the phone rang, drawing Donna Costanza into the house.

"I like your grandmother."

"I can tell." And looking over to the house, she began to relate how the old woman used to talk to her. "When I was little and came over to stay with her—she took care of me when my brother had chicken pox. I used to play right over there... well, actually they told me to stay there, but I went all over, getting into everything.

"Want to know a secret? I kissed my first boy in that field. Tony Rossuto. We were playing and it got really hot, so we sat down to cool off. They had corn planted then, and Tony told me my hair looked like corn silk. I thought he meant all wild and messy, so I got mad and told him to take it back. He wouldn't, because to him corn silk was the prettiest thing in the world, golden and soft and shiny. He told me it was worth lots of money, because kings and priests wore silk. Oh, how long I believed silk came from corn, but I couldn't figure out why my grandparents weren't rich when they had so much. Anyway, I told Tony to kiss me, because it's how grownups make up after a fight. He thought it over a long time before saying yes." She stared at the field, perhaps raising up high stalks of corn in her mind, searching between the rows. "I don't remember the kiss. Isn't it strange? Everything up to it, then Tony running away, but I can't remember his kiss."

I leaned across the table to offer her one of mine to remember instead.

"Silly, I remember yours all the time. And other things, too." She touched my ring to her breast. Instinctively I looked over to Donna Costanza's back door.

"Sometimes you really are silly, Paolino," she said, throwing her arms around my neck and jumping into my lap. She nestled her head between my shoulder and neck and began to hum *Volare*. We sat for a few minutes without talking, and then she sat up a bit, twisting her torso to face me, her arms resting across my shoulders. After looking me in the eyes a moment, with an expressionless look I had seen the first day we came, she started to talk again, picking up the thread of a theme she had left dangling some minutes back.

"Sometimes, when I ask her what something means, instead of answering, she tells me to wait for understanding. Give time time, she tells me, the future will take care of explaining all you need to know. Isn't she wonderful?"

I remember it all as wonderful. Sitting behind the house, under a tree, surrounded by the groomed gardens, orchards and vineyards of a couple of generations of one family and feeling part of it simply by holding Ann Marisse's hand. She was my connection. As I think back, I realize she must have been guiding me to this spot and moment from the start, and in the early spring of '59 she had brought me to it, an inner circle within the circle. I may not have had the time right then to think much about it, nor the perspective to appreciate it, but it was clear that this was her goal. The two of us in the center of all the things she held precious, the way of life she intended us to be part of. But it also was an invitation to go on, a key to another door. Across the threshold we were supposed to pass into yet another zone of...what? When? But her models were clear and I accepted the plan. I was happy there and would have stayed.

Donna Costanza came out to warn us Marianne's parents were coming out. We kissed her goodbye, and she blessed us both, making a small sign of the cross with her thumb on our foreheads. Then, with what seemed to be a reference to her doubts about the safety of my scooter, she cautioned me to take care of Ann Marisse or I would have to answer to her, even in heaven. She smiled as she said it, but I knew she spoke in earnest.

That night, when I called Ann Marisse, she came on angry. "You're really horrible. I know what you're doing."

My first reaction was to deny whatever she had heard as untrue, wondering at the same time what she could have heard and from whom. But then she laughed just enough to make me relax and play along, agreeing, yes, horrible, but that she had known it all along.

"No, I thought you could be trusted. You know what you did? You stole my memory. I've been trying to picture Tony Rossuto all night, but he's gone. I can bring back the corn field, the hot day, our conversation, but when I look for his face, yours pops up. It's the kiss. I knew it. You gave me your kiss and stole my memory."

She probably made the whole thing up, but I enjoyed it. She was fun, spontaneous and unpredictable.

But her accusation wasn't far off target. I did want to make Tony Rossuto disappear. The story of her first kiss made me jealous, and somewhere in those misty unconscious recesses of my mind, I meant to slip into her memory of it and substitute myself. The game of desire we had initiated led us there, to coveting the main spot in each other's primary images. I didn't want to be Rossuto, just the pleasure she felt in having convinced him to kiss her, of having desired it, that pleasure should have my face.*

Easter: Once again my brother dropped Alonzo and me off at the Donna's car-lined drive, now shaded under newly ver-

*Much later, working on a script that played heavily on memory and illusions, I realized that, while I was guilty of stealing one memory from Ann Marisse's past, she had stolen those of my future, possessing the image of every woman I have met since. The line between memories and what I wish

dant trees. Spry annuals cradled the porch in a blaze of color. We approached casually. The same kids with different guns didn't stop this time when we climbed the steps to the door. They even aimed a couple of shots at us. Alonzo clutched his chest and moaned. He tried for a suave Bogart, but came across more like Palance in *Shane*. Whipping out a comb from his coat, he squeezed off three quick rounds and flashed a sinister smile. The kids' eyes squared in amazement. As we entered, I heard one comment, "Grownups are weird."

Marianne greeted us. Everything about her bespoke a restrained, less fluid Ann Marisse, tighter within the outline of her body, as if hoarding her feelings within it. When Alonzo reached for her hand, she surrendered it without reciprocating, leaving it perched in his, set to take flight at an instant. Though she didn't turn her head, her eyes continually drifted, as if expecting someone. I never heard her express affection. Yet, she duplicated Ann Marisse in so many ways it proved unsettling. A different choice of neighborhood when my parents came from Mexico and I might have ended up with her. The thought made me shudder.

As we had planned, Ann Marisse remained across the room, standing to the left of her mother who sat among the matriarchal court. She observed us with a squint of scrutiny. From the sofa, Donna Costanza greeted Alonzo and me in Italian, focusing everyone's attention with this break in familial protocol.

"*Bon giorno,*" Alonzo answered, then switched to English to add an Easter felicitation. Marianne dropped his hand and drew slightly away, leaving Alonzo and me set off as much as we could be in the crowded room. The shoulders of our jackets touched in the mirrored reflection, like boys bumping each

---

were memories becomes too intricate, crossed threads in the weave of images created over time. Then there are all the memories I want people to remember as mine. Ultimately, it makes no difference, as long as someone remembers me remembering Ann Marisse remembering me . . .

other as they walk, each trying to push the other off the sidewalk.

Donna Costanza shifted her gaze to me: my cue.

"*Cara mia Donna.*" Ann Marisse described to me later how Alonzo's mouth dropped, but having to concentrate on each syllable made me too nervous to notice. "*Io vengo a desiderare per Lei un magnifico giorno di Pasqua.*"

"*Grazie, Paulino, e come sta la tua famiglia?*"

"*Bene, grazie, Donna Costanza, ciascuno multo bene.*" I expressed my mother's appreciation of the Easter sausage bread the Donna had sent earlier in the week, then asked if my parents could bring their thanks personally, all of which rang true because it was. She enthusiastically encouraged me to tell them to visit anytime and then, knowing the narrow parameters of my ability, cued the finale: "*Viene qui, figlio, e dammi un bacio.*"

A widening of Ann Marisse's eyes and the relaxing of her body as she shifted her weight onto one foot confirmed success. Her mother shook her head, but couldn't suppress a smile. Everyone seemed pleased with the performance. Donna Costanza took my hands in hers and, in a low voice, advised me to pretend to talk intimately to sell the act. I didn't mind, having grown quite fond of her. My own grandmothers were vague images, my father's mother having disappeared into a hushed mystery—divorce was whispered—and the maternal one spoke only Spanish or French, drastically limiting our communication the few times she visited us before she died. So if Donna Costanza cared to hold my hands, I would stay as long as she wanted. Finally, however, she signaled Ann Marisse over and passed my hands directly into hers. She held them clasped together between hers for a moment before waving us off in the direction of the kitchen.

With a look of disbelief, Alonzo handed me a Coke. "Here, *cumba.*" It was as gracefully as I ever saw him take anything, winning a momentary place in my affection for the whole family. We went out to the patio to partake of the type of holiday feast I was learning to expect. It was assumed you would bring a gargantuan appetite for soup and salad, pasta, three courses of meat and fish, garlic bread, four or five vegetables, topped off with nuts, fruit and pastry. There was even espresso to crown it all. As the women cleared the tables, the men removed them to clear a space for dancing.

On the table where we had spent afternoons learning a little Italian and a lot about Donna Costanza, they installed a record player wired to speakers secured in the low branches of the oak. Requests went up for songs from the old country, but Ann Marisse's uncles commandeered the turntable to play their music: Swing—*American Patrol*. Ann Marisse's father took her hand and danced her away in perfect synchronization, turning, spinning, coming together and twirling out, her skirt flaring up to gather upon itself and drop again. In his arms she looked like her own big sister, mature and years beyond me, to whom, nevertheless, she returned, breathing hard. Placing a hand on my shoulder, she lifted one foot to inspect her shoe, but lost her balance and fell into me, hanging on with both arms to steady herself.

"You did it on purpose," I accused, holding her close.

"Aha," she admitted, touching the end of my nose with her index finger. *Stardust* came on. "Let's dance."

Relatives greeted me as they danced by, many speaking my name. Ann Marisse acknowledged each with a smile and a glance. Her eyes had a way of changing, more than focus, the texture and the weight of her gaze, creating a difference between how she saw others—or let them see her—and the look she brought back to me. We danced relaxed, unconcerned with being watched, her body lightly delivered into my arms. It was a different style, a pose from an era we had just missed, the one lingering in our parents and older brothers and sisters, defining them as pre-us, a style dictated by their music. But when Alonzo dropped on *At the Hop*, few older couples tried to dance. We didn't care either way, but just then slow

swing better fit our mood, so we convinced Marianne to switch
it back.

At the front door, one by one families were taking their
leave of Donna Costanza. Ann Marisse and I moved forward
with her family, but the Donna signaled us to wait until the
older pair exited to the night from where a cool breeze drifted
back through the screen door. Then she smiled like a girl who
has played a joke on her parents, but it passed quickly in an
abrupt shift of mood. She raised her hands to Ann Marisse's
face, brushed back a strand of hair, straightened her collar
and slid two fingers under the silver cross as though noticing
it for the first time, turning it to read the inscription of my
name. Then she studied her face again.

"Don't tell your papa, *cara mia*, but you inherited his family's best: fair skin, light eyes. His mother, your grandmother,
came from Tyrol, like my husband, but she was soft, like you,
too giving and open with your smile."

Ann Marisse's eyes brimmed with tears, but she swallowed hard, brought her hands to her grandmother's, lowered
them, and said, "But my hands are yours, Nonna."

They embraced. Momentarily I played outside observer, yet
related and intimately tied to them. A last few relatives were
waiting in the living room, respecting the privacy the matriarch
clearly wanted. When she let Ann Marisse go and turned to me,
I expected some words of wisdom, an old saying, anything, but
she simply took my hand and said something in Italian I hadn't
learned yet. Then she waved us to the door with her familiar
hand movement and turned to the next in line.

In the back seat of her parents' car, Ann Marisse held my
hand and looked out the window, relaxed and secure. Her parents asked none of the questions parents think obligatory
when accompanied by their children's friends. Unlike mine,
hers still sat next to each other, like teenagers. They didn't
offer to take me home, going instead directly to theirs, where I
received a casual good night devoid of special attention. At the

door, Ann Marisse continued in her quiet mood, perhaps tired from dancing.

"I had a really good time," I told her.

She looked at me, her eyes slowly focusing on mine as if they had to travel over a great distance in her mind, and it took a moment for her to arrive.

"*Ti amo,*" I offered to guide her approach.

"*Dammi un bacio, dolce Paulino,*" she whispered. After we kissed, she took a deep breath and said good night.

❀　❀　❀

The boundary may never have disappeared entirely, as Donna Costanza had warned, but her patronage had slipped me across like an undocumented alien. To us it seemed just a matter of waiting a few years, because the grand matriarch's blessing graced our heads like the aura of the Holy Ghost. Feeling so grown up, looking forward to sharing school again and beyond, we constructed and reconstructed the future with an assurance I've never regained.

❀　❀　❀

The last speech meet before regionals, scheduled for early May, coincided with a make-up baseball game. Between baseball and debate, Alonzo predictably chose the former, leaving Dick partnerless. Sister Kate tapped me to fill in. I had qualified already for state finals in poetry, but Dick needed this last chance for points to get his certificate. Having fought the battle of Dunkirk for this woman, how could I refuse a peaceful debate?

We brushed our routine back into shape, but the second round made it obvious we wouldn't last into the finals. Dick didn't care, he had his points, and I had delivered on my word to Sister Kate. Now, there remained only empty time to wait for the van back to HTHS. That's how the official version should have read: *Nothing special, nothing significant, another Saturday with the Speech Club*. Not quite.

Life gets complicated when you have nothing to do. Every nun in every grade warned us: idle hands make the devil's workshop. Mine kept busy, but when your team gets eliminated in the semifinal round, it's out of your control. I'd have debated Soviet Education to semester's end, but the judges wouldn't let us. Other options were open, granted: a circuitous transit bus, via downtown and two transfer stops, would have delivered me home free; volunteer to be a timekeeper for the finals, as Dick chose; or scout my regional competition in poetry—my choice.

Scanning the participants list, I noticed a familiar name: Teals, S. After graduating from St. C's, Susy chose an all-girls academy. Unattractive in grade school—stocky, plump and tomboyish—over the summer she shot up several inches and pleasantly rearranged her weight. Her body still radiated solid physical strength, but she had learned to use it to her benefit. Looking at her, your thoughts ran to clean, sporty, and fun. She dressed out of prep-school catalogues and looked like she spent her off hours on tennis courts or sailing, although I wouldn't call it sexy. Our girls were sexy. Susy? She had acquired a certain class.

In December we had coincided at a meet, but I hadn't recognized her when, after first results were posted, she asked how I had done. A first and second, I said, repressing my excitement; two fourths, she volunteered, exhibiting her disappointment with "Damn." It would have been out of character for an HTHS girl, but prep schoolers were known to be more worldly. One expected them to say "damn" unselfconsciously. It figured into their elan, like dark blue sweaters, plaid skirts and penny loafers. She looked at me from the full height of her summer growth which had brought us eye to eye, then, in a barely discernible adjustment, like background movement just within the screen, she relaxed her body, tilted her head forward, and looked up from below square trimmed bangs, creating the illusion of being shorter than I. Though I still didn't recognize her, I liked her style.

In January, she lunched with our group. When I asked how she knew Billy, Alonzo and Dick, she gave me the strangest look. Dick clued me in by using her last name. Embarrassed by my stupidity and incredulous of her transformation, I tried to match her old image to the new Susy. "You never change, Paul," she commented.

She wrote her phone number on my program, with a note: "It hasn't changed. Susy," then her address, with "just in case" swirled under it. But my schedule left no time for another girl. It was hard enough keeping Karen restricted to between 8:00 to 3:00, plus a couple more hours at play practice after the end of basketball season.

So Susy's name on the list decided the session for me. I had suggested she change her poem: *The Cremation of Sam Maggie* might fit her sporty look, but comedic poems don't garner big points. She agreed and tried to string Dickinson poems together, anticipating *The Belle of Amherst* by a few years, but she still got eliminated. When the final round came, drawing kids off towards one event or another, we remained in the cafeteria, undecided.

"What are you going to do, Paul?" she asked me, taking a last sip of her Coke.

"Want to explore the school?" I asked.

"What for?"

"There must be some room in this place where we can be alone," I suggested, looking over at her to catch her reaction.

She looked up, smiled, and nodded. "I thought you'd never ask."

We ended up in a classroom, alone, for nearly an hour, admittedly a compromising situation. I concede it was a mistake, a betrayal of sorts. But that's far from what it got inflated into by the rumor mill. Later, Susy and I wondered why we hadn't done more, since nobody believed us anyway.*

....

*My editor wanted the juiciest rumors left in for porno appeal, but what passed for adolescent scandal over thirty years ago would hardly impress you. Besides, the details matter less than the ultimate result. Actually, I deleted

So? I could claim someone told Ann Marisse. I explained it that way several times, then and later, and convinced some people. They were ready to blame Alonzo as the most likely. He could have told Marianne, who would have phoned her cousin with the news, as she had on other occasions. It plays well, rings of common sense—pure Hollywood. It just wasn't true.

No one knew; worse, no one had to. Later, Susy heard what happened and called to assure me she had told no one, especially not her boyfriend. Somebody else took care of it for her in short order, which led to the feared confrontation between them, and word circulated that he was coming after me. He was a Loyola High junior, so it particularly upset him to hear I was only a freshman. My brother, usually uninterested in my kid stuff, caught the rumor on the street and offered help if needed. Things were getting out of hand.

Susy, despite her own troubles, became again the loyal St. C's classmate, inviting me over to find a way out for both of us. Her parents weren't home, so I took Dick along. While he watched T.V. in the living room, in the den we tried to figure things out. She called Ann Marisse, who refused to talk to her. Marianne did, but wasn't any help. Susy didn't have to do it, but she tried all the same.

Then Dick came in with the news: two guys in a '57 Ford had pulled into the driveway, right behind our scooters. Her boyfriend. Susy went to the door. From the den we could hear them arguing. Dick was admiring the Nazi war paraphernalia on the walls and in glass cases. Mr. Teals, a vet, liked to display his memories. Above the sofa hung a painting of Patton surveying tanks battling across a smoke-filled valley. Dick feigned interest, but I knew he had every nerve focused on the fight we both expected. We had tangled with older guys before, but neither one of us was carrying anything to equalize the situation, so Dick lifted small objects, feeling the weight and shape in his fist.

---

most of it because when I remember how stupid it all was, and that in spite of everything I somehow was to blame, it infuriates me even now.

"Think she'll let them in?" he asked while testing the edge of an SS dagger with his thumb.

"Would you stay outside if she was your girl?"

When they entered, Susy stood between us and them. She quickly explained that he had promised not to start anything, just talk. She insisted to him again that nothing had happened. We had walked around, talked, killed some time, period. We were old friends, she lied, so no big deal. Her boyfriend and his buddy wore letter jackets, tan pants and penny loafers, their hair, cropped close, military fashion—the preppie look, cute on girls but so uncool on guys. They sat down at the bar and helped themselves to a soda. Hating them proved easy. I remember thinking how well they fit into Nazi decor.

Susy kept repeating that someone had blown things way out of proportion. Under his breath, Dick said we should catch the S.O.B. and kick the shit out of him. It got us nowhere but closer to the edge. But then Susy's parents arrived, and the menacing preppies turned polite school boys, well-mannered and respectful. They asked her father questions about some of his souvenirs and listened attentively to his version of the war. Each of us waited for the others to leave, but Susy asked me to stay. She was determined to clear up in one night what had taken a full week to build into its own reality.

So they left, Susy walking them out, and Dick trailing along behind as far as the front door to make sure. I stayed behind, fascinated by her father's memories of Monte Casino and the Italian campaign. Dick interrupted to say our scooters were about to be smashed.

Outside, Susy stood between the car and scooters, her calves straddling Dick's taillight. The Ford's V-8 purred inches from her outstretched hands.

"Boys," Susy's father said, "I thought you had to go."

He stood erect but at ease, feet apart, weight centered, his hands together in front of him holding a Luger. Unloaded, he assured us when we returned to the house after they had gone, but I heard him remove the clip before putting it away.

Susy and I went over our story to get it straight. The version we agreed upon lacked titillating details, so it ultimately convinced no one. It mattered little that, as a summary of what had happened, it was fairly accurate.

Susy asked me to do her a favor, help her understand why she placed so low in every meet. Technically, we did find an empty room, and I admit I hoped for more than poetry—Susy is an attractive woman. But in an open classroom, I sat on the teacher's desk to read her poems as she listened from the back row. I read poorly at that, because I didn't know her new material, so she asked for *Dunkirk*. War poetry to a girl in an empty school room! But she begged and I complied. *Dunkirk*, start to finish. I've memorized only one other poem in my life, Shakespeare's Sonnet CXVI, which has the double virtue of far fewer verses and being apropos for seduction, but I wouldn't learn it for another four years. So *Dunkirk* it had to be.

When I finished, she sighed, "I can't do it. It's your voice," which sparked the conversation that led to the kiss, a single, perhaps extended, but solitary kiss. I told her, "So use your eyes, they're fabulous, especially that thing you do when you tilt your head and look up."

She said, "Talk about eyes. Yours always drove me crazy."

I admired her new look.

"My father has me in training for the Ivy League, though it would be West Point if he weren't stuck with a girl," she said.

"Christ, mine wants me to apply to the Point, too. He wishes he had stayed in after the war—still counts the months he'd have left if he hadn't quit."

Her face lit up. "Mine, too. He knows exactly how much retirement pay he'd be pulling."

We were quiet a moment, then I confessed, "I want to play football for UCLA, but he says if not Army, then at least Notre Dame."

In short, we talked about things we had in common, most of which, as I analyze the memory, kept swinging back around to the body, how we looked, how so much depended on how tall I might grow, how tall she was afraid to grow, how I thought she was just right, how she thought I had always been, too, and then we were next to each other at the door, about to leave, and we kissed. Doesn't matter who made the first move, everything led to this undeniable conclusion to the conversation. Yes, our bodies matched well, but she held hers at a distance, bringing her face to mine across an empty space we meant to respect. Yes, I pulled her closer and she didn't resist, but that, too, flowed as natural as the conversation, as smoothly logical and innocent as the kiss itself. And yes, her breasts were small and firm, but at that point I could say so only from how they felt against my chest through our clothing, nothing more. But her body held next to mine, touching without movement, sufficed then to set me on the path discovered at Ann Marisse's the day we cut school a year before. I tried to hold Susy tighter, but maybe she could tell what was about to happen, because she backed away, gently, saying *sorry* in what to me sounded so much like an apology for stepping on my toe that I laughed.

"What's so funny," she asked, still in my arms, but her body well off mine.

"Nothing, I just like the way you kiss."

She checked her watch. "Oops, it's getting late." She separated from me as naturally as she had approached, leaving me to contain my frustration quietly, while she dug some kleenex out of her purse to wipe her lipstick from my mouth. She smoothed the pleats of her kilt skirt, tucked in her blouse and tried to check her reflection in the glass panel of a door.

"I've wanted to do that since sixth grade, but when I got brave enough, you were going with that seventh-grader we all hated."

"I still do."

"I'm glad. Actually, you're really cute together."

I might have kept talking, but right then I wanted most to get out of there. Susy kissed well, but my interest was receding faster than my erection, and she seemed to be of like mind.

"I have to get back for the awards. We better take separate ways down, okay?" She didn't ask me to call her or anything, and although disconcerting to my self-esteem, it fit
perfectly my needs at the moment.

I came down in time to witness our senior debate team
receive first prize. Susy and her friends passed us on the way
out, smiling with the pert All-American buoyancy of Catholic
prep-school girls.

❉   ❉   ❉

In its pure form the incident holds little significance, better forgotten than centered as the source of so many memories
to follow. It merited silence more than words. So...

Why did I tell Ann Marisse? You can't imagine how many
times over the years I've returned to the question. The places
where it has occurred to me, cafes in Rome, a river cruise up
the Rhine, skiing in Aspen, writing in Paris, Denver, New
York, Cambridge, Berlin, Erlangen, our house in the Tyrol...
Though disguised for incredulous adult ears, it infiltrates my
conversations, my readings, my writings, my scripts: WHY
DID I TELL ANN MARISSE?

❉   ❉   ❉

Growing up Catholic, we learned to place a premium on
confession: it's a matter of eternal life or death. First, they
introduced original sin. We learned from a catechism reen-
forced with visual aids, most memorable of which were the
holy pictures awarded for good deeds or grades. Small, play-
ing-card-sized illustrations, gilt-edged, they served as book-
marks or stood by our beds on tables, exhorting us to defend
our pure souls. Original sin appeared as a dark, grotesque,
fallen angel who looked sinisterly back over his twisted shoulder as he exited the card to the left of a mother who had not
been able to prevent the monster from branding her baby with
the mark of sin. Baptism, the bright angel with the flowing
golden hair and a short white tunic under the sparkling armor

clinging to his torso, approached from the right, a basin in one hand and a pitcher of holy water in the other to cleanse the wound. But the blemish remained—a permanent inclination toward sin. The bright angel would guard the child forever, but, as other holy pictures taught us, guardian angels got drowsy and took naps, leaving a window ajar through which the dark foe flew in to scratch the never cauterized spot of vulnerability, making it fester anew. This drove the boy to skip out on his guardian angel, aided by other weak-willed friends. Since once reinfected total purification is impossible, confession is given us at what Catholics call the Age of Reason, around seven or eight, when guardian angels grow careless from years of sleepless duty, and the dark angel, who has been resting up in the shadows and watching for his break, swoops in like a vulture. Confession, we were promised, would strip our sins away, leaving us clean and refreshed, like Lysterine, to let us start again. Even the worst crimes are forgiven, never to be held against you. Ah, but if you died with mortal sin on your soul, the Dark One Himself would take it and your body as well, and kindle fire in your festered spot to devour your entire being, yet miraculously not consume a hair of it, so you could suffer infinitely—even longer: for Eternity. Confession sounded like a better alternative than hiding transgressions. Pinocchio's allegory rang clear: human boys are fated to sin, but confession can save them from temptations of the flesh and mind.

If this wasn't sufficient, hadn't Elvis' girl forgiven him when she found out the truth in each of his movies since *Loving You*? Didn't Robert Montgomery advise his children that truth made the sun shine on *Father Knows Best*? Had they talked things over, would Othello have slain Desdemona? Didn't the Platters sing, "Please be kind and I know you'll find it so easy to forgive," and wasn't *The Diary of Anne Frank* a confession of sorts? Confession pulsed through our veins.

Considering all that, guilt felt natural. It just shouldn't have happened. Susy was like Ann Marisse—good girls, the kind you go steady with and eventually marry. They end up somebody's mother. Now, Valorie had dropped into a different class, not because she'd let you feel her up, but because she chose public school without having flunked out or her father going broke or anything. And messing around with Karen, well that was different, too, though why is it harder to explain?

Making out with Karen whenever I got a chance, say during study hall, or when I wasn't needed at play practice, simply didn't count. It started at Homecoming when she kissed me and made me promise a refund on her investment. We worked out pleasurable installments and lost track of my balance. The chance that someone would walk in limited us to heavy petting and body rubbing, enjoyable and conveniently discrete. She couldn't afford trouble with her boyfriend, a high school senior from Jefferson who used to pick her up in a chopped, lowered and leaded-in '53 Olds. Different because... Karen chose to be different.

Other girls wore tight skirts. Others had dark hair or a promising smile, were more flirtatious or dirty-mouthed, but not many coordinated all features. Karen knew the impression she gave and enjoyed it, played it to the hilt. But what put Karen in a different class all together was that she was Mexican. There were a few others of us in the school, but she looked the part, milked it, exploiting our expectations. She consistently chose the wrong way: skirts, makeup, language, the total image. Just as Susy chose to look Ivy League, Valorie like a beach bunny, and Ann Marisse incarnated the All-American Teen Angel, Karen was the whore—a word I've come to respect over the years, but back then used with the same conviction as my friends. The dark vamp, the easy make, the bad girl who cools a boy's fire without cutting off his water, she came pleasure-ready...but in the end, she counted zero. I didn't have to tell Ann Marisse because, ultimately, Karen wasn't anybody. Nobody, no one, nothing. So much so that I didn't think about it in the least. Susy was something else: she merited a confession.

Saturday night I should have stayed home. Instead, I drove to Ann Marisse's, ran through the normal greetings and told her I had something important to tell her, committing myself to the scene. I still might have invented something, but my somber mood narrowed the realm of choices. I had fixed on the role of troubled-young-man-struggling-with-a-deep-inner-conflict, Dean in *East of Eden* or *Rebel*, and coming out of it without some self-destructive revelation would have betrayed the character.*

We went into the den. In black pedal-pushers, a button-down white blouse, tails out, and no shoes, she looked casual, her ponytail held with a blue band. She crossed to the HiFi, enjoying my eyes watching her move. To prolong the sensation, she delayed over details: needle, volume, the balance set. Johnny Mathis' voice flowed, mellow and sweet, my Valentine's Day gift, the album with her favorite, *When Sunny Gets Blue*. She returned to me on the love seat.

"Ooo, so serious. You lost the debate?" Feeling playful, she kissed me. When I didn't respond fully, she realized something was wrong and changed her mood. "Something happen at home?" Her mind seemed to inventory my areas of vulnerability, but she centered on what must have made most sense to her: "Did I do something?"

---

*If now I recast that night through defensive irony, it alters nothing. I wasn't playing a role conceived of in any terms but the painful ones I took seriously then. This pretense is for you. The problem is that what happened reads like a melodramatic cliché. My editorial sense tells me to edit before some clown at my publisher reads it, to reduce it to the trivial and incredibly light thing life becomes when filtered through cynicism and wasted years. Protect it, hide it, make it acceptable, publishable. Another voice tells me, however, that I fear less for the material than for myself.

If it smacks of cheap melodrama and that's too much for you to bear, skip a few pages ahead. If, on the other hand, your taste runs to youthful angst or you remember your first broken heart, continue.

"At the meet today I met this girl who used to go to St. C's, Susy Teals. Neither of us made the last round, so we spent the afternoon together."

Her body stiffened in expectation. The situation had been set, though nothing really said. She must have sensed the realm of our possibilities suddenly shrink to a tiny shell smaller than her heart where it lodged. Her breathing quickened as if she intuited a threat from the person she believed would shield her from danger. I intended to continue, but she could always guess my conclusions faster than I could explain a problem, and now was no different. Her mind raced through every scenario before I could speak another sentence, leaping past me to the end, to then circle back on herself, loop through, close the knot and slide it tight. She couldn't breathe, as though someone had strung wire around her chest and was pulling it tighter.

Her eyes took on a puzzled look, sort of gray and cloudy, as she listened to me explain, as if trying to place a face to the name I spoke. Nothing. Someone named Susy had crossed into our space, cut open her chest and was strangling her heart, squeezing her lungs, twisting her stomach, yet she was faceless.

I heard myself say, walk, look, just talk, kiss. I don't remember how much I actually told her. She stared at the floor, but there was nothing there. Silence, except for Johnny Mathis singing much too appropriately, *love is gone so what can matter...*"

"I'm sorry," I finally said.

Her eyes closed. Her hands were squeezed so hard, her knuckles turned bone-white. To my claim, "It didn't mean anything," Mathis commented, *somehow it's not the same.*

Her hands relaxed slightly, palms up, showing the imprint of her nails. She looked down to her hands on her lap as if discovering something distant, unfamiliar: the small arch of stones flickered on my ring on her thumb. I moved a hand towards hers, but they retreated to her chest, clasping each other.

"Don't. Please."

I don't know why I tried to touch her face, but she slapped my hand, then struck at it with her fist, missed, and pulled it back tightly to her heart as if reacting to a sudden pain. My ring pressed the side of her breast, while her other hand kept slapping at the air in front of her face. I don't think she realized that I wasn't trying to touch her anymore, because she kept moving one hand and clutching the other to her body, protecting herself against a touch she knew too well.

"No, no, no, nononononono..."

Later, she said, "I wanted to die. I wanted you to go. I wanted you to stay and let me kill you."

She wanted time to stop...

        to freeze and burn like a broken movie...

She wanted to rip my words like a cheap book...

    wanted to shatter the record...

    wanted someone to come save her...

        to make a wall out of her arms...

        to beat my words out of her heart...

            out of her head...

            out of her ears...

She wanted me to swallow them...

    to make them dissolve...

    wanted time to race backwards...

    to unlisten to the words...

        unsee me kiss a faceless girl...

        unfeel me hurt her...

            betray her...

She wanted me to not have come that night...

    to not have ever come...

        have ever seen her...

            ever loved her...

                learned to love her...

She wanted me to, "Please go away."*

---

*Editor's note. The author provided the following letter in response to my opinion that some scenes are "too emotional to believe in a twelve-year-old,"

I thought she hadn't heard me. She sat so quiet, so still. I
remember thinking, anytime now she'll open her arms and
forgive me. When she didn't, I tried to explain that it didn't
mean anything, which it didn't: one kiss. I couldn't believe it
could matter so much and so long.

Years later, when I needed information for a script, I
called to ask how she had felt, but she wouldn't say. In Rome
we had been discussing a similar scene. Bertolucci told me he
wanted nothing to happen on screen, yet everything to happen
behind it. My professors at UCLA used to say nothing hap-

---

i.e., their first break-up. No one, however, used the term "cheap melodrama."
Below we reproduce the unedited note from the real Ann Marisse.

April 19, 1974

Paul:

Your call caught me off balance, at a disadvantage: surprise attack.

When you asked how I felt the first time we broke up, I said I
couldn't remember. Not true. I just couldn't tell you. It came back to me
in a rush, a sharp blow to the chest. I didn't think I could still feel anything so deeply. It was long ago and should be forgotten. We were only
children. I thought I had it stored away, that other things that happened
between us since then were more important, more real. I'd never try to
remember that night; but you asked, and apparently it's important to
you, although as usual you don't explain why, just expect me to understand. All I could say then was I didn't remember it. I lied.

I felt the air being sucked out of me. I remember spinning yet not
moving, being tied in knots by my own body. You were saying you were
sorry while I wanted to die. I was sure my heart had stopped and I wanted to break everything, rip it to pieces, you included, but mostly myself. I
felt betrayed, worthless, stupid. I felt everything I was sure of suddenly
disappear. I never dreamed you would hurt me. We were happy. Maybe it
was nothing, but it didn't feel like it.

I loved you more than you deserved, and you broke my heart. It
sounds childish now, but who cares? It's true the heart can break, unfortunately more than once. The first doesn't protect you from the second.
You taught me what that feels like, too. I'll never forget. Anything since
is a mere reference to that first break.

After all this time, how can you call out of the blue and ask how I felt
the first time we broke up? Like the second time, except at least I knew
why the first, while the second remains a mystery, like you. I was thirteen and I wanted to die, yet I wanted you to save me, but you left, you
went home. You bastard.

A.M.

pens behind a screen, it's strictly a visible surface. But I remembered something once had, so I called Ann Marisse. It was, I confess, an excuse as well. By the time her letter reached me, we had worked out the scene on camera. But I discussed her answer with Bertolucci, and he said, "*Ecco*, Paolo, get this woman to write that scene for us and you'll have something." Then he talked about how adults learn to reserve emotions for closed rooms, out of sight. Public performances follow strict rules, Bertolucci said, like a tango without passion, danced in a ballroom. Rigid and lifeless. "Repression," he said, with a hand on my shoulder. "It's called growing up," and he laughed, but a serious, acid laugh. "A cliché learned for survival, but which must be unlearned to create art," he said—another cliché, but more difficult to achieve. "Write a scene," he asked of me, "where I feel both the learning and the unlearning at once—that's what you're looking for."

❋ ❋ ❋

Two weeks later Ann Marisse still wouldn't talk to me.

"I can't believe she's still mad."

"Man, you can hardly blame her," Dick replied. "The way I heard it, you had some orgy. Let her cool out."

I was fed up with continually having to deny versions of a story which changed with every repetition.

Two weeks later I was still asking myself how she could stay mad over a simple kiss.

"She ain't," Alonzo offered one day.

"What do you mean?" He knew something, but he'd drag it out. Craving the spotlight, he wouldn't deliver until everyone around surrendered it to him. We were at the creamery, and Alonzo waited for Dick and Billy to stop thumbing through jukebox selections.

"It's not Susy anymore. They talked it over and she believes her." He paused, prolonging the suspense like a bastard, but I controlled myself. "It's your Spic chic."

I called Ann Marisse, but no one would let me talk to her. I tried to see her, but her friends kept her well guarded. I even sneaked back into St. C's after school during graduation practice, but Sister Dolores caught me. She pretended to take my presence as a visit and complimented me on my freshman year. As usual, she was well informed. As she escorted me out, she recommended against expecting all my plans to come through right away. "God moves in strange ways and reveals His design only in the end," she consoled me, or maybe herself. She watched me until I was well off the school grounds.

Ann Marisse's little brother didn't understand, but he closed ranks in family solidarity. Her father would only nod, then look away quickly when we ran into each other. Her mother, not even that. It was useless.

I rummaged through letters, notes, books, pictures, presents, whatever would prolong the possibility of picking up where I had let it slip. I quit meeting Karen—a mutual decision. If her boyfriend found out, we would both be in for it. She fought a battle of containment to keep the gossip from reaching him or her mother, plugging all leaks until summer, when news spread that she had run away to New York. Others said she had had a baby. In the fall she didn't return. When I ran into her years later, the last thing she said before disappearing into a New York cab was, "Paul, I never told Ann Marisse."

From the first I suspected Alonzo, an intuition confirmed much later. Yet I have no one to blame but myself. Marianne did tell her, but only after Ann Marisse asked her if she knew Susy, so my pointless confession set the cycle in motion. Marianne confirmed the Karen exposé, information leaked by Alonzo. He supplied yet another name to bolster the effect: Valorie, though without reference to Malibu, himself or Sharleen. He claimed to have seen us together on my scooter the weeks Ann Marisse and Marianne were vacationing in Colorado. Recently, I discovered he piled on more names of girls from other schools, girls to whose houses, according to him, he had accompanied me. True, we had gone, but I went with him, taking him on the scooter. I had wasted hours playing with little sisters hardly old enough to kiss, or little brothers, or talking to mothers in kitchens, while Alonzo made it in some other part of the house! Then I got the blame, single billing and exclusive. Naive Marianne swallowed it, and, after the speech meet and my stupid confession, so did Ann Marisse. Taken in context, it confirmed the worst. No one asked me for a denial, since my best friend had supplied the proof. For that matter, no one filled me in on the plot for over thirty years.

※　※　※

Our first separation lasted nearly six years, although eventually we saw each other on the side, once, and it almost ended up in a passionate session of petting and some real sex. Chances are that not going together gave us more freedom. The need to wait, to control ourselves, which we hadn't observed well in the first place, made less sense now that we had nothing to wait for. Our plans had disappeared. Someone else took her to the dances. Someone else attended the family reunions and ate the fabulous pasta. I'm sure of this because other rings appeared on her hand, other letter sweaters over her shoulders. She was pictured in the annuals dancing with other guys. From above a caption "King and Queen of May Day Hop," she and someone else looked out, smiling from under crowns of spring flowers. The team captain their senior year walked her to the stage to crown her Homecoming Queen, but I only saw the picture in *The Catholic Register*. But when Donna Costanza died, Ann Marisse cried alone in church, unless you count Alonzo, who probably sat between the cousins.

One night, junior year, about eight o'clock the phone rang.

"Oh, Paul, she's dead."

Suddenly hearing her voice startled me as much as the cryptic news.

"My Nonna died," she added.

I still didn't know what to say. But she hadn't called for sympathy. In spite of everything, she knew that in me she could find empathy, and for that I didn't need empty words.

She asked me to come over, then abruptly changed her mind. We talked only briefly; their phone was needed for other calls. The rest of the week she missed school, and when she returned we didn't talk. I watched her rejoin the group as if little had happened. But long after others had forgotten, the memory persisted between us, in a quick glance, a convergence of our eyes, a sudden fading of the smile and a slight relaxing of the face and a refocusing of the gaze onto something just in front of her...and once in a while, too seldom, a searching for me in the crowd. I wrote her a note sharing recollections of Donna Costanza. She read it in study hall and looked up once to acknowledge the sentiment, nothing more.

Because much more had died with Donna Costanza. Certainly the past, her disappearance snapping a chord we might have used to trace our steps back to where I had taken a wrong turn. A certain future died as well, and somehow we were to blame. Maybe that's what she wanted to tell me when she called, or later with the glance—that, and a tacit admission of shared blame. We hadn't known how to nurture what Donna Costanza blessed. With every advantage and no obstacles to speak of, we had let it slip away. The old woman's warning resonated in my memory: I would have to deal with her even in death, a curse upon my head where I still feel it.

Her change of mind I took to be absolute, so I didn't go to the funeral either. Excommunicated, I had lost the right to share the present, as much as I wanted to. One of her temporary boyfriends may have gone to the church, even sat close, but it didn't mean anything. They could all go, any of them, but none entered the inner circle, I'm sure. Not even Alonzo, no matter where he positioned himself. Then or ever. Because the center evaporated into memories, locked inside itself like the lost answer to a forgotten riddle.

❄   ❄   ❄

Senior year started like one of those high school movies, but why blame us for achieving the full cliché: Alonzo and I, co-captains of a division championship team that lost state by a field goal. He finally got a shot at first-string quarterback, with me right behind at full, where I had started since the sophomore season. Just like old times: Dick at pulling guard, protecting me from Alonzo's unreliable blocks, and Billy, grown huge and strong, anchoring the line at center. We were picked from the beginning to top the league. Only one intangible could fail in this recipe for success: Alonzo, always working an angle to get somewhere the fastest and easiest way, couldn't string together two plays to make four yards, much less three for ten. After a disastrous first scrimmage, the coach started looking at him with "bench" written all over his face.

So at practice I started pointing out to him how to build one play off of another. He sort of caught on, but the first Sunday of the season his mind went blank. I could tell by his lost-puppy look after the first play. His eyes shifted around like they had when we got back from Malibu years before. On the way back to the huddle, I whispered a number. Then another after each play. Dick and Billy grinned at each other, catching on immediately; the rest of the team took longer to notice, but we won. By the second game, I called the plays in the huddle, and Alonzo added the starting number, an arrangement that served us right through to the championship. A dual voice, intelligence and brute practicality, who knows?

In the city championship, my play-calling won Alonzo MVP for "the strategy and daring of a Patton." Sports writers praised the last drive when Alonzo picked apart the defense with a brilliant sequence of plays that culminated in Alonzo's naked bootleg around end, straight onto the sports page with a three-inch photograph of him scoring the winning touchdown.

To top everything, the *ciùc* turned out really photogenic. I give him credit. He looked like a rock star smirking for an admiring crowd. No true Presley sneer, but not a bad imitation.

Public humiliation, however, came later at the pizzeria. Karl Sr., whose son played tackle, served us pizza on the house, reserving the back room for the whole team. We were downing dessert when Ann Marisse, Marianne, and a couple of other juniors came in. Alonzo had to call them over to show off his award. Marianne gave him a kiss, as could be expected from a steady, but Ann Marisse followed with another, on the lips. Then tossing a glance over the rest of us, the girls, in four-part harmony, granted us an "all of you played great, too." Damn!

Do you think Alonzo shared any credit or thanked me, even when we were alone? No chance. So for the second time in our life I used practice to get even. I hit him so hard on a drill that for a moment he seemed suspended horizontally in air before crashing on his back. This time, though, the coach reprimanded me for almost killing our star with the state championship coming up, and he let Alonzo skip the usual sprints at the end of practice. While the team raced up and back, up and back, Alonzo walked slowly to the drinking fountain, using his patented bowlegged limp for sympathy. Then he stood, watching us, one hand rubbing the small of his back. But no one could have made out, from where we sprinted across the field, the look of satisfaction on his face I knew so well. He might be standing still, rubbing his back, but inside Alonzo bobbed from side to side to the rhythm of his inner joy, planning his next move, believing that what people didn't know wouldn't hurt them. In addition, he had learned that it doesn't matter who does what as long as you get the credit. We had learned it together, but who was running sprints and who was cooling off at the drinking fountain?

When the Catholic all-state team was named, the only thing to spoil my making the first team was Alonzo's picture right next to mine.

Basketball proved a similar but less successful story. He and I, according to the coach, made one super player, I on defense and Alonzo on offense. "Now, if you were only the same person," he'd complain. With his height advantage, Alonzo got to play more, but we lost.

Although out of Speech Club since sophomore year—Sister Kate's replacement preferred grooming her own stable—I stayed hooked on poetry, even writing it on my own. English became my favorite class, and I signed up for the school paper. Sister Claire assigned me the sports page and expressed shock when I asked for clubs and functions instead. Susy, on the other hand, resolutely pursued poetry competition. The last semester of senior year she asked me to work on a run at state finals, a culminating award to prove she hadn't wasted her time. I accepted, but only if she would be my date for the senior prom. She placed second statewide a couple of weeks after impressing HTHS as the most beautiful girl at the dance. At least, she got the most attention, coming from another school, although for me there could be only one most beautiful, Ann Marisse. The two of them greeted each other like old friends, and at Susy's suggestion I danced once with Ann Marisse.

"Susy's very pretty," she said.

"But you're the most beautiful girl here."

Ann Marisse looked at me from the distance she held herself—it was a waltz, *Fascination*. The dim lights in the decorated gym ignited sparks in the jeweled tiara set in the weave of her up-swept and braided blond hair, dangling baguettes accenting the line of her face and a lavender velvet ribbon softly encircling her throat. With her hair arranged high on her head, she seemed taller, but from the angle her left arm drew in its rise to my shoulder, I could tell she had not grown much in three years.

"You're serious," she said, then smiled to herself, her eyes darting towards the bandstand, her mouth inhaling deeply. She seemed to be considering something, yet obstinately clung to her refusal to let herself enjoy our dance. As we waltzed, she moved her head from side to side with turns and changes of direction, avoiding my eyes. As the number faded out, she finally looked at me: "I like you better silly and foolish."

We didn't dance again for several years, until Marianne's wedding.

※　※　※

It would have been impossible, however, for Ann Marisse and me to be strictly strangers over the three years we shared the halls of HTHS. The school was too small. Everyone knew what everyone else did. When Ann Marisse arrived, she took over center stage, winning most popular freshman girl, vice-president of her class and a ribbon in poetry at the year's first speech meet. Over the years I enjoyed, even took pride in, watching her be the best: B-team cheerleader, president of the Speech Club, Valentine's Day Queen, May Day Queen, Latin Club secretary... our paths crossed often, officially for the most part, but informally as well. Mainly she went out with boys from her own class, although Karl Jr. from the pizzeria dated her for a while.

One night at a party, Dick told me to look at the door. Karl stood there with Ann Marisse. We saw them together a few more times, but for the weeks it lasted, Karl could hardly talk to me. It was junior year, basketball season, and he tried to avoid lining up near me in drills. He grew sullen around us, behavior incompatible with his gregarious nature. One night Dick and I went into the pizzeria and found Karl working tables, "learning the trade," his father used to tease. He came over, slipped a large pizza onto the table and with a happy, relieved look, said, *mangia, cumba*. The next day he confided to Dick that he had told Ann Marisse he couldn't handle it: dating his best friend's girl made him too tense. Dick related it to me in the same serious voice as when he had warned me about Alonzo.

"Face it, you two are fated, good buddy," he said, staring out the window of his '56 Chevy and sipping a Coke at the drive-in. Cars circled to the modulating sounds of their radios. "Why don't you cool whatever game you're playing and call her? She's so fine. I'm sure she wants you back."

"It's no good anymore."

"What do you want, man? Whatcha trying to prove?"

"Nothing."

I wondered why I couldn't just call Ann Marisse and say, *Take me back, baby, give me one more chance.* I didn't know how, so I suggested we gash down Main. Things felt better when we were moving, all the windows rolled down, eyes barely above dash level. I began to tell Dick how much I wanted to be back with her, talking, remembering, raging at being so stupid.

"Craziest two people I've ever seen," Dick shouted over the blaring radio. "Fuckin' A, man, you're something else."

We needed to release tension and found a couple of Loyola seniors who had challenged us after a game, then never showed up. In the chrome-flashing chase, the dangerous dance of bodies weaving, fists cracking, for a few minutes my mind dissolved to a blank; but with hands sore and shirt bloodied over a heart still pounding, the longing for Ann Marisse surged back stronger. Dick summed it up in a way I wouldn't understand till much later: "We've got it bad, Paul, and that ain't good."

❋　❋　❋

Although we couldn't avoid each other all the time, not having a steady among the HTHS girls cut down the odds of my having to watch her dance with someone else at a party, hold hands at a movie, or worse. Couples were the thing, so if you weren't paired, you didn't easily fit into the group's plans. This put Dick and me together often, since he didn't stay with

any girl long, drifting back to Janice between periods of restlessness. He seemed to be looking for someone who never
appeared. Always nervous and jumpy with a date when we
doubled, he calmed down only when the crowd would meet at
Karl's or someone's house. He danced with all the girls, talked
to the guys, avoiding only Alonzo, which to me proved his loyalty.

I saw a lot of Susy, though we only dated once, for the
prom. She had boyfriends, but she would let nothing get
between her and her goals. She'd complain about the guys
from the Jesuit school with whom her own school combined for
functions. Though they dressed differently, she said, underneath they were just as unbearable. I pretended to take it personally, and teased her. She apologized, explaining that they
all wanted to be lawyers or doctors and marry a college grad
to bring up their children to play tennis at the club. She wanted to be the doctor, and she knew the East Coast would let her
achieve her dream. Getting there was the first step. She
grilled me on what my dreams were, but I really couldn't see
them clearly any longer.

"Football?" she asked my senior year, trying once again to
elicit a commitment to the old illusion.

"Maybe, but not at UCLA. God, probably nowhere."

For Susy the future stood firm like destiny; she'd allow
minor detours, but no question about the means of transporta-
tion or points of interest to be seen along the way. My admission produced the most singular expression of shock I had
ever seen ambush her sense of control. It had come to be our
identity motif: she was off to the East Coast to make a future,
while I was to be an All-American at UCLA or Notre Dame.
Now, she stared in disbelief, as if I had lit a match to the road
map of my dreams and she feared the blaze might spread
cross-country to hers.

I tried to explain. "The first time we talked, I knew I had
to grow four more inches, and you were afraid to grow another
half. Remember?"

She did, because she still practiced her subtle bow-and-upward-stare gesture when introduced to boys.

"Well look," I said, pulling her to her feet to face me. "We're still almost the same height, and you've grown only your half-inch."

"Thank God."

"On you it looks great. On my scouting report it equals too small for the big time. I'm okay for a Catholic high like H.T., or small colleges like Dartmouth, but not UCLA. And if not for a good team, why play at all?"

She looked me in the eyes, without bowing, and watched me accept what I hadn't dared say out loud at home or at school. Always objective and ruthlessly analytical with herself, she had let friendship maintain an illusion around me. Another girl might have cried, and most likely I'd have joined in, but Susy overpowered problems, plowed right through, forced them into retreat. She hugged me, kissed my cheek and held her mouth to mine for more. This time there was no one who needed telling later. Besides, I had been cured of my obsession with confession. Susy may never have been my steady, but she was my first.

Susy's body had the tautness of the athlete she had become in her high school: supple, though unobtrusive muscles. And the stamina to push it to the limit. But we weren't competing, just spontaneously completing what three years before had begun in an innocent kiss. Her nipples rose to the brush of my fingertips over her blouse, a lesson garnered from Karen in the gym. Her breathing assumed a measured beat, harmonizing to mine. Her lips brushed my ear to say, "Get undressed."

We stripped down and she looked at me, admiring my muscle tone: at its lifetime peak, nothing to pinch but skin. She kissed my chest.

"Maybe we should have done all the stuff people made up back then, for all the good it did to wait," she said.

She kneeled to go down on me, rocking her body back and forth from the hips. She looked like a praying girl, kneeling and swaying. She looked up and asked me with her eyes to join her on the den rug. We lay along side one another and, as we kissed, I ran a hand down from her breast to her stomach and lower, and, in spite of myself, looked up amazed. Where I expected a tangle of pubic hair, my hand found her silky smooth. She actually blushed.

"Swimming," she said. "I read waxing gives you an edge."

"Does it?" kissing her.

"I win," she breathed the words into my mouth.

The explanation didn't matter to me. The feel of my hand sliding over her smooth, fleshy pad, one of the few soft spots on Susy's body, fascinated me, bringing me to repeat the movement more to feel the slide over clean skin than to excite her. Now she began to breath deeper, shifting to a higher rhythm. And when my middle finger dipped, she was just as smooth inside, slick and moist.

But she took my hand and moved it back up. I looked at her and she just nodded, trying not to interrupt her breathing to talk. Guiding my fingers, she taught me what Karen hadn't gotten around to: the marvel of a woman's clitoris. She stroked herself with our fingers interlocked until I felt the node of her clit respond. Only then did she stroke me. She guided me in, effortlessly, and I began to rise fast to match her excitement, peaking...when she pulled away. I groped to hold her, but came against her stomach as she hugged me tightly to her, out but solidly between our two bodies, as close to inside as she could have me without letting me back in.

"I just can't take the chance," she apologized as we lay on the rug, a cushion under our heads.

"It's okay, now. But good thing you didn't ask me a minute ago."

I still remember her there on the rug, as relaxed and natural as a nudist on the Riviera, shining moist from perspiration, her fingers drawing sticky white swirls over her stomach.

Before I could finish appreciating the spectacle, however, she jumped up and disappeared into the bathroom. She shouted to me to come wash up before her parents came home.

Like everything she did, Susy showered like an athlete, making no coy efforts to hide her body. She dried herself briskly, rubbing the towel hard over her skin. She moved about the bathroom in long, sure strides, reaching for a comb with a sweep of the arm, pulling it through her short hair with no quarter given to snags or knots. She went back out to the den, picked up her panties and started to get dressed.

From the bathroom door, I admired her form, intrigued by my lack of attachment, the absence of, not love necessarily, but the feeling that I should feel love. The freedom from justifying in affection what we had just done unsettled me, stirring a confused sense of guilt or regret. I didn't realize then that what I felt for Susy, what allowed us not to need to justify our lovemaking by calling it love, was exactly affection. We liked and cared about each other. I just didn't understand it yet, because it still hadn't entered into my repertoire of possible relationships.

"Where did you learn that?"

"To fuck?"—voiced as easily as "damn" three years earlier, embarrassing me. I ducked back into the bathroom and wrapped a towel around myself before reentering the room. She was dressed, except for her shoes, which she placed toes down in a magazine rack. "With a Loyola premed now in his first year at Johns Hopkins."

"No, the rest. How to touch." She looked up bemused and tossed me my shirt. "Yourself, I mean. From the premed?"

"Albert?" she chuckled. "No. From books. Remember Sister Charity in fourth grade? 'Everything you will ever need to know, children, is somewhere in a book.' She'll never know where her advice led. Albert didn't teach me a thing! Except to feel like a freak. As soon as he'd come, he'd start in with how I was too much: too wet, too big, too slippery. Funny, he never called himself too small. But my parents adored him. 'A match made in heaven.' Until they found out he was Jewish—wrong heaven. I'd be too much for him even if he weren't kosher; he couldn't last two sets."

The night of the prom, we considered doing it again, but the dress, the tuxedo, the rear seat of the car, it was all like a step back into kids' stuff between us. Besides, I had danced with Ann Marisse, made my play, as Dick said I should—a feeble, indirect, cowardly play, true—and had been turned down. My equipment may have risen to the cause, but my heart wasn't in it. Susy could tell, yet she gave it half an effort out of sheer loyalty before, perhaps for the only time in her life, conceding the game to an opponent who didn't even want to take the field.

I saw Susy last—until Vietnam—just before she left for Mount Holyoke. I had been working all summer at a cemetery, a job left over from years when the shoveling kept me in shape, while she had been taking intensive French at Loyola and improving her tennis. I picked her up and drove to the creamery. The guy working the counter told us they would close soon to remodel into a Italian restaurant. The news darkened our mood to low nostalgia. He offered us a double malt for the price of a single to revive our spirits, but it didn't taste up to par. Susy tried talking about college, but that fizzled as well. We drove around the neighborhood, down by the lake and around to my house. She'd never met my parents and thought it might be her last chance for a while. Through the picture window we could see my mother sitting at the piano, alone, my father probably in the den tinkering with his collection of shortwave sets. He never rejected communication as long as it didn't mean talking to someone in the same room; Guam, Alaska and Bolivia were among his favorites. I started the car again, knowing it was too late. In front of her house, we parked and listened to the radio. Surfing music was ruining the rock stations, so I tuned in some folk music and mentioned that it sounded more East Coast.

"What's wrong?" she asked.

"I don't know. Do you ever get tired of living the way people say you should?"

"No, because I don't think I do."

She was wrong, but at that moment it sounded right, and we kidded one another about still acting like seniors afraid of graduation, which at least described me accurately. Nothing I had planned remained, but I had no one to blame but myself.

"You'll have to get used to a life of surprises. Might not be all that bad. Want to start with this," she said, taking my hand and slipping it under her skirt: she had had herself waxed. She was no longer swimming, but she did it for me, she confessed, although it wasn't easy for her to admit doing something without a utilitarian reason. She still didn't let me come inside her, but I expected and accepted the withdrawal. We rested in each others arms for longer than we should have, but her parents didn't come home until, standing in the driveway, she was promising to write.

She kept her promise, though not often. Making her play for freedom from the California style of life kept her too busy. But she had overestimated her emancipation when she claimed she didn't live according to expectations. After graduating from college in three years and finishing her med degree, she served in Vietnam and eventually became a career officer. In the end, her father got his military dream-child, even though he had to settle for it being a woman.

I, on the contrary, would work hard at avoiding the war, dragging out film school until the lottery freed me, repeating courses to fill the required hours for a student deferment and fighting with my father, who branded me an ingrate and coward. It shamed him that neither of his sons would volunteer for Vietnam. Most people mourn loved ones or friends whose names appear on the Vietnam War memorial; my father mourns our absence. But that came much later.

✳   ✳   ✳

Under "Major," I firmly printed *undecided* on all university forms my first year, but even before choosing where to go, I
had accepted two things. One, football was in the past, which
linked to two: I wanted to get away from the group who,
among other things, would always see me as the football hero
who failed to live up to expectations. Susy wanted freedom to
create a future; I wanted a new past. Like my father, my
friends made me feel like a has-been at eighteen. When I'd tell
them I wasn't going to play at UCLA, they would ask things
like, Did you get hurt? or Why aren't you going to school?
They were unprepared for a decision not to play, but go to
school anyway. Maybe Alonzo got the same questions, but I
tried to avoid him as much as I could, so I didn't know. I just
wanted to get away. I don't know who told them I had enrolled
at Loyola. They must have asked themselves, "Do they play
football?"

I never promised anyone I'd play football at UCLA or die
in Vietnam or promise you every page full of Ann Marisse.
Who gives a damn about the first two...it's the last that drives me crazy... When I think back on those years of high
school and realize I went through them without Ann Marisse,
allowing it to happen and not making a better effort to get
back together, an abyss opens within me...

❋   ❋   ❋

Ann Marisse has the world's softest lips. It must sound
like another exaggeration, but no, positively the softest. In
1957, when we kissed for the first time, I anticipated tight lips
like the other girls'. It could have been the impression conveyed by the thin line of her upper lip, which only in high
school she would start fleshing out with accents of color. In
seventh grade she used no makeup, so nothing prepared me
for her lips; I expected her to squeeze them tight, as if to resist
intrusion. No way. A total surprise. Later, when those same
lips opened into my first French kiss on her sofa the day we
cut school to meet at her house, I discovered what priests

mean when they say, *Flesh of my Flesh; take this and eat.* To
be received, hosted as a Host within the warmth of her mouth,
her tongue retreating, leading me between her lips and teeth,
to play at knowing what we were doing...I came right there.
It happened to me first with Ann Marisse. Her lips took me to
the experience—or better expressed, to the sudden blurring of
experience in the expansion of sensation into...what? Nothing? Perhaps. But in my case, the nothing of orgasm took on a
face, a kiss, a name: Ann Marisse. Kissing Karen, Susy, Phyllis or names I can't recall meant nothing in comparison. I may
have touched other girls, but I discovered the softness of
breasts when I touched the softest breasts I've ever caressed
the first time I touched any girl's breasts, and she was Ann
Marisse, the same breasts that first attracted me to her on the
playground in seventh grade and still never fail to spark
something akin to electric current in my fingertips. Karen
may have taught me to excite a nipple, but I learned for Ann
Marisse. That's the way I thought about it without thinking at
all. It came as natural as the way Susy moved; or as studied
and learned and integrated into my essential pattern of living
as writing films has become over the years. Either way, it
makes no difference. My whole life has been spent searching
for the same softness of lips and breasts, the same warmth of
her enveloping body, her sex around mine like a custom-fitted
suede glove. When, in the process of memory, I try to recall
the latest women, Ann Marisse's image—no, the sensation of
her—imposes itself. Wrong word, *imposes*; she permeates the
others like a spirit made flesh to renew the soft permanence of
herself. Always, but always. Priests instruct, do this in memory of Ann Marisse, and I do, because my faith is sealed and I
have no choice. Go, the mass is over, they decree, but it never
really ends.

    And yet, Ann Marisse wasn't the first I made love to, and
I wasn't her first. *Not the first*—it doesn't matter in the way
we're brought up to think it should. I care zero about virginity;
it's less a thing than an idea, an attitude, an identity invented

and reinvented. No. It's that we were to be exclusive in our love; that's the failed heart of the matter, our dashed expectations of total exclusivity and a record of blown opportunities to fulfill them.

Yet somehow, in spite of the physical presence of other partners, I was always with Ann Marisse. And wasn't. But we almost were... first for each other, I mean. Almost.

* * *

We saw *Summer Place* the same day, though not together. I came walking out of the Sunday matinee humming its supreme theme song, holding my date's hand, but thinking if Sandra Dee, who looked like a young Lana Turner, were my girl, she wouldn't need tricks to seduce me like Troy Donahue, and when she called to tell him she was pregnant, I almost shouted, "I'll marry you." Then they ended up going back to the parents, the ones who still remembered what being young was like, who forgave them and let them have their baby in their house by the sea. With this swirling in my mind, I turned to tell Dick, there beside me with Janice, and I saw him looking over his shoulder: Ann Marisse was walking hand-in-hand with a senior, two years older than I.

On the phone, we wasted no time on her choice of date or mine. If I wanted to talk, okay, but not about anyone else, we had no right, she insisted, even if my date was, according to her date, so easy. We laughed together. In her own way she had admitted to not giving a damn about her date or mine. She sounded happy to talk to me. The movie had left her in a strange mood, she explained. Then, asking me if I remembered this part or that, she began to retell it. She was marvelous, parodying the way I used to tell her to watch this scene or notice some detail. She retold more of *King Kong* than Sandra Dee had in the film, criticizing Dee for picking clichés that would never convince her own mother if she came home at dawn with me in hand. She would have repeated the whole movie scene by scene, like the princess of the *Thousand*

and One Nights. And besides, "if Troy Donahue is anything like you, the last thing Sandra Dee should do is mention an old movie."

"Why?"

"Cuz you'd take me to see it, and then where would we be? No, I'd choose a ballet and hum the opening of *Romeo and Juliet*. And as you kissed me—what a kiss, wasn't it?, out in the watch house when she brings him down to her—my humming would become the theme song as they focus on the waves crashing over the rocks to let everyone know what's going on. It's probably easier to go from a hum into a kiss, don't you think?"

She took me completely. A year of missing her, and now, on the phone, she possessed me with her same conversation, the same racing at full speed, counting on me to be right behind her when she paused, picking up what I had seen and turning it around so I could see it again in a different way.

"But I'm no Troy Donahue."

"No lie! He's too sweet. He did the right thing when she needed him," she added, almost solemnly. "He could have walked out, like some people I know." For a moment we teetered at the edge of goodbye, silent phones suspended over the hooks.

I should have told her, But if you called me, I'd go back. I could have confessed, I've been waiting for you to call. But Ann Marisse didn't give me a chance, changing the subject with a simple, "But it always works out in the movies." That's when she began recalling other films, ones we sat through to the end, even when they didn't deserve five minutes of our attention, because I wanted to see if they'd get better; ones we loved and ones during which we started to make love.

"Our failed love," she called it, dramatically stressing *failed*. She was having fun, teasing me in character, perhaps Sandra Dee's. She laughed at the clumsy efforts of friends to bring us back together and Marianne's to keep us apart, the way we skirted each other at school, the uselessness of not talking to me but the pointlessness of trying to make it come back. It would be great, we agreed, if we could forget the betrayals, and I wanted to tell her I could forget anything, everything.

"Too bad we have to grow up," she said, "but you can't be Sandra Dee all your life."

Our conversation hit a snag, losing momentum, her mood descending to bitter nostalgia, the sophisticated-lady perspective. We were adults, she said in a sober tone, and we had to go on to something else, leave the past behind, forgive each other and accept that the future was, as she repeated, something else—we never stopped to define what. We both simply accepted it, as she maintained we must, and went on. However, she added, since we were sharing the same hallways, lunchroom, teachers and friends, and would be for a few years, why not be friends. I suggested, in that case, that it wouldn't hurt to see each other one more time.

She laughed. "I see you almost every day, even when I don't want to." But she understood what I meant and, after a pause, said, "Yes. Where? Not here. Out? Yes. Pick you up? Okay."

My motor scooter wouldn't do. Like Troy Donahue, I desperately needed a car, but I didn't even have a license. My mother? No, she hadn't let me ride the scooter without one. I could steal my father's, but with him you could never tell; he might decide to wash his car by moonlight. I tried the last resort, my brother.

I found him in his room, studying, and laid it right out: "I have to meet Ann Marisse and I could really use a car. Can I borrow yours?"

"Your girl, huh?" he answered. Perhaps he didn't remember my age or that I wouldn't have a license for a few more months. Maybe he just felt sorry for me. Whatever, he tossed me the keys to his cherry '48 Ford.

Ann Marisse and I parked on a side street not far from her house. We were both afraid to use major streets, and the police often checked cars near the lake for neckers, which in this case would have bought us a ticket to the station and calls to our parents. The night sky was shading in rapidly, so Ann Marisse suggested we drive to the mystery house. The neighborhood's oldest residence remained a relic from when the area had been farmland. Through a barrier of tall poplars, a Spanish-style mansion could be glimpsed during the day, its red-tile roof slanting down over once brightly whitewashed walls. The property extended far beyond the house, curving towards the park which once had been part of its grounds. By the time we sought the protection of its shadowy drive, much of the estate had been parceled off. Ann Marisse's father twice had purchased land from the original tract, and a third house would later slice out more. It saddened Ann Marisse to see it go in patches, "like a quilt sold at auction, square by square, unraveling someone's life. Wouldn't it be terrible if it happened to my Nonna's land. Someone should keep it all together," she whispered.

Not what I imagined we had come to discuss, but it was enough just to be there, the radio turned off to preserve the battery, listening to her talk and looking at her in the semi-darkness, sitting across the front seat from me, nearer than we had been in a year. If she wanted to talk about the neighborhood mythology, I'd listen all night. But she said she didn't want to talk about Donna Costanza. It made her sad, she repeated. "And I don't want to be sad anymore, ever, please, Paul," and she slid over next to me. We discovered steering wheels to be a hindrance for anything but driving, so together we slid back to lean against the opposite door, her body half-turned to receive mine, kissing again to erase time, as if nothing had happened. But it had, making me hesitant, timid to move my hands, afraid to adjust my body to hers, to do the one thing, whatever it might be, to bring this to an abrupt halt. But her lips hadn't changed. She began with a gentle, nurturing kiss, an I-wouldn't-do-anything-to-hurt-you-kiss, exploring only our lips, feeling the contact and trying to believe it. Slowly, she drew me out, my tongue following hers as it retreated between her teeth. No longer playful, she eased into a mood of recuperation. I, however, remained apprehensive, not sure of what to do and what to avoid, so I limited myself to reacting, unwilling to risk doing anything to upset her. Foolish. Stupid. True, but I didn't want anything to go wrong.

Of course, this was exactly where I went wrong. Ann Marisse offered a chance to make it all right, to obliterate the pain and disappointment with an ultimate first: sex. She had decided to bring us back, but not to where we had been, because I had cracked that mold and not known how to hold the pieces together. She wanted to jump to the end and backtrack to the middle, filling in the gaps together. The offer of a lifetime, and I was afraid... fifteen and afraid to make another mistake.

She pushed me back with her hand. In the dark I couldn't see her eyes well, but I could tell she was staring up at me. She took my hand and brought it up towards her face, kissed the fingertips, and moved it down. I thought she would place it on her breast, but she left it on her throat, and returned her hand to the back of my neck, finding her favorite spot. The feeling returned, just as she wanted it to, but this time merging with another: my fingers recognized a cross I knew to be silver with tiny facets and "From Paul" engraved on the reverse. She had convinced me. From buttons to the hooks to kissing her nipples, we flowed smoothly from offer to response. She held my head in both hands, her finger combing through my hair, content to receive my lips. She had me again, guiding my sensations, knowing we were gliding towards her goal. She brought my face up to hers and kissed me, bringing her body under mine and me between her legs so our hips could initiate a soft, undulating friction in rhythm.

Then I stopped: "We shouldn't, Ann Marisse. We have to wait."

She had as difficult a time understanding it as many of you, maybe worse. Her blouse undone, bra lifted to expose her breasts, skirt riding high on her hips, and I tell her to wait.

"Don't be silly and foolish, Pauly, it's not the time."

"I'm trying to be adult."

"It's all right. Come here, kiss me. Really." And she pulled my head back down.

It should have happened right there, but it didn't.

After a few minutes I sat back up again, and in spite of everything my body begged me for, I said, "No. We have to wait."

The mood shattered. She had offered me a chance and I blew it. Again. For all the right reasons, you might say, but at exactly the wrong time. How I've derided myself all these years with the memory of this failure, laughed at the praise for my insight in the light of this one moment when I should have known better and, instead, did what I thought right. Paul Valencia playing the honorable Catholic boy, stupidly urging her to wait. For what? Time? My reasons must have sounded to her more confused than the dialogue from those same movies that inspired us to go ahead while warning us to stop. Illusions over illusions over brittle celluloid.

❊   ❊   ❊

No, not the first, neither of us for the other, although we wanted to be and should have been.

❊   ❊   ❊

Our first separation lasted over half-a-decade. We often saw each other and almost always talked to or passed one another in groups. Not going together made it hard to be at close quarters, because there were always those among us who felt the tension. With the blundered attempt at reunion after *Summer Place*, it got worse. She avoided me more for a few weeks, while I tried to run into her between classes and after school, but soon our movements drifted back into the pattern set by our schedules, she usually taking subjects I had the year before. My need to wait was respected to the logical conclusion: no contact if she could find any way out. I might as well have died. She could smile through me with a look I came to dread. When forced to speak to me, her conversation was superficial, uncharacteristically measured, even tedious. She seemed intent on making me understand that our plans were canceled, wiped out. I had made my choice and she instinctively leaped far ahead. More than merely removed to outside the boundaries of her space, which would have left me oriented to her, she no longer held out even this comfort. For me there remained nowhere, in or out of her space.

True, at moments her defenses lagged (*A message in my yearbook: "No matter what, you're still* tops *with me"*), signaling a potential truce (*Standing in the aisle of a dark school bus returning from a weekend ski trip, singing old songs through a general state of exhaustion, Dick suggests "Loving You," but I claim to have forgotten; her hand grips my wrist in the dim light, gently intense, her tired eyes focus assailably uninhibited: "You have to remember, Paul,"—a plea or a curse?*), but I read them with caution (*Eight of us praying the rosary out loud in the back of a van on the way to regional finals in speech; her hand delaying on a bead to allow mine to slip over it and interlace through the last three mysteries*), because they faded faster than they appeared (*Making me up for the school play, she stared at my face but avoided my eyes until the end: "Too bad I can't redesign your heart as easily!"*). She worked so hard to eliminate them.

When I graduated, Ann Marisse must have found the hallways of HTHS suddenly wider, the stairs no longer a matter of memorized schedules of which route to avoid. Nothing left to shun. I wondered then if she felt an absence, even in her relief, but I couldn't ask her. She crossed me off her agenda for half-a-decade.

That's how it went for those years, a few chance encounters and one blown opportunity.

※   ※   ※

I had evaded telling people I would be going to Loyola on an academic scholarship. It wouldn't have impressed those who expected me to excel on a different field. My brother didn't find out until midsummer and then he just nodded his head. If he understood, he wasn't saying. Having been my father's favorite son for the first eighteen years of his life, until he also rejected West Point, had rubbed off in his style of communicating: eloquently silent and concise. My mother's reaction: "You can prepare to be a doctor or lawyer at any university." When she imagined my future, it was always through the examples of her brothers, my uncles in Mexico, and her own father, but never mine. She had absolute confidence that we would succeed at their level no matter where we studied. Besides, she didn't mind me staying home.

Another reason for keeping my decision a secret was to distance myself from Alonzo. During our last semester he ran a daily report on recruitment letters and calls. Offers came in from small state colleges as well as inquiries from the same Ivy League schools that had contacted me. That Dick received them, too, forced him into convoluted explanations of the subtle differences between their offers. No one asked about mine because my destination was taken for granted, so why would I bother to consider East Coast schools with second-rate teams. I figured Alonzo would accept one of the offers, so I was safe in choosing Loyola.

After maneuvering through registration lines, I reached the advising table. I was sitting in front of a black-frocked Jesuit who studied my file silently, when out of nowhere Alonzo hit me on the shoulder with his registration packet and said hello. Before I could react, another priest paused behind the adviser, looked down at my transcript and commented dryly, "He's one of mine." Father Boyle, the adviser informed me, was the English Department chairman. Alonzo didn't qualify as one of Fr. Boyle's, but he hung around anyway, just like in high school. We all shared lecture courses, like Western Civ, Psych, Theology I. On a campus as large as UCLA, chances are we wouldn't have seen each other, but at Loyola we might as well have been roommates.

Alonzo disliked strange places where no one knew him, so he looked for acquaintances he could count on in each course to avoid sitting alone. From there he worked the new crowd, to whom he'd introduced me as his best high school buddy. But soon the work load swept me up, and I found myself studying every moment. Boyle was pitilessly exigent, and his lectures on poetry drove me in search of more readings. He offered to meet with a group of us interested in writing. These sessions became my life center. Around Christmas, I heard Alonzo mention he had found a job. I didn't even ask what.

In my sophomore year, I declared an English major. On the first day of fall semester, Alonzo flopped down next to me in Elizabethan Drama, proclaiming his love of Shakespeare. I was convinced he chose the same major to ruin it for me. Neither of us discussed our plans, and I confess to not having thought about a profession. Someday I'd have to work. Like dying, the time would come and I'd find myself doing it. In the neighborhood hangouts, a new question arose: What are you going to be? It disconcerted me at first, because I had no answer to appease them. I tested the waters with "maybe a writer," and straight-away someone attached "sports" to the noun. I corrected them, saying anything but sports. The questioning faces reappeared, throwing raised-eyebrow and lifted-head signals across the take-out counter. They wanted something of value to replace the football career I supposedly had thrown away. For what? I had no reply.

One evening, while I was dining in the Italian restaurant that occupied the old creamery shell, Coach Purdy came up. I introduced him to Kandy, a diminutive but extremely alluring woman, and invited him to join us. He declined, but remained standing next to the table, reminiscing, asking the young lady if she knew she was with the best player he had ever coached.

Surprisingly, he recalled my high school games in detail. No one but Coach Purdy ever said, as he did to Kandy, "You should have seen the game Paul called in the championship." I'd have welcomed a play-by-play account to compare with my own, but he said goodbye and started to leave. Then he stopped, settled his feet into the ready position he had drilled into us—shoulders-width apart and left slightly ahead of the right, the one my body still reverts to in threatening moments—and delivered two verbal blows. "Sister Dolores says you're going to be an English teacher. Good. I always wanted to teach, but couldn't wangle a certificate." Then, drawing a quick breath, he turned his eyes to Kandy. "Young lady, you be good to Paul. He deserves the best."

I explained as little as possible over a pasta that made me nostalgic for Karl's. Kandy protested that she had enjoyed him. She had wanted to see my old neighborhood to imbibe the influences from which my "strange manner of being" had emerged, so running into an eye witness of my feats struck her as the perfect touch.

"He loves you a lot," Kandy said, transforming forever my memory of the man.

＊　＊　＊

With her perfectly proportioned, small frame, Kandy was what you might call cute. That her height and sweet appearance kept men from taking her seriously as an actress constantly infuriated her. She hated being cute. She froze when men called her little girl. She began writing her name with a K to forge steel into the servile spine of her first initial after a professor commented on how sweet and tasty she looked. Then she adopted *Kirsten*, the name she used when I met her, in order to excise the vulnerable open vowel, the endearing y, and the edible connotations. *Kirsten* came armored in five solid consonants around two sharp vowels that made the name hiss, like a striking snake. Its Scandinavian origin conjured images of tall, nordic Valkyries, "and nobody fucks with them," she told me. Little of her original *Candice* survived, but at four-foot, nine and three-quarters she knew it required radical change or nothing. To back it up, she black-belted in Akido and waited for the first director to try to cuddle her like a sexual child. She reminded me of a miniature Susy, although I would have never expressed it to her in those words.

Kandy had attracted me even before I had seen her face. In early 1964, Father Boyle recommended me for the drama workshop taught by a visiting professor from New York. Honored, I arrived to check it out and found the students standing in front of a low stage listening to a middle-aged, balding man perched on a high stool and explaining the workshop procedure. From my vantage at back, I noticed a young woman standing tall among the rest, then immediately I sensed the incongruity of the impression. Although the students around her were taller, she created the illusion of height, holding her body erect, stretched to its ultimate, yet relaxed within a rigidly perpendicular line traced by her spine. In a black turtle neck, black pants and boots, her short, straight black hair cut one length all around from cheek to cheek, drawing a sharp-edge along the turtleneck collar, she was a vision of a New York Beat, utterly out of place among Loyola students. The precision of her geometry aside, she seemed the epitome of the nonconformist. Then, as the professor gave his spiel about acting as psychological and existential self-knowledge through the manipulation of the human body's myriad potential and the psyche's suppressed, untapped resources, she turned her head and smiled to herself. I decide to take the course.

After the meeting, when I told her she had seduced me with the starkness of her look, so un-Californian, she said I was full of shit. When I explained how I had been observing her, she cut it to a simple, "Shit. Who gave you the right to watch me?" Although it was a question, she didn't stay for a reply. My first invitation met with a categorical refusal requiring no elaboration: "Fuck off." Experienced at reading such signs after years of Ann Marisse's, I gave up and talked to her only when the professor assigned us to an outside project.

She came on intensely distrustful of men. From glimpses of her life she permitted us, a series of traumatic experiences had convinced her that society existed as organized exploitation of women by their proprietors and agents, men. The professor doted on her as the solitary presence of authentic gut-level experience among the palm-oil slick, Californian-squeaky-clean, ambitionless youths whom he was condemned to nurse for a semester. Kandy became his soul mate, but they pulled and twisted each other like a married couple trapped in Edward Albee's imagination. He strained between expressions of sincere admiration for her "mature insight" and withholding praise to assert his power as director. Nevertheless, try as he might to distance himself from the rest of us bourgeois suburbanites, Kandy's sweeping indictments of males fell on his head as well. "Resentful" was not too strong a word for Kandy's vision of the society men had created for her and her sex. "Angry" fit her equally as well.

She and another student were assigned a scene: "Engaged couple; one of them breaks it off; don't act it, live it." A product of the New York Actors Studio, the professor peddled the Strasberg technique. Kandy broke it off first, efficiently, no nonsense, leaving her companion no room for response, alone on the stage, just as she had done to me. The students applauded, but the professor criticized her for egotistically nullifying her fellow actor's participation. She protested. She had not played to an actor, but broken up with her fiancé, in which case, she didn't care to hear his response. He knew her point paraphrased his instructions, but he wrested back control by contradicting himself, recommending that she keep in mind we co-existed in a workshop where she represented, after all, only one small person among many.

Kandy's head lifted higher under the lash of his words. They set up to replay it, this time her partner taking the lead. He cavalierly discarded her for another woman, better looking and more supportive of his career. Kandy listened, emotionless, then she blew up, spewing her anger in a rush of obscenities which backed the speechless student out of the circle and into a chair, where she finished him off with a brutally believable slap. Wild applause. This time the professor praised her realistic language and the slap, but, not willing to let her escape without criticism, he commented on her reaction: convincing, but too abrupt. She was advised to convey emotion outwardly while her fiancé talked, perhaps attempting to interrupt, instead of waiting until he was through.

I disagreed almost under my breath, but he heard and asked me on what basis.

"I can't explain it, but Kirsten's right, it happens like that."

"Anything more, Valencia?" he asked in his condescending way of feigning interest in students' opinions.

"Yeah. Cut the swearing and just slap him."

Kandy waited outside after class to invite me for coffee and to become friends.

"Why?" I asked, suspicious of the sudden change in her.

"Haven't you noticed? We're not only the smartest people in the workshop, we are the most sensitive."

Coming from her it sounded incongruous, and I told her so. Her treatment of me had displayed no such sensitivity, and I balked at offering my friendship again so easily. I had too many things to do, I told her. She sipped her coffee, thinking, then conceded my point. From that day on, in measured and not always easily extracted portions, she began to dole out her other side, the private person behind the public persona, starting with, "My real name is Kandy, with a K."

We were never in love, but in Kandy's way of dealing with the world, it was more important to be, as she put it, held in mutual trust—"The rest is shit."

One principle anchored Kandy's process of building trust: No Secrets. My foundation in the varied styles of confession proved, for once, an advantage. We agreed to share everything about our past. So, Kandy heard a lot about Ann Marisse, while she elaborated on her struggle to survive. But slowly I noticed Kandy's tendency to refashion episodes into ever-changing versions of her basic story. After a while she let slip she was not a student; she attended the workshop because her father had called our professor an extraordinary acting coach. This, in turn, unearthed another shard of information: far from being on her own, as she represented herself, she lived with her father and stepmother. None of the family information came volunteered. No, it was rather forcibly extracted after I saw the mansion she called home.

"Mutual trust?" I asked her the first time she let me drive her home—her old Plymouth had stalled. "Some shitty concept of trust you got, lady!"

"I couldn't be sure you'd be honest with a spoiled little rich bitch."

"Remember, you said little, not me."

"Fuck you, P."

"Any time, bitch."

Her eyes swelled with the peaking anger I recognized from the stage, so I spoke while I still had an opening.

"What about all those gut-wrenching revelations about growing up poor and pulling yourself up by the bra straps? Bull."

"Live the role, convince the audience. You can't pretend to hate, you have to hate."

"You can't pretend to lie, no, you have to really lie."

"Look who's talking. You expect me to believe all that crap about loving some chick next door you never see? All that teenage existential angst? I could puke. With a name like Ann Marisse! Go dish that shit at a coffee house, man. Get real."

"Yeah. It's real! Real coffee I pay for with real money from my real small scholarship to listen to real lies about mutual trust from a real rich bitch who's afraid to be real!"

She jumped out and slammed the car door, sending the inside handle flying across the seat onto my lap. I peeled out of the drive in reverse, then slammed into low to trace freshly laid rubber back towards the garage. Getting out of the car to chase her across the granite walk curving towards one wing of the sprawling modern structure, I yelled at her to stop.

"I never said she lived next door, and she wasn't even a teenager when we met, and her name is Ann Marisse... I trusted you, Kandy, and I want to know what the fuck this is all about."

We started over, beginning with her father. The house itself told a story of wealth and artistic sensitivity which Kandy omitted. Her version began with the distance she felt and the lack of expectations he had for her, before settling into traditional biography. As a copyright lawyer fresh out of the University of Chicago in the '20's, he joined M.G.M.'s office in charge of option contracts with authors, eventually taking it over. In the late '40's, just before the Supreme Court crippled the studios, he solidified exclusive personal arrangements with some of the leading literary agents, positioning himself as a key link between Hollywood and New York publishing. It proved very lucrative when the studio monopolies were broken.

Kandy, the second daughter of the first marriage, he loved devotedly, but he couldn't talk to her, even when she was young. Never requiring or demanding anything, he allowed her a limitless range of choices and action, perhaps because he was incapable of assuming a maternal role of nurturing when Kandy's mother and sister died. He recognized her talent and intelligence, but never pushed her to be anything but his daughter. He had more wealth than she could possibly need, set aside so nothing could deprive her of it, not even his second wife, who, to top it off, Kandy described as "very nice" and easy to get along with.

It sounded nothing like the lurid trash we've heard about the ugly truth behind the portals of the rich and decadent. I was prepared for tales of incest, rape, child abuse, abandonment, white slavery, anything but "Gidget Goes Beverly Hills." It struck me that Kandy's anger stemmed from thinking she had missed something by being rich, while I felt jealous at finding she had practically everything I wanted: a custom-designed home, art, a library the size of my parents' house, signed photographs of famous authors, actors and directors...I hadn't seen inside the garage, but I could imagine what she drove when not slumming at Loyola. And, to top it off, she was five years older than I and had already graduated from UCLA.

Kandy and I worked on building our mutual trust for over a year before a fateful staging of *A Midsummer Night's Dream* brought Ann Marisse back into the picture. She complained often of her father's silence, so I offered to swap parents. Since I had dashed my father's expectations, he had become exceedingly verbal, although one might question the advantage of the change. She thanked me but refused, offering instead to make the ultimate sacrifice and read my writing, which apparently I mentioned in every other sentence. We had met as aspiring actors, but one of the things I confessed was that acting didn't interest me as a career. I was in the workshop to pick her up. To her, on the other hand, acting was everything.

"I'm going to make something happen on my own," she said one night.

"No one is on their own. That's not the way the world is."

"I want to say I did it alone."

"Unbelievable! Someone in this room recently lectured me: 'the self-made man is worse than an illusion, it's a crock of shit. No one cares how you do it as long as you do it.'"

"One of your more profound statements."

"Yours! But it's true. As long as your acting is good, no one cares about your father's Calder next to the pool. If one of your father's friends can help you get an acting job, great!

Once on stage, you don't need them. It's you and the lines and the audience. Whatever helps you in, use it. I'd give anything to get someone to look at my writing."

While Kandy stubbornly refused to use her father to reach her goal, she had no such qualms when it came to helping me reach mine. She didn't get my permission to ask him to read my poetry, but then I had said I'd give anything if someone would.

"You know poetry," her father began. An auspicious start, but it marked the high point in his analysis, which continued with, "You just can't write it."

Her father studied me with the cool stare of a man whose reputation depended on recognizing assured value before signing contracts. After making the above observations, he proceeded to point out the why and show me the wherefore of his judgment. He was the best poetry teacher I had encountered, the last I consulted. I accepted his verdict: I am not a poet. It does no good to lie about someone's writing, because down the line a manuscript suffers unspeakable indignities in the claws of professional snobs with the tact of Godzilla. Sadists all, female or male, no difference. By being cruelly direct, Kandy's father acted kindly. My making love to his daughter had nothing to do with it.

From the center of your head, somewhere at a point marking the convergence of two lines, one crossing from side to side just in front of your ears and the other emerging from between your eyes, project a filament of your life energy honed to a needle point to pierce down through the back of your mouth, drawing it through your throat, descending along and just to the inside of your spine, to slide between your lungs, diving through your stomach, plunging like mercury time to the center of your body's hourglass, streaking to the vertex of groin and inner legs, to bend against G force, turning back along the searing surface, pulling gravity up to curve itself out into a shallow arc extending through your sexes to soar back through the other body you feel as your own, there just the other side, where your skin turns inside out, moving, racing, climbing, propelling the parabola spiraling through the throat, piercing to the tip of the tongue to explode back into your mouth…again…again…and again…

This is one way to imagine sex with Kandy. Perhaps because she introduced me to the Eastern-cults just starting to sweep into hip circles, I always had the sensation with her of spinning in a tight, perpetual yin/yang circle. Not that meditation interested her. The *Kama Sutra* was more to her taste. When she added some new pill, a present from one of her rock-musician friends, the impression exploded in psychedelic light-show effects: sensations/memories/dreams/illusions/ideals/*words of love you say whispered in my*/desires circling through our dual body at the speed of light…

Kandy and I would linger in each other, her head on my shoulder, mouth on my neck, my arms stretching over her back, hands cupping the orbs of her butt, her legs tucked to bring her knees along side my ribs, her feet next to my ass, our eyes open, not speaking, her lips over the vein in my neck, so close they named each pulse of blood. Nothing moving but the pulse and her lips. She never made me pull out, holding me in and asking me not to give up so soon, teaching me to use muscles that make my cock continue to pulse in her minutes after orgasm.

One night her father ran into me when I was leaving Kandy's wing of the house. He greeted me warmly, as if considering something like inviting me in for a nightcap, but then changed his mind and spoke to me there, on the granite walk. His words started off as directly as his critique of my poetry.

"She's always been a mystery to me, Paul. Whatever she wants, I give her, but she never lets me inside. I never succeed in eliciting a response. With you, however,…" and he paused. "It's all right. Whatever she wants is all right."

❋   ❋   ❋

"My husband used to say there was something wrong with me," she said once, still lying next to me, waiting for me to recover and filling the pause with self-revelation. "I wanted sex all the time, so in the divorce he charged me with being a nymph."

Husband? Trust, I came to understand with Kandy, is forged through continual tests of a person's capacity to absorb revelations inherently so charged with the unexpected as to undermine the image of the other believed and accepted up to any particular moment. Her first husband and her rock-musician friend were the same person. They met when she went to Radcliff and she brought him to L.A. to help him get started, transferring to UCLA in the process. It didn't work out because, according to him, his music couldn't grow in "the greenhouse of our love," his term for a situation where all he did was make love to her or rest up to make love to her again. He used words like that, she said, avoiding real ones. "A lot like you in many ways," she added, stroking my flaccid penis. She found him shacked up with the female singer he had contracted for a gig in San Francisco. She didn't contest the divorce, accepting that maybe she was a nymph.

"I thought men liked nymphs."

"Only in literature and bad movies," I told her. "There's a fundamental physical inequality that makes it difficult for men to satisfy the average woman, much less an insatiable one. Or in real words, men can't keep it hard long enough to fuck a nymph."

She was sexually demanding, no doubt, but giving as well, sensitive to details, taking time over the taste of herself on my mouth or fingers, swallowing my come and kissing my prick until it shrank, running her lips and fingers over it to feel how the skin changed as it contracted, showing no impatience or frustration. In the shower she'd explore my body, looking for tiny marks, scars, anything she could use to learn more about me, expanding our cache of trust. I explored hers, too, but she preferred to give her body directly, as real matter, instead of reified words. Ours were divergent systems: I was into representation; Kandy, presentation.

Then, still in her bedroom, we would work, I on my courses and she on my writing. Her father's daughter, she nurtured
my writing by ripping it to pieces. Naked, a red pencil in one
hand and my paper in the other, at times kneeling on the bed
to scribble a suggestion, she took on the character of a perverse angel, innocent in her nudity and all knowing in her cri-
tiques. Sometimes, I couldn't handle it and I'd get dressed and
threaten to leave. She'd ignore my reaction, track down an
example of her point and read me a sentence, repeat it, and
again, while she lay flat on her back, the paper held high over
her face at arms length. She'd repeat it until the criticism
sank in. I learned to read my drafts out loud, as if read in her
voice, then make corrections before giving her my essays or
short stories. The former improved immensely, and she gave
me topics to write on, as if I didn't have classes and term
papers already. She redlined my short stories as too *academic*.
She read me parts she branded repressed, or others she called
too modern novel, meaning pedantically overwritten. The
story ideas and the dialogue she liked, but the descriptions
and the narrative displeased her. She especially objected to
my reluctance to use direct, clear sexual language. She gave
me Henry Miller and instructed, *imitate*.

One night, she read a review she had asked me to write
on the new Stones album. Not brilliant, she said, but something might be done with it. Her ex-husband had quit music
and, with collateral Kandy had provided, had started a Rock
magazine. Cut and edited, the review became my first publication. The editors liked the material and asked for more, so
Kandy bargained for a better fee and steady assignments.
When she told me, still resting on top of me after making love,
I thanked her sincerely, telling her I trusted her even with my
writing, so much that she could be my agent. She rolled off of
me and went to sit down across the room, leaving me staring
at the ceiling. Having accepted her uncharted zones of hyper-
sensitivity into which the most innocent comment could drop
us, I assumed I had offended her. Perhaps her joy at doing me

a favor had been defiled by my reference to a commercial arrangement. She returned with a handwritten contract: I as writer; she as literary agent. Trust was one thing, business another.

Our relationship, call it what you will, revealed to her a career she has enjoyed ever since, one for which she had all the right contacts. She would use her father's contract forms when they became partners soon after; illustrious names have graced it over the years. But this first one was the only one we've ever made and the only one she ever signed, Candice. Soon after this, she legally changed her name to Kirsten. We had achieved mutual trust, but men, as she told me, men were a different story.

A few days later, we went to eat at the old creamery to celebrate my first publication. If she intended to handle me on more than a sexual basis, she should absorb the local color of my roots. She got a whole pallet full when Coach Purdy interrupted our meal. Another rung in our ladder of trust.

We were not in love, Kandy and I. We had more: a contractual bond on a professional level. And involved, sure... we used to call it screwing around, or just plain screwing. But no strings and, speaking for myself, we were straightforward and out-front with everything. So when I ran into Ann Marisse and invited her to dinner, naturally I told Kandy.

"She exists? I was starting to think she was as phony as your stories. What are you going to do?"

"See her."

"Just fuckin' see her! A poor choice of words. Conveys nothing. Worst, it's a fuckin' lie, or it better be."

"Are you mad?"

"Always. Angry, no. You've wasted half of your damn life—your own words—obsessed with this broad, and your only thought is to see her. What is she, one of your precious holy cards?"

"No, but what do you want me to do?"

"To write as well as you think you can. That's where it's at for us, isn't it? Our contract extends that far. A fuck today, a blow yesterday, but mainly writing."

"What are you saying?"

"I'm telling you to touch her, kiss her, fine, but fuck her, for crying out loud, and then marry the bitch before either one of you does anything else to screw it up... Then, if you have time, write, if you can write when you are living with your ideal. Shit, see if you still want it so badly. And you can see me, too, if she lets you. We have a contract. You know where I am."

※　※　※

Every spring the English Department's Shakespeare Conference and Renaissance Festival transported the campus into another age. Everywhere students turned, they ran into vendors and jugglers, multi-hued jesters and armored jousters from The Society of Creative Anachronisms. Plays could be viewed live or in film screenings. I helped design an outdoor staging of *A Midsummer Night's Dream* and went to catch it on a Sunday evening in early April. A small part of the audience occupied chairs in front of the stage, while the majority sat amphitheater-fashion on a grassy knoll. At intermission, when the crowd worked its way down to refreshment stands flanking the stage, I saw her, sitting alone on a blanket. Ann Marisse—thinner, hair loose and flowing, more blond than I remembered, a large suede jacket, obviously not her own, shielding her shoulders against the evening breeze rounding the hill. I weaved my way around blankets until I stood in front of her. In the same manner I had seen her read so many books over the years, she was concentrating intensely on the program notes.

"Hi."

She raised her head slowly; her eyes focused hesitantly in a gesture I had seen before, as though coming a great distance to see me.

"Hello."

We looked at each other in silence, both waiting for the other to continue. Then Alonzo appeared with two drinks and didn't invite me to join them. I left them there alone, together. But her one word, natural and open, had been sufficient to let me know where I stood.

A call the next day began our second sustained romance.

❋   ❋   ❋

Two days after the Shakespeare festival, I picked her up for dinner. Although she had her own apartment near the university, she waited for me at her parents' house. Respecting her mother's wishes, Ann Marisse had attended classes at a local state campus her first year, but intent on transferring to UCLA her sophomore year, she forged a compromise. Her parents let her share an apartment during the week with yet another cousin, if she spent weekends at home. Her mother maintained her room exactly as she had always had it. In that way Ann Marisse could step back out of a future her parents admired her for achieving but feared, lest it swallow her up. Ann Marisse didn't mind the arrangement, feeling no desire to distance herself from her parents. She also enjoyed the freedom of her own space in the apartment, defining it with the objects of her studies and interests—books, posters of campus events and a large reproduction of a Frank Lloyd Wright house thrusting its sweeping lines into the horizon. Yet Ann Marisse still cherished the security of knowing she could fall back into her old bed among stuffed animals. She moved from one space to the other with the same fluid ease with which she walked in and out of my life. She, of course, saw it differently: I did the walking through hers.

I dreaded having to greet her parents. We had never quit running into each other, as neighbors do who share the same streets and stores, but their manner remained tenaciously cool and distant. Ann Marisse must have known, because she came to the door before I rang the bell and stepped out ready to leave, handing me her white shawl. In a black dress, her blond hair like sunlight warming her bare shoulders, she walked just in front of me and to the right out to my car. As I began to step beside her to open the door, she leaned slightly into my path, turned to face me and kissed me on the mouth...the same constant softness of our memories, the same declaration of presence and offertory, her right hand on my chest and no other part of our bodies touching.

Breaking off the kiss in a hesitant retreat, then returning to let her lips graze my face for the length of a quick breath, more to avoid my eyes than to kiss my cheek, she finally leaned her body back several inches, using her right hand to push softly away. Her eyes searched mine, first one, then the other, then back, inquiring something at a level of communication only light comprehends. Upon finding the answer demanded of me, she smiled, not the same way I would have remembered her smile a moment before it curved the serious line of her lips, but the way she taught me to see it from then on: a smile of patient inclusiveness and acceptance, of knowing I loved her.

With a look of satisfaction, of finally being with the man meant for her, of having returned to the beginning, she spoke: "Oh, Paul." It emerged a breath above a whisper, and she paused, leaving the words floating between us, as if she couldn't bring herself to say what she wanted, filtering the sounds through a mixture of tentative happiness and lingering regret. "Oh, Paul, why have we lost so many years?"

"I don't know," I answered.

I never have been able to explain it, at least not when I've tried to focus on us, exclusively, the way we wanted it to be and the way she could mold it with the turn of her body, a kiss and a word, or the way we had danced secretly alone among friends. When I look at us, standing in front of her house in 1957, walking through a living room at Christmas, dancing at Easter or the Prom or in her den, watching each other in the arms of others, reading the same book miles apart, discovering orgasm before knowing the word and the nerve endings waiting to explode under enured fingertips, embracing in an old watchhouse overlooking the sea while discussing *King Kong*, reaching across a car seat to touch and wonder why/why not, we are always alone in spite of everything. If I study the image, hold it up to the light to see the transparent quality of the space around us, I can never explain why. This allowed me to say then, as it permits me to write now, sincerely, *I don't know*. There are moments when I have insisted on this frame, mimicking the way she could cup her hands around a rose and offer it to me as unique and perpetual; or the petals preserved in a key chain so I wouldn't forget California summers when I'd leave to become a writer—if I left to become anything. In the '50s Tommy Edwards sang, "It's only the good times I remember," but it's never so simple. As I learned later, it has less to do with good or bad than with the art of editing, of cropping the frame to turn the image 360 degrees around that dual, solitary figure, highlighting every detail. This image of us makes any other answer impossible.

She stepped out, in a black cotton dress that hugged her torso, emphasizing the mature narrowing of her waist, then flared slightly to end just above her knees. Her blond hair, swept back and to the sides from her high forehead, like waves breaking and blending into the late afternoon sunlight falling warmly to her bare shoulders; in her left hand a small clutch bag matching the patent leather of her shoes. She walked just in front of me less than an arm's length away and to the right, leading me to my car. I watched her pause, sensing, remembering her next step as she leaned slightly into my path, turned on her left foot and kissed me on the mouth: the same constant softness of memories of offertory, of presence; her right hand slipped inside my jacket, making a rustling sound on my shirt as it came to rest against my chest, fingers spread, and no other part of our body touching, leaving the space between unbearably perceptible.

Breaking off the kiss in a hesitant retreat, a return, and a final easing back, letting her lips graze my face for the length of a quick breath, more to hide her eyes than to kiss my cheek, she leaned her body back several inches, using her right hand to push softly away to the distance she needed to look at me. Her eyes ready to search mine, first one then the other then back, inquiring something at a level of communication only light attends, and reading the reply demanded of me, seeing in them the reflection of herself she desired, she smiled, the way I would remember her smile from then on, but not before it curved the serious line of her lips, not the way she had taught me to see it before; now, a smile of patient inclusiveness and acceptance, of knowing whom she loved and being loved in return.

With a look of satisfaction, one of finally being, of returning, she spoke:

"Oh, Paul," whispered in tentative happiness, "why have we lost so many years?"

1965, as I wrote then in my Rock review column, was a FANtastically INcredible, super-sensational, comer of a year with a bullet, NO 2 ways about it, with the British Invasion roaring through every Go-Go Club and backwater dive in the U.S.A. We welcomed it with open arms, longer hair and shorter skirts. But assimilating the new didn't mean we had to scrap the old. So when Johnny Mathis played the Hollywood Bowl, we fought the crowd to get in as if for the Beatles. And when he sang only half of the promised performance, we drove back to the old mystery mansion, parked, and danced in the street. We had doubled with a new friend from Loyola, Johnny, whose date complained about the rough pavement; but we didn't care, because we were searching for dropped threads, splicing loose ends, making up and out for lost time. Johnny understood and took his girl into the back seat to give us privacy.

✻   ✻   ✻

That first night I needed something special, different, so I made a reservation at a restaurant Kandy's father frequented, Chez Pierre. It became our weekly Monday date. Pierre, a real French maitre d'—Ann Marisse tested him out thoroughly—held our favorite table and greeted us like old friends.

Behind the sensual joy of new flavors in mouths hungry for exotic difference lay the desire to travel. We asked Pierre about Paris, and he switched into French to reminisce about his years as a student chef, forgetting I understood nothing. I didn't object, because I preferred watching Ann Marisse translate to me while keeping her eyes fixed on Pierre, her expressions mirroring the joy of his words, the humor of anecdotes and the timely metaphor to allude to love. She blushed, bowed and shook her head, singing a French *no, no, je suis Italienne* to his inquiry into her French origin. *"C'est imposible,"* he objected. Back in English, he insisted I take my young lady to Paris. His recommendation became a mandate: we would go, but only if I promised to take her to Italy first.

"Rome, of course, and then Florence. We could see it all, Paul. We'll walk down the Spanish steps... No, better, you stand at the bottom and I'll walk down as if we've never met, and you'll watch me like a stranger, then proposition me."

"And Trevi, from *Three Coins in the Fountain.*"

"Then to Germany—Heidelberg."

"The Student Prince..."

"No, silly, my uncle Joe was there after the war and says no one should miss the castle in Heidelberg at sunset. So we'll take a grand tour in the old grand style."

"A two-year honeymoon, at least."

And her eyes focused more intensely for a moment as she paused, waiting.

In a way we were still children in adult clothes, or maybe barely adults in children's dreams. Each meal was a voyage, tickets around the world and back for the price of pomegranates and bread sticks, Baked Alaska or Chateaubriand. We had it all in reach, there inside Chez Pierre, where no one cared to take it away.

How did they see us, Pierre and our waiter David, a southern Black with gray-speckled sideburns who flourished us with Louisiana refinement? We didn't stop to ask, never thinking it would differ from the way we saw ourselves: casual in formal clothes, grown up, but not old, the radiant blonde and the dark, Italian-looking young man. One could question the sincerity of their reception and cynically attribute it to the dollar amount spent over the year, but it was more. Dollars, yes, but more.

In July, three days before my twenty-first birthday, Pierre welcomed us, complimented Ann Marisse's dress, praised one of my reviews in a local magazine, and turned us over to David. On Ann Marisse's suggestion, we left the selections to him. After three months, he knew our tastes.

We were arguing over a poem I had written about friends and dogs. She wouldn't stop laughing to listen to my justification. Others had been more verbal in their objections to my poetry, but none more accurate. While David expertly sliced a Beef Wellington for us, Pierre approached with a half-bottle of Burgundy. Before I could refuse, David set one glass in front of Ann Marisse, a second for me, and winked. I hadn't arranged any of it, and in the end neither Pierre would charge us nor David accept a tip. "A gift to our favorite couple," Pierre told us when we were ready to leave.

Ann Marisse caressed the stem of her glass, absorbed in the reflection of the central chandelier floating in miniature, deep in the ruby liquid. We touched glasses and took a first sip. It was too dry for our palate, and David repressed a chuckle.

"A few things you still have to get used to," he said, nodding his head, "but you've got lots of time."

Donna Costanza's fruity Zinfandel was more to my liking, I reminded Ann Marisse. She agreed, but kissed me with a taste of wine to share on her tongue.

The back of my fingers traced the line of her cheek. "You arranged this for me, huh?"

"The meal, yes, but not the wine. How could I?"

"You have ways."

"I don't always get what I want."

"When?"

"Let's not go into that."

"Mes amis?" Pierre interrupted. "Our chef desires to serve you his new creation, Crepes Framboise Ann Marisse."

The chef narrated the steps of preparation. The flambé, the choreography of hands and utensils, the scent of Cognac and Crème de Framboise, the French-English mix of rich "r's" or "i's" melting into long "eee's," it all delighted and impressed us, as did the taste itself. We didn't stop to analyze how trite the performance might sound recalled out of context. We appreciated every corny, exaggerated "r," every hyperbolic sweep of the cook's hand, and the final kiss and snapping-quick parting of his fingertips to signal the peek of exquisite flavor. Most of all, we were moved by affection for people who, for whatever reason, made us feel like lovers deserving of a monument, if nothing more than a fruit-filled crepe named in our tribute.

My father, on the other hand, seemed to take offense at what he considered my exorbitant expenditures on dinner at Chez Pierre. "How the hell can a kid his age afford a place like that?" he asked my mother when he found a matchbook next to my keys. Perhaps it undermined his sense of paternal authority not to be asked for money for my dates. He had always relished the opportunity to counsel me about girls—"None of them are worth it" or "Don't get them expensive presents, they don't know the difference." I heard my mother tell him that I had a job.

It was true. Kandy's connection with her ex's new publishing scheme was paying me off royally, more money than I had ever made at one time. My reviews of concerts and new albums appeared statewide—no personal billing at first, but steady money. We're talking a hundred a week in 1965, enough to cover tuition for a summer course, work on my writing, and expensive dinners once a week. But to my father it was too easy, more like stealing than work.

I took a UCLA course to be with Ann Marisse. Modern English Novel: Virginia Woolf, D.H. Lawrence and Malcolm Lowry. While she traced existential motifs or explained literary techniques, I found myself imagining screen adaptations. For Boyle at Loyola I had compared the film and text of Shaw's *Caesar and Cleopatra*, and it made such an impression on me that I had trouble concentrating on the novels as novels. As film they required different approaches: synthesis, dialogue, reinvention. Ann Marisse tolerated my intrusions on her academic analysis up to the point when my musings folded themselves into the actual novels in her mind, irremediably confusing the versions and forcing her to reread to draw clear distinctions. She forbad me to change a character or a detail of a plot out loud until after the final examination and went screaming from the room. The night I began to transpose *Orlando* into a contemporary story about two students and a lecherous old teacher, she threw me out. She intended to write a term paper on *Orlando*, so my interference infuriated her.

"Some day you're going to have to accept reality, Paul. You can't rewrite everything," she screamed before she slammed the door.

Then, looking down from her apartment balcony, she apologized for yelling at me. From the parking lot I asked if I could go back up. "No," she said, barely controlling herself. Back home, my mother said "the blonde" had called and left a message: "Tomorrow."

It didn't always end in balcony scenes or apologetic phone calls. Earlier in the summer, the following exchange had occurred by the pool.

"*Under the Volcano* would be a bitch to make into a movie, but I've outlined *Women in Love*..."

"What do you know about women in love?" she interrupted me with a laugh. She used laughter as a critical weapon, and usually I agreed with her judgments, but now I didn't understand her point. I was on a towel next to her, face down, studying my notebook. She rolled over on her side, flipped her hair back over her shoulder, and waited for me to look up or turn over.

"All my life I've loved you, Paul. But you? Nothing, as if you didn't even notice." Her intense stare meant she was serious. Maybe I had offended her.

"It's not true...." Disconcerted, I reverted to her favorite Shakespearean sonnet: "Let me not to the marriage of true minds..."

"No minds or neverminds," she cut me off, sitting up and closing my notebook firmly. "What interests me is your body, stupid, without impediments." Her voice dropped from aggressive to solicitous to ask, "When are you going to realize it?"

So we finally made love a few months after getting back together. The same soft lips, same lush breasts, the line of her body drawn along mine, like a dream repeated, but for the first time.

In the morning, I awoke first, got up very carefully so as not to disturb her, and went to the kitchen. Her cousin had gone home for the summer, so we were alone. I foraged through the cupboards as quietly as possible. I wanted to surprise her with coffee in bed, but the electric pot refused to perk. I found an old-fashioned Italian one for espresso and studied the strange design, filled it with water and coffee, placed it on a burner and turned it on. If it worked I could wake her with the smell of fresh coffee, but it didn't turn out as I had intended. Nothing ever did.

Before the damn water came to a boil, suddenly from the bedroom I heard a desperate, "Paul, Paul!"

"What happened, honey, what's wrong?" I tried to comfort her. She was sitting up in bed, so I reached out to put my arms around her, but she blocked my efforts, opening both hands flat against my chest to hold me back.

"Nothing," she said. "Nothing. Just, I've always wanted to wake up next to you. Sometimes I even pretend it's you. Now I couldn't find you." Her eyes, somewhere between gray and blue, very clear and hard to define in this light or any other, slowly filled with tears and kept me from asking with whom she pretended. Her hands slipped down my chest and settled, palms up, on her naked thighs. She stared down at them while I watched the tears well to the breaking point and release their tension over her cheeks, streaming down to drip onto her breasts. I loved her so much I didn't know what to do.

"You're rotten, Paul, such a *ciùc*. You always hurt me, huh? No, don't say anything." She paused, still staring at her hands; the little finger of the right one trembled. "Worse still," she continued, "I know you'll never change. You can't."

"But how, when?..."

"Shut up," she commanded softly. "It doesn't matter, not anymore," and she kissed me.

The coffee boiled away and ruined the pot.

I tried to understand, not right then, but during the long drives home from her apartment. In another age, the one that burst upon the scene a couple of years later, but too late for us, we would have moved in together. But we dragged around the ball and chain of our generational attitudes. Even though they suspected what we were doing, our parents would not have understood, or even tried had we gone public. She kept coming home on weekends and I kept driving home during the week. The times I spent the night, I had to contend with my mother's silence and pained facial expressions the next day. She blamed herself for my sins. When I confessed to staying with Ann Marisse, she sighed, relieved. She thought I had been with prostitutes, because to her mind a Catholic girl wouldn't let her boyfriend stay all night. Yet, she was happy with my choice of fiancée. She stopped referring to Ann Marisse as "the blonde," using her name instead, and when Ann Marisse came to the house, my mother called her *hija*, considering us already married. Ann Marisse loved her for it, and I loved them both in their affectionate interaction. I don't know if my father noticed my absences; he never said, not even when intoning the litany of my transgressions. Perhaps he considered staying all night with a "girl" a fitting activity for a "boy," at least a normal one.

On one of those long drives home, I decided never to ask
with whom she pretended. I wanted to know—it festered in
my memory—but I refused to risk what had taken so long to
retrieve on questions when the answers were guaranteed not
to please me. I figured, it cuts both ways: "What I don't know
won't hurt me." With the painful thought that I might know
too much already, I set adrift out into the flowing freeway
lanes, letting it get swept behind me and away. It heartened
me to feel how easily it seemed to disappear into the traffic.
Only one thing stubbornly hung on, like a bumper sticker on
the car ahead of me: the present tense. "Sometimes I even pretend it's you," she had said. Not "pretended," I'm sure, so I
changed lanes and concentrated on *Under the Volcano*.

You're jumping to conclusions, but then it's what we've
been trained to do. We learned to analyze everything, as if life
were a detective story with clues, and our mission, to break
the code before the end. Too bad we're not taught to turn back
at the second-to-last page and start again for the pleasure of
staying in the world created when we give ourselves to experience without asking anything in return. But we're taught to
push on to the end.

While we never quite forgave life its grave misprint in our
sexual record, we didn't discuss our disappointment at not
being first. Perhaps neither of us cared to invite alien spirits
into our bed. Maybe as students of the modern novel we realized the ephemeral quality of love when confronted by the
word *betrayal*, be it based on truth or fiction. Or we were just
too afraid to know. Whatever. But we didn't separate over sexual infidelity, mine or hers, no matter what anyone says.

Despite what people might have thought, dating Ann
Marisse did not affect my writing. I met my review deadlines,
rewrote a few stories, and read even more than before. The
best school for a writer is reading. Experience is overrated by
non-writers who assume writing comes from living. Interview-
ers often ask, did that actually happen, or, is this character
real, or who is this woman? As if one could only write about

flesh and blood people. Actually, real types just clutter your memory with sticky details they consider unexpendable, unlike literary characters, who are malleable and open to invention. They live in books, not in life, but then for writers the boundaries blur like tie-dye stains charting fluid patterns of new territories across old divisions, leaving insignificant difference. Years ago a friend used to warn me, you can't make love to a book—I couldn't agree less.

Ann Marisse's studies kept her just as busy, so our schedules and interests were quite compatible. If I sensed a change after renewing our relationship, it was the intensity. Ann Marisse's image had always centered my thoughts. In the spring of '65, body and thought coincided, the image assuming a corporeal substance, a physical presence with its own weight, three dimensions, movement and irrepressible free will. I didn't love her more now, nor was I obsessed with her to a lesser degree, but now I could pour my desire into her body instead of a memory. I didn't have to create the image. She was there...

❊   ❊   ❊

In 1950, our yard had flourished, one among the many, when a Japanese family cared for the lawn and garden. Nostalgic for the flowered patios and parks of her youth in Mexico City, my mother wanted the bluegrass carpet and mountains of roses my father had promised when he courted her. On their wedding day, looking at the roses of her uncle's home where they dined, her husband spoke again of the garden they would have in his native California. Under the skilled hands of the Japanese, my father's promise bloomed, until they asked for wages to match the quality of their work. My father replied that he and his sons would take over, thank you. My brother cut the grass for a few years until I grew strong enough to push the hand mower. The lawn stayed green, but grew ragged along the edges. The lawn's scraggly teeth mirrored the voracious pests blitzing the garden. By 1952, a

botanical cemetery framed our frazzled lawn. My mother for-
ayed valiantly into the devastation, spraying every inch with
the latest guaranteed cure-all, but soon she comprehended the
forked tonguedness of garden-shop owners. Yet she couldn't
bear to invite the Japanese family back. They had lost face,
she said, an expression garnered from the World War II
movies my father dragged her to so she could appreciate what
he had participated in his year at the San Diego Ship Yards.
She came to accept the distinctive identity of her home, an
oasis of brown-bordered green among the neighborhood's mul-
ticolored gardens.

In '64, at the cemetery where I still worked summers, the
boss ordered us to clear an area and get rid of the plants. My
mother smiled when she saw them transplanted in her garden. She kissed my father on the cheek, assuming that he was
finally attending to his promise. Surely the rose bushes could
not be far behind. I overheard her say as much to herself one
night a year later as she placed dishes in the washer. She
recounted his promise of thirty-five years earlier and assured
me roses would appear shortly. She thanked me for helping
tend the new plants, since my father had so much to do and so
much on his mind. No ill lasts a hundred years, she told me,
nor could any person bear it.

According to the florist, rose-planting season was waning,
but I bought them anyway with one of my writing paychecks
and hid them in Ann Marisse's garage. We planted them all
one Wednesday in my mother's absence, Ann Marisse and I,
digging, fertilizing, blending the planting mix, unwrapping,
holding them straight while the other shoveled in the soil, patting the mounds with our hands. We admired our work, thirteen rose bushes encircling the yard, strategically patterned
into my mother's dream.

After dinner, when Ann Marisse and I were reading out
on the patio, glancing up occasionally at the bushes, half-
expecting them to wither and collapse, my mother emerged
from the house with two cups of iced coffee. She stood next to

us, looking out over the yard which had become the home of her exile. "It won't take long for them to bloom," Ann Marisse said, breaking the silence.

"They are beautiful already, *hija*," my mother replied.

She walked out and looked at each bush, one by one, walking, pausing, walking on, balancing precariously in high heels on the lawn, her arms crossed at the waist, standing and looking down, moving a hand once in a while to her face to place her index finger alongside her cheek. When she returned, she squeezed Ann Marisse's shoulder softly with one hand, thanked us for the lovely roses, and went inside.

The plants had ignored the seasons, blooming like a cover for *House and Garden* to provide the petals Ann Marisse gathered secretly for my birthday gift. Four petals of glorious crimson floated in a pocket of crystal almost two inches in diameter and held in a sterling bezel. A short chain joined the bezel to a ring for keys. From the start, Ann Marisse intended to catch the moment and hold it beyond itself. When I opened the package in front of the family after dinner, my mother complimented Ann Marisse on the fine silver work; my father asked why I needed another key chain.

"To remind him of California when he's off to New York," Ann Marisse said, surprising everyone. "All writers go to New York," she added.

Johnny admired the bezel in his gentle, would-be surgeon's hands. "The West Coast was good enough for Robinson Jeffers, but you're right, he started in the east."

"I hate to travel," my father said. "It's never done anything for me."

"But one can travel with someone else, like a wife," my mother said, and the conversation shifted abruptly to a real wedding: Marianne and Dick were engaged.

I moved my keys on to the new chain while my mother and Ann Marisse carried dishes to the kitchen. Johnny and I joined them. As they talked about wedding plans, I marveled at how rapidly a life could change directions.

❋ ❋ ❋

Dick and I still ran into each other once in a while, and when we did the same old subject dominated: women. Many of our friends were already married, some with babies, so he'd tease me about never getting married, and I'd kid him about being next, since he and Janice had been together on and off since grade school. He kept saying, maybe, why not? I tried to draw some of the old '50s slang out of him, but couldn't penetrate his new somber exterior. He had cut school back to part-time so he could work, but when we spoke of marriage, he projected it into an indefinite future, after something just as indefinite, maybe law school.

Then prefacing his question with, "Really, Paul," he asked me when I might get married, and I told him the same went for me: after I finished. What? he asked me. I don't know, I told him, teacher training, I guess. To whom? he added. We looked at each other, and for a moment the old Dick surfaced in his knowing, Elvis smile mirrored in my own. "Shit, as if I didn't know," he said.

Now he was going to marry Marianne and hadn't included me in the wedding.

❋ ❋ ❋

"He's always liked her," Ann Marisse told me in front of the country club before the reception.

"I never noticed."

"You hardly notice anything outside of movies or books."

"I notice you. Want me to prove it?"

"Later, Paul. I have to be with the wedding party." She started to go in, then looked back at me. "I can't believe the way you and Alonzo acted during mass."

The four of us, Dick, Billy, Alonzo and I, had been together since forever, but only Billy stood by Dick in the wedding party. Marianne excluded Alonzo. They had gone together too long for her to feel comfortable with him standing near Dick during the mass. I could have matched up with Ann Marisse, but in weddings so many touchy relationships must be juggled. Dick's brothers had to be included, and Marianne's. Besides, Marianne never quit suspecting me of two-timing Ann Marisse with Kandy.

"You weren't invited to be in it either?" Alonzo had asked as he slid in next to me in the pew at the church earlier. I sat with my parents, but he had come alone. The priest was starting the service and the congregation focused on the wedding couple kneeling at the altar.

"Dick wanted me in it..." A girl in front of us looked back at him, and Alonzo flashed her a smile; when she looked away, he continued. "But I might make Ann Marisse nervous."

Two pews away, Mrs. Lombardi turned to see who was talking and gave me a silencing look.

"We should be up there," he said. "Dick's our best friend, no matter who he marries."

This time my mother leaned forward to look at him. He greeted her and my father, asking them how they had been. She thanked him, more with eye movements than her barely audible whispers. Then she received a shushing from further down the pew, to which my father responded with one of his own.

"Have you met the Colorado cousin? She's bitchin'. Maybe we could double before she leaves, like old times. Have some fun over at the apartment."

The priest turned to the bride and groom to recite some prayer—I had lost track of the mass—and shot a censuring look in our direction. Members of the wedding party followed his eyes our way and whispered to each other.

"At least Dick could've asked us to serve mass. Think you could still be an altar boy? I bet you'd still look like an angel, Pauly."

After all that, Alonzo still tried to hitch a ride with us to the country club, a couple hours drive into the mountains. I avoided answering him by nodding towards the altar where the priest sliced the air above the couple with a final blessing.

During the ceremony, Ann Marisse looked radiant next to Marianne. The contrast of the latter's white gown and Ann Marisse's rich, Aspen-bronze dress underscored the difference within their similarity. Marianne seemed cooler, colorless in spite of her black hair and darker complexion, rigid in her body movements, reserved in her gestures during the vows or the exchange of rings. When Dick kissed her, she offered strictly the surface of her lips, no more. When they turned to the congregation, her joy was held in the eyes, with only the faintest lines of a smile teasing the corners of her mouth. Next to her, Ann Marisse's emotions respected no decorum. The affection and happiness she held for her cousin flowed through her hands as she straightened Marianne's veil, impulsively kissing her cheek when she finished, touching Dick's arm as she passed, beaming as she watched them descend the steps from the altar to begin the recession. But just before she took Billy's arm to follow them out, her eyes raised to find mine and she winked, bringing the ceremony to a close, our ritual sealed.

At the reception dinner, Ann Marisse sat with the wedding party at the head table, set last-supper fashion on a platform at one end of the dining room. Unfamiliar names flanked my place card before I went through the buffet line, but when I returned, there sat Alonzo, waiting. Reading my expression, he shrugged his shoulders and pointed to his card. When I protested it hadn't been there before, he admitted the exchange.

"Old friends..." he started again.

"Knock it off. I'm not nostalgic."

"Nostalgic. An English major's word."

"You ought to know."

"I changed to business, in case you haven't noticed."

An older couple sitting across the table, relatives from Colorado, asked me if I was the same Paul whom the cousins used to talk about when they came to visit. Alonzo reimposed his line of thought even after several minutes had elapsed, minutes pleasantly devoted to memories of Ann Marisse and Marianne's Colorado summer of '58.

"You don't keep up with old friends, Paul, except one."

"School and work keep me busy."

"And your little girl friend, what's her name, Kristen? She looks like she could keep a man busy. Now that you can't give her your full attention, mind if I ask her out?"

"She doesn't date illiterates."

"You never know about women, Paul. Not all English majors are snobs. Some of them can still talk to us regular people."

"I'm sick of your games, Alonzo, so why in the fuck don't you say what you mean?"

"That's good English."

"You wouldn't know the difference."

Ann Marisse's relatives diverted their eyes down towards the table, then, making some excuse, rushed away. Once again we were attracting disapproving looks.

Ann Marisse appeared where her relatives had vacated their chairs, her smile rigid and forced—I never saw her look more like Marianne.

"You act like you're still in seventh grade."

"If we were," I answered, "he'd be on the floor by now."

"Want to try it again, just once when I'm ready."

"Paul, don't, for me, please. Alonzo, grow up!"

"Now I'm supposed to grow up. Not what you were saying a few months go."

"Paul, for me?" Her hands pressed mine, her eyes pleading to let it pass, to ignore him and not embarrass her family, telling me that no one else mattered...

Dick's hand came down on my shoulder: "Come start the dance." His wide smile spoke of having waited out his time to get what he wanted; now he could live the rest of his life according to design. Our tradition, the way everyone we knew dreamed it would be. He didn't have to tell us, probably couldn't have, especially after downing a dozen champagne toasts. He said he wanted to dance with Ann Marisse right after dancing with his wife and asked me if it was okay. With an arm around each of us, he walked us away from Alonzo and into the ballroom.

"Ann Marisse, if I hadn't seen Marianne in eighth grade, I would have fallen for you. But you were already Paul's girl, so it would have been worse than falling in love with Marianne. I knew you two would work it out. Like I told you both, fate."

The wedding party was waiting for Dick to start the first dance, but he called for champagne and insisted on another toast.

"To my best friends, Paul and Ann Marisse. May the next wedding be yours."

Everyone agreed, except Marianne, who pulled on Dick's sleeve to keep him from drinking, whispering something which caused him to shake his head and try to kiss her. Taking it as a signal, the band broke into *Fascination.* After a minute of letting the bride and groom dance alone, couples joined in, filling the dance floor next to a curved wall of glass beyond which stretched a terrace overlooking a large pool and the club gardens surrounded by forest.

We slipped into an embrace with natural ease, all hesitation forgotten after six months of being back together. I shifted one hand to the side of her waist and extended my arm into the classic waltz position, allowing a space to open between us. She looked at me from the distance it had created, smiled and assumed her role, body formally erect, head moving from side to side as we turned in the dance.

"Remember?"

She focused her gaze on me, saying nothing for a moment. Then: "I like you better silly and foolish...but I like you most when you look at me."

"I looked at you that whole night."

"Sure. When we danced, once. You brought that Susy. She was beautiful."

"Not as much as you. You're the most beautiful girl in this room."

"You're serious."

My arm slid around her waist, collapsing the space between us as the band modulated into *Over the Rainbow*. Dick looked over from where he was dancing with Marianne and nodded, as he used to on the field when he understood my signal for a defense without asking, and kept dancing.

"Everything," she said to herself. "I remember every second. That night, dancing, wanting you to hold me, to forget the way you rejected me..."

"I didn't..."

"Don't," she pressed a finger to my lips. "You spoil things so easily when you talk. For once, let me. I'm dancing at Marianne's wedding with the only person in the world I love more than her. The only boy I've ever loved, Paul. No matter what."

She hugged me close as we danced. For wanting to talk, she was grimly silent as the band played through a medley of romantic standards, stretching out the bride and groom's dance. Dick and Marianne were embraced like teenagers, barely moving.

"Do you know what it was like to want you and not be with you?" she finally asked.

"Exactly."

"No. You couldn't." She was so close I could only see her eyes. "It was different for you. You heard Dick. To him I was your girl from the start. Nobody in this room has ever seen me as anything else. Not even me, and certainly not you. I'm not blaming you; it's what I wanted to be. That's why it hurt so bad when you didn't want me. Then, as hard as I tried to cut you out, to be me alone, I was always Paul's girl. I can't remember being just Marianne's cousin or my brother's big sister.

"When you left school, I became Paul's ex-girl. Twice you've left me behind. But I was your girl. It doesn't matter who I date, it always comes down to you. After senior Homecoming, I cried because you hadn't been there to see me. I wanted you to come to the window and tell me I was yours. But I swore I wouldn't ask you again. When I need you most, you're never here. It's not fair. Do you realize this is the first dance we've come to together? All that wasted time, Paul."

She buried her face in my chest, her body shaking softly in my arms.

"Please," I whispered.

She took my hand and led me out to the terrace. Shadowy fingers were reaching in from the mountainside where a breeze had set the trees swaying, wafting pine scent over the scene.

She placed both hands on the terrace railing, leaned her body against it, and waited to regain her composure. I knew it wasn't the right time to interrupt. Since freshman year she hadn't talked to me this way, going back over what we were to each other, and I wanted to hear her. The lights around the pool blinked on to a soft glow while waiters lit torches around the terrace perimeter and down in the gardens below.

"None of this makes sense, but then for years we haven't made sense. We know what we want and still mess it up." Then interrupting her train of thought with a smile, her body relaxing, she turned her face towards the overlook, offering me her profile and feeling me watch her.

"After the prom, Donny and I parked in front of the house. He noticed the night light on inside and asked if my parents left it for me. I said, no, for Paul. He didn't think it was funny at all." She laughed at the memory.

"I hated you at those dances, the way you always stared at me. But when you left, Donny took over a team that couldn't replace the class of '62, and I became the girl who couldn't replace just one of you, although I hadn't really had you for years." She looked around at the forest.

"Without you, days are just time to fill and forget; mark them off and wait. It makes me desperate to get back on track. But when we do, in the middle of everything that makes us happy, and I am happy with you, I start waiting for something...for the crash.

"Do you really know anything about me?" She turned to look at me. "What I feel, what I want, what I'm capable of doing, the lengths you drive me to when you turn our plans upside down without warning? Being in love with you is like, like standing on a gallows and not knowing why or when the floor is going to fall out from under me. Can't you see what havoc you cause?"

With a breath she looked away, then glanced back at me before turning her head to look in the other direction. When she resumed speaking, her voice sounded distant.

"Remember when we saw *Summer Place*? I was scared, but I told myself it's simple: just say yes and close my eyes. Make it easy. I got so nervous...I can't describe it, something right here." Turning to face the forest again, she placed her hands open on her lower stomach, as though feeling for the memory with her fingers to let it dictate words to explain what she had no words for. Her hands moved again to the railing and she breathed deeply, exhaling as her body came to rest back against the railing.

"Then you said no." She turned on me. "Paul, it's not the way it's supposed to happen. Even Sandra Dee handled it better."

"She had King Kong's help, but look where it got them."

"I wouldn't care, even now," she said, pounding her fists twice on my chest, not at all gently. Then, leaving them there, she leaned forward against me, her face turned back towards the ballroom where the reception continued, couples dancing to the kind of rock music acoustic bands imitate, the muffled sounds reaching us on the terrace.

"You just had to be Elvis to the end, Mr. Nice Guy even when I didn't want you to be. You can be such a fool, Paul, but it's okay, really, because you're a sensitive fool. Put your arms around me, Pauly, its chilly. We're impossible. Do you think we'll ever work it out?"

"I hope so."

As the dancers adjusted for a slow number, her mother came out to tell us that Dick and Marianne would be leaving in about fifteen minutes, so she would be throwing the bouquet soon. She left the door open, boosting the music's volume into the night.

We started to move towards the ballroom, but Ann Marisse turned in front of me and stopped. She stared up at me for a moment, her same gesture which always arrests my breathing in anticipation; but instead of a quick phrase and twirl out, as she had done so many times before, she remained there, facing me, looking up, waiting, separating the world into our private circle and the rest. Then she slipped both arms around my shoulders, as though she wanted to dance.

"You know..." I began.

But she brought a finger to my lips again, not demanding silence, rather something else. I could read it in her face, held just below mine, looking up.

"Remember," she commanded.

I read the desire, but not its object. Which of the memories did she want to hear?

"Remember." She held me close, her hand traveling up to the back of my neck, under the longer hair I was wearing by then, to find the exact spot she had claimed as hers. I looked over her head, searching for some image to offer her from so many.

"I've loved you all my life. That's what I remember."

"Are you serious this time? Pauly, are you finally sure?"

"Yes."

She held me tight for a moment, hiding her face away from my eyes. Then I think I heard her say, "I wanted you first, really, but I didn't think you were ever coming back."

"It doesn't matter," I told her, holding her head to my chest and stroking her hair.

I meant what I said, but perhaps it wasn't true. Sometime you don't know exactly what you're talking about, but you try to say the right thing. Whatever we were in, we wanted to be in it together, serious and sure. I would have said anything to make her feel it.

❀   ❀   ❀

"You can't be serious, Paul." —Kandy's reaction to the scene you just read when we met to discuss the first half of the manuscript four years ago in her New York office. She tried reading some of the dialogue out loud, but I waved her words away with my hands and told her it wasn't meant to be read out loud, it's not a script.

"I've read the manuscript and I'm leveling with you. You narrate a twenty-year-old scene and can't muster a grain of irony."

"I don't want irony," I responded, irked by the familiar scalpel precision with which she has sculpted my writing for twenty years. "I want it the way it happened. That's it."

"No, because I'm the one your editor will call. I can hear it already, this is melodramatic sentimentality."

"I don't care."

"This isn't a novel, Paul. You're writing romance."

"Call it whatever you..."

"Two decades of a solid career in film, and now you give me a fuckin' romance."

"Why don't you stop talking like a fuckin' teenager?"

"Because your fuckin' manuscript makes me feel like one."

"Good!" I shouted as I got up to leave her office. She followed me to the door and stood there, looking up at me with a pleading expression of, reconsider. Instead, I kissed her. Not a light kiss of goodbye between friends, but a sexual kiss between old lovers, a remember-this kiss, a who-the-hell-cares-how-old-we-are kiss, a why-isn't-your-office-still-in-your-bedroom kiss; and she responded in kind. When we broke it off, she shook her head and said, "Okay, I'll keep reading."

"Thank you. That's all I've ever asked of you."

"The fuck it is."

I walked out, turned on my heel in front of the secretary, and opened the door again. Back at her desk, Kandy stood looking down at my manuscript, the scattered sheets forming a wedge across the polished mahogany surface.

"It was a romance," I told her. "I could never fool you."

❉   ❉   ❉

I know about romance. I've adapted more than a few, good and bad, pruning turgid narratives into the simple plots required by producers of T.V. mini-series and feature films. People call it frivolous, but they read it all the same. Who can blame them for wanting to escape the mess surrounding us. When I agreed with Kandy, however, I wasn't referring to marketing categories but to the texture of what I gave her to read. We, Ann Marisse and I, lived a romance, the people kind, the cry-on-your-shoulder-and-swear-eternal-love kind. They share in common escapist desire. We wanted to exist by ourselves according to one rule: love. We wanted it so badly that everything we did was affected and everyone around us was affected, but we didn't want them to affect us. That it's so painful at times you want to die is easy to call trite, but that offers no consolation when it's happening. There are no trite expressions of affection or suffering between two people when they're in love...and alone. Lift them out of context, print them in the pages of a book, and things get sticky, literally too sweet, and problems arise.

We weren't alone. All around us our friends were living their romances as well, at least those who weren't married. Not yet the love-in craze that swept the late 60s, but more mellow and old-fashioned: a sitting-in-the-park, strolling-down-a-shady-lane or dancing-in-the-dark type of love, closer to private courting than a free-sex happening. My friend Johnny also had lost his high school love, Marilyn, but encouraged by our renewed affair, he gave it another shot.

Johnny and I planned a candlelight seduction, six courses, three wines, continental to the hilt. Between classes we rushed back to his apartment to check on the sauces, set the table with crystal and roses borrowed from home, pick the records—ballad singers, Piaf and Katyna Ranieri. The late afternoon was spent in last-minute preparations, tasting food, sipping wine. Ann Marisse and Marilyn were impressed. Johnny played host, toasting them, us, the food, anything to keep the glasses filled, his own more than the rest. He was ecstatic, reunited with his love and flying high. When evening light faded, only the stereo's tiny red dot glowed in the living room to set the mood of romance, why call it anything else?

Ann Marisse suggested we give them some time alone, so we took a walk and came back to find them on the sofa, sipping cognac, talking intimately. So we closed ourselves in the bedroom until lured out by the aroma of the fresh coffee Marilyn was brewing for Johnny. We followed her to the living room, where he waited on the sofa, his head leaning back, his long legs stretched out in front of him. Marilyn held the cup out, but before he could take it, she turned it over in his lap. As he yelled and Ann Marisse ran to get a towel, Marilyn calmly asked me to drive her home. Something he said or did—he couldn't remember. I tried to talk to Marilyn for him, but she refused to explain or consider seeing him again. Months later, Johnny still couldn't remember what he had done in the rapture of three wines, cognac, and the warm flesh of his lost love. Pure romance and, if once in a while the flesh burns, it's just one of those turns in the game, *"...all in the wonderful game that we know as love..."*

* * *

Ann Marisse and I found ourselves between two worlds: our old friends and the university. But what she took as momentary, with her studies eventually leading her back home, I preferred to see as a permanently broken circuit. When we were alone it mattered little, but around Dick and Marianne the pressure grew. They took us as their mirror couple, those old friends newlyweds bounce their married image off of to check how they are changing, growing, and how much happier they are married. For Ann Marisse the scene was intense because the newlyweds became the clan's new focal point when they received Donna Costanza's old house as a wedding present. Then, with sinister family logic, the seasonal feasts were renewed after a six-year hiatus. Dick and Marianne's beaming example sparked constant questions about our plans at each family gathering, my own included.

Ann Marisse countered by avoiding their house after the first few weeks. She invented excuses to meet at the movies or a restaurant, or let them visit us at the apartment. But their mere presence constantly reminded us of expectations postponed, ones that we didn't entirely disdain. In desperation, she announced she had to go into academic hibernation to finish the term, and we holed up in Westwood, sallying out weekly to the Film Club and Chez Pierre.

Christmas lurked on the calendar like the grimacing Fallen Angel sensing his opportunity to pounce. Nothing short of leaving town could protect us from the first full-scale family reunion since Donna Costanza's funeral.

"Don't you have relatives in Mexico?" she asked me.

It signaled despair. Sure, we had relatives in Mexico, but I didn't know them and had no desire to pursue the relationship. I countered, suggesting skiing in Colorado. I didn't realize she had considered it seriously until in a fit of anxiety she tore up a letter in which her cousin informed her of the family's plans to attend the Christmas reunion in L.A. We were doomed.

Not that my home was carefree. As if in revenge for the roses, my father intensified his communication with me. When a twenty-one year silence you've come to rely on as a pillar of your everyday existence crumbles, the other columns feel the strain. Ann Marisse sensed the stress behind my words, in my body, but she had to drag the cause out of me. Kandy would have advised me to tell him to fuck off, but Ann Marisse, viewing fathers through the Kodacolor slide of her own exceptional model, couldn't accept that mine resembled hers only as his opposite. She urged me to talk it out, making me promise to try.

How could I talk out things like: "Too bad you didn't accept your appointment to West Point. You'd almost be out by now and the young officers will get first crack at Vietnam. Mark my words, we'll have a full-scale war soon, and it could be your only chance to serve." Or: "I came across these pamphlets down at City Hall. Officer's training for college graduates. I didn't know students had it so soft. Says here you could still get commissioned with less than a year of basic. The Marines look the best. Join the Navy and you might miss the real action."

Karl Jr. showed me one, too, down at the Ristorante. He said if he didn't have Carmen and the kids to take care of, he'd join. He couldn't be an officer without college, but, he said, maybe we could serve together, like in the old days, "You call the plays and I'll run interference."

Before the casualty list started sounding like the roll call of an entire generation, we thought it would be another war fought in Hollywood cutting rooms. We looked at it through *The Flying Leathernecks*, *Guadalcanal Diary* and *The Halls of Montezuma*. The futile ending of *The Bridges of Toko-Ri* hadn't registered on us. Many of us were ready to play war. Some of us were lucky enough to get distracted.

Johnny, the well-balanced, brilliant premed and my closest friend, joined the Navy. My heart sank when he told me, not because I disagreed with the war—no war existed in the winter of '66, just an escalating police action—but because if going was inevitable, I wanted to go with him. He read philosophy, smoked a mellow pipe, hummed old songs to define the moment, and talked about life like a modern novelist. He

drank Chivas Regal with me over blue ice cubes and knew I
loved Ann Marisse more than anything in the world. The first
time he saw her, he smiled, nodded, and said, "I love her, too."
He was sincere and I didn't mind. No one else ever shared
Chez Pierre with us, and we would sit and talk, the three of us
until early morning. They would chat on the phone, Johnny
sending me messages through her. She pronounced his name
with an affection reserved for him alone. After completing one
of those officer training programs, he came back through L.A.
on his way to report for duty. He invited Ann Marisse and me
to the Officer's Club and was sorry to see me show up alone.
He spoke about Lotus Elans, East Coast girls, and how they
had assigned him to a ship which in all likelihood would
spend the next few years docked in Hawaii. A great place for a
honeymoon, he suggested, urging me to forget everything else
and marry her, no matter what. He celebrated his in Ensena-
da a few weeks later: two hurried days with a girl he had met
in San Diego. They even had time to send a postcard with the
news addressed to both of us. Two honeymoon days were all
they had before he shipped out to cruise the Vietnam coast
doing saturation shelling, for which his ship was awarded a
string of dried ears of "slain Viet Cong." And he came home
still loving his wife and still loving Ann Marisse and still loving me in spite of my dodging the war.

But my father wasn't going to let it go at that, even before
it was a war. Because he wanted at least one son to fight in
what he knew was becoming a war, which meant me, the only
one who could. And even if I had been "afraid to play college
football, Vietnam can give you another chance to be somebody." And, "What the hell is wrong with you?" And, "Answer
me, damn it, I'm your father!" Years later, he sent me a photo
of himself next to the Vietnam Memorial, with a note written
on the back: "Paul, your name could have been here too had
you gone. Love, your Dad."

We also kept disagreeing over money. He never asked me
for rent, but the subject of when birds should leave the nest

surfaced a few times. And then came his interminable praise of whichever of my old classmates he had run into who was already working or already had a family or already had a new car or already was buying his own house or already enlisted... But his favorite subject was my old friends who still had short hair. Why my long hair bothered him almost as much as my refusal to die for my country has remained with me as the symbol of just how fucked up people get about superficial values.

"Talk it out," Ann Marisse said.

Sometimes... Sometimes I preferred Kandy.

※　※　※

Christmas Day, 1965. The blacktopped road was lined on both sides with cars, newer models in the old formations. Across the way where there had been fields, short wooden stakes linked with white string outlined construction lots for new homes. A second row of sites some fifty yards further out confirmed the future existence of a street between the rows of houses which would rise in the spring to clutter the view of the mountains from Donna Costanza's front windows. Her house, however, looked the same. Christmas lights outlined the eaves and the wrought-iron railing of the front entrance, but nothing structural had been altered. We drove past the house, made a U-turn, and parked at the end of the row of cars. We were already late, but Ann Marisse suggested we wait just a while longer before going in.

"I'm not ready for this," she said.

"We'll say we haven't set a date, and we want two kids, but will take as many as God sends. Will that keep us out of trouble?"

"Don't tease. If that's all I have to face, I won't care."

"What then?"

"Mom's been telling me how much they've changed the house. I love Marianne, but sometimes she has the worst taste."

As we walked down the driveway, I told her how I had felt the first time I came, all nervous, and how she had saved me. She remembered my terrified look. We approached the front steps, and I warned her about the gangsters who guarded the door. She gave me a curious look, which turned to embarrassed amusement when we saw two teenagers necking. They looked over at us when we rang the doorbell, but didn't separate.

Dick greeted us and asked us to find our own way in. After all, Ann Marisse probably knew the house better than he. It wasn't so much a matter of taste. Marianne hadn't disposed of the old furniture in favor of modern, or hung black velvet paintings or anything outlandishly offensive, just one major alteration: the mirrored tiles had given way to wood paneling. As a consequence, the center of gravity had shifted to the small fireplace, which had gone almost unnoticed in Donna Costanza's time. Now, as you entered the room, you turned to the left to find the heart of the reunion, a modest fire.

We stopped short at the threshold of that sacred room where Donna Costanza had received me twice. Assaulted by the wood-paneled wall, both of us were reluctant to proceed. I felt Ann Marisse's hand reach for mine and clasp it so hard that pain shot up my forearm. Any moment she would turn and run; I could feel it coming. But then Marianne came to say hello and asked me if I wouldn't mind if she took Ann Marisse to join the women. Ann Marisse studied her cousin's face as if suddenly recognizing an assassin who no one else suspects. As they began to move away, I said, "Ann Marisse, remember, my mother is expecting us, so we can't stay long."

A lie, of course. Marianne guessed it, but Dick teased her about acting as though hers was the only family to celebrate Christmas. Besides, he said with a wink to us and a pat on Marianne's behind, they're not married yet, they still make out. She hit him with an elbow I had seen her use once on Alonzo, but she must have loved Dick, because she restrained it into a gentle, playful tap.

Back in the car, we lingered awhile, staring at the house, the flickering string of lights lending it a festive air. We had nowhere to go. My parents were visiting my brother, so my sister had invited a group of friends in. Ann Marisse's family had stayed at the party.

"Let's go home," she said.

"The apartment?"

"No, my parents' house."

On the way, we talked very little. I mentioned listening to her father and Dick's match stories of how they just missed the real action of W.W.II, graduating too near the end. Dick's father had been recalled for Korea with his reserve unit, but only made it as far as Japan. I told Ann Marisse I felt almost as left out as when Alonzo had pulled the Italian shtick on me, but not even this memory rescued her out of the blue funk. She sank deeper by the minute, staring out the window and cultivating a depression.

When we reached her house, she asked me if I wanted something to drink and told me to get her one of whatever I chose. I went to the liquor cabinet and picked the bottle with the most class, clean lines and simple label: Grappa. With one brandy snifter half full for us to share, I went to the den to put on some records. I opted to avoid nostalgia and picked classical: no memories attached, for me anyway.

When Ann Marisse didn't return, I went to see if she was all right. Her father had repeated his floor plan to me so often I could have found Ann Marisse's room in the dark.

In the soft light of a table lamp, she lay on the bed, crying. A pride of stuffed animals cowered at the far side of the bed in a helter-skelter pile, betraying the sweep of an angry, perhaps despondent arm. The lone survivor, a limp spotted puppy, clung to the headboard with padded paws; the faded name on the heart dangling from its collar showed signs of having once been crossed out.

I sat on the edge of the bed and touched her shoulder.

"I loved her, too," I said, which produced the opposite reaction I had intended. Her crying intensified. "She wouldn't want you to cry. She was always happy. It's not your fault."

"Marianne shouldn't have her house; she doesn't even like it. She used to call Nonna the Queen of Hearts, because *Alice in Wonderland* reminded her of Nonna's, like going to a garden run by a mean old lady with her own rules. She hates gardening."

I hadn't shared with her another discussion among the males: the surveying of lots in the fields behind the house, part of Ann Marisse's father's largest project of his career. Nor had she noticed how the old barn had given way already to a modern garage.

"Donna Costanza told us our world would be different. To pick what we need to travel and take it with us. I have what I need. You. Everything else we can buy when we get there."

"It's not funny," she protested. "I don't want to go anywhere. They ruined her living room."

"No, they just made it in their own image, like God."

"Don't be silly."

"I can if I want. But seriously, Donna Costanza held the center of the family in her hands for each of you to touch when you came to her. Now Marianne has it, but she doesn't know how to share it. She never shares anything. You're so busy giving her whatever she needs that you don't notice. She takes, but gives nothing back, not to Dick, or Alonzo before, not even to you. You've shared our whole life with her, but I bet she doesn't tell you half. Maybe because being the way she is, she doesn't have half as much to tell." I had begun inventing consolation, but found myself speaking the truth. Mine.

"I suppose she took the mirrors up to her bedroom."

"Not a bad idea, but she doesn't strike me as the type."

She turned over and gave me a disapproving shake of her head, then waited, silently demanding a better interpretation.

"When you took me to meet Donna Costanza, we stood in front of the sofa waiting for her to talk to me. In the mirror I saw us together for the first time as a couple, the way we look to other people. You know what I thought?"

She shook her head, staring up at me with a reserve stubbornly anchored in self-commiseration.

"We look fine together. We still do, you know, even if we can't see ourselves in the Donna's mirror. Maybe Marianne doesn't want to see herself, with Dick or alone. I don't know. She might see what I do. Or..." I was talking because Ann Marisse had asked me to, searching for an explanation through words, trusting them to tell me something I didn't know yet. And before I realized it, they had led me into a danger zone I had always avoided, perhaps because it hovered at the edge of our relationship without interfering, or at the center of their relationship where I was afraid to trespass.

"Or? Come on, oh wise one." Her mood was passing and I didn't want to trigger a relapse.

"Truth?"

"Always."

"Maybe she doesn't want to see herself next to you. Don't turn away, listen. I've watched the two of you side by side, lots. It's okay most of the time. Together you're...tough to choose between, objectively speaking. But then, something happens. You smile in that soft way your lips have of easing into affection or surprise, and she crumbles, like a castaway broken toy."

"You're crazy."

"No. I love you, yes, but I've seen it happen too many times to have imagined it. You smile and she fades away. It must be hard to grow up with someone who can make you disappear, even in your own house."

"Maybe she just doesn't want to see herself get fat. She's pregnant. She's going to announce it tonight, a special present for Dick. That's why she got so upset when we left. She wanted me there when she tells the family."

"We could have stayed."

"No. I couldn't bear it after the mirror. Besides... well, let's not talk about jealousy."

❀   ❀   ❀

Notwithstanding my prejudice as to the distorting and sinisterly absorbing quality of one of the figures in question, the cousins held each other up as clear, mirror images of themselves, judging and seeking their reflection in the other. They saw their relationship as love. Who am I to say it wasn't?

We, too, saw our relationship as love, and for whatever reason, Ann Marisse wanted me then, and I planned never again to oppose the way she wanted the world and us to be. Ever. Amid the slowly unraveling fabric of my own familial and social life, I had decided categorically to stand wherever she wanted me to stand, as long as I could.

❀   ❀   ❀

[The following dialogue originated as hypothetical, becoming accurate later when Kandy, upon reading it, agreed she couldn't have said it better.]

Kandy: "You treat Ann Marisse's character like a saint."

Paul: "That's not true. I've said we made love."

Kandy: "Shit. You describe the position of my knees, the size and texture of Susy's pussy, Valorie's raspberry nipples and Drea's exquisite predilection for sodomy, but with Ann Marisse you pull the old Hollywood bullshit, cutting to an image of a boiling coffee pot."

Paul: "Christ, you're right! It's probably my respect for her."

Kandy: "Fuck respect. You're afraid of her. You never could treat her like a woman, so you kid-gloved her out of your life. I'm not saying it's what happened back then, but you sure as hell are doing it in this book. If you don't want to wake up someday, with the book published, to find you've missed your chance to be with her again, the only place you'll probably ever have it, in print, rewrite."

Paul: "What should I change?"

Kandy: "I told you years ago: Don't just look at her and quit making love to her—trust me. After two hundred pages we damn well know you love her. Fuck her. Can you do that for me?"

Paul: "I don't know."

Kandy: "Try."

[So, respecting her opinion, I wrote an alternate version. Both are submitted for your perusal. I leave it up to you which you prefer to remember as the authentic image of our love.]

※   ※   ※

"Make love to me, Paul."

It occurred to me to raise the question, *Here?*, but I had learned once before what my objections could lead to, so I suppressed my reservations and complied.

I looked at her, watching her eyes study mine. She waited for me to speak or move, her hair disheveled and eyes still showing the last traces of tears. Her hands rested just below her breasts, the fingertips barely meeting along the row of buttons fastening the bodice of her dress. When I looked from her eyes to her hair, her glance followed mine, and she lifted a hand to clear away strands fallen across her forehead. I stopped her, catching her hand in mine and shaking my head. She looked back up at me and let her hand drop open on my thigh. Our silver cross rested on her throat. I ran my fingers over the cross, then under it, as Donna Costanza had done when she inspected it as if weighing my sincerity. Ann Marisse watched me inspect it, her eyes taking on the joy of the memory lightly balanced in my fingers. Leaving the cross gently niched at the base of her throat, my fingers began to undo the many small buttons, slowly. Neither of us cared to hurry anywhere. The row ended at her waist, exposing a V of flesh crossed in the middle by the narrowest ribbon of untanned skin. No bra—an unexpected revelation. She smiled at my surprise. "No hooks to..." and my finger silenced *her* lips. She kissed and bit the tip, then her eyelids almost closed as my hand slid under her dress and over her breast. Her nipple needed no wakening, meeting my fingertips dark and erect; my lips framed the circle's tip for my tongue to draw spiraling labyrinths. She arched her back, bringing her breast firmly into my mouth, but then sat up on the bed, took my head in her hands and kissed me, with scarcely a trace of gentleness or patience, searching out my tongue before I could respond. Moving much faster than I, eager to make me catch her, jumping ahead as always to points she intuited or created beyond my vision, she fought with my shirt, battled my belt, and finally made me stand up as she slid to her knees on the floor to challenge it directly and free my erection. She took it in one hand and pressed it to the side of her face, her eyes closing as she passed it along her cheek, running the tip just under her mouth to feel it on the other side of her face, then back, this time over her mouth, her lips parting to shape and cover the head. My thighs pulsed, the muscles of my stomach tightening, sensations traveling too fast to identify the spot they had already abandoned, though their passing left vibrations slow to dissipate. She moved her head back, turned her body to bring me around with her and pushed me back onto the bed. I reached for her, but she refused to let my fingers ensnare hers, and without a word signaled me to lean back on the bed and finished removing my clothes. She crossed the room to finish undressing in front of a full length mirror, moving deliberately, leaving her dress and slip on a chair, as though leisurely changing for bed. I watched her and her reflection take their time unsnapping the tops of their nylons and then rolling each down their thighs, over the knees, past their calves and off the feet. In a moment she had her garter belt and panties off, then she filled my arms with her body, touching places she knew well already, but licking them to make sure they were just as she remembered. She lay beside

me and pulled me over, guiding me in. "Oh," she cried, making
me hesitate. "No, don't stop...come," she whispered, clutching
me to her, bringing her legs up and over mine, high on my
thighs, then shooting down along them to lock at the back of
our knees, and pump, slow, around, then faster, until she
pushed me up and arched her back. I was leaning up on my
rigid arms, my hands open next to her head, but she pushed
harder on my chest. I lifted back, bringing my knees up under
me, sliding my hands down her back to lift her hips, while her
hands reached back against the headboard, knocking the spotted puppy aside. When our movements combined, she half-
moanedhalfcried...oh no, nonononono, and brought me down
to her, repeating, yes, yes, in my ear, kissing me, yes, holding
my head in her hands, pulling my long hair, yes, as I came.
"Ann Marisse Ann Marisse," I gasped, trying to catch my
breath, but dying so quickly, so soon, too soon, too damn soon,
and she, saying yes, yes, it's all right, Pauly, it's all right, yes,
it's all right now, love, yes. I contracted those small muscles in
spurting rhythm to make her feel I was still coming and she
laughed. "I love it when you do that."

We laughed together between gasped breaths, and edged
down slowly, I trying to stay with her, telling her not to quit,
touching her to help her soar, to not come down just for me,
and she said it was okay, she didn't mind, but closed her eyes
and inhaled deeply, allowing me to circle her clitoris into a
rise as she let slip the string she had tied around me years
before to anchor herself down, and she came, moaning to herself, humming and pronouncing things I couldn't understand
because they weren't said for me, talking to herself by herself.
Her hand moved down to pace my fingers, lifting them to rub
lighter, and with a voice not unlike anger or pain, she voiced
her orgasm in a sound I can't contain in a word...then I was
telling her I loved to watch her come, to go into herself, to forget me—she protested, but I said it was all right—so amazed
at what I had just seen, what she offered me when she
thought only of herself, that I touched her clitoris again and

she said, "Aouch, don't, not yet." So we rested. We said we loved each other, made promises and rested.

✻   ✻   ✻

"This is it?" Kandy asked over long distance after receiving the passage.

"I tried, and it's the best I can do."

She sighed. I could hear her breathing at the other end of the line and imagined her holding the pages up with her other hand and scanning back across the sentences.

"Really, I tried, Kandy. I just can't do it your way. If you don't like it, we'll forget the whole thing. I don't know where it's going anymore. I don't know what it means. And I can't see an end. Two hundred pages, you said. This can be filled out to two hundred pages. But I can't do it your way, so send it back and forget it."

"It's all right, Paul, calm down. It's fine."

"You liked it?

"Yes.... But you didn't fuck her. She fucked you."

II

"... I remember ..."

"Hello," Drea said, kissing my cheek, abandoning her purse on the patio chair beside me and then serving herself from the bottle of mineral water on the table where I had been reading over the script for the scenes to be filmed the next day. Holding the glass to her mouth with both hands, she went to stand next to the railing and looked out at the darkened Mediterranean seascape that during the day spread to the horizon from the balcony of our suite. A few specks of light dotted the immensity of black waters below. The difference between them and the infinite points scattered across the dome above lay in their slow progress on a straight line that in a matter of minutes led them to flicker out miles beyond the earth's curvature. Above, lights scintillated in the illusion of movement, but it was the entire sky that revolved, its circular passage taking all night to trace. Centered, like a moon dial of orientation, stood Drea, in violet hot pants and a sheer purple blouse.

We were several weeks into the shooting of *La passione e la riva*. She had accepted the contract because they offered to let me assist in reshaping the script to Drea's satisfaction. That evening we had reviewed the day's rushes with Carlo, the director. After, while she finished changing out of costume, he asked me to go on ahead. He wanted to talk to her alone.

"Tomorrow, as you know, is the first nude scene on the beach," he explained, "and I don't want her to be nervous."

Back then I didn't know Carlo well enough to speak frankly, as I would now, so I couldn't tell him not to worry about Drea. She only used to get nervous when someone tried to cover her body. "Eet's my most valuable assssset," she had put me on with her Italian import accent the night we had met at Kandy's in L.A. She was wrong, because she already could act. Like her accent, it fooled me. Pretty convincing for a native New Yorker.

Drea turned her back to the ocean and asked, "What are you doing, darling?"

"Nothing, darling."

We also accepted the contract because it allowed us to honeymoon in Italy, expenses paid by the people who brought you Beach Party Passion Italian-Style and so many other forgettable thrills.

Drea was…is lovely. Tall, tanned, her natural auburn hair blackened to jet for the initial scenes of her role, a model's high cheekbones, her frame carrying more weight— not the old-style voluptuousness we grew up with, but a newer, slimmed down and firmed up version just as exciting, tending towards hard-edged, more angular and not always as inviting to men. The next week her hair would be tinted blonde for the rest of the film. Her lips, I told her when we met, don't look Italian. She took offense and cursed me in a native accent, pure Abruzzi. Adorable lips, I assured her, sensuous and desirable, but more northern, not cutely puckered a la Bardot, rather wider and provocatively threatening, like Susannah York's. She smiled and kissed me. A camera flashed and she struck a pose, thriving on the attention. Even now, paparazzi ask me my name. My face is familiar, but it remains more that of the man often seen with Drea than that of Paul Valence, script writer. Few people read credits beyond stars and directors.

"Come look at the ocean. It's beautiful."

"Come look at this, it's beautiful, too."

She put her arms around my shoulders from behind and, with her face next to mine, skimmed my notebook.

"You're writing about me?"

"Just a description to keep in practice."

"I like it when you describe me. Like a photographer taking my picture, but you're kinder than a camera. No flaws, never in bad light." She rested her chin on my shoulder. "I'm so very tired, darling. Will you come to bed?"

As we walked to the bedroom, she placed one arm over my shoulder while her other hand caressed my chest, her weight thrust on me like a drunk's. I left her on the bed to go into the bathroom. In the mirror her reflection lay back, then rolled over to pick up an envelope marked FORWARD over the Rome studio's address, itself scrawled over that of my parents. It had arrived in a packet with other envelopes that now lay opened and scattered on the desk against the wall. This one I had left sealed.

"It's addressed to you, darling."

"You can open it." I began to brush my teeth and waited for her to tell me what I knew it said; the return address and the size of the envelope were message enough. She wouldn't read it to me, I knew, because scripts are all she'll read out loud. Everything else she scans at incredible speed. "How do you think I survived Barnard?" she told me the first time I saw her pick up a typed sheet, glance at it, then hand it back, fully read.

"Oh, too bad. It's a wedding invitation, but I'm afraid you missed it. June 24. We were already here. They must be good friends, Paul, they wrote you a note. Look."

I had prepared myself for the news of their wedding, but the mention of the note brought me out to sit on the bed opposite Drea, who held the card out and watched me read it, my hand still toweling my face dry. I wasn't sure yet, but I suspected Drea of reading people as easily as she did words.

Dear Paul:

We know you're busy, but it would be good to have you here to share this happiest moment of our life.

Ann & Alonzo

Both signatures were, however, in the same hand, Alonzo's.

"Old friends, darling, yes, very old friends."
"Tell me about them tomorrow. I'm really much too tired."

❋   ❋   ❋

Ann and Alonzo? *Ann*?

❋   ❋   ❋

In 1969, I bumped into Alonzo. After dropping some materials off at the UCLA Film Restoration Project, I walked over
to the Westwood Theater to catch a film I had previewed at
the studio, but hadn't experienced in a real movie house. A
fair review could have branded it a waste of good film stock.
Friends of mine were sitting on their hands or tearing their
hair hoping for a chance to shoot half the footage swept off the
editing-room floor for this bomb. Many of them never completed their degrees in film for lack of funds and a break. I
dropped out of film school for the opposite reason: too many
opportunities tendered by Kandy's well-heeled friends—plus a
military lottery system that freed me from the draft.

The only merit in this particular example of Hollywood
forgetabilia appeared at the end, next to the unillustrious title
of assistant screen writer: my name, for the first time briefly
and rather illegibly clearing the screen bottom to top in less
than five seconds.

Three years since graduation from Loyola. Three years of
attending graduate courses to maintain draft-deferred status,
learning the little they could teach about writing, jobbing
small assignments on films being made locally, especially
when they needed my research skills or the Italian I had
taken in college, and letting Kandy manage my career. By the
end of 1966, after a series of violent confrontations with my
father, among others, and with my closest friends married or
gone to war, I had reached the conclusion that running my life
demanded full-time concentration better left to someone more
objective, sober and with a talent for organization. Someone I
could trust—primarily that. More than under her wing,

Kandy took me into her home, giving me space and the not-so-gentle care I required. She compartmentalized my efforts exclusively into filmmaking.

From a term paper on adapting fiction to film I had shown her in '65, Kandy had shared with her father the treatment for *Women in Love*. He passed it on to a friend at Universal who advised that I learn the art of screen writing before trying it again, although in private he agreed it was promising enough to apprentice me, if that's what Kandy wanted. Her father relayed everything to Kandy, who then shared it with me. I dropped my teacher's training courses my last semester and loaded up on creative writing seminars. When the war got hot, I enrolled at UCLA, where the film school admissions director had once worked for Kandy's father at MGM. He gave me a full fellowship.

My first on-screen film credit came for straightening out a script left in mid-revision when the writer overdosed on a combination of uppers and downers. I stepped in to sort some papers, connect the plot line, dice the dialogue with more contemporary slang, but still got second billing to my predecessor's ashes, already sealed in a porcelain urn by the time the picture booked into Westwood. It was bad film, but a good break.

Three years had hardly changed Alonzo: same short hair, sneering smile, familiar stiff bowlegged walk, only now sheathed in polyester pants. I had no idea if he realized how much I resented him. If he did, I'm sure he enjoyed it. A fear suddenly gripped me that he might follow me into filmmaking and end up producing my next picture. He had the face of a producer, that certain used-car salesman look.

"I like to know my customer's work environment," he said, handing me his card: *ALONZO MONTE, Independent Agent*. He too had been visiting professors. Fortunately for the arts, Alonzo had dedicated himself to the vulgar commerce of insurance. Over coffee I told him about my hit film opening at the

Westwood, and then he sold me an extravagant policy I could hardly afford right then.

"With this you're fully protected, buddy."

"How about insurance against you hanging around the rest of my life?"

Not for a moment did he take it seriously. Apparently he had forgotten our last arguments, suspended over the edge of mayhem, restrained by the voice and hands of Ann Marisse.

"Now then, if you get married or contract any illness listed right here, we'd have to make an adjustment. You have my card, but let me write my home phone. Aaa, are you thinking of getting married?" He left the question suspended over the table where he stirred his empty cappuccino glass. More than his inquiry into my personal affairs, I resented his supercilious attitude.

"No," I responded with mounting impatience.

"Really? It's just whenever you come up in conversation, someone wonders if you're married yet. You know how it is in the old neighborhood. Karl Jr.'s son is so big, his grandfather says he'll have him waiting tables before he starts at St. C's."

"Who?" I asked.

"You know Karl; we were in his wedding. I'm little Karl's godfather."

"Who always asks?"

"What? Oh, no one in particular. The old crowd, the one you wanted to forget, remember? No offense, Paul. We can't all travel in the Hollywood set. Did you know Billy got wounded in Nam? A real mess. No insurance company will pick him up now."

As he talked, I recognized the old Alonzo, the lunch-room con hoarding information, the suspense expert demanding your undivided attention—so I gave it. He'd take his time, but deliver sooner or later; if not, there would be no point to his game. He mentioned helping Coach Purdy, since he could set his own hours as an independent agent. Besides writing it off as a charity deduction, it padded his community-service record and set the players' parents up as new contacts. The team had done well in the fall, coming in second. It's not as tough as when we played, he told me. Fewer Catholic schools made for a short season. Besides, he said, they're mostly little squirts, few bruisers like us; a lightweight squad was the best they could field. But he enjoyed treating them to pizza at Karl's—he was bringing it back around—because the gang still came in regularly, even Dick with his kids. His eyes raised. "I sold them the policy on their new house. What a beauty." Then finally: "He married Ann's cousin, remember..."

I should have killed him for abbreviating her name: *Ann*, snipped off to fit in his book of clients—as if she had ceased being the same person.

Actually, though, I shouldn't have resented him his pathetic gesture of possession. Among those stagnant and boring friends from so long ago, Ann Marisse must have been someone else. Maybe truly a simple Ann, if she could ever be anything simple. Just as the girl who held hands with a senior during *Summer Place* or the one who parked with Donny must have been someone else, and the one who danced with her boyfriend, any of them, while staring at me over his shoulder surely was another in the body they held, just as I am someone else with other women.

The rest of Alonzo's neighborhood update buzzed at the periphery of my consciousness until I found my hand being pumped by a standing salesman, holding a briefcase in his other hand and smiling down at me. He repeated something about recommending him to my friends and gave me yet another of his cards.

"Besides, you know where we are."

Which one of them wanted to know what had become of me? The thought lingered beyond the irritation at being reminded how Alonzo could rankle me at will. I had extricated him from my life since college, and now... If Ann Marisse wanted to know, how did she ask? Who? More than how or who, I needed to know what expression accompanied the words, what gestures? Did she look at anyone, or stare nowhere in particular, searching for that invisible point she pursued in front of her as she walked just ahead of me? What did she really want to know when she asked? Who asked, Ann or Ann Marisse?

Only one other person had ever called her Ann, and I'm sure Kandy's purpose was malicious.

❋　❋　❋

"Where are we going?" Ann Marisse asked?

"To Kandy's. She's having some friends in and wants us to go."

"Do we have to?"

"No, but why not?"

"I don't know her and I'm not sure if I want to."

"She's a good friend. Come on. You'll like her house."

The publishing crowd was supposed to be there, but the cars in the drive predicted a much faster Hollywood set. After kissing me lightly on the lips, Kandy greeted Ann Marisse with excessive enthusiasm, linking arms to present her to people I already knew. I went over to say hello to Kandy's father, stepmother and my editors, all the while visually tracking Kandy and Ann Marisse as they ambled through the room to pause at clusters of people for the ritual of introduction. Ann Marisse looked a little nervous at first, pleading with her eyes to be rescued, as I planned to do by working my way around to head them off. By the time I reached them, however, she seemed well in control of a conversation with a young man who was trying to come on to her by offering a part in a film. He refused to believe she wasn't an actress. I stole her away to show her the rest of the house. It overwhelmed her as it had me the first time. Staring out at the pool area where more guests mingled, she finally asked, "What does her father do to make this kind of money?"

"Market other people's work. Not bad, huh?"

"I never imagined people lived like this, except the stars."

A band started playing in the living room, attracting a crowd of dancers. We joined them for a while, but the pungent smoke drove us to the staircase to watch from above. I went to get her a drink, stopping to talk to Kandy's ex on the way, who introduced me to his new young wife, yet another singer, clearly too young to be as drunk as she acted. When I returned to the stairs, Ann Marisse turned her back on the party to look at me, squinting her eyes.

"What's wrong?"

"I'm trying to see you without your new friends. Do you think I'll still be able to find the Pauly I'm used to?"

"I'm right here. Why?"

"They're so different, and you look different when you're with them."

"You don't like them?"

"I don't know them, but you move through all this like you belong. Doesn't it feel strange to you?"

"Yes, still a bit, but I could get used to it."

"Could you?"

"So can you."

"If you want me to, I guess I can. But I don't think Kandy would like it."

"Why?"

"She's nice and everything, but underneath her sweet act, I get the impression that she would have preferred you not to bring me. She obviously wants to have you to herself."

"Everything between us is strictly contractual."

"Come here."

She pulled me forward and kissed me. Then, holding her hand to my cheek to study my face as if trying to find me behind a mask, she added, "You couldn't see how much I loved you either until I almost ran you down on the playground. Someday you might drive Kandy to something just as desperate. Can you be so blind? She loves you, Paul. I could tell right away. And I can't say I could get used to that part, although I

can understand it, because so do I. Be careful, Paul. Don't
hurt her. But for that matter, me either, okay?"

She pressed her thumbnail into my chest and kissed me
again. Then she asked, "Can we go home?"

We left without saying goodbye. I told Ann Marisse that
Kandy wouldn't care, although I knew she would.

On the way home, Ann Marisse became pensive, resting
her head on my shoulder and not responding at length to any
of my comments. After we made love with a noticeably urgent
intensity, she returned to her silent mood, hugging me and
kissing my shoulder.

"She doesn't like me," she said finally.

"Kandy?"

"Know how I can tell? She kept introducing me as Ann,
even after I corrected her."

I rolled on my side to face her. "I'm sorry."

"It's not your fault. You didn't do it."

"I'd never do it. I can't imagine you except as Ann
Marisse, both names, like both eyes," and I kissed them, "and
both breasts," and my mouth moved down to fuse word to
flesh.

"You kiss pairs exclusively?"

"No. You have only one mouth."

"Ummm. Good, but not what I had in mind."

"Oh."

After a stormy scene I had with Kandy, she has never
again referred to Ann Marisse as anything but Ann Marisse,
although in truth she hardly ever mentions her by name.

❈   ❈   ❈

Drea can pick up a prop and bring it to life in her hands.
She has the touch of great musicians: what in another person's cold palms thunks solid and dead, in her fingers sings
resonant. She infuses the same vitality into her lines,
although when we first arrived in Europe they preferred to
see her body burst from mundane restraints. She can sing like

a Rock diva or dance like a young Cyd Charisse, but they wanted tits and ass. She took it as part of the game. For a Barnard grad, I thought she was playing it stupidly. But I watched her work the roles, as inane as they were, and fashion them to her benefit.

Although the point of *La passione e la riva* was to exploit the nude scenes, the plot demanded a difficult transition of Drea. From start to end, the time supposedly lived through in the film took her from an adolescent to a woman in her late twenties. That day they were shooting a scene which would establish the starting point of the character's emotional evolution. I watched her rework her face at the last minute. She had no time for conversation, so I just observed. She brushed and blended out the well defined lines, so when she answered the call, a fresh young face appeared on the set, one made up to look untouched by cosmetics. Throughout the day she played the scenes as directed, posing no prima-donna resistance to Carlo, smiling at his instructions and carrying them out faithfully. Yet, she modified and molded the character to give it the young naiveté it needed.

They had worked up to the climactic scene in the sequence. This one over, and we'd wrap for the day. But suddenly nothing worked. It can happen. Everything goes smoothly until, for no reason, it falls apart. Lines falter and refuse to flow with the scene's tempo, movements contradict the lines, actors can't catch their rhythm, not to speak of technical glitches at the worst moments. Drea tensed up more with each delay. I could see it in her shoulders between the failed takes.

"Relax, Drea," Carlo counseled, walking her off the set for a short break. "It's not you. It's the stone wall of an idiot you're playing to." He left her next to me and went to soothe "the stone wall," probably with the same words. I rubbed her lower back softly, careful not to raise marks which the camera could pick up, silently respecting her concentration.

"What do you think?" she asked under her breath.

"You're tight."

She shook her head, indicating a different subject.

"The scene? You have to convey fear of desire and desire. It's a cliché."

"But I don't want it to look like a clumsy cliché. Suggestions, professor?"

"Don't grab his shoulder, you're not his guardian angel. You need lyric innocence and desire, like a ballet." I told her to try:

> Drea kisses him, but holds him away with her hands on his chest. He turns to leave, but before he moves more than a step, she takes his right hand in her left and turns him back, her right hand coming up and forward, drawing his left hand instinctively up to meet hers. She kisses him again, lightly, moving one hand to his cheek, then letting it slide down to linger low on his stomach. She turns and exits through the door into what is supposedly her mother's home.

"Where is she going?" Carlo yelled. "Drea, come back."

"Cut?"

"Yes, of course!" Carlo waited for Drea to reappear, shaking his head. "Again," he ordered, "but hold the kiss; let him caress you. It's your first time to be fondled. Don't run."

They shot again, Drea obeying Carlo's wishes. Nonetheless, when the film premiered, the fondling and caressing had been snipped out in editing. Amid the mediocrity of the finished product, the scene passed like a brighter shadow in a nightmare, barely distinguishable except to us. We had completed our first major European project.

Just months earlier I had been struggling to adapt a mystery novel into a T.V. pilot to be set in Washington, D.C. Had the series sold, our detective would have been in the middle of the world's most exciting political city during the crime-ridden start of Nixon's second term. When Watergate began topping the daytime ratings, a few network execs had to explain how they had missed the boat on a natural, but by then Drea and I were in Italy.

My denial to Alonzo in Westwood aside, the studio people took my engagement to Drea as inevitable. For a quickly rising young actress to pursue a mere writer promised no return, but we got along. We had met at another of Kandy's receptions, those parties she staged to present her new clients in the flattering light of a performance she alone choreographed. She had branched out into representing actors and musicians, fields she knew from direct experience. Drea was introduced to me as Kandy's hottest new property—a term I despised, more so because we were just that. Drea played her Italian self the entire evening, breathing fully resonant "A" and "O," and long "E" where an "I" should have been, pretending to see the United States from a European perspective and prodding me to explain our politics and society. By evening's end I had had the best conversation since Johnny had sailed for Vietnam.

"You object to being Kandy's property?"

"Anyone's," I nodded, refusing to speak more on the subject.

"You're an actor, no? Kandy calls you her hot Latin Lover."

"Shit. I hate it when she does that."

"But she told me you're Mexican."

"Actually I'm Italian American. Maybe we're related. What part of Italy are you from?" I looked around for Kandy, furious that she had made revelations to a stranger. Besides, how many times had I told her, "I'm Mexican American."

"Same fuckin' difference," she'd always answer.

Drea worked the crowd with her smile, watching me out of the corner of her eye. Meanwhile, I took long draws of Scotch and noticed how she nursed what looked like gin and tonic. Only after we had dated for a while did I discover she drank nothing but sparkling water with wedges of lemon or lime, allowing her to pretend to get tipsy to the point of frankness without being drunk beyond the pale. It served her well, like displaying at strategic moments more breast than she apparently intended.

"Kandy warned me about you. If you get maudlin or existential, or start sounding like a modern novel, I'm to kiss you. Do you always forget your problems with a kiss?"

"Just my ideals."

"Such a cynic."

"Such a bitch. Not you, Kandy."

"How do you know I'm not?"

"Because you're not at all alike."

I can be wrong, especially when confronted with the perfect imitation of a foreign accent pronounced directly above a neckline plunging to the navel and a hemline rising to not very far below that. Together, they distract your focus from evaluating the subject behind the phenomenon. Time would prove Kandy and Drea durably compatible. Although their way of approaching the world seemed radically different on first impression, they had more in common than the Ivy League experience. After getting to know Drea, I recognized they shared the quick mind, an intense love for acting and the determination not to let anything keep them from their goals, especially their physical appearance. Drea had the body in demand, but Kandy never resented Drea her natural gifts. Quite the opposite, she helped her exploit them to advantage. I'm sure she vicariously has lived Drea's career, becoming her closest confidant and friend, maybe more. Their plan for the '70s called for Kandy to make Drea a star who eventually would act in nothing but my scripts. No objections here. Especially persuasive has been their willingness to share me—not at once, although the thought crossed our collective mind on several occasions in particularly romantic locations around the world—but during any given period of time...like the rest of our lives.

Drea has the sometimes pleasing, sometimes disquieting, custom of living in private her public image of lustful starlet,

even now when she has developed into a full star. It's the Liz
Taylor tradition she plays to, and although she has avoided
the required scandals to maintain the image, I can vouch for
the fervor of her passion off screen. She lives her sexual pleasures unrepressed. After a time, she came to read my needs
for silence and distance as well as I now can read hers when
she's working, but it didn't always come easily for her. At first
she couldn't tell I was actually hard at work when it seemed I
wasn't doing anything other than sitting and staring at nothing, or listening silently to music, or walking from one room to
another picking up junk mail and perusing advertisements. It
can still unsettle her when, in the middle of a stroll, for example, I fall into silence or begin singing the lyrics of old songs
quietly to myself, staring at the ground, my arm around her
waist still, lost, as she claims, in another world. I don't argue
or try to correct her; we get along in our love, all of us. Drea
now understands that I am letting the words sort themselves
into dialogues, listening to my characters discuss their lives
with me or each other, providing them the background music
they need to remember where, how and who they were at a
certain moment of their lives, all of which duly appears on the
computer screen, trimmed of my excesses and interventions,
in the orderly fashion producers require. In 1970, however,
she would often take the opportunity of my apparent lack of
anything to occupy my time to initiate sex. Drea is extremely
good at her pleasures and likes trying exquisite things beyond
what even directors have requested of her as yet. But back
then I had that novel to reduce into a T.V. pilot and it wasn't
turning over on schedule; it was no time for pleasure.

Faced with the script deadline, I asked Kandy to book
Drea into some out-of-town interviews to get some time alone.
One afternoon, fed up with vainly searching for a new twist to
the crime-series clichés, I went out to eat. Afraid of running
into someone from the studio, I had to avoid the usual places,
so I turned onto the freeway. The sensation of being absorbed
back into the soothing rhythm of anonymous traffic, the secu-

rity of moving along automatically, took over. Years had passed since I had abandoned myself to a long drive to let ideas bounce off the cars and formulate in the pin-ball of brake lights and turn signals...and I found myself going home.

My mother's roses had taken root and spread with a fury, betraying a purpose beyond nature: the blood-flamed scream of an otherwise silent, patient acceptance of non-life. I drove on, pulled, perhaps, by curiosity or desire to the pizzaria. As though he had been there waiting for me, Karl Jr. received me warmly. Karl Sr. stared a moment before recognizing me, but then warmed just as friendly, whipping the menu out of my hands and boasting, "As if I didn't know what you want." He strode into the kitchen to make my pizza himself. Karl Jr. showed me pictures of his son and wife and talked about old friends who still dropped in frequently and those who were in Vietnam, and then asked me, "You know Alonzo is in the hospital, don't you?"

No, I didn't. Ask me about his polyester suits, his walk, his surprised eyes in seventh grade as my fist connected, yes, but his present life drew a blank, other than he helped Coach Purdy and sold insurance. To tell you the truth, which is what this has been all about from the start, it didn't interest me in the least.

The next day, however, I phoned St. Anthony's to get his room number. Visiting hours hadn't changed, although now they were open to more than family members.

By mid-afternoon the freeway had sucked me into its processor again, catapulting me through fluid channels of transit, coupled and uncoupled randomly with nameless fellow travelers whose thoughts would go unknown to me forever, exactly as they should. I drove to the hospital for the only reason that made sense: Ann Marisse. I was hoping we could run into each other in a more natural manner than my searching her out or calling. I never doubted she would be there.

Alonzo greeted me with the smile of a salesman sure of his advantage. He controlled the set, the lighting, and the script. Already Dick and Marianne stood at the bedside, and next to them two strangers who turned out to be old school friends who called me Paul with disquieting familiarity. I avoided first names altogether, a habit Kandy and Drea continually try to break me of still—bad for business, they scold. We talked some ten minutes, during which Alonzo used his body's sudden betrayal to persuade us to increase our insurance coverage while we still could.

Bored and impatient, I was about to leave when Alonzo's mother arrived, escorted by Ann Marisse. His mother couldn't have been more than sixty, but looked aged and frail. She asked my name twice and still couldn't recall me, forcing Alonzo to remind her with anecdotes from our past. Ah, she finally said, although the connection still evaded her. Then, for the second time, I saw Ann Marisse kiss Alonzo on the lips, touching his cheek to ask how he felt. For a moment they talked privately, ignoring us visitors. After, without dropping his hand, she stayed by his side, acknowledging the rest of us with a general greeting. Almost half a decade and not even a kiss on the cheek, just a glance across the room, a panning glance at that.

The situation defined itself all too well: stage front, visitors in supporting roles and bit parts; center stage, the bed with the patient/protagonist (an overhead spot, sufficiently bright to illuminate, soft enough to flatter); behind the bed, the suffering mother, seated, watching her sainted son; and the star, the ever-beautiful...what was she playing? Her part remained unclear, in the process of definition. Friend? Lover? Ann Marisse asked him how his day had gone, drawing all eyes to herself, but only to deliver our attention back to Alonzo through her solicitous inquiries.

The tritest scene imaginable, yet the actors took their roles seriously. Except me. No way would I follow a script that reduced my presence to a cameo walk-on to enhance Alonzo's image. I had played this hospital years before, with better taste, more intimately, but less pathetically. Ann Marisse had played it with me, too, and I wasn't going to let her rewrite her part just for Alonzo. I wouldn't stand for it. This hospital routine belonged to me, copyrighted in my memory.

So I set out to attract and hold her gaze. I had learned the technique from an expert, Ann Marisse. The fixed stare and cool commentary to draw energy to a single axis of perception. Within minutes, conversation began to lag in steadily longer pauses, gaps, unsettling the cast. The first to leave—flee— were the old friends. Then Marianne dragged Dick out to the corridor where she tried to force him to "Do something about it, he's your friend," unclear as to which of us she referred, but it didn't matter because Dick refused. Their voices faded down the hall. In the room, silence thickened like lead, the longer we stared the denser it congealed, until Alonzo's mother began to whimper, a soft, frightened-dog whimper. To the rescue came a timely nurse, bobbing her head into the room to warn us visiting hours were over for all but the immediate family—the rules hadn't changed all together. Ann Marisse stayed, confirming her in the worst possible role in the scenario.

When the elevator opened on the ground floor, Marianne accosted me: "Leave her alone. You leave her in peace."

Departing visitors quickened their steps towards the exit; a nurse looked around for an attendant. Dick implored her to lower her voice, so she yelled the louder: "Who the hell do you think you are, Paul? You know they're engaged. Why else would you show up again? I know you, Paul...I've always known you, and I'm not fooled, not a..." The elevator doors mercifully cut her off; her muffled voice filtered through to us as it ascended skyward like the levitating angel of doom.

Dick walked me to the parking lot, perhaps out of loyalty to a camaraderie for him kept fresh through continual evocation at Karl's. As he made excuses for Marianne, I fathomed for echoes of his old Rock cadence, but his monotone sincerity intensified the sense of loss knotting my stomach. He tried to make me see what I preferred to ignore.

"She's very nervous. She cares for him a lot, too, always has. You remember?" He looked up at the hospital, as if expecting to find Marianne spying on us from a window. "And she's pregnant again, our third."

"Aha," I answered, following his gaze to the upper stories, wishing the non-existent face at the window would be the lighter side of the pair.

"Yeah, but you were brutal, Paul. It was a little too much, even for you."

I studied him out of the corner of my eye, waiting for a comment on Alonzo's part in the farce. Dick's warning from years back came to me clearly over his words there in the parking lot.

"Look, Paul," he continued, leaning down to talk through the window as I started the engine. "Alonzo's not so bad. A good friend, actually. He's great with the kids. You two were always best friends. Don't do anything to mess it up for them."

Without saying goodbye, I pressed the button to raise the window. The rearview mirror swallowed Dick in a slow fade-away.

❋   ❋   ❋

"I can't. We're getting married."

She could, I insisted. "Just to talk for a while."

Summer Place and Sandra Dee...but now we were adults and nothing could be forgotten, she claimed, and one more time could hurt Alonzo seriously, particularly in his condition. Her unfamiliar fidelity to someone else exasperated me.

"But how can you marry Alonzo?"

"Easily. Just watch."

"No. Don't invite me to the funeral."

"I wasn't planning to."

"Do you love him?"

"This is pointless, Paul."

"You can't even lie about it."

"..."

"And me? What about me?"

"Yes, what about you? Paul Valencia? Or is it Valence?"
She laughed. "You?" She laughed again. "One never knows."

"You still love me. I can tell."

"Goodbye, Paul."

I called back, but she answered without speaking. There
was a silence neither of us broke. After a moment I hung up.

※　※　※

Shortly after Alonzo was released, they were married, at
St. Catherine's Church. My invitation came signed with both
of their names in Alonzo's handwriting. It caught up with me
on the Italian coast, where Drea and I were honeymooning.

"Signora, this envelope, it was under the bed."

Drea looked up from the reflection of her face, which she
had been making up for the party to celebrate having filmed
her first starring role. In the mirror the maid stood with a
bundle of towels under one arm and a small envelope in the
other hand. Behind her, Drea could see our luggage prepared
for departure. She returned to the pleasure of accenting her
best features, leaning forward almost into the mirror itself.
Her blonde hair was pulled tightly along the side of her head,
held with brass clips from which it fell over her deeply
bronzed back. She brushed gloss on her lower lip to give it
more volume, like Susannah York's.

"It's my husband's, but don't bother him now. He's working."

※　※　※

Dec. 7, 1975

Dear Paul:

Just saw *Il Fine della Innocenza*. Better luck next
time. You need more control of the production. The young
girl is superb and the last scene, brilliant. I recognized
the slap from the Loyola workshop. Whose idea was it to

voice-over the letter so it extends into the next scene? Good work. A bit "modern novel," but not to excess. Now, write something like that for Drea. She's not a child, she needs adult material. A good director wouldn't hurt, either.

Kandy

What Kandy and a few critics saw as a perfect climax, to me turned out to be my delicate trailer on a sledge-hammer vision of innocence, full of torrid relationships among the working class. They had used my script, but shot it in the slums to give it believable ambiance. I knew I had lost it when the director kept enhancing the plot to fit the setting. My straightforward, contemporary story about middle-class urban youth, devoid of class struggle, fell into the hands of old-guard social-relevance ideologues. I quickly learned that unlimited creative freedom was an illusion for a writer, since directors reserved the right to reinvent the script on the set.

❋   ❋   ❋

In early 1966, our Loyola film club fell under the foreign film spell. Films like *Jules and Jim, Hiroshima Mon Amour* and *La Dolce Vita* conveyed the kind of intense focus on love we were discussing endlessly in our courses on existentialism. Gone was the technicolor world of make-believe and happy endings, stripped down to the dull contrasts of black-and-white "real life." We talked endlessly about the futility of love.

Ann Marisse, on the other hand, detested these films, their chic ennui and estrangement from emotion. She countered Sartre's existential nothingness with Shakespeare's ironic plenitude of nothing in Sonnet CXVI. And in private I agreed, especially when we talked in bed after making love. Ann Marisse teased me so much about the club's obsession with *Nothing* that it turned into our private code for *everything*. We looked it up in other languages: *rien, nichts, niente nada intet gornit*, secret synonyms for love. At film club meetings, however, I'd slip back into black-and-white cynicism.

Towards school year's end, the club met to wrap up the series. Each student was expected to prepare a paper. When I began to read mine on the European vision of life over the American film version, Ann Marisse narrowed her eyes as if she were having a hard time bringing me and my ideas into focus.

"You can't believe that," she interrupted. "Those movies don't show the way life is either, at least not the way it has to be. It's absurd to think they're any more real than ours."

The club's discussion abruptly cued on Ann Marisse. After the collapse of ideals and the apathetic abyss we would plunge into at the end of the '60s, a generation, far from lost in space, mired in the fetid earth shoveled over friends and our illusions, it's difficult now to recreate the sincere energy we invested discussing the possibility of love, happiness, meaning. Recently I've been invited to universities to meet with film majors; they "go into film" not to make movies, but because it pays well. They study with a sense of purpose which never revealed itself to me, except in the image of Ann Marisse. I never thought about what I would do, but I knew with whom I'd do it. The one sure thing in my future was to look at her forever, although I never dreamed it would have to be through so many mirrors. Students now want the bottom line, so talking about the possibility or impossibility of love is pointless to them—you can't define it, so it doesn't exist. Our old concern for the question smacks of being "too '60s," a euphemism for bogging down in useless idealism. But no one can deny that we endlessly discussed such arcane subjects so seriously... and what I have been avoiding for a hundred pages is the confrontation Ann Marisse drew between my words and my beliefs.

Was I a cynic? How could I believe in two-year honeymoons and deny love, she wanted to know? I had no defense, but something in those films convinced me, and I argued for them.

"You don't believe what you're saying," she interrupted again.

"Okay. It doesn't matter. It's only a movie."

"But you're talking about them as if they're real, something to imitate. Why turn life into something tired and dull and sad? It's crazy."

"We weren't saying that."

"You were! I don't want to struggle every minute for meaning or consciousness. I don't want to struggle at all. You make yourself miserable."

Some students nodded their agreement, some played with their coffee cups to stay neutral, and others looked annoyed with her refusal to accept the obvious: life as conflict and struggle. I needed to refocus their attention.

"According to the French existentialists," I began, but she had heard it all before and wasn't in the mood to let me run on.

"The French?" she began with a sardonic smile. "Behind the *haute couture ou la musique classique ou des paysages exhaltants, il n'y a que du vide. Il faut l'admettre. Il y a bien une autre façon de voir les choses, mais si tu penses que non, alors pourquoi est-ce que nous faisons comme si la vie avait un sens? Moi, je ne veux pas faire comme si; pas avec quelqu'un...* You'd make me like you."

She had me. She knew that my French barely extended beyond the Chez Pierre menu, but she just stared at me, neither relenting nor translating. Johnny and a few other students also knew French well and might have intervened, but none of them volunteered. Recognizing that their public discussion had become our private impasse, they began to drift away.

"Does love really make you miserable?" she asked me in the car, her body half-turned in the seat. "It doesn't me. I'm usually happy, in spite of the way you are."

"Can we forget it? I'm not unhappy."

"Then don't say we're impossible."

"I didn't. I said modern society bleeds the intensity out of existence and marriage condemns people to a life of boredom. Like Zorba says, he's been married with children and everything, the complete catastrophe."

"I rest my case!"

"But not us. We won't let it happen. We'll find another place, another way to live."

"I like the way we live. I like the way my parents live, or Dick and Marianne. They're not bored. They just love each other. Maybe they don't question everything they do or worry about being conscious of every moment. It's hard enough just living to have to worry about that, too. All of you think you're so superior because you study with Jesuits. We might not have to take philosophy at UCLA, but at least we don't go around saying nothing is real. If you expect life to be nothingness, you'll end up making it nothing."

"Whose nothing, Sartre or..."

"Don't change the subject. I'm serious."

"All right. What about getting away from all this? Going to those places we talk about? Living our way? We both want it."

"For a while. For a honeymoon, a weekend in Canada, a change of scene...but we can't live all alone in another world. I won't. I wouldn't be happy that way."

"Wouldn't you like to live in Rome?"

"Which one, *Three Coins in the Fountain* or *La Dolce Vita*?"

"It's the same one."

"No, Paul. The same fountain, but what a difference. One's happy, hopeful, Technicolor! The other is sad, gray and drab. One is us; the other is...someone else I'm not sure I like. No, I am sure I wouldn't like them, because they don't like themselves. You can't always be out of place, like some stranger. This is our home."

I surrendered with, "You're right."

We sat silently in the car in her apartment parking lot. She made no move to close the gap, and I couldn't bring myself to initiate a physical reconciliation. She finally said she had an early class and lots of reading yet to finish, so I walked her in and kissed her good night.

Standing by my car, I looked up to find her watching me from the balcony. Once again we were playing Shakespeare in the middle of Los Angeles. It was too much for either of us. I looked down and shook my head. What did it really matter to me if love was an impossible concept, when Ann Marisse was there above me, much more than possible, real, waiting for me to improvise something to erase the night?

"Do you love me?" she asked.

"Yes."

"Do I love you?"

"I hope so. Yes, you do."

"So now what?"

"I'm sorry."

"That's not what I want."

"I want you."

"Then why are you always running away when I want you to stay?"

"But you said..."

"Don't accept what I say, *sciocco*, and don't go, please."

❄   ❄   ❄

Disillusioning experiences with the European film producers taught me Ann Marisse was right. I had been seduced by form more than content, sugar-coated by distance. Once I got there, her question resurfaced: "You don't really believe what they say about love, do you?"

I found that I didn't, but no one was going to let me make a film about my version, at least not right away. So I took refuge in small scenes, gems cut and polished for friends and professionals who shared the same frustrations. The art of scamming producers by working cameo scenes you collect into a celluloid portfolio of signature pieces I learned from watching Drea. Observing the way she controlled her appearance despite makeup men, how she added the small gesture or the strange inflection to make herself the most memorable element in a scene, it struck me she worked on her image more than the film.

When I mentioned it, Drea responded, "Of course, darling, it's called becoming a star. I won't have to steal scenes when you write all my scripts. What a difference it makes to have material created just for me. Like playing myself through your eyes, and I love the way you see me. If I can get it across to the camera, we've got it made."

I promised to write her at least one superb scene in each script, something unforgettable. That's where the idea was born: intense, almost self-contained showcases for her. I remember explaining it to her. I even remember the fascination in her eyes as she listened... What I don't recall is if it was also then I began recreating Ann Marisse in every female character.

Certainly I can trace it back further for you if I try. She originated the idea for the culminating scene in *La passione e la riva*, yet she also was behind my suggestion to George Lucas that every American boy from the class of '62 has a blonde ideal he can never quite catch. She cruises through his life like a car forever going the opposite direction, or leaving you at a red light as she speeds ahead, turns the corner and disappears, while you sit envisioning "what if?..." Or you're riding with someone else while knowing she's out there, just a block or two away, moving in the same grid of streets, but unseen, an image you almost forget, until a car the same color swerves into your lane to set it off again, the memory, the chase, your life. She becomes the motivating force behind and the goal ahead of the recreation of the story, all your stories. Without her, there would be no creation.

❄   ❄   ❄

We were at another of Kandy's infamous parties which over the years had grown larger and more uninhibited, apace with the '60s. She had persuaded me to attend by mentioning that Lucas was going to make my kind of movie. No Broadway production numbers danced across theater sets to phony rock music composed for a studio orchestra. He planned to hit the streets in cars, plotting it to happen all in one night of crisis, love, drag racing—and it would have a sound track of authentic rock. Maybe he already had in mind the lost ideal who drives the young writer out of his mind, but he didn't say so. When I saw the film, the blonde in the '57 T-bird was perfect. Ultimately, it's not the memory of friends that draws the writer back to invent the script for the movie; it's the blonde who leads him back to write a film about the ideal who always gets away. Not even that—he writes it just so he can watch her drive by one more time, a one more time multiplied into forever, repeated somewhere every day, at least for a long long time. Someday she will see herself and remember when she was the blonde who one night on the phone could have changed two lives, but instead hung up too soon, and would spend the rest of her life fighting off regret. She would watch it until she remembered, not as it happened, but as she was watching it happen. Later, her memory would mix watching, doing and remembering into one interwoven event, all with the same weight in the single image of desire. That's American film in its soul-possessing greatness. Film about the absolute need to make film. Film about me.

So I put her there, an Ann Marisse in every film, maybe for only an ephemeral second, in a gesture, a smile, a word, a movement of a hand or finger. At first it sufficed that I could see it, if no one else. Another possibility of Ann Marisse, one who exists only in the screen image drawn from my writing, an Ann Marisse so convincing that other players involved in the dialog take her for the real thing—perhaps even Ann Marisse herself.

❊   ❊   ❊

The rest of the scripts, the parts that didn't interest me
except as excuses for the key scene, nevertheless attracted
more attention than I thought they merited. Each script
seemed to multiply the offers for work. Drea's insistence on us
working as a team had a lot to do with it, but sometimes producers called me first. The demand from both channels grew
so heavy that we found our honeymoon in Europe had turned
into several years of wandering around the continent. It was
exciting and highly profitable, but soon, moving from a villa in
Italy to a hotel in Germany or a friend's home in Paris, and
then back to another hotel in Spain started to grate on us.

"Face it, darling, if you're tired of this, we either get something of our own over here, or go back home."

"Over here," I answered. "It too soon to go back."

"Too soon?"

"Not for you, maybe, but I'd be back where I started."

"So what do you suggest?"

"You fly to Munich to meet Wolfgang. I'll take the train
and join you there. On the way, I'll stop and see if that mountain chalet we liked is still for sale."

"You could call."

"But you know I prefer to go by train anyway. I think better on trains. It helps me write."

On that trip to buy our home in the Italian Tyrol, I discovered once again that, in spite of my schemes, I didn't have full
control of all the scenes from the past. One of those unfore-
seen, distasteful incidents we can't prepare for sprang its trap
and snapped me out of my customary musing when riding
trains. First-class compartments have the plush comfort of a
Victorian parlor. They lull you into assuming your fellow passengers will comport themselves with the etiquette befitting
the setting. Only one passenger had been sharing the space
with me for several hours, an elderly woman who had shown
the conductor a U.S. passport with her Eurail pass. She fit

perfectly in first class, but not so the pair of French soldiers who entered the compartment about ten minutes outside of Verona and took the seats next to the door. When the conductor returned to check the soldiers' tickets, they showed him second-class stubs. I smiled, remembering Sunday trains from Paris filled with soldiers who seemed to exploit a tradition of the military riding first-class, sometimes with no ticket at all. The Italian conductor refused to honor such an absurd idea, and the confrontation escalated menacingly, compounded by the soldiers' scant comprehension of Italian and the conductor's refusal to continue speaking to these *"cani testoni."* I intervened, with my rudimentary French and fluent Italian. The soldiers sulked away to a lower class—where they truly belonged. As he left, the conductor thanked me and remarked how one could recognize the difference between French scum and an Italian gentleman like myself.

At first I basked in the compliment, but then its ambiguity puzzled me: Had the conductor just told me, ironically, that as a foreigner I should mind my own business? His statement left me perturbed. Kandy would brand what followed modern-novel window dressing, but the conductor's comment left me literally pondering my image in the compartment's large window as the train progressed north towards Bolzano and the Tyrolean Alps. At times the forest closed tightly on the train, turning the glass into a pine-green mirror, extending a duplication of the compartment out into the corridor of air formed by the speeding train. Then the mountainside would collapse into a valley, the forest retreating swiftly before the onslaught of cultivated fields, swallowing my image and isolating the compartment into singularity. As I watched my face appear and disappear in a dance of masks across the northern Italian landscape to the steady underbeat of the rails and the arbitrary melody of my floating image, I fell into a classic flashback.

❄   ❄   ❄

Between Christmas of 1965 and New Years, Ann Marisse and I made time for each other every day, reading and making love in her apartment, playing at being married. I told my mother I needed to do research at the library and wanted to stay in the city to start early and work late. She told me to be careful nothing happened to Ann Marisse which would force us to do sooner what eventually we would do anyway. It's better to be able to plan a wedding than have to rush, she commented. I promised her we would be careful, although we never were.

The last week of 1965 flowed into the first week of classes, and when the Italian Club met to nominate a queen candidate for the prom, I suggested Ann Marisse. Alonzo, who hadn't spoken to me much since the wedding, supported me, as did several members of the Film Club and some old friends from HTHS who knew her. The majority approved and, although we had all semester, we moved immediately into the campaign. I didn't even bother to ask her if she wanted to run. That she went to U.C.L.A. presented a major drawback, but we postered the campus, handed out autographed glossies, brought her to functions, had her going through the motions like a presidential contender, and in the end, she won. I knew she would as soon as the men on campus saw her as I did— the most beautiful, seductive, desirable American Dream on two feet. They would kill for a chance to dance with her. But since that probability hovered somewhere around zero, at least they could watch her dance with me in the middle of their collective admiring eyes, paired with the jealous, but equally admiring eyes of their dates. We had nothing to worry about in the contest, but I worked my tail off to make sure, making the rounds daily of the main corridors, replacing posters. When the vote came in, the club met to congratulate ourselves for winning.

Ann Marisse came to the start of the meeting to thank us personally, emphasizing how much it meant to her, as an Italian, to win for the Italian Club. We cheered, she almost cried, and I walked her to the parking lot. As I re-entered the room, I noticed how quiet the meeting had become. Then I heard the president say, "You mean Paul's not Italian?"

"Not unless he's been holding out on me all these years," Alonzo answered.

They both turned to me, along with about thirty-five members in good standing, presumably all blood-tested descendants of immigrants from somewhere on the Mediterranean boot. Their eyes were trained on me as on a Black discovered at a KKK rally. Male eyes only, because the Italian Club in 1966 was still restricted. I wouldn't know until later that Alonzo had raised the question, but I got the strong impression he had been talking about me the entire time it had taken me to see Ann Marisse off.

"No, not really," I confessed, recalling a similar situation with another group of Italian Americans whom I expected to be my relatives someday, among whom Alonzo had moved from the start like a long-lost cousin. Some members didn't care. As far as they were concerned, I was more Italian than most of the Italians on campus. Others said I had nominated Ann Marisse, so I should escort her. Alonzo suggested the club president should do it, since he was the elected leader. The argument took up the rest of the meeting, but I couldn't concentrate on the discussion, a nauseous anger rising in my chest. No one asked me not to participate in the discussion, much less to resign from the club, but after minutes of yelling and fighting, I walked up, handed the president my withdrawal from membership and left. Later, a couple of old friends tried to change my mind, but I said I had no time for an identity crisis. I had too much to do.

Ann Marisse was furious. She called Alonzo and accused him of starting trouble again. They talked for a long time, but I heard only Ann Marisse's side of the conversation. She said that he insisted he hadn't started it and turned it around, claiming he had argued in the end for me to escort her, leaving it up to me, so he had done all he could. True again, technically, but he knew I wouldn't go back. It was probably the only time Ann Marisse's persuasion failed: I refused, flatly.

When I asked her what else they had argued about so long on the phone, she said, "Nothing important, old business better forgotten."

Why I didn't ask what business, ask until she answered, or accept and forget once and for all, are two more unanswerable questions. I felt too exhausted to pursue it and even now it makes me physically tired to think about it. I went home that night for the first time in a week. My mother, who had heard from Ann Marisse about the election, congratulated me, noticed the lack of enthusiasm, and asked if I wanted to talk about it. I wasn't up for it. I wanted to talk, but not confess.

Johnny invited me in, offered me a chair and brought a bottle of Cutty Sark and glasses filled with blue ice cubes. "For the mood," he said. Black might have been more appropriate. No need to explain what had happened; Ann Marisse had already called him. It seems each of us wanted him to find out what was wrong with the other. He lit his aromatic pipe and we sipped Scotch.

"Why don't you talk it out with her? I'll never understand your inability to handle problems with words."

"I don't like to ask her questions and I hate to demand explanations."

"She had nothing to do with what happened. That should make you happy. But, it's not just the club mess, is it?"

"No. It's Alonzo in general, or maybe in particular, but I don't want to talk about him either."

"Is it so important? If anything happened between them, it's over. You know there's no one else in her life. Never has been. The rest were substitutes. Even when she calls me, she's just talking to you. I haven't been around the world or anything, but I've never seen anyone so in love. What more could you want? Christ, I'd give anything for that kind of love...for her. You're too lucky to believe."

"Will you find out for me?"

He caressed the bowl of his pipe, watching me through the aromatic smoke. Instinct told him to refuse, but then I had done the same for him with Marylin. He shook his head.

"Do you really need to know, do you want to know? Wouldn't life be simpler if you accept what you have? Paul, if I could, I'd take her right now, knowing she loves you."

We talked until he had to be to his eight o'clock morning class. I drove him over to the university and left him off. The blue ice cubes had darkened our tongues, made us look like victims of a plague.

"Johnny," I called him back to the car. "Find out, but don't tell me unless I ask again. And, Johnny, if you think it's better, tell me lies."

The president of the club was supposed to escort Ann Marisse to the crowning and the queen's dance. As their names were announced, the court and queen emerged from behind a curtain with their escorts. How the announcer knew Alonzo's name as Ann Marisse's escort is a question I must have been too angry to think about until the scene came back to me in the train, projected on the compartment window as clearly as the computer screen in front of me now, growing ever more brilliant as night works its way up from the snowed-in valley far below our villa home. No longer were my eyes focusing on the compartment's image playing tag with the landscape or my face in the eerie game of sitting on the outside watching me watch it from the inside and pondering which was more real. I was staring at Alonzo dancing with Ann Marisse, he pretending to be doing her a favor and she smiling for the crowd as if nothing had happened and looking for me over his shoulder, perhaps wondering how she had been maneuvered into this mess.

The conductor's voice came in over the speaker, announcing our arrival in Bolzano. As I slipped on my coat and slung the long strap of my briefcase over my shoulder, I could hear three voices arguing and yelling across the barriers of consciousness and reality, trying to maintain open the rapidly

shrinking channel of communication linking two moments
widely separated in time and space, two moments momentarily fused by the provocative comment of the conductor who
smiled again at me as I passed him on my way off the train.
Voices spoke a melody of words no longer distinguishable in
the slowly rising clatter of the train escaping towards Inns-
bruck and points north. Voices that must have remained
aboard, trapped between the double glass panes of the window
where they could continue to haunt a face much like mine I
saw staring back at me from the window's inside surface
behind which the American lady waved goodbye as I walked
along the platform in one direction and the train carried her
in the other, alone and now unprotected by the man she may
have described back home as that nice Italian gentleman who
accompanied her all the way to Bolzano.

❋   ❋   ❋

While I was framing Ann Marisse's image in luminous
scenes on countless theater screens, Alonzo was plying his
own trade. He was trying to frame his own Ann into a ranch-
style prison, PTA, the women's-auxiliary, and mount her on
the wall of his rec-room alongside his trophies for MVP, All-
State and Salesman of the Year.

I had something quite different in mind. My goal was to
attract Ann Marisse to herself in the image I created. Yet,
speaking frankly, more than anything I did it for the sheer
pleasure of seeing her reappear near me, in a place of our
own. To see her walk, smile...I wanted her to see herself
stroll the Hackteufel along the Neckar River where swans
swim in pairs for life, down to the Old Gate and out to the center of the bridge, then turn to see the castle high above the Alt
Stadt just as sunset flames it to the fiery-red memory of
ancient battles, just so that millions of eyes could see her eyes
open in surprise and excitement at the vision of Heidelberg in
the spring.

"Cut. *Gut*, Drea, *sehr gut*. Now, take *einen moment*, relax, recompose your hair, *dann ein mal, bitte*. Last time, I promise. The walk along the river was fine, the gate, *alles, ausgezeichnet*, really, *wirklich*, but if we're lucky the sun will cooperate this time. We'll take it from Drea looking at the *Schloss*. But don't go away, *Liebling*. Paul, Paul, no, please, stay back. I can do almost anything, but I can't control the sun. Only the producer could do that, and he's in Berlin. Ready, everyone. Remember, Drea. Turn, look up, turn back, see him, wave. *Fertig!*

The sun exploded from the clouds like a million spots flashing on Drea turning to catch the castle's red sandstone torch to glory, its crystal windows a blaze of reflections. Then she turned back, searching for her lover on the other side, down by where scull crews practice on the Neckar. She found him with her eyes and smiled. With the look—no wave—the scene closes.

"The wave, Drea. Drea, wave. *Scheisse!* We've lost the sun, Drea."
"Oh, Wolfgang, *ich habe vergessen! Es tut mir leid!*"

* * *

"Nice touch, Paul," Kandy said when she saw the film, "the look, the meeting of the eyes and no wave. It's like an intimate code between lovers."

"She can't wave," Drea explained. "Just before the last take, Paul came and told me to forget it. Someone might see her and mention to her husband that they saw her waving to a man. Oh, but Wolfgang exploded. All I could say was I forgot."

"Another day to set up the shot, if we got the right sunlight, would have cost a fortune. What else could he do? But it gave us the right ending."

"He even thanked me for it later," Drea added. "He said, 'mistakes always help a film.'"

* * *

Rome in the dog days of summer, when Bertolucci wanted Drea, as he said, "For anything, I don't care, just so long as she's on screen."

It was the only time I have appeared in one of the scenes. At the last minute, the actor who played the reporter got sick the day we were to shoot. So with my hair restyled and with the character's jacket on, I assumed his place at an outdoor cafe on the Piazza di Spagna. Heat radiated from the surface of Bernini's Barcaccia fountain, making its ancient scow shimmer mirage-like in its marble bath. The scene was shot over my shoulder so only my back showed on screen. Later they spliced in the actor's face, his eyes staring upward to watch Drea:

> Walking down the tiered Scalinata in front of the Convento della Trinità dei Monti. Her body glides along the line between sun and shadow, drifting left or right to avoid tourists or Roman pedestrians. Her sheer white dress floats from radiant to mute like a swan flirting with the sun. When the breeze rising from the Piazza teases her hair, lifting and sweeping it to the side as she balances on the axis of dark and light, her figure ignites in a trail of golden flame…and she pauses on the last landing to search for someone among the tables of the outdoor cafe where he sits, pretending he doesn't know her…for a moment her gaze finds his, absorbs it, then breaks off to glance down over her own body, then, with a smile, she looks up and takes a step towards the camera…

Or in Madrid, the spring after Franco's death, when we shot the final scene in our BBC remake of *The Sun Also Rises*, Drea in the role of Brett. Brett stepped to the cab, turned and asked, "Oh, Jake, why have we lost so much time?" Jake looked into her eyes and answered, "I don't know, Brett, I don't know." It's nowhere in Hemingway, and Ava Gardner never said it to Tyrone Power, but we froze their image in that pose, rolled the credits and theme music over it, and no one complained.

Then, in screening rooms in cities across Europe, I would study the scenes, watching Ann Marisse: the delicate shift of moods in her eyes, her smile, the timbre of her laugh. I could feel the touch of her fingers on my cheek, across my lips, could see her discover the cityscapes we had promised each other and speculate how far I could lead her.

❀   ❀   ❀

In Florence, 1979, April was still struggling to warm itself into spring. Kandy and I returned late from Bologna where her flight had landed and I had picked her up to drive across the mountains to Florence. During filming we had the entire fourth floor of a house reputedly built by the Free Masons. A magnificent suite of rooms interconnected Borgia-style, with sliding wall panels between bedrooms, bathrooms with two way mirrors and peepholes, and a kitchen so grand it promised more an orgy than a feast. But we kept it for just the two of us until Kandy arrived to spend a couple days on her way to Israel. She had invested in a new fashion line and was off to the 1980 beach-wear preview.

We found a table set for us with cold meats, cheese and fruit. Attached to a bottle of Bardolino, a note from Drea welcomed Kandy, but excused herself: she had a predawn make-up call the next day. A p.s. told us she had left the scene on the projector, if we felt like viewing it.

"Which scene?"

"Let's see."

Drea stands facing a full-length mirror; shot of her back and reflection. Cut to a close-up of face framed in blonde hair; slow dissolve to bring into focus what she sees: a man across the room, sitting at a table, writing. Logs burn in a fireplace, casting flickering light across the floor's rich, polished wood surface. A lamp illuminates the table top and the ceiling above, its parchment shade giving off an amber glow. The wood-paneled and bookshelved room radiates a warm mystery born of the play of shadow and golden light in the lush tones of the materials, accentuated by the contrasting austerity of its furnishings. Drea looks at herself in the mirror, studying her image, then turns to approach him.

Drea: "It was difficult to come. Leaving him for good won't be easy."

Man responds without looking up from his writing: "He watches you."

Drea: "No, he guards me."

Man, still writing: "It's the same."

Drea, stymied by his indifference, looks around, serves herself a glass of cognac from a crystal decanter on one of the shelves and walks back across the room.

Drea: "No. It's not. You used to watch me. Remember? You watched me grow up. And when we made love, you always kept your eyes open. I thought you would watch me forever. But you left, for no reason. I never knew why. What had I done? What went wrong? Do you know what it was like to depend on your presence, and have you disappear with no explanation? You left me no choice. When I married him, I expected it to be like everyone else: we'd learn to love each other through children, a home... But you were still there, somehow, watching. I could feel it. You. And your books, like letters in code. Now I'm here and you won't even look at me. I thought you wanted me!"

Man: "I do."

Drea: "Then what are you doing over there?"

Man: "Look. Come here."

Drea comes around the table, behind his chair to read over his shoulder. Her free hand moves to rest on his shoulder, her upper body leaning down. From in front of the table, we see their faces side by side, her blonde hair falling over his shoulder on the right. She reads, her lips moving, and he, his head turned to the right, watches her read, their faces receiving the light from the lamp and its bright reflection from the table surface, and profiled against the shadows of the wall and ceiling.

Drea: "It's me? You're writing about me?"

Man: "All my poetry is about you."

Drea: "Sometimes I feel it, but then I'm not sure. I know you have someone else and I convince myself you write for her. It's been so long and people change." She kisses his neck, forcing him to look up and turn in the chair, then brings her body around and down until she is pressed against his chest, the brandy snifter still in her hand as her arms encircle his head. Some of the liquid spills on him and they laugh, but only for a moment.

Man: "I used to miss your laugh, but I learned to hear it in my head and let it create the rhythms in my poetry."

Drea: "But I haven't stopped missing you." She kisses him again, then stands, as if considering what to do, or where. Her eyes study the stark room. "Do you always work in such monastic surroundings?"

Man: "Yes."

Drea: "Then we'll just have to make it do." She leans over, kisses him, and while the camera focuses tightly on the head and shoulders, the movement of her hands and arms can be perceived.. She breaks from the kiss, stands and then comes back down to straddle him, kissing his eyes as she guides him, easing herself on to him. She looks up and closes her eyes, feeling him inside her. He kisses her neck. She is biting her fleshy lower lip, then her eyes squeeze tight in a gesture of pain or intense emotion before her smile begins to form slowly, her eyes relaxing and opening, her hands running through his hair, over his neck and shoulders, her fingers at times clawing into him. We can see her moving her body over him, her legs extending and falling under her skirt, and hear her saying, "Yes, yes, it's all right, don't hold back, it's all right, love, yes." His body convulses, hands gripping her shoulders, his head flung back, eyes closed tight, as she kisses his neck and ear, and repeats "Yes, yes, yes..."

Camera circles the two figures; a play of light and dark on their faces set against contrasting backdrops makes their images seem to transform and multiply in spite of remaining absolutely still. Their heads face opposite directions, side by side. She still straddles him, but neither moves. His eyes are closed, his lips barely touching a vein in her neck. They relax in the extension of pleasure, not moving in each other's embrace.

Drea: "I remembered the first time. My first time with anyone was with you..."

Man: "Our first time was with each other."

Drea: "Oh, Jean, why have we lost so many years?"

"Paul, do you know what you're doing?"

"Why, does the writing sound bad?"

"No, but what you're creating. I've seen it before, but this..."

"It's my style, Kandy."

"Fuck style. Don't you think Drea knows?"

I looked over at Kandy for a long time, weighing how much she saw in the scene and what I should admit to.

"You saw yourself?"

"That's not what I mean."

"You're there, in the way she..."

"Drea doesn't care. She knows you and I mean nothing..."

"Untrue."

"She knows what we mean to each other because she's part of it. Believe me, she doesn't care. This is different."

I preferred not to answer, not to talk out what was on the screen and had spoken for itself.

"Be careful, Paul. She loves you."

"Who?"

❋   ❋   ❋

April 18, 1981

Dear Paul,

The new script is your best ever. A young actress will have to play the part of Francesca as a girl. It was bad enough to make Drea play an adolescent when she was in her twenties. Now it would be madness. She can carry off everything else, from the university to the present. Sometimes I forget she is so much younger than we. By the way, you're an irredeemable, unrepentant thief, but I should know by now not to tell you anything I don't want shared with the world. A writer, after all, you fucking scoundrel.

I'll negotiate with London, the most likely place if you keep the story's Scottish location. I would recommend resetting it elsewhere. Scotland offers such a short season for location work. Spain is always good, and since that bastard Franco died, the money is flowing. I know you don't like to think about these things, so not another word. But consider a change; or shoot in Spain and say it's Scotland. If the coast of Galicia can pass for Dunkirk, they can make one of those old walled cities look like Edinburgh. From over here, it all looks like Disney World.

You also should think seriously of turning this into a book. Ghost written, if you want, but the potential royalties are attractive.

When are you going to put a phone in the chalet? Mail—even Express—is too fucking slow. My love to Drea; a separate letter for her is on the way.

Kandy

May 1, 1981

Dear Kandy:

Since when does FUCKIN' end in G? Getting a little modern-novel pedantic in your middle age? And Drea is not so much younger than we, she just ages in reverse. Perhaps she has found the secret of youth in the sexual exploitation of a good man. Who could he be? I don't want a book with my name on it that isn't written by me. If I had time I would see to it myself. Until I do, please don't propose it again. (How attractive?) About the script. I want more control with this one, director if possible. I insist on two things. 1. Fidelity to the script, especially no changes in scene 34, for any reason. 2. Final say in the choice of the actors to play the girl and boy. I want it all in the contract or no script. With the prizes last year, and the work already contracted—and investments, thanks to you—I can afford to wait it out. Okay? I recommend, however, you try an interested new backer, Mr. Alessandro Portini, at the Banca Centrale, Verona.

When are you coming? We miss you. I'll put a phone in if you promise to spend the summer with us. You can't imagine the Tyrol; like Aspen without kitsch or Republicans. Lucky Drea speaks German, too!, because the people in the village don't take well to Italian. A dear friend once told me her son-in-law spoke Italian like a pig. Maybe his family came from here, although they sound more like dogs when they'll lower themselves to speak it at all, snarling and growling. Drea says it's just me. Of course, everybody loves her. But the atmosphere helps me work, and train connections are as good as almost anywhere. I stay less on the sets now, preferring to see them shoot only those parts I'm most interested in. If you get a contract for this, however, I think I would oversee the whole thing.

Please do come.

                                            Paul

p.s.: Thief? Agreed, but what's with "unrepentant, irredeemable thief?" Way overwritten! And at your age.

                                            May 20, 1981

Dear Paul and Drea:

Will be there June to discuss details of film. Can
promise everything you asked, including directing, but
you must guarantee timely selection of girl—and tele-
phone.

                                            Kandy

p.s.: It ain't how you spell it but how you do it that counts.
And wouldn't you like to know who he is? You'll never
wring it out of me.

Timely selection? I already had her picked out.

We were in Milan for the film festival in 1980. Before the
limousine door fully opened, flashing strobes bursting on auto-
matic focused a rapid-fire spot on the main attraction: Drea. I
escorted her into the exhibition hall and delivered her over to
the reporters. She winked and puckered her lips, our ritual
code. (We understand the duties of stardom, and resistance is
pointless.) From a passing tray of champagne flutes, I scooped
off a pair, feeling once again very much the stereotype of a
film star's husband, relatively anonymous but content in the
role. It couldn't last, but maybe before someone discovered me
I could down enough alcohol not to mind. Too soon, however, I
ran into the producer of several of our pictures over the years,
the kind of independent impresario you can't afford to snub.
Wasting little on small talk, he reaffirmed his interest in seeing anything I might be working on, and then, almost as an
afterthought, introduced me to a striking woman in her thirties, tall, regal in appearance and demeanor. As I held her
gloved hand, I heard the producer say she wrote fiction. I apol-

ogized for being unfamiliar with her work, a laguna I would remedy as soon as I could get to a book store. She offered to send me copies in exchange for a candid opinion. When I heard the producer say they were thinking of adapting some of her stories into a film, I realized I'd been waylaid. We all use tricks in the trade, but it never fails to irritate me when I'm the victim. Nevertheless, I accepted her offer, pledging utter frankness, more to honor her beauty than my word.

With the film festival weeks behind me, I had forgotten the encounter when a package arrived by private car, a chauffeur walking up to the chalet to deliver it personally. The plain brown paper package contained four books and a note apologizing for her associate's lack of taste in discussing business at our first meeting. She sounded either skilled at seduction or naive about the film industry, where social events don't exist, just tax write-offs. At the bottom she had printed an address, but no phone number. Perhaps she knew I dislike phones. Then again, it made a trip inevitable.

As I considered the elegant swirl of Francesca's signature, I found myself anticipating something along these lines: a reading of the books, a visit to thank her and comment on them, a discovery of our common interests and aesthetic affinity leading to a physical attraction too sweet and passionate to resist, etc. However, I found a type of literature I detest. The stories were contrived parodies of myth and folklore, with a strained oral tone tending to wander off the subject. I recognized in one of them a polished version of a piece I had declined to script several years before. The novels took lengthy excursions into the same kind of orality, continually mixing fantasy with reality, with superficial references to political issues and feminism interspersed apparently more for effect than genuine concern. She rambled on about generations of grotesque lovers with super power in their loins but nothing in their heads, and women who could fuck all night, clean house all day, and still find time to fight with Garibaldi's revolutionaries, whom they also bedded and advised

simultaneously, liberating Italy in their spare moments. After
their death, the Pope declared them saints in ceremonies
which the deceased attended in full celestial regalia. I couldn't
see myself rewriting her works into film until she rewrote
them into a literature halfway interesting to me. Yet, her
beauty, not her prose, attracted me, so I decided to overlook
my adverse reaction and pay her a visit. How to avoid sharing
my opinion, so ardently solicited at the festival, would come to
me in route.

At the Rovereto depot, I rented a car to drive up to her
home near Monte di Nago. After the woman's imposing presence and the chauffeured delivery of her writings, the opulence of her residence was not unexpected: an
eighteenth-century chateau of Italian style, with vast English
gardens and a picturesque lake curving itself like a disguised
moat from the front of the structure, through a small valley,
around and below the terraces off to one side, where it emp-
tied its waters over a damn or through the sluices of a mysterious old mill on their way to Lake Garda. The road
approached the chateau over an elegant stone bridge span-
ning the lake at an angle to allow passengers a kinetic view of
their destination. I had sent a note saying I would arrive one
day during the week, if business permitted. Leaving it vague
seemed less compromising.

Francesca received me in a small drawing room. The
upper half of the fifteen-foot walls was covered with rose
satin, and tall French doors opened onto garden terraces. She
was every bit as lovely as my first impression, but instead of
her hair up, as in Milan, it cascaded over her shoulders, a rich
black mane stirring in me cravings unrelated to literary dis-
cussions. She prefaced our conversation with yet another apology for her friend's rudeness, protesting that business should
be handled in business settings so as not to distract from pleasure. At that point I wasn't sure whether she considered writing business or pleasure. I placed her books in neither
category, counting their reading as acts of *a priori* atonement

for unforgiven sins. From her bearing, the way her hand allowed itself to be caressed when she passed me a cup of coffee, or the way she took my arm to lead me out to see the lake from the terrace, we both seemed intent on quickly dispensing with the preliminaries to mutual seduction. I was thinking that I wouldn't have to stay the week as I had advised Drea this business might take. As it turned out, however, I did stay on a few days. I had hardly imagined the extent of Francesca's creativity.

We were watching swans fly over the hills beyond the lake to settle on its surface, when from the garden a young voice called, "Francesca, Francesca," and a girl came running, not towards us, rather in a line which led her in front of and past us, a large golden retriever bounding at her side, sometimes breaking into a run, to then turn and loop back around her to pick up the race again. Her blonde hair, held tightly to the sides of her head with barrettes, danced out behind her as she ran. She wore a Scottish plaid jumper whose straps had slid to the sides of her precocious breasts. She couldn't have been more than thirteen.

"My daughter," Francesca answered to my unspoken question. "Her school mistress is ill, so she has the day free."

I looked from her to the child disappearing onto the lower terraces, juxtaposing their contrasting images.

"No, not at all, she takes after her father, my first husband, and inherited his most attractive, Scottish features." Francesca possesses an uncanny ability to converse as if my words are conveyed to her without me needing to vocalize them.

I accepted her offer to stay to meet her husband, Alex, a banker from Verona who spent long weekends at her estate during the school year. Summers, she and the girl lived in Great Britain because Francesca wanted her daughter to grow up speaking English and thinking like a democratic woman with no tolerance for chauvinist Italian men. I recommended the States, but in her opinion the British accent conveys more

charm, especially with a touch of Scottish lilt. We had been
speaking Italian, but when Francesca switched to English, it
confirmed the truth of what she said: the lilt charmed me.
Francesca had grown up with her own nanny, one who
entered the house under the guise of being British, only to
reveal herself over the years a closet Highland Scot. She
taught her ward to read with Sir Walter Scott and Robert
Burns, leaving Francesca a lifelong yearning for a heathered
heath that she resolutely maintained, not just in her mind
and the estate she had acquired in the highlands, but in her
daughter's fantasies.

That evening I met Jeanne, a vivacious child, intelligent
in her conversation, quick and clever, with an engaging open-
ness for adults she derived from having too few playmates her
age. She took great pleasure in testing her knowledge and
readings on an adult who knew the same novels and poetry
she had talked about previously only with her teacher and
mother. When I responded that I, too, had read *The Secret
Garden* after seeing the movie many years ago, her eyes
opened wide for a moment, returning to normal in an effort to
rein in her excitement.

After a recital of her best Brahms pieces, she braved to
question me about my work and if I had children. When she
heard Drea's name, however, all restraint disappeared. The
polite, well-schooled discipline crumbled, and she poured forth
her star-struck admiration for the image of the woman I actually lived with.

Yes, Jeanne did look like Ann Marisse. Not exactly, but
for those searching for the right correspondences and willing
to overlook minor differences, she could have been our daughter. When she reluctantly retired for the night, I remained
under her spell. Francesca and Alex entertained me with
pleasant and, for a banker, unexpectedly literate conversation.
We discussed Margaret Atwood, Italo Calvino and Gabriel
García Márquez, the latter being her undisputed favorite—
which anyone reading her fiction would have guessed. But I

listened with only my ears, my mind overhearing another conversation taking place as if in the room below us, muffled yet
near, voices distinguishable in tone and rhythm, characters
arising to take on flesh and assume positions in the script
writing itself out at a level somewhere beyond speech, a pre-
verbal conversation of figures and images, situations and
motives, all the pretexts for a scene which had presented itself
fully formed and dialogued the moment I saw Jeanne. It
turned out to be scene 34, unaltered from the moment on the
terrace to now.

Three days followed of activities I hadn't prepared for at
all: touring the estate, talking, walking and even working in
the mornings. Francesca's immutable schedule demanded four
hours of writing daily; but her husband being home made it
difficult to do everything else she had planned for us, or so she
told me. I offered to keep him company, which she encouraged, saying a story insisted on her immediate attention.

Alex took me riding, suffering with good humor my lack of
equestrian skill. He showed me the estate's income-generating
sector that he had developed to insure Francesca's possession
of it in a world no longer so respectful of old titles without for-
tunes. He had established a dairy and Europe's largest pres-
surized geodesic dome for the cultivation of wild mushrooms,
a delicacy more profitable than beef, he explained. Hidden
from the chateau, the translucent dome and the dairy
appeared to spring naturally from the humid green soil, like
mushrooms themselves, except with the humanly planned and
molded quality of a Hepworth sculpture. The architecture
betrayed a willingness to budget above the dictates of function
for the pleasure of beauty, even whimsy. Alex sat astride his
black Arabian and admired his achievement, explaining how
he had done it to secure Francesca's dreams of economic independence that allowed her to devote her time to writing and
Jeanne. There was more, however. He had made a dream
landscape materialize from one of her books. In his fashion,
and according to the fancies of Francesca's writing, Alex had

created an architecture of love. He was a man so willing to be possessed by his lover's imagery that he would go to any length to make her imaginary space real for the gratification of living in it with her. By the time we returned from our ride, Alex and I were talking like old friends who share a common purpose.

Then Alex brought out a horse of a different color, his Ferrari, to drive me to Bolzano, where I could send a telegram to Drea and look for books. I found some titles to present to Francesca, but not the ones I sought for Jeanne. As an afterthought, I asked Alex if he knew a good jewelry store. He took me to Francesca's family jeweler. When we met, the jeweler asked two things, what I had in mind and for whom. Upon receiving my answers, he opened his hands in the air like a magician and said, *Gut*, followed by rapid-fire sentences in the Tyrolese dialect. Alex shook his head, but interpreted for me. The jeweler was raving about how God had made him start working on just the right thing three weeks ago, as if he had been ordered to prepare for our visit. Alex shrugged his shoulders, made a gesture signaling "crazy," and then, pointing all around us, added, "All of them, the whole north, superstitious primitives."

Perhaps, but the old man's hands were pure inspiration not unrelated to the divine. He brought out a cross, modestly but finely sculpted in silver, with a delicate chain. The piece shone against his fingers like an apparition. By then it wouldn't have surprised me to find Jeanne's name etched on the reverse side, but only an open space shone, awaiting the tool and challenging my vanity. I hesitated, but Alex insisted that if it was to be a memento, nothing could be more appropriate. The old man inscribed "von Paul."

"How splendid," Francesca told Jeanne. "Silver becomes you with your coloring and hair. Nothing can compete with the gold God already gave you."

Jeanne kissed her mother and tendered me her hand with sincere gratitude. Her mother suggested she find a more fit-

ting manner to thank a gentleman and friend of the family for
such an elegant gift. Jeanne then kissed me on the cheek.

When I returned home, the memory of Jeanne lingered
over all others. Beyond what she represented to me personally, she had that intangible something that lights sparks in a
casting director's eyes and fixes an actor's image in the audience's mind. They might not remember details of the plot, but
they never forget a face like Jeanne's. No one else could play
the Ann Marisse I was already creating for the next film, but
it would be only the first of Jeanne's career if her mother
allowed her to take the chance.

❋　❋　❋

By the time I wrote to Kandy, I had sealed a bargain with
Francesca. It took another trip, but I didn't mind. Her chauffeur, Danillo, met my train to drive me to the chateau.
Francesca received me in her study this time, sitting behind
an English Regency desk. The script lay on the richly grained
surface, Francesca's thick Mont Blanc resting like a paper
weight on the cover. In all probability she had marked certain
passages with a professional eye. The use of her name for the
protagonist and the setting in Scotland had pleased her. She
offered her highland manor as a location site and even suggested I approach Alex with the venture. Then she said, "You
want something, Paul. Why else would you send me this? You
need neither my approval nor these other things I have
offered you."

"Maybe it was an excuse to see you."

"No. It's not true. Later, I'll allow myself to pretend it is.
It will affect no one, I promise. Once I told you, however, that
I fancy everything in its place. This is the office where I con-
duct business, so now tell me what you want."

"Jeanne. You're not surprised? No, you wouldn't be. I'll
ask for the right to choose the actress to play the ingenue and
insist we use an amateur for freshness and authenticity.

You've read the one difficult scene. Is it too much for her? For you?"

Francesca stood up, walked to the window and looked out.

"It's acting, I know, but to make it seem real she must make love to the boy. You don't resort to allusions, Paul. The writing is explicit, direct, even coldly objective, yet I can feel you care for the girl in this one scene."

She looked at me a moment and then back out the window. "Can you accept criticism, Paul, from a friend?"

"About the script?"

"This one and others."

"Oh."

"We've avoided talking about writing because you don't like mine. Yes, it's true, don't deny it, but I admire yours. Until now I had only seen the films, but I always recognized one of your special scenes, carefully constructed and filmed. Always I ask myself, why doesn't this man write an entire film the way he has written this one scene? You could make great films instead of...good ones."

I listened, watching her stare out the window and talk to me as though placing me there, just outside the glass or within my own reflection, casting a spell for future reference. Could there be women who exist at a higher realm of consciousness, perform miraculous deeds, read men's minds? More likely, as an intuitive artist, Francesca read me exactly as I unconsciously wanted her to. Yet her question couldn't be answered, because I had given up hoping for the individual control it implied in an industry where the product passes through too many hands to qualify as a personal creation. I had influenced and manipulated directors to get the little she saw, and only now, on the basis of those few scenes, could I demand more. But outsiders can't understand, so I responded with a question of my own.

"Now, what is it you want, Francesca?"

"Three promises to begin with."

She returned to her desk, picked up her Mont Blank like a black wand, aimed its white-star at me and enumerated the requirements for granting her permission.

"First, Jeanne will do nothing she does not care to do. You alone will explain the role and direct her. No one shall abuse her in the name of any goal, not in the slightest." Her face had assumed the stern insistence and concern of a loving parent.

"My word on it. You can even be there to supervise me."

"I trust you, Paul, or I would not permit Jeanne to participate under any conditions. It's clear you are as fond of her as you are of this character, although surely you are aware that many women will misunderstand this type of affection. I fear they won't understand my allowing Jeanne to collaborate either, but the decision will be hers. I will counsel, but never persuade or censor her."

Francesca's face softened when she addressed the second demand, reflecting a different kind of concern, more personal and intimate, while at once eerily objective.

"Second. You must write a complete work. For yourself. Or for this woman you love through your writing. Promise?"

"And if I break it, what?"

"A Scottish-Italian curse on your head, sworn in ancient Celtic against which all known antidotes are in dead tongues no longer spoken. Do you communicate well with the dead, Paul? You dismiss my writing as fantasy, but would you dare to find out if it is true? I would not advise it."

I laughed, but her smile reflected no humorous intent behind her words, echoing a similar threat many years before.

"And third?" I asked.

"Actually, payment of an old debt: the frank opinion of my work you promised in Milan. Such a face, Paul! Is the prospect so dreadful?" She rang a bell for the maid. "I like that face. It shows we are friends and have no need to pretend any longer. Coffee in the drawing room, Angelina," she instructed the maid.

She stood up, signaled me to accompany her and took my arm in the same fluid manner she had used the first day to lead me outside to see the lake—or to wait for Jeanne to appear from my dreams.

"Now," Francesca said as we walked towards the satin-paneled doors dividing her study from the sitting room, "before we cross from work space to that of pleasure, a last demand." With her elegant hand flat against the panel, she eased it open, revealing the coffee service waiting on the small table in front of the French doors. A flood of sunlight washed high on the walls, taking on the golden-rose glow of the satin and brocade curtains closing off the secret alcove on the far side of the room I hadn't noticed before. "Our imaginations open with this door into a space unrelated to any other, even to our writing. An entirely private place. Promise?"

※　※　※

Drea, who was in Rome that week planning the campaign to launch her own line of cosmetics, took the train to Verona where Francesca, Alex and I met her. She had wanted to meet my new collaborator of whom I had spoken so highly without telling her much at all, except that her daughter was going to be a star. Drea and Francesca greeted each other like sisters, with kisses on the cheek and tight pressing of their hands. Later, after the opera and a late dinner, Francesca and Drea walked a few paces ahead of us, arms entwined, heads moving in unison to see the bats or ghosts disturb the shadows high above us in the colonnade of the ancient coliseum. They paused in the circle cast by a street light, turned to look at each other and spoke in whispers.

"Francesca's world," I thought out loud as I watched them share their secrets, "take it or leave it."

"Paul, my friend," Alex said, taking me by the elbow and holding his other hand out towards the two women, "it makes no difference what you decide once she has you inside her world. Our choices have already been made for us. The best we can do is hope it never ends."

*　*　*

When we returned home, Drea asked me for the script and retreated to the study. The next day, other than the usual questions on mood and motivation and what liberties were to be left to her discretion, one scene peaked her interest. Not Jeanne's, around which all the rest had been devised, but another she herself would play at the beginning of the adult life of Francesca Moore.

"This episode, Paul, at the university? Where did it come from?"

"With the professor? Can't you guess?"

Drea removed her reading glasses, brushed her hair back from her face with the little finger of each hand, and looked at me as if to plumb my meaning. Reclined as she was on the sofa facing me, the panorama of the mountains behind her opened a vast background through the large window. The pines drooped under the powdery weight of an early snow. Her legs were drawn up on the cushions, a long beige silk skirt covering even her feet, her back propped against the sofa's high arm. Although two huge logs radiated heat from the hearth, we both wore heavy, loose sweaters over turtle-neck liners, layered against the inevitable draftiness of Euro-pean houses. Her auburn hair contrasted brilliantly with the off-white Scottish wool and the pale pink silk turtleneck rising to outline the perfect sketch of her chin. Unlike mine, her face betrayed no sign of age, skin as firm as the night we met. She really did seem to be getting younger, the reading glasses the solitary hint of her aging like the rest of us. Her eyes are a fla-grant blue that ignites like exploding Lapis Lazuli when she's angry. A metallic-blue eyeliner and mascara designed espe-cially for her by Laroche highlight them to unforgettable.

Drea had kept her eyes leveled on me for minutes, and then said, "I know you don't like to ask questions. It's fine.

From the start I've appreciated the way you don't probe, just
listen and absorb whatever I tell you. I might have told you
more had you asked, but then I've never liked being grilled,
even by caring men. Like my father. He used to ask me at dinner, Diane, what did you do in school today, did you learn anything new? It got so I dreaded the moment he would ask the
question. It's not that I didn't tell him what happened at
school, but I hated to be questioned. When I got older, he
stopped asking. At dinner, I'd watch him and wait. One night,
my mother found me crying because Daddy had stopped loving me. It's strange the way we come to desire even what we
dislike, those rituals we build our life around. So I started
asking him what he did every day. It took time, but he finally
opened up. Then my mother cried: She hardly knew her own
husband until she overheard Daddy describing to me his life
outside the house. She wasn't angry. She thanked me. And
now you and I sit and talk across a table daily about everything we do or read or even dream. Maybe it works because
you never ask trivial questions like what did you learn today?
But there are things I haven't told you. How you seem to know
anyway, I've never asked. But this you could have only gotten
from Kandy. I knew she passed on many things to you, but
this was from when I first met her and had nothing to do with
you. At the time, you and I weren't yet even a press item."

"Mutual trust. Kandy tells me everything except the full
truth about herself, and I tell her lies which might turn out to
be true some day. She told me a little after you and I met."

"That's how you knew!" She flashed her professional sex-
goddess smile, perturbing me, tipping the conversation off
course towards another possibility. She read my expression
like a poem, all at once, and eased her stare as if to say,
maybe, but not yet. Then she began to talk, in a form reminis-
cent of a soliloquy, placing me outside the story, but clearly in
the speaker's presence, a boundary she'd cross once in a while
to break the frame. She knew how to excite my interest and
play on my curiosity.

"When I graduated, I went to L.A. People warned me it would be hard, but not impossible. Too many girls, more beautiful, more talented, maybe, but certainly more willing to do whatever they had to for a chance. There's no such thing as a director's couch, darling. King-size waterbeds glide out from their walls. I'll do anything for love, but not for money. So I came over here. The business isn't easier, but on the way I picked up some names from a friend of a good friend, which made all the difference in the world...before Kandy found me.

"I've never told you about Trish, my friend from high school. Over-sexed and verbally obscene, yet brilliant, a lot like Kandy. We hung out together, which puzzled our teachers no end. When Radcliffe accepted her and rejected me, the senior adviser predicted Harvard would go down the toilet. Sometimes I'd go up to Cambridge, or she'd come to New York for a show or exhibit. She stayed on at Harvard for a doctorate in Comp Lit. After my Hollywood disaster, Trish took me in. A couple blocks from Harvard Square, she had this beautiful apartment. Twelve foot ceilings, wood paneling, the works. I knew her family couldn't afford it, so I naively asked how she managed.

"Her answered surprised me, even for her. Her dissertation director was paying for it."

"She was sleeping with her adviser."

"Not much different from Hollywood, don't you think? Anyway, when she talked about him, he didn't sound so bad at first. And when I met him, he was charming. He knew a lot about Hollywood because he taught a film course, too. Well, it turned out that he had lots of European connections. When I told him what had happened in California, Piet was sympathetic, Paul, and offered to give me several names. He seemed so nice, until later, when Trish told me what the names would cost. 'He wants you,' she said. I'll never forget her face when she told me. I was too shocked to react, so she repeated it in all the languages she knew.

"I didn't want to understand in any language. You know what I mean, Paul? My best friend tells me her lover wants me...but she wasn't just telling me, she was asking me to do it, asking me to understand and not cause her any more problems with Piet than she already had. She had more than love invested. Love, too, I guess, because Piet divorced his wife in '74, but Trish refused to marry him. She had the doctorate and a job by then, and didn't want to give up her position at Duke."

"She told me she didn't mind. One more between friends, she said. She meant Rick, my high school boyfriend. I don't know what hurt more, Trish asking me to fuck her lover or telling me Rick was pathetic in bed. But she assured me that Piet was an expert."

"I don't know if you can understand why I agreed. But if you want to get it right in the film, Trish has to look trapped, like an animal in a zoo. In all the years I had known her, I'd never seen that expression on her face."

Drea stopped talking. She wanted something to drink. In the kitchen the maid offered to prepare it, but I preferred to do it myself, heating water with a slice of lemon the way she likes it, and giving Drea time. Although I had heard much of the story from Kandy, I wanted to compare Drea's version.

"Piet was good. The stereotype of a European lover, taking his time and knowing how much time should be taken. No passion, but then I didn't love him. We did it several times before I left for Rome. Being good at it helped. He made it a pleasure most of the time.

"Does this bother you, darling? No? Too bad. Try to let down your imperturbable cynicism, darling. It's me, Drea."

"Go on."

"That's just what I couldn't do, go on. Dr. Riviere was a Harvard Don with a passion for introducing his students to new experiences. Piet taught me something all right, something I didn't tell anyone until I met Kandy. Trish and I kept writing, but we never hashed out our memories from those weeks. Then, when I went back to L.A. as Kandy's Italian import, she and I talked about everything, but mostly you. I don't remember how it came up. I remember we were talking about your love, Ann, the one she called your dream girl, and how you were still running away from her. I do remember that she made me curious when she described her as fuckin' beautiful, the ideal girl next door, first love, wife and mother type. Supposedly you had blown up because Kandy set her up with some director. Kandy hated her, I could tell, but it was obvious, too, that she was more scared of loosing you."

"She didn't have me."

"Maybe not, but she didn't want Ann to have you either. Christ, Paul, everyone knew. I don't know how many people warned me to stay away from you or get dropped by Kandy. But she's the one who started talking about you. I mean, talking about how you and I should get together."

"It was her idea? I thought she was against it."

"Part of the plan. You were sure to chase me if she said you couldn't. I didn't need tricks, but I did want to know why she wanted you to be with me when she was in love with you."

"Somebody else told me that once, but I didn't believe her."

"Kandy denied it, too. When I asked straight out if you made love, you know what she said?"

"I can imagine. Something like, we fuck."

"Her exact words. She made you sound so fantastic, that you liked to try everything, and, somehow, I told her about Piet. It was like when women start comparing their experiences and you need something to top their stories, you know? I asked her if you and she went in for kinky sex? And of course she had to elaborate on all the positions you so dearly love. I guess I felt I had to shut her up with something, so I simply said one word: sodomy, Piet's favorite. It worked. I don't know if she believed me, but at least she quit raving about you. She was even more stunned when I told her that with the right person I liked it. When we made love the first time, I thought you seemed to know, remember?"

"In Kandy's guest room, yes. You asked how I knew, but I avoided answering."

"Would you have told me that Kandy had told you if I had asked again?"

"Yes. It's part of the same trust thing Kandy likes."

"This scene you've written, it's straight from my story, isn't it."

"Yes."

"It helps build the character, to understand her determination to experience what she's forced to do, but with someone she loves. The same action within love changes value. Yes. But will you do me a favor?"

"What?"

"I've never asked you to change anything before, but could you change the professor's name and the university? Piet's dead, but his wife and daughter aren't. Why hurt them? And don't make me do it on camera. I'll give it facial expression to convince the camera it's happening, but I don't want a full body shot, okay?"

"Why? You love your body on screen."

She got up and came to sit on the arm of my chair.

"It's just one thing I want to reserve for us. Private, for you, me and Kandy. Such a little thing, but I want to keep it for the three of us, alone."

I caressed the back of her knee. "You make it sound like Kandy and you are lovers," I teased her, half-serious.

"Aren't the two of you?" She turned and slid down across my lap, her upper body facing me.

"We were." My hand found the hem of her skirt, slipped beneath it and followed her calve up between her legs, which she spread to let it pass, and I began to caress her silk-covered sex with my thumb. She was already damp.

"You are." Her hips responded with short strokes to the pressure of my thumb, rubbing my erection with her side in the same motion.

"Would you care?"

"Would you?"

"I don't know," I answered, searching her eyes for a clue to her thoughts. Their seriousness fascinated me. She was playing, but I wasn't sure what kind of game. She moved her hips further back with one stroke for me to move my hand inside her panties. My middle finger pressed between the orbs of her butt.

"No, you don't know," she said through a soft sigh, more like a heavy breath, and a smile began to form on her lips, but still not in her eyes.

"If I asked, would you tell me?" I probed.

"You would have to persuade me. Bribe me." Her hips moved now more with the rhythm of my finger than my thumb, a reverse stroke of rear more than forward opening.

"What do you want?"

Her eyes softened a little as the smile grew more definite. "Want me to show you?"

"Yes."

"Really?" She kissed me, then took me down to the floor and taught me what the scene had finally allowed her to ask me for without asking. Later she told me she has never liked to ask for sex. She tasted like the smell of old wine bottles brought from a dank cave after years of storage, something dark and aged for a special palate. And she taught me that I, too, like the taste of my secret self on her lips. Most of all, I like the insinuation in her eyes, wherever we are, when she looks at my hands and runs her fingers across her lips.

She didn't tell me if she had used Kandy to tease me into seduction, but then again I didn't ask. Not that I prefer not to know; I enjoy wondering, fantasizing when I watch them together, and I wouldn't want to find out for certain that they aren't.

※ ※ ※

Piet's name was changed to Etienne, and the university
became Yale. It satisfied Drea, while retaining enough clues to
guide the discerning viewers back to the real culprit in this
filmic search-and-destroy mission. Then last year at a film
conference in Boston, during the question and answer session
a young lady asked me if I considered my denunciation of sexual harassment to have been instrumental in the judgment
against the Yale professor. I protested that I knew nothing
about the case and, moreover, the episode, being fictional,
bore no relationship with any Yale don. The audience chuckled knowingly, or in this case, mis-knowingly. The more I
insisted, the less they believed me, citing one of the graduate
student plaintives' reference to the film and a possible no-com-
ment confirmation by a Yale graduate now employed at
Duke—the one name I left unchanged. My only defense would
have been to denounce the late Piet Riviere in public, but the
deceased couldn't have come forward to confirm his well-
groomed reputation as a sleaze. Besides, I had promised Drea
not to mention him.

※ ※ ※

Jeanne's acting debut was traumatic, not for her but for
Francesca. The sophisticated mother watched her daughter
give an erotic performance for the camera with such precocious joy in the sexual play that Francesca was left quite visi-
bly shaken.

As the barely adolescent Francesca, Jeanne is spending a
summer at the family's Scottish manor with her cousins. With
the only boy her age, she explores the countryside and every
dark room of the old house. Towards the end of their vacation,
they quarrel, but he begs to see her one last time before he
leaves. The scene opens with Francesca leading him into the
garage where their grandmother's old Rolls is stored. In the
back seat, she tells him that if he wants her to forgive him he

must kiss her, because it is how adults make up. He's not convinced, so she proceeds to explain how it is done in her mother's books, which she reads in secret. He protests that it's a sin. But she caresses him, telling him that it couldn't be wrong for people in love, because then their parents would be sinning all the time. She asks him if he loves her, to which he ardently responds yes. As she moves closer, her hand lightly slips between his legs, while with her other hand she leads his under her slip. The seduction is over quickly, the boy coming almost immediately, while she tells him it's all right, she doesn't mind, that the books say that when they are older it will be better. The next day, he leaves without saying goodbye. They meet again only when Drea is playing the adult Francesca, a successful professional who retains perverse sexual tastes, spurred on by her mentor in the Yale Law School.

After the shooting, Francesca looked drained, pale. It was as if she had experienced the scene the same way it later appeared on the screen, fluid and undisturbed by cameras, lights, and interruptions to replace the real Rolls-Royce with a cut-away for the inside shots. Between takes, Jeanne inquired about everything. Acting was a new adventure for her, not work. Francesca, however, winced each time I called for another take. To speed up the process, I allowed Jeanne to improvise more than I had been prepared to permit, but it only made things worse. When Francesca realized that the sensual gestures of persuasion sprang directly from her daughter's imagination, she began to move her lips—whether praying or pronouncing incantations, I couldn't tell.

Later that night, Jeanne was again the same vivacious girl, shy with strangers, open and effusive with the adults she knew, and the epitome of classic loveliness at the piano. When we had a moment aside, I asked her where she got the idea to say she had learned to make love from her mother's books. "It's true," she said, and asked me if I had read all of Francesca's stories.

Francesca also wanted a moment or two aside with me, but insisted I go to her room. Luckily, Drea was still in Paris finishing shooting on a commercial for her new perfume line. The first thing Francesca said when I entered her door that night was how fine is the line between the erotic art of her stories and the camera's pornographic eye.

❋   ❋   ❋

"You had no right to it!"

"Paul, darling, I've never seen you this angry over so little. And this really is nothing. Isn't it, Kandy?"

"Drea, you can't use this," I insisted. "I won't allow it."

"Darling, they spend nearly as much on the shooting of one commercial as we do on an entire film. I'm truly sorry, but it's too late. Kandy can tell you, it's all sealed and delivered."

"These are my lines; this is my scene."

"You can't copyright an idea, Paul. Besides, they are my lines and my scene as well. Why do you think they chose them? They took a lot of care to go through my films to find the most memorable image. It's a line I've used twice, once in..."

"I know where I've used it. That's not the fuckin' point."

"What is? That your writing has become a commercial for cheap perfume? Well it's not cheap, Paul, $150.00 an ounce is par with the best. And what do we do that isn't commercial? The only thing you've done in fifteen years that wasn't is your interview with the nurses and doctors from Vietnam, and only because Susan asked you to do it."

"I never would have approved."

"You did, Paul! Not only approved, you signed the contract. Kandy made them acknowledge you as co-author, didn't you?"

"True," Kandy replied, trying to stay neutral.

"When?"

"Two years ago."

"When I was preparing *Francesca Moore*?"

"Exactly."

"You know I couldn't think of anything else...anything so..."

"So trivial as a million-dollar perfume line? You said it looked fine. I trust you, you said."

"I do."

"*Bugiardo*. At least admit it's a quality production."

"Granted, yes, but I could have reworked it, given it a different look."

"We did. I insisted we not use the same settings from either film. Imagine, one producer wanted to do it just like the scene in *Il Ritorno*, in the writing room, with the same lighting..."

"And the same fucking."

"Of course. But this is elegant, don't you think?"

Search lights crisscross a theater facade: an awards event, with limousines pulling up, stars exiting, waving, making their way through reporters and photographers. One attracts the people more than the rest, forcing the camera to shift from a male star, whose face momentarily fills the screen, to Drea as she steps from her limo, richly sheathed in a black strapless gown, and moves through the flashing cameras of the paparazzi, past the actor—who looks at her appreciatively, longingly—and into the theater. Cut to Drea receiving the award, alternating with close takes of the actor from the opening shot. Meanwhile, a voice-over narrator speaks of the lost excitement of young passion, of the first great romance. Drea exits down the aisle, past the actor again, glancing at him, setting off a quick cut to a memory sequence of the two of them—younger, somewhere on the banks of the Seine, the Parisian skyline as a backdrop—cut back to Drea approaching her limousine and the actor reaching out for her hand. She turns, smiles and says her only line in the commercial: "Darling, why have we lost so many years?" As the limo departs and we see them kiss in the back seat, the narrator's voice returns to affirm, "Don't lose time, return to the fragrance of years past, of true love, DREA, the perfume tradition you thought lost forever."

"Not bad at all," Kandy said. "Daily national exposure on all the channels. And it has a sort of fifties' retro-feel."

"Paul thinks it's crass and commercial. And plagiarism, besides."

"Whose?" asked Kandy.

"What do you mean?" I asked. "You know where that line comes from."

"Do I? The old question, which came first, the fuckin' chicken or the chickens fucking?"

Drea looked from Kandy to me and back, waiting to be let in on the conversation.

"It's a scene Paul wrote—or lived?—years ago. It could have been the script for the last segment of the commercial."

Kandy knew what, knew whom I had seen on the screen. I listened to her explain it to Drea after asking my permission with her eyes. Kandy's version, while accurate, had an unsettling tone, as if she were watching it from a distance. But then Kandy had heard me tell it for the first time years ago, and retell it later, when it became nostalgia and, finally, the essence of loss.

"You should be happy, darling," Drea said to me when Kandy finished. "I've given you your Ann Marisse on more screens than we dreamed possible. She's bound to see it now. I don't know what more you could ask me to do."

Drea left us in the living room. With her hand, Kandy motioned me not to follow.

"Give her time. She's used to you and she loves you. This won't change it. Let her absorb the shock. This was her baby. It's rough to discover you're just a repetition of someone else's memories. She's accepted it before, so I imagine she will now. I told you years ago it was dangerous."

❋   ❋   ❋

Jeanne won an award for her role, traveling to Los Angeles to receive it in March of 1983. A second film awaited her, to be shot in Germany, one I had nothing to do with. But she was convinced I had arranged it, since she considered me her guardian angel, the person who had made her an actress.

Francesca found her daughter's new career distracting from her writing, but she accompanied her to accept the prize, as she had earlier on a publicity tour around the premier. They both invited me to the award ceremony, but I begged off. As usual, another project had already taken over my life.

When a Nobel-Prize-winning novel must be adapted for film, no one emerges unscathed, but if there was one book I wanted to script it was *The Unbearable Lightness of Being*. I suppose I expected it to fall into place without special effort on my part, so I left the business end to Kandy and didn't bother to contact Kundera myself. Instead, I went from a sketchy treatment straight to scripting. Strangely enough, I couldn't bring myself to intercalate a scene of my own invention, because Kundera's work seemed to already capture what I wanted to show, albeit by inversion. It would be my subtlest work ever. For example, men in my scripts usually leave women because they desire to move freely, freed from the restraints of domesticity, but in *ULB* a woman leaves a man for the same reason. When her lover divorces his wife to come to live with her, she abandons him without so much as a note of explanation. Then there are the two women, studies in contrast—the light/good/moral wife and the dark/playfully bad/amoral mistress. He loves them both, but feels drawn to the one who needs him, the photographer dependent on the world of social reality inherent in the media in which she works. He is happier with the free-spirited painter who can ignore or run from the exterior realities; yet he stays with the other. In my scripts the decision usually goes in the other direction. However, the point is both women fuse in the image of love he pursues. At one point the two women leaf through an album of the artist's paintings taken by the photographer, the one's work within the other's. The two women, their faces side by side, are reflections of each other in the eyes of the protagonist who contemplates them. The multifaceted image of his love in this scene fuses them as one possibility before time assumes its progress towards fragmentation. The audi-

ence should want to keep them together, make them realize
there is no contradiction between the two halves of one reflection when held in the admiring gaze. But it's only possible in
the personal space of art. When the Soviets invade Czechoslo-
vakia in 1968, art becomes social and the lovers are torn
apart. In my case, the forces that upset my plans were more
pedestrian: the producer contracted the script to someone else.

I was working on the difficult concluding scenes, on how
to kill off the protagonists without melodrama or stamping the
film with an image of sadness that would betray the erotic
energy of the story, when Kandy called with an urgent message. It was like the death of a friend. Losing time wasn't the
point, nor the prestige of scripting a Nobel Prize. It was having to accept that those characters I had come to know, had
lived intimately with to the point where I could recognize
their voices in the dark, would never exist in that space of
light and sound, never become images in the audience's memory. They were fated to remain in the limbo of an unfilmed
script.

When I saw the film, I confess, it was close to what I'd
have done. In the end, who remembers who wrote what? But
this one I would have liked to claim.

The same night Kandy called, I floundered around quite
out of character for myself. Drea was in Paris doing a television special. I had refused to accompany her to stay and finish
the now stillborn script. I tried reading Francesca's latest
novel, but just could not force myself past the miraculous
rebirth of a dead baby on the first page. So like many times in
the past, I turned on the computer to lose myself in writing.
Memories of Ann Marisse appeared on the monitor screen,
arranging themselves into scenes, but more to be read than
filmed. Hours later, I noticed light beginning to profile the
shape of individual trees outside my window. I had worked
through the night and felt at once light-headed and leaden,
my mind was still racing, while my fingers ached.

I lay down on the sofa. On the desk, the computer monitor still glowed, white lines of electronic print strung across a sky-blue background. It had that strange capacity to fascinate and dull the senses simultaneously, like an old television test screen, and I stared at it for who knows how long? In its dim light the phone sat, quiet, waiting. What happened next, I remember like something from a dream.

The international operator connected me with information in Los Angeles; a staccato, mechanical voice fed me the ten-digit number I had requested; then suddenly I felt shamefully anonymous, a silent caller in the darkness halfway around the world.

"Hello..." A startling voice, matured after almost two decades, lower, deeper than the silence into which I hung up.

I stared at the phone and wondered if Ann Marisse was doing the same. I imagined her asking herself "who?" before replacing the receiver, or remarking to Alonzo, "It sounded like long distance." I wondered if she perhaps remembered having heard an identical silence before? Did she, in that flicker of an instant, scan the space around her for some key to explain the unsettling feeling that somewhere in the night someone was watching her?

I began to type, but now a script. A woman, staring at her phone, saying to herself, "It's happening again." And in a dark room a man depresses the button on his phone, and only then speaks into the receiver, "Its just me." I tried to create the sense of impending crisis in a woman's life that springs entirely from her imagination or intuition after receiving what she perceives to be a mysterious call in the night. Whether my writing was reflecting reality or vice versa, the fact was that the women in my life were as on edge as the one in the script.

Drea was searching for what she could only describe as, "Something different, something not me. Don't you ever get tired of the same me?"

"No, never, really."

"You're impossible."

I suppose I was, but no different than ever.

Francesca had parlayed her authority over Jeanne to commit me to writing this, a novel that was sliding irretrievably into something between romance and autobiography. When Kandy, who had encouraged me to write a book, read early drafts, she jumped on the phone, warning me to reconsider.

"It's getting out of hand," she said.

I agreed and quit writing. But I sent her a copy of what I had done, what I calculated would be the first third. She sent it back with a cryptic note urging me to continue, so I drew up the file on the computer and started again. We met after I finished the first half, and she called it a romance, but let me continue. When I sent her a preliminary draft of the rest, she was back on the phone, raving.

"Listen, Paul, it doesn't make any fuckin' sense to go on with this."

"Too late now. Besides, I thought you liked it."

"Sometimes I do, but this is business and as your agent I have to watch out for your interests. Why be so stubborn?"

"I promised."

"Promised who?

"Francesca. I had to promise to write something all my own before she would agree to let Jeanne do the film."

"Next time check with me first before you make promises you can't keep."

"I can."

"Shouldn't keep, then. It doesn't work even as a romance."

"So call it an autobiography, if you want."

"Maybe nobody will publish it."

"That's okay. I only promised to write it."

"Well, promise me you'll think it over."

"It's a promise."

Actually, I think the new films disturbed Kandy more than this book. Years before, in Florence, she had warned me about pushing Drea too hard, yet they both have always understood that my work feeds off of my obsessions.

❀   ❀   ❀

Drea, meanwhile, works as hard as ever, and has committed herself to a French television series which will require she spend months in Paris. She teases me about having to dye her hair blond for the role—"Like a second honeymoon, darling, remember?"

Well I do. Passion on the beach, in the same bed with an auburn-haired wife playing a blonde sex kitten; making love in the pool in clear sight of the cast; petting in the back seat, with Carlo sitting on the other side, pretending to look out the window; her parody of *And God Created Women* at a brunch for the production team, Drea in a sheet serving herself food, just to prove she could pout as well as Bardot.

Now, she's ready for a new part, a challenge. She is tired of her routine, or maybe she's searching for a new form of expression. Her restlessness affects me because we have become accustomed to sharing the same space for our reading and much of my thinking. She knows I'm working on something different. She can tell from the long, continuous paragraphs in place of short dialog phrases. She watches and wonders where it will lead us. She insists she isn't interested in reading this book until it's finished, but Kandy reports, as Drea must know she does, Drea's inquiries into what I am writing. Kandy shares with me what she tells Drea, but within our mutual trust, how far can I trust her? Kandy rarely lies, true, but she delays key information long enough to create erroneous interpretations.

One thing is for Kandy to read my life, ordered neatly into perfectly horizontal rows of elegant roman typeface filing into a continuous column against the background of quality, 100% rag, white bond, with only my voice in her memory as a reference for intonation; quite another for Drea to hear it from Kandy over a transatlantic phone. The slightest change in presentation, a minor alteration of camera angle or pitch in the audio, can turn reception a hundred and eighty degrees.

✳   ✳   ✳

After meeting Kandy and my publisher in New York to discuss the book you are reading, I was scheduled to speak at Trinity College, Hartford, CT. An old friend, Paul Lauter, invited me to participate on a panel dedicated to film in a symposium on non-traditional writing. The panel went well, good-humored and less pedantic than I expected. Afterwards, they hosted a dinner and poetry reading in one of those fully automated buildings Hartford ballyhoos, a high-rise belonging to the Associated Insurance Brokers of America... and yes, another meeting took place the same day, a convention of regional representatives to honor the Top Salesman in each of the fifty states.

After the poetry reading, I stepped out of the hall to take some air. As I walked back, I heard a voice addressing someone in a mixture of familiarity and aggressive disdain.

"You bastard."

The hallways were thick with people from the insurance convention and our symposium mixed with building residents strolling through the mall-like ground floor, so the words could have been aimed at almost anyone. As I reached the banquet hall door, however, the voice spoke again, but louder and closer than before.

"Don't run away, Paul, you filthy bastard."

A hand grabbed my shoulder and spun me around. Just as I recognized Alonzo in front of me, the door struck me from behind, hurling me towards Alonzo. Looking back on the whole affair, if this were a film at my disposal, I would turn it into a slapstick farce in the fine low tradition of pie tossing and waiters tripping with trays of drinks. But that happens only in the movies.

Alonzo was serious, deadly so. He backed up a step and swung at me as I attempted to regain my balance. The blow surprised more than injured me, his fist grazing the top of my head and spinning me again, back towards the door and into the open arms of Judy Hortís, a Puerto Rican poet who had given a reading at the symposium. Apparently she was leaving, because she had donned her rain cape, and Lauter was escorting her to the door. I can still hear her exclamation of *"¡Ay, bendito!"* as she caught me in an embrace neither one of us had planned, although earlier, listening to her read in a sensual mixture of Spanish and English, I had entertained a foray into my Hispanic roots. Alonzo reached for me, but Hortís placed herself between us and menaced him with her umbrella. An Easterner, she knew how to face down muggers.

Alonzo squinted his eyes to take her measure, bared his rabbit-like front teeth, and snarled, "Another chippy from your harem, Paul?"

The metal tip of Hortís' umbrella cracked over Alonzo's right shoulder, staggering him a moment before a quick follow-up thwack to the left clavicle dropped him to one knee, as if she had knighted him for some deed of valor. Lucky for Alonzo, Lauter restrained Hortís and tried to restore order.

I almost felt sorry for Alonzo, he looked so pathetic, genuflected on the floor. But what distorted his face, more than pain, was rage. Rage and a smoldering hate that, denied a physical outlet by Hortís' imposing figure, spewed itself into a bilious harangue.

"I know what you're trying to do, Paul," Alonzo accused in a pitiful voice that gathered confidence from its own venomous accumulation. "You never give up. But she's my wife, no matter what you put on television. I know it never happened. I know everything she's ever done. You liar."

A couple of his colleagues, the lapels of their blue suits emblazoned with the shield of the AISA, rushed to Alonzo's aid, helping him to his feet. One of them tried to calm him down, advising him to be careful what he said in public.

Alonzo's face twisted in pain as he rubbed his left clavicle with his right hand. His other arm lifted an open hand to

point five accusing fingers at me in a melodramatic gesture
that underscored his next barrage. "Filthy pornographer, child
molester. Tell these people how old that little girl was. Thirteen? Maybe twelve? But we know why you seduced her, don't
we?" He looked around to gather support from the spectators.
Then, satisfied that he had the crowd waiting for the answer
to his question, he shifted their stares to me and he added,
"She looks like Ann, but I have the real one. She's my wife,
and that's what you can't take."

Hortís' umbrella seemed to wilt and drifted downward, as
though she were starting to wonder at which of the two of us
she should point it. A crowd continued to gather, most of them
coming up in time to hear only Alonzo's raving lies.

"He's insane," I told Hortís.

"And he's a terrorist!" Alonzo retorted.

In the background, someone said, "Call security, hurry,
get the police."

"Ask him, any of you. Ask why he won't leave us alone.
Why he makes her do those filthy things in front of everybody.
With strangers!"

Alonzo was winning over the crowd. I could feel them
glaring at me, judging me through his words. Hortís had
turned halfway toward me, her umbrella once again balanced
on the floor cane-like and neutral. I was loosing ground. There
was a pause which I suppose I was expected to fill, but what
could I say?

"Liar," he repeated. "Everything you write is a pack of
lies. I can prove it." He was obsessed and swelling in confidence, feeding off of his ability to swing the crowd's senti-
ments. Looking around him, past his friends to the strangers
who had gathered, and even at those standing near me, those
assumed to be on my side, he put on his most appealing voice
to explain to them, "Paul chased my wife for years. But since
she chose me over him, he makes up lies about her, about us."

A security guard pushed through the crowd and stepped
between us. Sizing up the situation, he spoke directly to

Lauter and Alonzo's friend from the convention, advising them to take each of us in separate directions and make sure we stayed apart. The alternative was to bring in the police, and he gave the two of us harsh looks to underscore the threat. A couple more guards were dispersing the crowd.

Alonzo, however, wasn't quite finished. He had one last item to add in this sordid affair. As our respective groups retreated into the spaces reserved for them, Lauter and Hortís escorting me back into the hall, Alonzo yelled his last denunciation. "I don't care what you wrote in *The Diary of a Mad Housewife*, we're happy. She's never seen you again. Liar, liar."

❋   ❋   ❋

Where to begin? The assault caused little physical injury, other than a welt raised on my scalp from Alonzo's wild swing. The verbal assault was the more furious of the two, but in reality it sounded a lot like what scandal rags published about me once in a while. At least the part about pornography and even my supposed affair with Jeanne. Trash, but great for their circulation. No one, however, had raised the obvious analogies to be drawn with *The Diary of a Mad Housewife*. I confess they had never crossed my mind.

If I remember correctly, the film deals with a bright young woman, married to a supercilious bore who drives her crazy with his social climbing and paternalistic condescension. She finds a lover, a writer capable of awakening her sexually but unwilling to become emotionally involved, if it means he must make compromises in his life style. Eventually, I think, the marriage breaks up, or she breaks down, or the husband commits suicide, or perhaps they just go on in their boredom, miserable forever after. It stirred a small controversy in 1970, with its nudity and nonjudgmental depiction of adultery, and continues to draw a cult following. However, I am not the ideal person to discuss it with you because I didn't write the script and never particularly liked the film. In this case, Alonzo's accusation is accurate: It was a lie. Not mine, but a lie, nevertheless. His own culpability in creating the lie by draping *The Diary of a Mad Housewife* around Ann Marisse's image is a question for her lawyer or his confessor, but not for me or this book. I interpreted it as reinforcement of a feeling that it might be time to return home. If Alonzo's distress was any indication, the woman in his life was restless as well.

What disturbed me most, however, was his calling me a liar and my work a pack of lies. True, I had made film after film about Ann Marisse and was already writing this book that carries her name as a title, but none of it was lies.* It grated on me so much that I called Kandy's father to ask if I had grounds for a suit. He recommended the law firm to whom he had sold his copyright practice when he retired. A Ms. Whitney asked for copies of the films to prepare the case. Kandy reassured me that she has excellent credentials, a Stanford Law graduate with a Ph.D. in Literature and Film from Wisconsin. Her preliminary opinion was that we could sue for defamation of character and damage to my professional reputation. Alonzo counter sued for bodily assault and mental harassment.

❈   ❈   ❈

"Why do you want to come back?" Kandy asked, directly and aggressively when I told her I might move back to California. She needed to know what it would mean for the contracts she was working on and the network of relationships she had woven around us, Drea and me, and our home in Europe. Behind the business tone, I knew there was also concern for what it might mean for Drea and me personally.

"You're chasing a nightmare, Paul, one you couldn't live with twenty years ago. What makes you think it'll be any different now?"

---

*The publishing house exercised its right to change the title. I plan to cross out the new one and write in ANN MARISSE on every copy I can get my hands on.

"I'm tired of Europe. I want to go home."

"Don't give me that home crap. This is Kandy, remember? I know your home better than you do. Want some reminders? Reread the pages of the book you've been sending me. Planning a reunion with your father? Think he's forgiven you? Do you think it will make any difference if you come home now? She's dead, Paul."

Kandy knew she couldn't change my mind by focusing on what really concerned her, Ann Marisse, so she tried a low blow. If I didn't love Kandy I could hate her for it. I don't remember if she heard it from me or from Drea, but I guess it makes no difference. We should expect anything we tell our lovers to be used eventually against us. It's only just.

❊   ❊   ❊

Madrid, summer 1986. *Madrileños* leave in the summer. Traffic thins out and businesses cut back to a skeleton crew. Tourists often think Madrid is a slow city, with fewer people than other major capitals. They don't realize that vast numbers of city dwellers flee to the mountains to await autumn far from the stifling urban heat. If you stop looking at tourist attractions, and if the pickpockets, purse snatchers and muggers give you a moment's peace to concentrate on where you are and what is happening, you might feel like a character in one of Francesca's stories: a forlorn pilgrim trapped in a ghost town of the soul. That's Madrid in the summer: hell on earth, a joke played on masochistic tourists who thrill at being part and parcel of the Hemingwayesque Spanish spirit. Madrid: a life/death crisis. It may be all of these things and more, but the ones who suffer are the tourists who pay dearly for the privilege.

Our accommodations were located near the main drag where the night life plods noisily on until early morning hours—exactly what you don't need with pre-dawn make-up calls. The suites themselves turned out to be circa 1940s. Our first night, we pulled the mattress from an unventilated bedroom, laid it on the enormous dining room table, opened the

windows and balcony doors, and tried to pretend we were on
location in the Sahara, a cool memory in comparison. Then,
while in Segovia to scout a location, someone jimmied the locks
on an entire street full of parked cars, ours among them,
removed their contents, including floor and trunk rugs in some
cases, and departed, all under the unseeing eyes of the city
police. The embassy told us it was Spanish business as usual
since Franco's death. They recommended not going out alone or
with anything valuable. The Spanish co-producer hired thugs
to guard the equipment, but they looked more like the culprits.

In the middle of this, I received a message. My mother
had fallen and they had taken her to the hospital. She had
been tending the roses, my sister said, when her heel caught
in the grass. The fall snapped her hip. Where were the gar-
deners I sent her money for, I wondered. Every day I called
the hospital to check on her recovery from the emergency
operation. My mother was happy I was back in Spain, so I
silenced the truth, speaking instead of the imaginary beauty
of the flowers. Drea talked to her in Spanish, telling her we
would go see her as soon as the picture was wrapped up.

"Go now, Paul," Drea urged me. "We can shoot it without
you. I'll catch up as soon as we're finished."

"No. Just a few more days to make sure there aren't any
questions about the last couple scenes."

The operation went well and she was recuperating in the
hospital, her spirits rising. I talked to her attendants and
nurses, insisting on every precaution. But they took her home.
I called to protest: she was fine in the hospital; she needed
professional care.

"She'll be all right," my brother reassured me.

"Why didn't they leave her in the hospital?"

"Dad's insurance will cover just so many days."

"Fuck the insurance. I'll pay for it."

"You know how he is."

Yes, I knew how. We hadn't talked for over a decade, but I
knew. First there was the war, then films about the war. He

sent me reviews clipped from the local VFW papers denounc-
ing films I helped make and some I knew nothing about. He
made a package of photos of the patriotic celebrations of the
bicentennial to mail to me with a message, "The Real America." Then there was the photograph and message from his pil-
grimage to the Vietnam War Memorial. I knew. Money I sent
was returned or ignored; tickets for them to visit us, cashed in
at the airlines or left unused; gifts—expensive or not—were
returned because it would upset him to use them. The only
things she kept were the rings and a watch, which my brother
found later with a bankbook detailing the deposit of the money
I had sent, all labeled "return to Drea." The paint brushes, the
finest I could find, were returned after the funeral. There were
signs of recent use in traces of paint. Yes, I knew.

The day they brought her home, she confessed to me that
she was in pain because no one knew how to move her. I told
my brother to get a full-time nurse; he said the insurance
would pay for a day nurse to start the following week. I was
beside myself with anger at their acquiescence to my father's
pettiness, when it was simply a matter of leaving her in good
care and letting me pay for it. What could it matter? They
said they understood, but they wouldn't try to convince him.

We were just coming in from a day's shooting, about ten
at night, when the phone rang. It was my mother. She talked
to Drea for a moment, reassuring her everything was fine and
she looked forward to seeing us.

"Is anything wrong," I asked?

"No, *hijo*," she said. "I just want to talk to you. I haven't
told you how beautiful the roses are this year."

"But you shouldn't be out there taking care of them. Hire
a gardener. I've told you before, I'll pay for it."

"Yes, yes, this time I will. Why are you always so angry,
Pablito? It's not good for you. God didn't make us to be unhappy. You have so much. Drea, your career, your beautiful home."

"So when are you coming to see it? You can paint there."

"Your father says maybe we can afford it next year."

"I'll send you a ticket."

"No, *hijo*, but if you're not too busy, you might come and see me soon." Her voice changed, becoming a hushed, secret plea. "It scares me when they move me. It hurts and I'm afraid they're going to drop me. Your father, he's not good at these things. Maybe you could show him how."

"I'll be there tomorrow."

"Thank you, *hijo*."

If you're not too busy, she said. Drea called the studio exec. and made arrangements for me to leave the next day.

The phone woke us at one in the morning. She was dead on arrival at the hospital. I refused to return for the funeral. She was no longer there and I couldn't have tolerated their efforts to comfort each other with pieties no longer of any use to her. I would have been a stranger among them. But neither could I leave it alone. I wanted to know how it happened. A heart attack, my sister said. I demanded the medical report. Be reasonable, my brother wrote me. My father refused to send it, so I wrote the letter accusing him of. . . of still living.

I said much more, none of it capable of bringing her back and all of it amounting to the same recrimination. I was angry because he had outlived her. She had waited for the end and been beaten by the luck of the draw. I was angry because I wasn't there to help or even to do nothing but be there and watch. Perhaps I wanted to be the last image she saw. But I was too busy, and then it was too late.

Kandy did have the right to say it. We've earned it with each other. She could be cruel because she wanted to save me from losing more. However, if she was serious at all, then she had mistaken my motives. My going home had nothing to do with my mother's death. Revenge held no interest for me by then. I didn't plan to see the roses or my family. Kandy was only right about one thing. She was dead.

July 18, 1986

Dear Paul:

I am so sorry about your mother. It was a shock. She seemed so full of life, so young in spirit, so much fun. Some people forecast their death, it comes as naturally as waking up, but not your mother. I know how hard it must be for you. When my grandmother died, at least I had you to share it, to call, your note. We can't talk, but I can return your gesture of writing. Remember her face the day we planted the roses for her? She went to each one and stood for a moment. They looked so small next to her, but she was happy. Then she came back and thanked us, and I'll never forget the look on her face or the touch of her hand. You should see how they have grown. She was proud of them. She always remembered that day. She told me I could come by any time and cut some for myself. They are yours, yours and Paul's, she told me, and she often recalled your birthday and the key chain. Somehow I think she saw it as her gift as much as mine. She told me so much about her life in Mexico and when she came to California. Mostly she talked to me about your work, where you were traveling and your home in Italy. I would take her reviews of your films, and she always searched for a mention of your name. She was so proud of you and loved you so much. I'll miss her.

Ann Marisse

Not once did my mother mention having seen or talked to Ann Marisse. She must have felt torn between Drea, whom she loved and talked to on the phone more than to me, and Ann Marisse, whom, it turned out, she saw frequently. Their relationship was a mystery, as was as well my parent's relationship, before and after I left the house in a rage against my father.

My mother never spoke of her life after their wedding, those first few years in Mexico, when my brother and sister were born and before my father decided to return to the United States. And of the years before, her memories were centered around her brothers and sisters, cousins, and famous figures she knew as classmates or friends of aunts or uncles. The Mexico City of her childhood was a relatively small place, and the circle open to the girls of upperclass families was tiny. Even so, her reality turned into a fantasy world for me, fully populated by exotic figures and strange events, bedtime stories of a past devoid of a trace of my father. He appeared later, but her life seemed to have come to an abrupt halt shortly after they left Mexico. I was born into those years devoured by silence. I learned not to ask questions which might lapse her into vague denials justified with claims of failing memory. I preferred to listen instead to the detail-rich tales of children playing tag and searching for buried treasure in gardens of roses and bougainvillea, of hunger so painful when the revolutionaries cut the capital off from supplies that a ray of sun became a piece of cheese, transformed by a compensating hallucination; of adolescents trying to recover from the trauma of revolutionary chaos and still maintain a sense of class; and of early adult jobs sought and held before marriage. Yet she spoke to Ann Marisse also about those later years, the ones she kept back from me. What kind of fidelity to her husband called for a silence with me? What woman's or mother's lesson did she need to pass on to Ann Marisse that she refused to impart to me?

❀   ❀   ❀

While my mother's memories blurred to a close for me shortly after her marriage, mine began the moment I saw Ann Marisse cross the playground. I hardly ever bothered to try to reconstruct my memories before that point zero, but when my mother died I took out some old photographs to find some clues.

Another smile defined my face before Elvis, a natural smile, as spontaneous as the one paparrazis catch as I walk with Drea or address a conference. A candid shot, for sure, because I detest posed pictures, refuse to oblige when asked. Once, I searched old photos for that boy's smile, only to find my mother's mouth. That's why I recognized it easily, having seen it every day for years without realizing that it molded my own before I acquired the skill of imitation. Before Elvis. But what did I do before seventh grade? I was waiting. It seems that I did nothing but wait for life to begin. It can't be true, but it's fixed in my memory. I read ancient history, admiring the Trojans and preferring Hector over Achilles, learned Latin prayers to serve mass, performing them with intense belief until the pastor commented, "Don't take it so seriously." It distressed me for weeks. Football, yes. I shouldn't admit it, but I remember the pleasure of throwing the block—which Ann Marisse described to me two years later—and feeling a leg give way, snapping in three places. I remember pairing up with O'Brien to wade into the eighth graders when they tried to break up our game, the sound and feel of fists smashing; Sister Dolores pulling us out of class to warn us if we ever beat up her boys again we'd have to answer to her and she wasn't scared of either one or both of us. I remember the books in my father's study, especially the Fascist propaganda from Franco's Catholic Church, his navy manual on hand-to-hand combat that I tried on friends at school and another on safe sexual practices I shared as well, provoking yet another visit from Sister Dolores. Cherry Cokes at the creamery and the first wet dreams. That was sixth grade. Some time in seventh, a Japanese geisha taught me to dance the Continental to "Honky Tonk." Before her, my body lacked direction. I was thoughtless, belonging to no one, not even myself. I didn't know I was alive until she ran across the playground and made me follow her. Since then, it hasn't made more sense, perhaps, but the direction has been clear. I was drifting before Ann Marisse; I didn't do much worth remembering.

❋   ❋   ❋

Whitney, Whitney & Daughters
Attorneys At Law

April 17, 1988

Mr. Paul Valence
C.O. Hill & Hill Associates
37 Rodeo Drive
Beverly Hills, CA. 92916

Mr. Valence.

Records show that you have received a report on the favorable disposition of the defamation suit, and another addressing the question of mendacity in film, rendered moot by the courts. My sister Rebecca, who handles all real estate transactions, will contact you about the Carmel property. Below, I remit the final segment of my report containing: I. Summary critique of: 36 films, 43 collaborations, 45 episodes for television, 9 miniseries, and 1 documentary. II. Summary of personal reaction, as requested. III. Appendix: detailed commentary on each item.

I. SUMMARY CRITIQUE

Before proceeding with the critique, I will dispose of the legal questions of pornography and child molestation.
A. Pornography. Nothing in the listed materials falls under the Supreme Court's definition of pornography. However, considering recent rulings in related areas, it is possible that conservative local courts could declare some of the scenes in question pornographic. Cases in point: the child seduction from *Francesca Moore*, the depiction of sodomy in film of same title, the fellatio scenes in *Die Alte Brüke* and *Dinner at Chez Pierre*, and the poet's studio scene in *Il Ritorno* (examples not all inclusive). However, it is my opinion that none of the above scenes is legally pornographic. The matter of ethical or social standards is addressed in S.II.
B. The court could interpret the depiction of sexual acts between children as abuse of the actors who participated in the performance. However, since the scene in question was filmed in Scotland, U.S. courts lack jurisdiction. In addition, if the scene from *Francesca Moore* is placed in the context of, for example, Zeffirelli's *Romeo and Juliet*, or the recent *Blue Lagoon* remake, it falls within the socially accepted standards of sexual interaction.
In summary, I find nothing legally objectionable.
II. PERSONAL REACTION TO VIEWING THE MATERIALS
Mr. Valence requests a personal, yet professional, reaction to the viewing of his material. I began viewing the

films as an attorney, found myself analyzing them on aesthetic values, then discovered myself reacting to them as both a female and a feminist. My attempt to delineate and separate myself into distinct perspectives produced a convoluted statement of purpose and definition of each perspective. Therefore, I jettisoned the approach, opting for a unified summation of the material, which, I fear, turned into a personal essay. A desire to be free of the chaos of sentiment and emotions once led me to choose the legal profession over literary analysis.

While not legally pornographic, the sodomy scenes are morally reprehensible. Sodomy debases a woman, reducing her to a sexual object of unnatural abuse. To place in the mouth of a female character the desire to engage in the act forces the victim to assume the blame, a standard tactic of patriarchal domination. That a woman would, of her own accord, speak these lines is improbable and incredible, ultimately unbelievable in a realistic film. It turns the entire episode, and the motivation for subsequent actions by the character based on it, ludicrous.

This notwithstanding, the sodomy scenes, both the first with the friend's lover and the second with the husband, were well realized as film. The camera avoids exploitation of full body shots and details of entry. I felt that the actress undermined the script at this point, giving a convincing portrayal of emotion and suffering without resorting to visually offensive acts. The result was a sensual beauty, both attractive and sinister, more sinister because it is so attractive. Finally, *Francesca Moore* deserves credit for exposing the insidious sexual harassment tolerated at institutions of higher learning, like Yale, where the professor in question was subsequently exposed and dismissed.

However, in as much as Mr. Valence's films create a seductive image of sexual practices which are harmful to women, they are ethically unjustifiable. It is reprehensible to suggest that through perverted sexual behavior a woman can win love and affection. While the prospect of sharing forbidden actions with a lover may seem appealingly romantic, it is dangerous as a social norm and potentially disastrous to psychological integrity.

It especially appalled me to find Mr. Valence's name linked to *Nine and a Half Weeks*. While his collaboration was limited to one scene, any association with a blatant sexual-exploitation film is a dubious distinction. It imitates poorly French literary eroticism, but with none of the intellectual depth. Superficial treatment of the substantive social and philosophical questions raised by the erotic style of life is characteristic of U.S. cultural production. Yet, his career is distinguished by an admirable desire to distance himself from the U.S. film industry and to assume the European tradition. Why, then, collaborate in this U.S. imitation?

Your scene, I admit, transcends the rest of the film, which may ultimately be the signature of your career: scenes of high aesthetic value intercalated into a generally average context. Seduction through the viewing of art and the lover's imagined presence is credible. The effect can be frightening in its capacity to render a normal, rational person orgasmic. Your scene can provoke the same effect. Yet, as film writing it displays an insightful appreciation of the female psyche.

I was particularly impressed by two projects. First, your BBC production of *The Diary of Anne Frank*. You introduce inchoate attraction at an early age and subtly imply the possibility of them having shared more than a desperate kiss as the Gestapo breaks in. The scene when she tries to initiate a sexual encounter, which Peter refuses out of some misguided moral restraint, was, in the context of her fate, desolatingly moving. You infused the miniseries with a subtextual desire missing in the Hollywood film, and probably in the book itself. After watching the series, I reread the book and discovered your images where I did not remember them being fifteen or twenty years ago.

Second, your documentary with Major Colonel Susan Hollingsworth, M.D., was ground-breaking and timely. This story of female military service should have been entered into the record years before. Your rapport with the Major Colonel revealed an unexpected side of you, free of the sexual obsessions dominating your work. The unencumbered flow of conversation and eye contact creat-

ed an intimate but respectful portrait of her, showing how
well a man and a woman can relate professionally.

Finally, your films are lovely and ultimately seductive. At
first I objected to female characters being reduced to the
stereotype of love goddess or the mythical abstract
WOMAN. After repeated viewing, I realize this is not
your intention at all. By having your protagonists share
common features, you have created, not an abstract myth,
but variations of one woman. Over time she becomes
strikingly recognizable in her idiosyncrasies, such as the
touch of the finger to the man's nose or lips, the use of her
body to influence the man by merely moving it closer or
further away, the way she intellectually races to the conclusion before the man has time to work up to the end of
the proposition, the way she moves as though following
the choreography of a dance she teaches the male character to perform with her in a duet of desire. Her one fundamental preoccupation is the loss of time they could share
together. Her passion for an extraordinary life is menaced
by a society of the ordinary. I attributed much of this to
your wife's persona as an actress, until I observed the
same characteristics in actresses featured in films or
scenes in which your wife did not appear. Your wife, in
turn, has her own variations of movement and expression,
a semiotic code which distinguishes her signature from
yours, although the two are like first and last names.
Together you have created a woman I would recognize in
a restaurant if I saw her. If she corresponds to the wife of
your attacker in the previous suit, then one could almost
call his actions justifiable self defense in the face of your
unrelenting homage to his wife.

The woman's every act plays across the screen of the
man's vision, yet she also creates the possibility of his
vision by her movement. She can be the image of herself
because he is there to imagine her and watch. The key in
their game is the final turn of the head and the
exchanged glance. It is not the norm to find a man so
intensely focused on the subtleties of a woman's life.

If I were this woman, I would feel strongly bound yet free,
his stare ready to incorporate any action into my multiple
self-image. Bondage, voyeurism, life based on sexual

attraction, these are dangerous concepts, but danger holds a certain fascination, one that pervades your films.

Sincerely,
Sarah Whitney

When I showed Drea Ms. Whitney's letter, she glanced over it and said, "Of course, darling, but you've known that all along."

❋   ❋   ❋

"Why are you going back?" Francesca asked the question as well. We had walked to the terrace overlooking the mill. Above the hills beyond the lake, the air sparkled a lavender and pink tone, ice crystals suspended in refraction a moment before dissolving in the warmer temperatures rising from the earth. Pensive and preoccupied, she had spoken the question from deep within her mood.

"It's time," I responded.

"Yours or hers, Paul?"

"What do you mean?"

"You're a sensitive man capable of great insensitivity, Paul, brilliant yet stupidly blind to the obvious. You expect the world to be like you create it, without extending to others the same authority. You believe in rules, logic, sincerity, trust, fidelity in your own fashion, and love, especially love, all of which makes you admirable and desirable..."

"But?"

"Let me tell you a story. Don't look away. Nothing in this valley will save you. Everything you see is mine and in my service. It won't take long.

"An exile came upon a house so similar to his home in the mother country that he bought it, moved in and filled it with reproductions of the objects his family had owned. One day, an itinerant dealer sold him an original item made centuries before by a master craftsman of the mother land. He paid dearly because it reminded him of the piece he had seen as a child in his living room. As his wealth grew, he replaced more reproductions with originals, until he exactly duplicated the memory of what he had lost. He found a wife, had a family, made friends, entertained, took a lover, and they all passed through his house, touching the fine Chinese porcelain like he had once had in his home in the mother country, playing the hand-inlaid clavichord of his youth, drinking the best wines imported from the vineyard of his region, admiring the chapel with an original medieval triptych carved, painted and gilded by the master sculptor of his home village and the suffering Christ reputed to bleed from Good Friday to Easter yearly, the model for all the bleeding Christs of his homeland. His house invited envy and he was happy, except he wanted to see his real home again. But no exceptions to exile could be acquired. One day a woman arrived, dressed in the native costume of his homeland and speaking the native dialect of his region. When he asked for proof of her claim to cross borders freely, she displayed Christ's stigmata on her hands and said she traveled by divine right. He placed his finger in the wound and it passed through her hand. Wiping blood from his finger, he asked, 'What do you want of me?' 'Nothing,' she answered. 'It's what I can do for you.' She offered to let him see his house again. He had been so faithful to his memories, even down to the daily rosary he prayed in his native dialect, he was to be rewarded. 'Would he travel with her?' he asked. No, she would bring it to him. He accepted and she disappeared. His bloody handkerchief told him it really had happened. He set about to wait for the miracle. He prayed, but nothing. Seasons came and passed. He lapsed into a deep regret, unable to appreciate his life and home. The man's sadness discouraged visitors. At Easter, the Christ bled, yet he took no joy in it. He stopped praying, stopped drinking, stopped living. After his death, when his homeland reformed, the new government, in its zeal to reestablish its lost identity, purchased his home to bring it back to his village as a museum, the only authentic home pre-served exactly as before the revolution, with the finest original pieces from the region. They set it next to the man's old house in which visitors could see the poor imitations of the originals that were displayed in the new one, everything in exactly the same place."

"That's it?"

"Yes."

"All that to tell me Ann Marisse is no longer the woman I remember?"

"No, to tell you the real Ann Marisse is here already. Why do you hate my writing, Paul?"

"I don't hate it. I just don't see why you hide it under mystic fantasy. I deal with reality."

"In celluloid."

"Okay, images of the real."

"You make images real. You seduce people into becoming the image you hold up for them. You believe in magic as much as I do. More, because you insist it's reality. So why turn your back on the reality you have created? We all love you. You and your obsession. Somehow it's the center of all of this, an invisible center you place in everything you write. You seduce us through the intensity of your desire and your pigheaded, single-minded vision of love. What you can't see is what you created, your life, ours, Jeanne's. Look out there, look at the ice making love to the hills. Where do they touch, where is the act? Is it real? Am I real to you or did you create me? Or did I create you? Isn't our mutual creation real?"

"I don't understand."

"We love you, Paul. Jeanne, Alex, me. If you wanted to get away, or to just leave Drea, you could come here with us. But I know it's not that."

"I'll be back. I promise."

"You're only good at promises you want to keep, Paul. I still have a couple outstanding."

"This one I want to keep. I'll be back."

"It took so long to conjure you up, and now you're leaving. Time is an unforgiving labyrinth whirling around death."

She kissed me on the cheek, took my arm, and we walked back into the house where Jeanne waited with tea and Scottish shortbreads. She showed me a picture of her new boyfriend, but complained of his naiveté. Out of the corner of her eye she looked at her mother to see the effect of her words, but Francesca betrayed no sign of agitation. Jeanne's adolescence, she had decided years before, would be left to her own invention. She instructed her in birth control and told her to make her life as happy as she could, because in the end it's the only one she would remember, even if she lived many more. Jeanne accompanied us to the front door, kissed me goodbye, and told Francesca she would wait in the library.

We walked out to where Danillo waited to drive me back to Rovereto. Francesca told me I could have him for the whole trip if I preferred, and I accepted. The car's plush comfort and driver's silence would allow me to relax and think about Francesca's story, free of ghosts who haunt the train lines. I kissed her goodbye and turned to leave.

"Paul, if you must go, be careful. There are death signs in the cards."

❉   ❉   ❉

May 10, 1988

Dear Mr. Valence:

Rebecca advises me that the Carmel property is fully secured, albeit at a higher sum than we projected. I fly up the coast weekly and have been checking on the house. Restoration is progressing on schedule. Be sure to let me know when you will arrive.

Sarah Whitney

❉   ❉   ❉

"You want to go back, darling?"
"Yes, Drea, I think so."

"You think so or you've already made up your mind? Is this something we're discussing or a *fait accompli*?"

I reserved my answer for a moment. Her question tested my resolve, forcing me to decide for the both of us, which I have never liked to do, preferring to let things just seem to happen.

"I want to go back, but it's not an ultimatum. We can talk about it."

"Darling, I've wanted to return several times, but you had your reasons for staying in Europe. No complaint, we have a good life here, but we can have more than one base."

"True. We can keep this house."

"I wouldn't sell it even if you wanted to. I love this house."

She got up and walked to the large picture window overlooking the valley. Spring usually comes late to the Tyrol mountains, but this year the first flowers would bloom well before May. She stood with one hand on her hip and the other on the upper frame of the window, her body half-turned towards me, yet looking out, her blonde hair radiant in the spring light. Suede boots sheathed her calves. The shorter fashions of the recent years allowed her to display her legs high above the knees to where the hem of a tan suede skirt circled her mid thighs. A loose-fitting natural silk blouse with long sleeves filtered the light and revealed the outline of her body under the cloth, the slim youthful lines, her firm breasts, nipples erect under the fabric. She placed herself on display, like a memory of the late 1960s.

"It's hard to believe we've been in Europe almost twenty years. Remember when we planned the decade? Kandy would arrange the films for both of us and I'd become a star playing the parts you wrote for me."

"We did it."

"Did it take longer than we thought, or have we just enjoyed ourselves too much to give it up?"

"I took longer. You were a star from the beginning."

"You know I can't go right away."

"Yes, but I can wait if you want."

"No, you have things to do before I arrive."

"Drea..."

"Darling, I've memorized so many of your dialogs, but I can't find any for the character you want me to be in this situation, because, frankly, I'm not sure which role you're playing. I've known from the start someone else was living with us, but you've never been one to talk about your past. It's all there in the films, I suppose. Your mother warned me you were quiet, more expressive with things than with people. I couldn't understand it, because I had read your treatments and scripts, but your mother knew you well. You never ask me about my past, so I accepted your game: we would learn who we were by being whatever we wanted to be together. Besides, we had Kandy to relay messages whenever we needed to bypass the rules. The only time you're really open is when you talk about film, and that's because it lets you talk about yourself through other characters. We can relate through every image ever held in a frame. You mention a scene from *The Barefoot Contessa* or a line in *Summer Place* and I know where we are and what you want to say."

"Do you?"

"Yes, darling, I do. It's a world of ghosts we share. I don't mind, really. Would you have me cut Sandra Dee out of each frame or Ann Marisse out of your mind? Then reshoot all the scenes in your memory with me in the starring role? I don't have to. You've given me the chance over and over, and there they are."

She nodded her head in the direction of the video tapes in the book case behind me, the collection of our films.

"The images of our life. Can I say our love? That's another thing I liked about you from the start. You could say the word love in public without apologizing for it. Of course, it was the '60s when many of us could, but you've clung to it longer than most. After a while it stopped bothering me that you thought of her when you said the word, because she became the image we created more than a real memory. The more we worked together, the more we remembered the women in love with the men who watched them, and they were all you and I, no matter what name they called each other. With the poet in *Il Ritorno*, I was coming back to you. Remember the rave reviews about my love scene: such a convincing performance. What acting? I made love to you, in that dark spot you dug out of yourself and rebuilt on the set, then sent me into to make love to you. Poor Charles, I don't think anyone had prepared him for so much realism. Have you noticed how he's avoided working with us since?"

"Too bad. It was the high point of his career."

"You could say that."

She turned to face me, crossing her arms under her breasts, leaning her weight on one leg, then bringing one hand up to touch her lips with her fingers, as though considering her next words.

"We've built a good life. I know you love me in our own convoluted and multi-channeled way. For a private person, you have introduced a lot of people into this love affair of ours. It's like the cast of our private film, working out the master plot as you envision it in your mind. Sort of a family."

She moved to her left directly between a brilliant ray of sun and me. She spoke from the shadow of her figure profiled against the sunlight reflecting in a clear mountain sky.

"But Paul, I want my own family. We agreed, without stating it anywhere along the line, that children would have to wait. Well, I can't wait any longer. I'll be forty soon and it already may be too late, although over here they don't seem to think so. We don't need any more security. I can take as much time out as I want, and you, well, I think you could work through a hurricane. I want to have a child. Two. It sounds horribly bourgeois, but I was an only child and I just want two. So I see no reason to wait...except one. You."

"I..."

"You have your book to finish, and Kandy tells me you're not sure how it's going to end. I want you to find out, because I can't wait much longer. So will you go and get it over with before I turn into a bitter old woman? If it works out, I'll join you there for a few weeks before the season starts in July. We can celebrate your first birthday in Carmel."

We made love gently, perversely taking our time, working through a new image being added to our repertoire of possibilities. It was the beginning of a goodbye before my trip, the outcome of which neither one of us could predict.

May 25, 1988

Paul,

Rumor has it that you're planning a trip, so I won't try to change your mind. Long ago I learned how pigheaded you can be, so let me talk business. This book you're preparing is not some sacrificial lamb. The public could give a shit about you or your life. Still there? Don't close up, you bastard, read the rest.

Your novel is about wanting rather than having. I'm glad, because all good novels are about the writer's desire. But I crave a semi-humorous ending: they meet thirty years later and she's ballooned to 200 pounds, or she's a secretary, fuckin' brainless, rude, efficient but vulgar. It happens. A month ago my first husband dropped by—remember the publisher? He's slimmed down, he says, so now he looks only six months pregnant instead of nine. Thank you, God, for putting me here and him elsewhere. But if I loved him back then, would it matter? Probably not, and that's fuckin' dangerous, because it should. Why? Because I'm selfish, as are all artists—you included, perhaps more than any of us. It's just the way it has to be.

So perhaps your other Paul—please consider changing the name—sees her and realizes that all his life he's chosen the right person. Not his wife or his agent or his lover, but himself. His selfishness lets him make ideal films for an audience of one, the perfect dream of a woman who couldn't have been so perfect had she actually been there. Had she lived with him, she would have fucked it up. That's what humans do who can't stop the film to rest off camera. And Paul would have had to stay in her mediocrity. Most critical, though, would be the lack of those films Paul never would have made. I remember you half-drunk, telling Coppola how every artist needs an idealized person for whom to create an ideal art. It's another way of reaching for perfection, yet maintaining the wanting, the desire. Once you get what you want, desire disappears and so does the reaching to grasp for perfection. Remember when I tried to tell you this years ago? Well, you found out for yourself. Look what you've done since. Point taken? But don't think I'm resting my case.

You've fixated on Top 40 Golden Oldies, but you used to listen to more back then. You drove me crazy with Dylan's "Blood on the Tracks" album, his pining for his lost Joan Baez. The hypocrite could have been with her anytime he wanted, but he knew better. Missing her produced great songs, while being with her would have only given him pleasure. Their separation pierced him to the heart, but that's where she still lives, so they've never been apart. Sound familiar? But you can't say it if she's there, and if you don't say it, who will know? Not even she. And remember the one about coming in from the void to the comfort of a good woman, his shelter from the storm, the woman who could relieve him of his crown of thorns? What is Dylan without the thorns? Exactly what he's become, a pathetic parody of himself. Does Paul want to lose his crown of thorns to live safe from the storm? I think not. It's your style, you wear the crown over your heart like a badge of nobility and the storm in your eyes like constant seduction. Who would you be without them?

In the end, what do we make our own? The lover? Love? No, just work. The biggest mistake would be to bog down in sweet contentment. Get happy, Paul, and your work will be shit. It happened before—remember, you're so good at it. Your characters in this misguided novel haven't fallen permanently into each other's arms as much as they would like, but that's exactly why their story can be written. You're so damn smart, can't you see it? What the hell do you think they're all about? Petrarch, Shakespeare, Anne Frank, Elvis, the Beatles, you? Desire and absence. The rest is shit. You want "Paul" to keep making films, don't you? He won't if he gets the girl. Leave him alone. He knows better. So should you. End of lecture? Not quite.

Another scenario: Paul gets the girl, but leaves her when he realizes that by habit, the habit of departure from non-ideal women, he's become a stranger. Maybe he leaves because she blocks his work; maybe that's why she left him in the first place. What's so fuckin' scary, terrifying, is when we leave ourselves behind—love always forces us to do that. Maybe his perfect woman commits suicide when she realizes her Paul is sacrificing his creative edge to live with her. Maybe she leaves because what she really loves in him is her image on the screen, the one he creates of her as she wants to be and can never be again, the image that ages and dies when he brings it to his bed every night. Have you thought that perhaps your Ann Marisse feels most alive when she watches herself as your ideal—Paul's ideal? How fuckin' confusing you've made things, my whole life, damn you. If they get back together, she might fade like those old photographs until she's a cloudy blur, a ghost. Have you thought about that, Paul? What the fuck are you going to say the next time you walk out on her? How many times do you think a woman, any woman, can survive your putting the knife to her throat? Is it for real this time, or is Paul sailing back to his Summer Place to test the old appeal? But while you cultivate memory, she's probably nursing forgetfulness. The bitch will take you back again, but what will you do when she finds the stranger waiting in your eyes? We all get old, Paul, but some things don't change.

Myself, I'd settle for a sense of humor these days. Funerals and feminist art and rap music and the death of too many friends...I don't want to hear one more dead name. I need to see you soon and forget for a while. Can your blood still pace my lips? Are you still a good lay? Am I? I'm so glad you finally decided to write a book. I was wondering how you were going to live without it. I'm happy you're writing, really, but keep it a novel. True autobiographies end only in death.

Love, Kandy.

p.s. Maybe Paul gets a letter from Ann Marisse telling him that all this time he's just imagined her and that since he's successful now he no longer needs the illusion, and the only evidence of her is this real letter from an imagined ghost, the novel as a long letter. Maybe she wrote the whole thing. No, forget it; much too modern novel!

Kandy is right about one thing, this book seems to want to become one long letter from characters who demand their point of view. Democracy is no way to run an autobiography.

❋   ❋   ❋

Before I left for California, Kandy asked me to do her a favor. She had been trying to contact Max Frisch, the Swiss novelist often mentioned as a Nobel candidate, to secure his permission to adapt one of his novels. Surkamp, his publisher, referred her directly to him, but Frisch hadn't answered her letters. Getting through to him on the phone was impossible, since his family and secretary guard his privacy with the ferocious zeal of Dobermans off leash. Kandy knew I had met him on the set of the German production of his *Homo Faber*, which Wolfgang directed. Frish is a stern old gentleman, given to reminiscing about his life with harsh, nostalgia-free objectivity. We didn't become friends or anything of the sort, but we were communicating on a last-name basis by the end of the week I visited the set.

Wolfgang provided Frisch's number and divulged that he receives calls only between 3:15 and 3:45 in the afternoon. The rest of the day he devotes to writing, reading, and visiting with his family and close friends. I phoned, fully expecting to be put off as an intruder on the open time reserved for important calls. When Frisch himself answered with characteristically Swiss abruptness, it took me by surprise, which he must have discerned in my voice.

"Yes, yes, Valence, I'm here. I am not dead yet, no matter what the critics report."

"Frisch, I wanted to talk to you about your novel *Mautuck.*"

"I called it a novel only because publishing it as a memoir struck me as presumptuous. A beautiful young woman she was, Valence, and as surprising to me as I tried to convey in the book. A man my age, even twenty years ago, does not deserve such good fortune."

"Frisch, a close friend of mine is interested in a film adaptation. If she can negotiate a contract with you, I would do the script, with your approval, of course."

"No, I don't approve at all."

"May I send you a treatment before you make up..."

"Have you read the novel, Valence?"

"Yes, of course. I've read all your work."

"Then you should know it's impossible. You remember the story?"

"Yes."

"Then you must not know your trade, Valence. It is nothing more nor less than an affair between an old man, of little import other than having his novels in translation, and a beautiful young woman who should know better than to get involved with him. They eat, they fuck, they drive up the coast and take a walk. Nothing more."

"Yes, a simple story, but so well-balanced and structured."

"That's the writing, man, not the story. What could you do with it in film? An old man bedding a woman in her twenties is fine on paper, where you see none of the wrinkles, the tired flesh, the blotched skin. On the screen it would become an obscenity, an unspeakable crime to ask an actress to play the role. A *Last Tango in Paris* without the redeeming parody. And if you take years off the man's life, say down to thirty five, even forty, it destroys the story, undermining the narrator's self-critical irony. The magic of the encounter springs from the great disparity in age as he imagines it. No. In America even less, with your insane obsession with youth. Absolutely not."

"You won't reconsider, Frisch?"

"Read one of my other novels."

"I've read them all."

"Well, read them again."

On that recommendation Frisch hung up. Kandy did receive a reply a few days before I arrived in Los Angeles expressing the same succinct opinion.

❋   ❋   ❋

Although I was about to turn forty-four when I arrived in Los Angeles, I felt somewhat like Frisch's protagonist, older than he really was, as if the years of residing in Europe had gathered on me like weighty moss, leaving me aged with the tradition and history I had come to view almost with European eyes. I had grown accustomed to buying my bread from a Tyrolese baker whose earthen oven had fed French invaders in the sixteenth century, and to staying in the homes of friends whose families trace their presence in the buildings back to the Middle Ages. More than this, however, I carried the baggage of a pending decision, one I had postponed for over twenty years, delaying it into a life's preoccupation—all right, an obsession.

In 1966, I delayed making a decision and found myself swept into indecision which, with the authority of years, threatened to solidify into my epitaph. In choosing not to choose, I had removed myself from the role Ann Marisse had ceded me, that of controlling the choice. But I thought we would always have time, that eventually our lives would tumble back into alignment within the kaleidoscope of our relationship along the lines of the sharply etched design both of us assumed to be understood and accepted by all concerned—or at least I assumed. Once again, time and people moved ahead as I watched and waited from a distance, unprepared to take by force of possession one path—to keep me in the same space, same neighborhood, same way of life—if it required the abandonment of another. I believed that nothing could alter the essential pairing of our lives. It was simply a matter of time until I had accomplished enough, accumulated enough, proved enough...forgotten enough. Then from the solidity of my position I would reach out and fine tune our picture back into focus. I never counted on the sheer weight of habit depositing its debris around our feet to fix us in an identity we never consciously selected. Back then, however, it was easier to turn the decision-making over to Kandy and wait for things to blow over and readjust. Two and half decades later—with the forms still tumbling within the scope of possibilities, still unsettled because I had refused to accept the finality of an arbitrary character and kept the mirrors turning—when time seemed ready to venture another swing to view the facets of choice profiled against the sun, Kandy received me back again.

❋   ❋   ❋

"This setup is overwhelming, Kandy. I didn't know our commissions could keep you in such opulence. The New York office is a garret in comparison."

Kandy had met me at the airport and driven me directly to her office. The bronze-tinted windows of the penthouse sweeping the length of the wall behind her black and mahogany Italian neo-futurist desk cast an aura of technocelestial magnificence over the setting, like an ultra-contemporary version of St. Peter's reception hall.

"Business could be better, but who's complaining? Did you read my letter?"

"I dutifully read everything you send me."

"You might have answered. I love sending earnest pleas for sanity into the fuckin' void. But I see it's done no good."

"There wasn't time. So, I'm back."

"You've always had a weakness for the obvious."

"You know what I mean."

"No, I'm not sure what it means. Do you? What's your plan?"

"I haven't mapped one out yet, at least not in detail."

"Could it be any other way? Let me tell you then. I heard it some, what?, twenty-five years ago? My age has doubled since, and you're not far behind. I asked you the same question and you answered, see her. You still don't have a better plan, do you?"

"No. In fact, back then I had our meeting arranged. Now I don't have even that."

"Do you want me to..."

"No, thanks. I don't know what's going to happen, and although Drea isn't a woman to hold grudges, if worse comes to worse, I don't want you to have to say you helped me. She loves you, too."

"Too?"

"Ah, the ambiguities of dialog. The audience is supposed to pose those questions, not have them asked by characters. Yes, too. I know you abhor the word, but now that you're twice the age, and I am passing you quicker than you realize in my sedentary life style, don't you think it's time we quit being so cynical? We're a pair, a threesome. We've loved each other for almost thirty years and we still fear the word. If Orwell was right, Big Brother has reserved for you a torture-chamber sound booth repeating one word: Love."

"In your voice."

"Or Drea's."

"Or Ann Marisse's?"

"I'm not sure I still hear it clearly, or if it's Drea speaking her words. Can't be your voice, you never said it. When I try to figure it out, the words blur: mine, hers..."

"Well, lover, you can stay at my place as long as you like and work on my vocabulary. Father is looking forward to seeing you again. Physically, he's not strong, but his mind and memory are sharp. And I'd like to have a few days with you to myself."

From the flat tone in her words, into which she normally would have infused a melody of playfulness, I could tell she meant the offer seriously.

"It's tempting."

"But you have business to take care of?"

"For now, yes. I want to go to see if the house is ready. They've been restoring it."

"I know. Sarah keeps me informed of everything."

"She, too? You brought Ms. Whitney into the loop. Kandy, you're a meddlesome lover."

"How else can I know what my prize property is doing? I trust you, but you're not the most forthcoming man. Actually, she should be waiting outside. I told her you were arriving today. You haven't met?"

"No."

Kandy pressed a button on her desk and instructed the secretary to show Ms. Whitney in.

To his credit, Frisch captured with precision the surprise one feels at discovering a young and attractive woman's interest in you, in spite of your age—the sense of undeserved good fortune. Sporting a Ph.D plus a law degree, Sarah had assumed in my mind the image of a woman my own age, or in her late thirties at best. Later she admitted to having just turned thirty-one, but she had that California air of youth and good health that belies trivial chronologies. She walked into Kandy's office, shook my hand, and took charge of me with the strength and agility of a youthful master of the art of taking control of lives in crisis. As she spoke to Kandy, I tried to picture her in court, a business suit instead of the silk dress which now softened the lines of her trim body, her strawberry blonde hair gathered close to her head to avoid the sensual feminine impression she conveyed with it combed in the flared, lion's-mane style of the day. She wore almost no jewelry, except for a gold bracelet and a thin wedding band.

Jet lag doesn't affect me greatly, but Kandy and Sarah had pressured me to rest before continuing the trip. Also, there were papers to sign on the house and a couple of meetings with producers that couldn't be postponed. The house had waited all this time; it would not disappear in two nights.

My bags had been taken to Kandy's, but Sarah drove me to her office first. If they wouldn't allow me to travel to the house immediately, at least I wanted to see the photos of the restoration work, so we went to pick them up. As she gathered the materials, I examined the video tapes neatly aligned on the bookcases across from her desk, copies of the material I had provided her for the suit. From her desk she pressed a remote and a panel slid back exposing a fifty-inch monitor.

"Don't take all the credit. I use it for many cases."

"It's better than mine back home."

"But not as good as your new one."

"Which?"

"I had it installed in the study. The previous owners had remodeled the room, so it would have been almost impossible to restore it exactly according to Wright's plans, which he redrew twice anyway, did you know? I think you'll appreciate the results, a virtual projection room. How could you survive without films? I can't imagine you not watching them. You do watch films, don't you?"

Right then I was watching her intently as she placed a tray of slides and a videotape into her briefcase and then held a rolled-up set of architectural designs out to me to carry.

After dinner, Mr. Hill ordered the butler to set up the slides and the video in his private projection room. On the large screen, the house on the beach flashed magnificent, profiled against the sky and sea like a grand ocean liner, the sweeping line of its outer wall, which first attracts the eye at the approach to the driveway, stretching itself into a massive ship's-prow terrace thrust high over the ultramarine waters of Carmel Bay. An emerald-green metal roof floats its gradual, tiered incline above a contrasting red soffit and long horizontal rows of glass. Two chimneys create the impression of dual smokestacks, crowning the ocean-liner effect.

From the beach perspective, the structure rises from a finger of rock pointing northwest, far into the bay. The sharply chiselled, tan-colored stone foundation seems to cut a path through the foaming breakers that rhythmically shatter on the wave-gnarled rocks that extend southward along the shore from the base of the promontory like a colony of petri-fied Triceratops beached headfirst in the sand, their spiked tails trailing out into the water. On the tape, the rise and ebb of the waves created the illusion of movement, swishing the rocky tails through the water.

Water lily-like pads of granite float on the gravel surface of the terrace leading to the double glass doors of the front entrance. Inside, the brown hues of polished wood flow unbro-ken in all directions, outlining the vast spaces of the glass outer walls, tiered as well to reprise the wave motif and the massive central fireplace constructed of the foundation's same tan stone. The nautical theme continues in the built-in furni-ture, the economy of detail and the way the glass walls of the dining room form a sharp angle to create the impression of a captain's bridge directly in line with the terrace's bow-tip visi-ble several yards beyond. The horizontal rows of windows, stepped out like inverted pyramids beneath the roof's can-tilevered overhang and forming four sides of the pentagonal dining niche, fracture the reflections off the water into a kalei-doscope of prismatic colors. Looking out from the dining room through the video's eye, with the lines of waves advancing against the terrace's prow, I felt an almost physical sensation of sitting in a ship steaming seaward.

Shortly before he died in 1959, Wright had refashioned the original gallery of bedrooms that lay behind the fireplace into a library study that looked out through its own prow of windows and glass doors to another terrace with vistas of the bay, the city and beyond to Pebble Beach. Bedrooms were added on a lower floor hewn out of the rock foundation, with windows and a shared, terraced pathway looking out to the sea. Except for the uncharacteristically large bedrooms, the style was classic Frank Lloyd Wright.

"How did you know about it?" Kandy's father asked.

"I did location research on it when you got me started at Universal. Luck and Sarah's firm did the rest."

"The state helped when I promised you would restore it as closely as possible to the original designs. The caretaker was delighted. His father still had the original keys with Wright's initials on them." Sarah laid the keys in my hand. While we watched video of the beach, I slipped the set onto the ring dangling from a silver-encased crystal bubble.

"What do you plan to do with it, Paul? It's rather far out of the way," Kandy's father said.

"No difficult questions, father, he's not ready for the answers," Kandy told him, then walked him up to his room. When she returned, she took her leave of Sarah and kissed me good night. Sarah stayed.

When Sarah and I left for Carmel the second morning after my return to California, I promised Kandy to take a whole day just for her when I came back. She made me repeat it in front of Sarah. You're my witness, Kandy said to her. This time she kissed us both before we left.

We flew up the coast to Monterey in a private plane Sarah piloted herself to avoid the inconvenience of public transport. The caretaker picked us up at the airport and drove us over to Carmel and out to the beach. I gave him and his wife two weeks off before I would return from Los Angeles to move in. He told me I could reach him in town via the radio in the study, since Ms. Whitney had not renewed the phone service. Sarah had respected my unvoiced wishes.

❀   ❀   ❀

Watching the white, foaming waves explode against the rocks and dissolve high in the air, Frisch's summary of his novel kept coming back to me. They met, they ate, they made love, they traveled up the coast and took a walk. It says it all, but not really, not accurately. It's in the telling of the action where art lies, not the action itself. Life is not inherently interesting; the artist makes it so, and Sarah worked her project like an inspired artist. My dilemma as I'm writing it now places me between granting her the space in the text she merits—which could expand voraciously if left on its own—or skipping over her to maintain the narrative flow. Could I merely reference Frisch's summary to explain our day together? A different coast, different lovers not so obscenely mismatched, different food, of course, and a walk which resembled his in no detail except the proximity of an ocean, although such a different one at that. We walked along a beach of pulverized stones deposited over centuries, fossilized rocks which Robinson Jeffers considered more essential and lasting than human kind— in all likelihood a correct evaluation. The presence of a threatening, northern sea, with its dense banks of fog, creates the necessary mood for such contemplation, unlike the inviting southern waters and clear skies of Malibu. But essentially speaking, Frish was right on target.

The first day, we had strolled along the beach hand in hand, like old friends. Now, as I watched the sea from the balcony, three days after arriving in California, Sarah walked into view far up the beach, a solitary figure in white pants and a blue windbreaker, her hair blowing over her left shoulder, her hands deep in her pockets and head bowed. My heart went out to her with an affection as wide as the vista, yet also as turbulent as the waves against the rocks. I knew she must be feeling hurt from the night before, but there was little I could do about it.

Now, as Sarah approached the beach below the terrace, the scene from the night before replayed in my memory. She had stocked the kitchen with everything necessary for a fabulous inaugural dinner, but she confessed to not knowing how to cook, so we prepared it together. Later, we sat for a long time in the glass niche of the dining room, talking and sipping

champagne as if toasting the outset of a voyage about to weigh
anchor and cruise into an uncharted, starry night.

"Sarah, I want to tell you how grateful I am to you for
making this possible for me."

"Repayment for the pleasure you've given me. I didn't
realize how much I missed thinking in terms of creativity till I
worked on your films."

"Also for the last few days."

"Don't. It's nothing we have to thank each other for."

She kissed me and we began to fall into familiar, albeit
still new patterns of finding each other. But then I stopped.

"Is something wrong, Paul?"

"No, but I think we should stop."

"Why? Are you sorry we started?"

"No, not at all. I just didn't expect this. I wasn't prepared.
Actually, it's that here, in this house, I want things to be different."

"You mean reserved for the real thing? For someone else?"

"Something like that. I just would rather stop."

She slept in one of the guest rooms, and in the morning,
when I came down, she had already gone out for a walk. Now
she was sitting on the water-sculptured outcropping of rocks
on the beach below the house, her legs drawn up in front of
her and hands clasped in front of her knees.

"Hi. Can I join you?"

"Sure," she said without looking up. "It's your beach, as
far as the state law lets you use it. The ocean is moody this
morning."

"Isn't it always rough this far north?"

"Not this bad. There's a storm brewing."

"You're a sailor, too? You can read the sea?"

"No, but I can listen to the radio. A light weather front
with small craft warnings. The edge moved in last night, if
you ask me. I hope it passes quickly."

She finally looked over at me.

"Sarah, can we talk?"

"It's not necessary, Paul. I'm over thirty and old enough to take affairs lightly. I learned from my ex-husband. Don't worry about it."

"Sarah, I'm working on forty-five and I'm still not old enough to take things that lightly. Please let me explain."

"If you must."

"For over thirty years I've thought of living with one person, with one woman."

"I know her well."

"Yes, Sarah, you do, but this isn't a competition. I'm not even sure if I play any role in her plans. It's been a long time. Even if she doesn't want me now, I'd like this house, this place, still to be special, something extraordinary, cut off from my past of ambiguous relationships. You'll probably think this sounds foolishly romantic, but I would like to have a space of love. With one person. So until that one person is clear in my mind, I don't want to make any false starts that might fill the house with echoes. Already your presence is here in a generous way no one could object to. Can you give me a little time to clear my head? You've happened to me so fast I'm not sure where I'm going."

"I am."

"Where?"

"Back to L.A. You've seen what you need to see here. I want you in my space with no restrictions or excuses. But, Paul, you're wrong. This has been a competition from the start, in many more ways than you know, and none of us likes to lose."

A storm did blow in, stronger than predicted, keeping us there another two days. Sarah hadn't been flying long, and the prospect of maneuvering a light plane in the strong costal air currents made us both nervous. We delayed our departure forty-eight hours, which we spent viewing old films—not mine—reading, and watching the storm perform for us. We relaxed comfortably in our nearness, although I confess that finding her so close, our arms or hands touching at times, sitting on the sofa watching films or the fire, an arm around her shoulders, or just sharing a bottle of wine, seemed so right that not making love became an absurdity. The storm never let up, at times threatening the house itself with crashing swells pulverizing themselves against the prowed terrace. The rocks below, although battered mercilessly, weathered the two days with no sign of major damage. The lay of the sand and pebble drifts, however, altered considerably, giving the beach a new appearance of dunes piled in successively larger rises out towards the sea, then falling off into a smoothly swept border running the length of the beach. When the morning of the fifth day cleared, it left an infinite horizon unlike any European vista, the sky a medium blue with as much height as depth, giving the impression of profundity where the Mediterranean sky always appears to lay itself thin, flat, like a veil so close you could pierce it with a strongly hurled stone. This was different, vaster and less accessible.

It took only those few days to learn that the house, while comfortable and amenable to human use, remains more faithful to nature than to man, taking its form and spirit from the surroundings. It would never permit me to survey the horizon from the terrace and declare, as Francesca can of her lake and hills, that everything within my vision is at my service. My new home has ways of reminding me that I am, at best, another caretaker lucky enough to be chosen to serve its purpose. Yet, it is also in the house's nature to offer something in return: a haven, distant and different and unpredictably beautiful.

❋   ❋   ❋

When Sarah dropped me off at Kandy's, there was a message for me to call her office as soon as I came in. Something in my lungs reacted like the time she called about the Kundera failure.

"What's wrong, Kandy? Drea?"

"No. Alonzo Monte is dead. I know you told me not to, but I made inquiries. It seems he'd been in the hospital for months. If you had returned last week, you could have seen him."

"It's okay, I didn't want to see him. We had nothing left to say to each other. Do you think he knew I'm here?"

"Maybe, if he read the *Times*. They published a picture of you and Drea announcing your move back to Hollywood. I don't know who leaked it, because nothing came from this office."

Dead. I had wanted to see him dead more than once; I had tried to kill him at least twice at football practice. He, in turn, might have killed me in Hartford a few years back if friends on both sides hadn't intervened. Actually dead, however, was more than I expected or had hoped for. Yet as much as I might try—admittedly little—I couldn't feel it; inside me nothing happened that could be associated with sadness or regret. If I had arrived in time to see him, what kind of conversation would have been possible? Alonzo, old friend, I'm here to gloat over your bad luck and reclaim Ann Marisse. Would he have turned generous and, like John Fowles' dying man, ask an old rival to take care of his wife? People once thought we were best friends. That could be, but every time I've tried to remember him that way, I find nothing but the image of Ann Marisse in his arms. No, neither one of us would have forgiven the other, even in the face of death.

What I found out later about his months of illness confirms to me the fruitlessness of any effort at reconciliation near the end. Death brought out how intolerable, how brutish, in short, how much a son of a bitch hid behind Alonzo's congenial mask, the one everybody else mistook for his real face. Instead of dying quietly, calm and brave, dispersing some last words of wisdom—like Gary Cooper entreating Bergman to go on for both their sakes before sacrificing himself for the cause in Civil-War Spain—Alonzo shouted curses and moaned insults, first against a deceiving God in whom I'm sure he never believed, and then at Ann Marisse. From his hospital

bed, Alonzo reproached her for the sons he would have wanted
to leave behind to assure she remained the grieving widow, for
the money she would enjoy without him, and, finally, for her
beauty and perpetual youth he considered the ultimate proofs
of a vendetta he claimed she had plotted against him from the
start. Moreover, he had the bad taste to die slowly, hanging on
much longer than the most optimistic doctors had dared speculate. Persistent to the end. Just three things salvaged his
miserable existence: if not a good death, certainly a marvelous
funeral; the incredible luck to have married Ann Marisse; and
that, all things considered, I didn't kill him sooner.

※　※　※

"Bone cancer," Dick told me, responding to a question I
hadn't posed. "Remember when he was hospitalized for it
before they got married? But we thought they caught it. He
always had that limp when he walked, even in grade school."

The funeral was scheduled for the next day. Dick thanked
me for coming such a long way for it, speaking both as a rela-
tive and long-time friend. I didn't try to correct the false
impression. In the end, we didn't talk long.

※　※　※

Skipping the mass, I borrowed Kandy's car and drove
straight to the cemetery. A large, somber crowd was filing into
a chapel that had not existed when I worked there in the early
'60s. Striving to convey a Christian ambiance without restrict-
ing the denomination, it was constructed as a modern, round
structure of smoked-glass walls, with a black-marble floor
which threatened to absorb you if you looked down too long,
and a sky-blue ceiling of indefinable height, translucent like
onyx—and in the center awaited the casket. Over the casket
floated high an enormous, plexiglass, Christless cross suspended by invisible means. Higher still, a halo of recessed
spotlights illuminated a circle around the casket, the spots

reflecting softly in the thirsty black floor. To one side a row of empty chairs awaited, reserved for the family.

I drifted forward through the people, exchanging a hushed greeting every so often with old school friends or forgotten acquaintances who all seemed to remember my name. I took up a place among those standing directly in front of the chairs and waited.

Ann Marisse entered, easily distinguished from Marianne and other black-clad women by the elegant and simple design of her dress. The half-veil covering her eyes provided, at the risk of appearing camp, the perfect dramatic touch. The total effect: stunning. Awe-inspiring, devastating, she captured the audience's attention, only to lend it lightly back with a glance towards the casket, from under the veil. But there were no tears in Ann Marisse's eyes. Her concern seemed to be solely for her mother-in-law, whose arm she supported in consolation as they entered.

I was relieved to see no children near her.

After the family members had been seated, a silver-headed priest appeared and began to recite a monologue which he probably had repeated hundreds of times in his career. Shortly after he started, Ann Marisse began to scan the crowd unobtrusively from under her veil. I didn't know if Dick had mentioned to her that he had talked to me, but considering his straightforward manner and courageous disregard for the fierce tensions binding and dividing what had once been two teenage couples, he probably had. Her head moved until she caught sight of me, then she diverted her eyes—not to the casket, no, but rather to herself, as if to inspect her dress or body; perhaps it was to her hands resting palms up, one cradled in the other on her lap. Then, without further hesitation, she raised her veil, reestablished eye contact and maintained it, returning my stare to link the poles of the axis of vision. Time swung back through memory to fix itself into an old pattern, jolting the present off its foundations as it swept into an altered rhythm. The old priest became nonplused, losing the thread of his talk; he extemporized to regain his composure, repeating himself and even commenting on the repetitions. Dick encircled Marianne's shoulders with a firm, restraining arm, and Alonzo's mother resorted to her pathetic whimpering. A whisper of apprehension set heads turning among the crowd, eyes searching discretely for the source of distress in the deceased's family. Yet decorum held sway, that is, except over Ann Marisse. She went on staring, as she had in the hospital room nearly twenty years before, in the outdoor theater five years before that, and at dances in high school and on the grade school playground before I can begin to remember starting to live.

The floundering sermon halted abruptly, punctuating itself in a final blessing and farewell fitfully thrown over the nervous crowd. A slow ebbing was already flushing the chapel through several exits.

Outside, to one side of the double doors in the front, I joined those awaiting the casket before going to their cars to follow the hearse to the grave site. The pallbearers appeared, loaded the casket, and disappeared into a limousine. The family, nevertheless, did not follow behind in the accustomed procession. A mortuary employee checked his watch, looked anxiously at the driveway, as if expecting another cortege to drive in at any moment, then retreated into the chapel. When he came back out, the family finally emerged behind him, a rumbling black cloud storming around Alonzo's mother.

Ann Marisse, after attempting to kiss the old woman, separated herself from the black-draped arms trying to keep her within the dark mass. Glancing around, her head held high, calm and self-assured, she located me and began her approach, equally as deliberate and unrushed. A path gradually parted through the crowd, closing back behind her as she passed, forming a moving circle with Ann Marisse at its core, coming closer and closer, until the outer edge broke like a wave to encompass me, leaving the two of us looking at each other across its new center in the space between us, she in front of me, just a step away. Her hands reached out as I offered mine in an almost normal reaction, unconscious at that moment of the unbearably melodramatic aspect the scene had taken on in its spontaneous development.

She spoke first: "Oh, Paul, he suffered so much."

"Yes, I can imagine."

In Kandy's car, before leaving the cemetery, she kissed me softly, lightly, not yet with desire, still contained and struggling with the possibilities suddenly reopened. With a sigh of relief that tried to resolve itself in a smile, her body relaxed into the seat, her head bowing for a moment, her eyes once again finding her hands in her lap. The open convertible, the afternoon sun, the lush green lawns surrounding us, mounds of roses in full bloom—the sparkling highlights in her familiar blonde hair freed from the black veil and the sky playing reflections in those same eyes when she lifted them, turning her torso slightly towards me and leaning back against the door, those eyes staring, waiting, watching me and waiting.

"Why did we lose so many years, Paul."

❊ ❊ ❊

Yes Alonzo was despicable, and in death even more than I had imagined. But I'll always be grateful to him for having died, if not as soon as he should have, at least not too late.

III

"... I guess we'll always wonder ..."

"Almost finished?" she asks me, touching my shoulder as she pauses by the table where I'm correcting galleys for what I hope will be the final time, aiming for a promised publication date before Christmas. If I don't insist again on more changes or last minute additions, the publisher guarantees the schedule. It's up to me. I've tried to stick to correcting typographical errors, limiting additions to small items that come to mind when I read over certain passages. Sometimes I feel I have to explain more or add information. If the book doesn't come out until next year, it won't matter much. We'll consider it a present for our daughter's first birthday.

In this light, the two of them look all the part of madonna and child. Francesca Ann, born in September of 1989, is still nursing. She doesn't realize she must share those breasts with her father, who thought the milk too sweet at first, but has developed a taste for it and the effect it has on her mother to suckle me like a child and then make love to me like a man, or both at once. They sit in a rocker designed by Wright, a gift from Kandy at the birth. If my mother were alive, she would paint a portrait of them in her last style, expressionistic impressionism she called it. Jeanne, who was in Hollywood to shoot exterior scenes for her latest film, stood in proxy for her mother at the baptism, her boyfriend—lover if you read *The Enquirer*—watching her affectionately as she held little Francesca Ann, who comported herself with quiet dignity. Kandy's father did the same for Alex. Francesca is pregnant herself and her doctors advise that at her age they shouldn't take unnecessary risks like transcontinental flights. Instead we may visit them soon. I've been fashioning an adaptation of one of her stories and would like to present it to her in person. It's about a woman who finds herself repeating scenes of her life in exact detail, but out of context and with different people—the plot lends itself to my obsessions, allowing me to create a scene perfect for Jeanne and Drea to play opposite each other as the same person at different times in the same place, together on the screen at once. Besides, I miss Tyrol. Drea is right, there is no reason to cut all ties with Europe. We can have both.

A child changes your life. I've been told it will get progressively more apparent as she acquires mobility and takes on her independence. Will she tire of my questions about her school work, or learn to play on my emotions with the movement of her young body, a touch of her hand? As for us, I notice the change most in the opening of a separate channel of communication, not in place of direct expression of affection, which continues its own course, but a new one, apart and distinct, perhaps drawing from but not dependent on the other. We're not fulfilled through the baby, rather expanded, multiplied. She waited a long time and now has what she admits she wanted all along. I waited as well, though differently, not knowing what I was waiting for, perhaps fearful of becoming what my father became to me.

He refused to attend the baptism, but a note arrived expressing congratulations of sorts: "I am surprised to see you still believe in the sacraments. Glad to hear you had a girl. They cause less grief in the long run." Certainly it's been a long run for us both, but he won't stand down. Doesn't know how. Even in my desire to begin a new phase of my life in which the past is reconciled with the present, I'm at a loss to find a similar channel through which to reach him. I concentrate, instead, on not repeating his model in my own family. Perhaps he is right, daughters are easier on fathers, although from what I know of the women in my life, I can't agree. We'll see.

I leave the galleys on the desk and walk over to them, place a hand on her shoulder and lean over to ask if there is anything she needs, but before I can speak, a finger tip rises to my lips. Francesca Ann has fallen asleep at her nipple, and if we let her settle into a firm rest, we can leave her to nap with the caretaker's wife, and walk along the beach. Looking back down at the baby, she begins to lower her finger as well, but I take it in my hand to kiss the swirls of its print, then slip the end between my teeth and gently bite down.

"That's what she'll be doing pretty soon, but not to my finger," she whispers.

I lean down, nudge her hair away from her ear and as softly as possible say that I can show her how it will feel if she wants to be prepared. She shakes her ear loose from my lips, which find her neck to kiss; but then I silently signal I will leave her alone to let Francesca Ann fall deeper into a momentary escape for us. She touches my nose just barely with the same fingertip, nods and smiles.

Down on the beach, several sea gulls arrogantly dispute the outcropping of rock with me, strutting their challenge to my intrusion. I can't tell if they are permanent residents or part of an ever-migrating population; over time I may recognize more of them as individuals, but for now we maintain a strategic distance, working out the terms upon which we will eventually share the rocks and beach as, if not old friends, at least tolerated and familiar neighbors. After all, they own the sea and air, while we only ask for the house and some land. They remind me of readers in their feigned indifference, masking an intense and judgmental concentration on my presence, going about their business, but reacting to my every adjustment of position; they scatter if I clear my throat, only to return, most of them, clicking their tongues and flapping their wings at my startling expression of physicality. One I call McQueen, because she is the portrait of my editor, head aloofly cocked to the sky to keep nature's beauty in full view and me and my indelicate intrusion at the periphery of her concern, as if she had much more important things to worry about, but will condescend to grant me a moment of her day. Yet, if I too try to focus on the sea, her stupendous, jaundiced eye revolves towards me in furious interrogation, posing the perpetual question: "What are you doing here so out of place? Can't you recognize it's all wrong?"

Yes, I do. And I've tried to write a more acceptable, fictional ending in the contemporary mode: irony, futility, disillusionment, an acknowledgment of time and change, neatly suspended finales a la Marianne Wiggins...but then why shift from one cliché to another just to please the gulls in my life? We have the money, so before the Japanese or Koreans buy up the entire coast, why not secure a small beachhead on the dream? If I learned anything from my mother's life it is that you can't waste it trying to meet someone else's expectations, especially if you have to give up the roses to keep them secure.

I watch the waves burst and roll over the fingers of rock, feel foamed droplets blow across me on the breeze. Kandy was right, I admit, a letdown follows after you achieve the ideal, but it lasted only a few months at most. Time and memory retreat, like water filtering from ebb-tide pools stranded by irresistible cycles; the past continues as remote as ever, absent even in presence. It remains there, just out of reach, a step in front of me, to be replayed over and over on the screen or the printed page, repeating the unanswerable question, why? The why of loss, unmitigated by revelations of gain.

A voice comes to me during a momentary break in the waves. She is standing on the prow of the terrace, pointing down to a stretch of beach sixty meters north. I nod, say goodbye to the gulls, who scurry forward to compete for my abandoned place on the highest rock—McQueen invariably wins, a bully to the end—and I set off to meet her. As she walks, with her blue windbreaker zipped up against the steady breeze, I think to myself how incredibly young she looks, profiled against the sky, her blonde hair blowing and her firm strides propelling her down the path. I find myself standing still, watching, wondering how she sees me. Supposedly, I have aged gracefully, but it's been some time since anyone has expressed surprise at my years as they used to even up to forty or forty-two. She is the young woman at my side when we go out, but then from the beginning she was younger. There will be, however, no growing old apace; she is vehemently not for it, I can tell. Her youthfulness pleases her and she means to preserve it.

She stands where we were to meet, relaxes her body into an exasperated pose and waves me forward to hurry. Before I reach her, however, she turns and begins to walk, north again. Any moment now she should spin around and wait for me to find her, offer a hand or both, and perhaps a kiss... Yet she doesn't, forcing me to catch up to her on the seaward side to match her stride. I study her profile as she stares ahead, as if concentrating on the effort it takes to walk on the pebbly strand. I say nothing, waiting for something, perhaps an explanation. Finally, she reaches out, puts her arm around my waist as her other hand caresses my chest, and leans her body against mine, burrowing her shoulder under my arm to bring it around her back. When I still don't speak, she looks up, without a smile, a serious look in her eyes, focusing slowly to recognize my own gaze waiting for hers, and says, "I wouldn't want to be totally predictable."

❋   ❋   ❋

Rereading the galleys has proved difficult. For almost a year I have not spent much time on remembering, with so much present to watch. Her body slowly transformed, rounding, blossoming in an unnatural beauty... I don't care what they say, it's the abnormality that makes it beautiful, extraordinary, so special: two hearts in one body, two centers sharing the same space. And then rediscovering her body after the birth as it reverts to its previous state, yet not exactly, hips a bit wider, sex more open, breasts still full and fertile, but now sweeter to the lips. She is richer than any obsession of memory as she daily feeds me future memories. Yet the galleys evoke other images, from so many other settings, and they are us as well. We are, no matter what Francesca Ann brings and changes and creates, the product of this life and, now, this book....

FINE